To Paul
with much love
Suzanna

THE AKASHIC RECORD

THE
AKASHIC
RECORD

S. M. SAUMAREZ

Matador
9 Priory Business Park
Kibworth Beauchamp
Leicestershire LE8 0RX, UK
Tel: (+44) 116 279 2299
Fax: (+44) 116 279 2277
Email: books@troubador.co.uk
Web: www.troubador.co.uk/matador

ISBN 978 1783063 987

British Library Cataloguing in Publication Data.
A catalogue record for this book is available from the British Library.

Typeset Aldine401 BT Roman by Troubador Publishing Ltd

Matador is an imprint of Troubador Publishing Ltd

This book is for the 'special needs' children with whom I lived and worked, for the underprivileged children of the Glasgow and Dundee Docks, for the children of the Circus and the children from the London estates where we so often worked. It is for Sophie, Daniel, Chris, Poppy, Sylva, Simon, Will, Alicia, Laura and Diego who are the Rough Puppet Theatre Company, and for the many other young people whom it has been my pleasure to teach and who in return have helped to shape my life.

Credits

I am grateful to NASA and their marvellous Hubble telescope for the photo 'Starburst Cluster Show Celestial Fireworks' which appears on the front cover.

Cover design by Brian Gold and many thanks to Brian for his patience and the sensitive enhancement of my photographs.

Thanks also to Ellie for being the perfect model for the cover.

I am indebted to Dr Patrick Curry for his unwavering encouragement and editing skills.

I would also like to thank Tearlach Flockhart-Byford for his artistic input and enthusiasm throughout this project.

Contents

Milo de Fer (age 17)

A flotilla of barges makes its way slowly upstream, straining against the emptying tide and casting long shadows in the low light of the Michaelmas sun. They come to rest in the lea of Blackfriars Bridge, where the ice-cool river Fleet bursts up from its subterranean course and flows into the Thames. Shouldering their guns, the crew moor up and the old barges heave a great sigh, relieved as their heavy cargo is unloaded. The bulk of it is yellow and red iron-ore, some smaller quantities of copper, tin, silver, a few gold ingots, Spanish mercury and a leather tote-bag of meteoric iron.

My father Jean de Fer is master of the Wayland Forge, cavernous vaults bored out by the racing waters of the river Fleet which courses its way beneath Fleet Street. Curiously, though, for a place that had once been so alive with news, reeking with rumour and committed to all of the little details, them quivering-nosed newshounds never did suspicion (even when one or two of their very own buildings took on a tipsy listing look an' they been obliged to sidestep a growing amount of steam jets that came blasting out the storm-drains) that deep underground my grandfather Volco, a lunatic with dynamite, been limping about with his three young sons' assistance, exploding the rocks, blasting out tunnels and generally rearranging the course of the river in order to drive the forge of his dreams.

When he were all good an' ready, grandfather Volco said to his boys, "Time to release the flood and find out if we are sinking or swimming folk." To which they says, "Okee dokee," an' in apprehensive elation they's released the flood. Well, collecting the Grandpa, my father an' his brothers along the way, the waters swept them helter-skelter down the tunnels, shot them through the

1

chicanes like cannon-fodder an' catapults them into the white water mill-race.

The collateral damage been well worth the pain, though, when the force of the water began to turn the great mill-wheel which drove the bellows to draw in a first long deep breath and exhale with the unhurried dignity of some ancient kraken discovering that it is okay to breathe on land. Then finding their rhythm, the bellows settled down to fan the flames of the mighty blast furnaces, an' in an obliging co-operation of rock, water, air an' fire, the forge came to life.

First time I heard that story I thought, Grandpa Volco musta had a wife. My father and his brothers musta had a mother. Where were she when the waters came down, and where did she get to? But my father buried the subject of Grandma Amber, deep in a cask within a cask within a cask, sewed it all up in a bag of lead weights and cast it to the bottom of the sea. "And don't go there," he warned. But I did go there, and asked around.

Grandma Amber, I found out, had her very own set of values to which she remained true an' stuck to them like glue. Totally unfortunately, these values was from a parallel universe to everybody else's an' a double edged sword, for while it were her unique take on life which allowed her to see Volco (who measured about 5.7 on the Richter scale, been a handful by any standards and not every woman's cup of chai) in the light of love, it were also these same values which caused old Volco to fall into episodes of jealousy, for Grandma Amber been a blinding beauty who attracted a number of admirers. But the place been terrible rough back then, an' a bit of colour been good for the soul an' cheery, an' while Volco fumed darkly about them "loafing loons," Amber absorbed the conflict an' transformed it into works of art.

Their stormy weather relationship blew itself out an' a peace treaty had been hastily drawn up when a girl child arrived. That was my Aunt Reema, who came into this world like a dainty sparkle out of black coal, with plans of her own to pursue. The birth of Reema had been immediately sobering for the whole family, who united in their efforts to take care of her. She were fragile an' looked on the verge of pegging out twenty-four-seven, an' being a rare bird she reacted to any tension by making it worse, collapsing like a broken elf, wailing piteously an' piercingly in forlorn bereft despair, making it absolutely worthwhile to maintain a sane an' peaceful atmosphere.

My father Jean been close to his sister right from the beginning. They's appreciated each other throughout the rough-an-tumble of family life, an' they's valued one another when they was left alone in the world. By the time she were nine, Reema were taking bit parts in the warm heart of the theatre an' by fourteen she were well on her thespian way. Like her mother, she'd learned to put her feelings on hold, offloading the lot on her staggered audiences who either tumbled in mirth or wiped their streaming eyes with the pain an' sorrow of it all, until one day the theatre sank without a trace.

Reema lives with Uncle Cole now. They settled in the Chelsea Physic Garden to raise their children Eden and Ariel an' teach us theatre studies, but I ain't an actor and she is an aunt of empathy. "Milo," she says, "I am very much hoping you will be in charge of the lighting again."

I have a brother Column, soft spoken with a creative imagination straight out the One-Off Department, but he keeps a lid on his light. He don't need no approval, for the art in his bones. He sees things differently. Give him anything and he will turn it into something else. He is sociable when he wants to be and wears his trousers about half way down his bum or lower, a big challenge for Dad an' the laws of gravity. Column is overbonded with Mum and makes her all kinds of trinkets. He do seem to have a magnetic effect on the maternal instincts of all womankind, shamelessly basking (like a shark) in the glory of their protection. At fifteen years old he is nestled snug and safe between me, age seventeen, and our younger sister Phoebe, who's thirteen an' a Goth, an' takes great pains to appear like she's just risen from the grave.

Grandfather Volco were a blacksmith through an' through, generous with his warmth and liberal with his thunder and lightning, whereas my father is a foundry man an' you have to look at what happens all around him to understand what he's about. The power with which Jean drives the forge is the same power with which the forge drives Jean. They is fine-tuned, equally matched an' has a working relationship that concentrates on the smooth running of rivers of molten iron, rushing waters, coal fired furnaces an' the eking out of flaws, an' listening carefully for the change of tone that signals the danger of a major blow. It takes more than this, an' more even than being born in a forge, to become a master. It takes invention, shaping iron, forging a future an' real inspiration, an' that's what caught the attention of the Worshipful Company of Blacksmiths, who made Dad a master craftsman.

Emerging in his wake comes my sister Phoebe, who is the unrecognized natural journeyman in this outfit. She do have a rapport with iron too and wields her hammers with a perfect precision, scattering cascades of sparks around her, like she's throwing stars.

Phoebe de Fer (age 13)

Fire comes in many forms. When we was little Aunt Reema took us to see the Chinese Water Puppets, an' part of that show included a underwater fire-breathing dragon. I don't know how they done that, but the quality of fire were a magic flare in the water, which is kinda like my Ma, who can find beauty in unlikely things. She built her own business, overbridged the millrace an' tamed the forge, and she made our home a subdued place of glints an' comforts that call you back with their inviting glow.

The air between my parents is busy with a language of unspoken words. They is easy together an' understand each others signs and portends pretty well, but it ain't all heavenly harmony an' the occasional fire-ball do get hurled. That is because from the oldest spearhead to the coldest of bullets, the history of war and the history of iron goes hand in hand, an' if iron do have a warlike nature, then to understand the nature of love one must check out the history of pots and pans of which my father has cast an incredible amount as gifts to smooth away the stormy waters of love.

Everyone an' his mother, an' especially my father (who do have a special relationship with electricity), is engaged with the problem of energy, and besides the pots and pans of peace, we produce propellers cast in alloys for wind turbines, four by fours an' suchlike for the building business, fancy filigree gates an' what has you. But mostly we cast the massive girders for shoring up the sea defences, and any one of us can shoe a horse or donkey in our sleep.

It were a great relief to see the iron barges coming up river in the sunshine. The journey is chancy and they'd been a long, long time coming home. We are few and far between an' just about everyone I knew been standing on the quayside, illuminated in the Michaelmas sunset, their sharp shadows falling across the waters, awaiting the return of those barges.

Canada Blanch waved from the wheelhouse, mighty delighted by the assembled delegation, an' said "Am I late, is it my birthday, or were you worried we been annihilated by the harem-scarems?" Captain Canada hopped ashore an' gave Mara his wife a grizzled hug, while his twin boys lost themselves with tying up the boats, just in case he tried to hug them too.

Chances were that Canada had been wheeling and dealing his way down the eastern seaboard an' were likely to have bought back some smoked and fresh fish, samphire, cheese, fresh apples, cider, plums, pears an' maybe even some wild mushrooms.

Among the crowd were Peeking Ducky, come to pick up some shrimps for his stall, an' Dorcas an' Tobias, who drew up their donkey cart with their daughters Angelina and Gloria ensconced in the back, leaning up on their elbows an' holding their faces to the sun, soaking up the rays like a couple of solar panels. Brother Sebastian and Brother Dominic was also there, all swathed in their gothic habits an' debating a Michaelmas theme. "When Archangel Michael cast Lucifer out of heaven, what happened to him, where did he go? An' where is he now, I wonder?"

"He's over there." I thought I'd try to help, an' pointed out a distant figure who were walking away down the wharf in big pair of hobnail boots. Brother Dominic stopped, an' holding his hands to his eyes like a pair of binoculars, he says, "Oh yes, so he is." He squinted through them, then focused on me. "Well spotted Phoebe, what good eyes you have."

"Mind if borrow them for a moment?" asked Brother Sebastian. "'Course I do. You've got a perfectly good pair of your own, hasn't he Phoebe?" They moved away slowly down the wharf to collect a box of fresh fish for that temperamental cook of theirs, who has the Michaelmas feast to prepare.

They is humble now, but once upon a time them Black Friars

walked the line between God Almighty and Almighty Westminster, and for a while they enjoyed all them power-sharing perks. Money, influence and generous gifts of land an' property came raining down upon them, an' the Pope even donated his very finest chef to them. Until Westminster discovered what a excellent venue the Priory been for a few covert executions, after which them Black Friars threw up their hands in horror and tipsy-toed away in their soft suede boots to concentrate their attentions exclusively on God. But not wanting to seem rude, I suppose, they sensibly retained the cook, a descendent of whom (a liability called Vatican Jack) still reigns in the kitchen.

Times has changed, governments an' popes is history, and though Brother Sebastian certainly do believe in a Michaelmas feast, he don't believe in God. An' just lately my father's been squelching about in the low-tide mud, helping them Brothers fix up a rig to harness the tides into generating some power for their freezing dark Priory.

I been quietly watching the hustle an' bustle on the wharf. The crew hoisted the loads skywards and lowered them carefully into the iron wagons where the drays waited to haul it all away, when Canada called, "You has the right idea Phoebe," an' came up to join me with his sons. Harley and Tyler been toting a heavy leather bag between them and sitting down, they says, "Look at this, meteorites for us to deliver to the Chelsea Physic Garden."

"I've an idea that Cole could use them to make a remedy, maybe you'se could take them on up when you go to Theatre Studies?" asked Canada, releasing the drawstrings to reveal the lumps of meteor iron.

"Where did you find them all?" I been amazed at the quantity.

"I didn't exactly find them. They came hurling out of the sky and almost killed me up on Psycho Charlotte's Beach."

"It's a wonder you survive, Dad."

"I know, it's a kinda miracle. Bless you, boys."

"I never even seen a shooting star, you is lucky." I felt wistful.

"Help yourself. They can be forged, if the nickel content ain't too high." Canada handed me a few good-sized lumps, and then shielding his eyes he looked up. "You're off. Look, here comes your ride to class. Good luck." Angelina and Gloria was trying to maintain their dignity as their donkey cart approached at a unusual sideways angle, for Delilah the donkey were casting long spindly shadows which were frazzling her nerves. "Well done, ladies," said Canada, an' stowing the meteors in the back of the cart he ambled off to join Mara, Tobias and Dorcas and my parents, who were sitting on the dock having a well-earned cup of chai along with the crew an' Albin and Tobin, the gunners.

"Bet they get the wine out the moment we is gone," Gloria remarked, moving up front.

"Abandon hope, all ye who enter here." Angelina invited us like we was going to hell.

"Here I am my darlings," said Milo, squashing hiself between them an' taking up the reins.

"And here I am MY darlings," said Column, an' keeping a firm hold of his trousers he clambered into the back with Harley, Tyler an' me. We knew where we belonged.

We moved out, an' even if Delilah do have her issues I been grateful for the donkey cart. Besides, it weren't like we had options. There were no boats available and the bus runs on chip oil, which leaves you smelling highly fishy by the end of your journey.

I love this city. It is beautiful to me, the lingering sun on the vacant windows bringing a little warmth into the empty spaces, and for a moment the broken-tooth skyline looked almost romantic in the evening light. The wavering silhouettes of tower blocks reflected along the straight-and-narrows of the old canals and where the banks had long caved in, the water eddied in an' out of the dereliction on its way through the uptown dusk.

Eroded by the constant washing and rinsing of the waters, the older buildings sometimes give up the ghost and fall flouncing down, exhausted, folding in on themselves with a roaring an' downpouring of dust that chases along the surrounding streets and takes forever and a day to settle.

Now and again one of us had to jump out to get some flotsam out the way, for the recent equinox tide had left the streets awash with all kinds of debris, delivering timber through the unhinged doors of empty homes. It even bought a couple of skiffs to rest halfway across the road, their owners onboard, pulling on their pipes, discussing how to get afloat again. "Land Ho," called Milo, which relieved a feeling that someone were watching us from one of those empty windows.

The Mantle was lighting the lamps up ahead, and bearing their

 long torches aloft they came snaking and swerving along the debris-littered road, peddling towards us on their strict service bikes with a squeaking and rattling that were doing the donkey's head in. "Evening all."

"Respect," we returned.

"Off to theatricals?"

"Yeah."

"Move along then." They rode by an' we relaxed. It's best to avoid the Mantle. Milo shook up the reins and Delilah moved off willingly, pricking her ears towards the warm stable she knew awaited her at the Chelsea Physic Garden. An' a good thing too, because the evening would not last forever and at night the Big Smoke disintegrated into a twilight zone. Across the river the chimneys of the Projack building flashed on and off with the words "Projack. Polluting the Place with Pills and Powders."

Well ahem, actually what they says is, " Projack. Paving the Way to a Pain-free Planet."

Column de Fer (age 15)

Everyone could see them mighty chimneystacks of Projack spewing out an unending plume of sherbet yellow smoke which undulated over the city and often ended up hanging eerily over Twilight Town, to come hissing down as acid rain upon the poor, Projack's walking, talking, wheezing human laboratory. The corporation maintained a breezy, upbeat, we're-working-on-it profile of non-complicity, and busily experimented with cures that came rolling off the lines at regular intervals for all of them breathing disorders they'd caused.

Everybody agreed that the puffers worked hard in their labs, and no doubts about it but some of the stuff they made was remarkable. Everyone also thought it were a front, the endless research a thing-in-itself an' the writing on the chimneys was ignored. An' everybody suspected they was behind the disappearances of people, in particular a friend of ours called Hope who been a little boy when he just vanished. We knew for certain that in the name of medicine, animals were subjected to experiments from which they perished, because every so often somebody inside Projack would liberate these sorry creatures into the Big Smoke where they was taken in and nurtured, for we are the capitol of survivors, after all.

It were common knowledge that the Mantle was cahooting with Projack for solutions to the energy problem, and we suspicioned that this was where their hush-hush real objectives lay. It were also rumoured that the Oligarchs was providing them with the uranium and plutonium that they was gonna need to make some amount of nuclear power. Even Projack knew that conflicts and natural disasters been the cause of leaks an' explosions that left pockets of land and poison towns all over the Earth that was no-go areas, silent graveyards for them glowing-boned skeleton people and their radioactive lands. Nuclear power were banned by international law, which for Projack meant Put On Hold. The spin were all so clever an' dazzling, nobody questioned or challenged what they was up to. We all knew all that, no theory, straight up an' dead cert, without no need to set foot in the place for the verifying.

Angelina (age 17)

The Mantle is the law an' a law unto themselves. They runs a racket an' has big fish to fry, while the little fish is better off looking out for themselves.

Time were when the whole shebang been ruled and regulated up to the hilt. No doubt about it, our ancestors was a Nosey Parker, Peeping Tom society. Man, they was as suspicious as a gangland boss, with everybody crawling about surveying one another probably the number one top-earner occupation. The roof-tops was littered with cameras an' a little digging often uncovers some old surveillance device disintegrating in the rubble. I guess not everyone went with it, 'cause a lot been vandalised an' buried in the ground, but any rate we is free to roam the iffy terrain.

My sister an' I is used to fending for ourselves, for Dorcas our mother been a midwife and we never really knew exactly were she was from one moment to the next. Sometimes, 'bout four in the morning, a frantic father would come pelting up the steps, banging on the front door an' yelling, "Helpity help help," all out of breath an' hyperventilating with the panics. "Take it easy," Dorcas would say " New baby on the way? A rare an' precious event. Have some chai why don't you, I'll just get my things together." And then she were gone, sometimes a long time.

Ma and her colleague Doc Cole worked up at the Horse Hospital and were committed to healing every extreme person which came their way. They were often paid in chickens, cabbages and once a piano even, but Dorcas kept us well away from her midwife duties and it weren't till much later, too much later in fact, that we found out why.

We live down a cobbled lane which runs up from Embankment

Gardens towards the remains of Charred Cross Station, where our father Tobias and Jean de Fer been stripping down a steam-engine wreck an' (supposedly secretly) rebuilding a very probably highly dangerous machine of a locomotive nature.

Tobias do love his gardening but he is actually employed to survey, explore and chart what remains of the railway system after global weirding. That consists of pumping his way around the railroads in a hand-car until the tracks run out where a bridge collapsed, the tracks disappears under water, the tracks fall into a ravine or the tracks come to a buckled and twisted end. Pa could be gone for weeks and he didn't necessarily hand over all his mappings to the Mantle.

Sometimes when we was younger, we'd go with him. Our singing beginnings was about filling up the empty spaces while pumping the hand-car through them rusting corrugated iron depots or past the disused platforms an' waiting-rooms of silence in old forlorn stations. " Hush and let me think a second," he'd say, consulting an old map. "Crawley! What the heck are we doing here? And what kind of a name is that to give a town?"

"Is we lost, Dad?"

"No, angel, but we ain't exactly found either."

The remains of Crawley looked enchanted by recent snowfall, with everywhere carpeted by a variety of white winter flowering heather that spread over buildings an' tumbled through the ornamental glades of Japanese Maple, hoary Magnolia and Ghost Gum trees. It swept around the Black Bamboo and giant clumps of Pampas Grass that occupied the open spaces an' crept for miles between the train-tracks, rustling dryly beneath us when we moved along. These parts once been teeming with people moving off to work in their shoals, off to the shops, off to school, coming up for air then off to sleep like fish in the sea. But like most places in the south, it been abandoned long ago, first from lack of water, then from way too much.

Every so often we'd stop for Dad to find his bearings or illustrate his maps with drawings and take notes on what we saw, while Gloria drew her own kind of maps of how these places felt in words and tunes, pulling her songs from the realm of inspiration like a fisherman reeling in a line, sometimes playing it in with hours of struggle and patience. But it were always worth it for the quirky glittering creations she eventually landed.

An upgrade in fortune took us off the rails, when Gloria and I started singing for a band which been in demand for its gentle tones and unique contemporary style. Just about every musician we knew had learned their stuff inside out with Brother Sebastian, who lived and breathed music, and with the help of what he called the Bazooka Method, i.e. an impressive vocabulary interspersed with threats of Hell and eternal damnation. Brother Sebastian been responsible for shaping hordes of grimy guttersnipes into angelic choirs whose voices rose echoing through the Priory. Some gone on to form bands like Full Metal Racket, Northern Rock or Soft Sloth, the band we sang in, which Brother Sebastian turned out to be very proud of, for he and his sidekick Brother Dominic never missed a gig.

You don't fraternise with the Mantle, they operates like a occupying force. But the lamp-lighters was harmless, almost normal. Why, at a distance they could have been mistaken for Will-o-the-Wisps, holding their tiny blue flames aloft and leaving a line of twinkling lamps and flaming braziers in their wake. They'd been right about getting a move on to the theatricals, though, for a posse of Smokes appeared astride their Skimmers, jumping over the wide wake they carved in the river an' firing off a random shot or two.

Delilah reacted to the gunfire like a starting-pistol at the Donkey Derby an' took off at a thrilling speed, catapulting the kids in the back clean off their seats and landing them in a heap on the floor with the upended bag of meteorites. Which they didn't seem to mind particularly, being the best of friends. They share the same sense of humour, they has secrets and places to go, an' for reasons I has never fully understood, they believe that Harley and Tyler's Grandma is watching over them in some kind of heavenly protection racket. Which I hope is true, because polite as they are, them kids is up to something and discreetly engaged in illegalities.

Harley (age 14)

"There is a place," our Grandmother Tookie told us, "that is completely out of time and space, and everything that we do is written down there in a starry script that's called the Akashic Record. This is where you'll find me when I'm dead and gone, for of course, I will be reading all about you. So make sure you do something worth reading about or I shall be dead bored, so to speak."

"We'll do our exceeding best," we assured her.

Grandma were a Parsee with Theosophical leanings. Grandpapa were a Zoroastrian with no leanings, an' just in case Grandma had been infecting us surreptitiously with Theosophy, he been keen for us to take on board that we had inherited magic fingertips because, he explained most earnestly, the ancient Zoroastrians were weatherworkers, every single one of them. "Well Grandpapa, I'll be," we said, delighted by the news.

When Grandma died Grandpa buried her in full Zoroastrian style, first the water then the fire, there being no handy Towers of Silence to leave her body on for the eagles an' elements to devour. Grandma Tookie would have preferred something a whole lot more Theosophical with her friends down at The White Eagle Lodge. She must have been peeved about it. There were no point in upsetting Grandpa any further, though, for they'd been born for each other, an' while death were obviously taking Grandma to new places, Grandpa were at a loss and going nowhere. He wasted away after her death and died of grief a couple of months later.

We was terrible troubled, we been empty and sad, but we's got it, for I'd die of grief too if Tyler carked it. Then no sooner had Grandpa been restored to the Light than one awful day, Hope, who were just

15

a nipper, disappeared, an' we's been looking for him ever since.

Our lives was all about loss, our minds was loud, angry an' sad, so in honour of Grandpa we put our minds to learning some basic coin manipulation an' sleight-of-hand techniques. It weren't exactly weather working, but it placed us in the present an' held the sadness at bay. An' just knowing that Grandma were in her starry library, reading about how sad we was an' what we was up to, been a big comfort an' a encouraging thing to us. Later it was sometimes embarrassing, and one just hoped she had the good sense to skip a few lines.

We was born in the Horse Hospital, and the day we came back to our home in Limehouse, our father added our names to his sign: "Canada Blanch, Shipwright, Haulage & Sons."

"And what happens if they decide to become ballet dancers?" Ma asked.

"No problem, we got room for all sorts in the haulage business." Which been true, for Dad were a equal-minded man, and having sorted out our careers, they set about equalising their identical twins in a process of blindfolded exchange, parcelling us around between each other until they no longer knew which of us were born first. Then they tattooed a blue dot on the wrist of one of us and a green dot on one of the other's. The one with the blue dot they called Tyler

and the green-dotted one were me, Harley. And till the day they died both Grandma and Grandpapa were never sure which were which and who been who, even with the dots.

Canada Blanch an' Sons operates out of Limehouse, an' we is chock-o-block full of all sorts of boats: sailing barges, steam barges an' combinations of both, a couple of old Lugers an' a number of small flat-bottomed River Lighters, some to be fixed an' some to be sailed. Pa's work is mainly ocean-going. But the day Grandpa died, our Ma became heiress to the Carma Co Empire, a train of barges which she runs up the Regents Canal, through Twilight Town an' on to Paddington Basin, trading for grain, coal, wool, scrap metal, livestock or whatever produce may come floating down the Grand Union with the outlanders. As a matter of fact, Tyler an' I been apprenticed to her.

Once or twice a year, the big rafts of logs would come down the Thames an' when they misjudged the tide by as little as ten minutes, the whole lot would float straight into Limehouse, which had them loggers hopping off their rafts and standing about on the corniche looking sheepish. At such times, Dad would say, "Mara my dear, you got the whole goddamn forest floating about in here. Super duper," an' rub his hands together gleefully, for his (an' her) solution to log-jams were to chuck in a few sticks of dynamite an' see what happens. "Clear!" Dad would shout out without no warning, giving no time at all for no one to get out of the way or stop up their ears before the mighty *Kaboom*. Which did work sometimes, with the whole lot floating off nice an' easy. Mostly, though, it was, "Sorry boys, you is stuck till kingdom come or the next tide to pull them off again." "Well thankee dankee for your efforts, Mara, Canada, and for not killing us all in the process," the tearful loggers replied, gawping at the wreckage of their logs.

Unfortunately, it were not all blowing things up or ferrying goods up and down the broken back canal. Our mother is a great believer in free will, an' when we were not working she made sure we went to every class available: medicine with Dr Cole, theatre studies with

Reema, farriery with Jean De Fer an, unbelievably, ballroom dancing and cooking with that demon Vatican Jack up at the Priory. Because the more education you has, the more informed your choices is... apparently. But there *is* magic in our lives.

The Big Smoke do have a whole chiasm of waterways to explore. Some are rivers that burst out of their straightjacket existence in underground pipes and head for the surface where they is meant to flow, like the Walbrook, which runs clear through St Stephens Church an' eddies round its pagan rock alter on its way to the Thames. Others are hidden beneath a overhang of thorny trees and chocked with the river-weed. Most of these were roads that long ago gave way to the sewers below but now gurgle clear between the walls of leaning alleyway, deserted by people. The water is teeming with little fishes an' home to a few Old World monkeys, an' our presence acknowledged by the restless flustering of nesting Chimney Storks an' the shadowing paddy-pad footfalls of Serval, Lynx or Maine Coon Cats, who has become warily accepting of the tasty scraps we bring for them. The Orientals use the larger ducts to ferry produce in from their water gardens, but the spaces in between is empty an' free for Tyler, Phoebe, Ariel, Column an' me to poll along, and I has a feeling that the magic of the water maze comes close to what our grandfather had in mind.

In them times when secrecy is required, Column do even have a hideaway deep underground for us to go, undisturbed by memories of Grandpa an' concealed from Grandma's watching eyes.

Mistral (girl age 10, origins classified)

You don't necessarily actually have to be all that dead or gone to read the starry writin'. There is some like me, perfectly live an' well, as can read it too.

Soon as that were found out, was I squirreled away, vacated, diskappeared an' vamoosed likerty-split! That's because there is some psycho's in this world what can't wait to have the likes of me down at the lab, stuck full of needles and wielding them awful sharp scalpels in a bid to find out what makes us tick.

Man, I been off the grid so fast, I never been in the system and there being no notion I been in existence. I ain't on no missing person list, nor is a single body looking for me nowhere. Total tragic an' all good.

Soon after I split, the boy called Hope been stolen away. Howevers, he do have one or two missing person posters and is likely alive, for he leaves traces of faint wavering starry writing which is unreadable, but we appears to be linked, for our stories overlap an' are inextricably entangled in the same chapters, but I can't find Hope nowhere. Which ain't about the looking, for I has a perfectly clear twenty-twenty view, for instance, of the theatre studies ensemble bolting toward the Chelsea Physic Garden in one runaway donkey cart.

Grandma Tookie (the Akashic Record, Chelsea Physic Garden)

Volco de Fer and later his boy Jean had blasted a home out of the rock with water and dynamite, but the Chelsea Physic Garden could not be forced, and neither did it happen over night. It came about in secret, under the earth, with the hidden splitting of bulbs and the minute shifting of seeds yearning for the sky, with blind roots finding an anchor in the earth, with modest little saplings growing into stout-hearted trees, with the woody sap that flowed through their core, with the unfolding of leaves that breathed out a canopy of green, with the blossoming of flowers and the ripening of its fruits and seeds. And every single seed that fell contained life, death and the absolute assurance of continuity.

A great deal of the Chelsea Physic Garden came floating in over the watery main with the great explorers. It took its time, and hundreds of years, to establish hundreds of medicinal plants, and at somewhere along the line it had attracted an' attentive guardian, Solo, the gardener, who had a feel for its needs. Thanks to him and the capable hands of its present curator, Dr Cole Levet, the Chelsea Physic Garden remained a tiny bit of paradise, shimmering in a city that was nearly dark.

Eden Levet (age 17)

No pressure or anything but I do feel the weighty doctoring ancestry breathing down my neck. But on the subject of free will, I and the lovely Mara Blanch is at one. I has a few strings to my bow an' is passable at a number of things, which don't indicate a flippant or flighty mind. It means some folks has no calling, an' is waiting an' seeing where they belongs an' where it feels comfortable to be. It is a matter of identity.

The first Levet took a long time to find his feet too. Robert emerged from Yorkshire, metamorphosed into a Parisian waiter and transformed himself into an apothecary. His love life (like mine) been one long turbulent tragic disaster until, rescued by his friends, he came under cloak-and-dagger to the Big Smoke, where he began to practise medicine with grace amongst the poets an' the poor.

Grandfather Owen gone his own way an' Grandma Dr Clara Levet re-located up north, but my Dad's knowledge of apothecary and medicinal plants eventually earned him the job of Curator of the Chelsea Physic Garden. Which suited everybody just fine, for it was an institution, an' once Dad took over nobody need bother think about it or him again. The Institute of General Practitioners enjoys an air of the magus status, though, which my father ignores. He gets on with the job, tending his plants through the revolving seasons, treating his patients through the ups and downs of their ailments, preserving old remedies or making new ones. He also works as a street doctor, slipping off at night, a lone wolf in a leather jacket, to his clinic at the Horse Hospital to work with the poor.

There is a sign carved over the door of the teaching lab which reads, 'As Above So Below'. For years I believed it were a reference to the Antipodean plants we has.

Dad teaches short courses in basic grow-your-own-medicine to anyone who fancies a go, which is where I learned that 'As Above so Below' were actually a profound metaphysical maxim that explains the entire workings of the universe, and over the years my father gave us a thorough grounding in biology, first aid, bone setting, stitching, splinting, resuscitation, dressing wounds and the ongoing study of the Materia Medica – in short, all you need to know for a career as neo-medieval medicine man.

As young students we was rewarded with a series of individualized ornate certificates, leftovers from a harvest festival called the Chelsea Flower Show, which read things like, "Column has achieved a Silver Medal for identifying the internal organs correctly." Or, "Gloria has received a plot of her own, for learning to identify twelve herbs and their medicinal properties." After which I got one that said, "Eden has achieved a Bronze Medal for being so helpful to Gloria in her garden." Boy, I was so overcome with love for her it hurt, my heart fluttered, my knees trembled an' I turned a cabbage-crimson every time she graced the scene – a state, I's sorry to report, she took full advantage of, and had me carting compost hither and thither like a lowly numpty creature. I been obliged to hop it for a while and return to a kind of glacial relationship of uptight normality.

Sometimes, with no apparent particular reason, the Institute of General Practitioners bestowed (like star dust) a sprinkling of funding (never quite enough) for education, which triggered a flurry of activity between us and Kew, with all the herb barges shunting up an' down river, some on gathering trips, an' shared advice an' exchanges with the seed banks. A whole lot more funding goes towards research by them puffers in Projack's dark satanic mills, but we do not lose out by occasionally being paid in animals, minerals or vegetables. We has a number of chickens and ducks living the life of Riley on the wild side of the garden, which also houses an old sluice gate through which I slip like mercury, in those times when I has to be alone in a secret life away from here.

Ariel Levet (age 13)

There were times when my brother Eden was gone for days, but wherever he went, he always came home safe an' his sporadic vanishings meant no one ever raised a eyebrow if I disappeared with my friends for a couple hours hanging out on the herb barges, exploring the unchartered waterways in a leaky Lighter or lingering in the oriental markets or, more often these days, dabbling in the risky underworld of pirate radio in Column's hideaway. We kept our profiles low, low as a hunting snake, for we was not prepared to let no menaces or fears rule our lives, no way.

If you happen to end up with a name like Ariel, chances are your mother is a lovey whose theatre been carried away by the river, and my Ma is called Reema. When Dad first came loping out the wastelands to take his medicals he also met Mum, and without the aide of no rose-tinted spectacles he beheld her as a glowing creature, and she recognized him as the man of her dreams. It been a rare case of the dye being cast, an alchemical distillation, a mutual compatibility and generally an earth-moving-under-one's-feet sort of moment, properly diagnosed as love at first sight. Dad sloped off (in his leather jacket I suppose) to the theatre every single night where Mum were appearing in the role of Titania, and thus he always did treat her with the greatest respect. Although she is not exactly a fairy queen, being the sister of Jean de Fer and bought up amongst the fire and brimstone of the Wayland Forge an'all that racket.

The Michaelmas sunset flared down the Thames in reds, oranges an' lilacs until, tipping out of sight in the west, a big pink moon rose in its wake, which filled the sky an' hovered almost stationary above Twilight Town. It were a friendly sight. Eden and I sat up on the garden wall, waiting peaceably together for the arrival of our friends an' enjoying the sky, knowing it could be a very long time afore we caught sight of the sun and moon again. The lamps had been lit an' the moon went on her way, drawing the tide and the nightlife out beneath her, when rounding the bend like the Four Horses of the Apocalypse came Delilah, clattering up the road so fast her little donkey shoes were sparking, an' with a muffled shout of "Don't wait up!" from Column, they's shot past the gates with most the cast all tumbled in the back.

They was back again soon enough, though, and at a more sedate pace, by which time Eden had combed his tawny hair on account of Gloria and we had raised the mighty iron flood-gates to let them in. Delilah made straight for the stables and Milo, Angelina and a darkly glowering Gloria gone inside, while the rest of us greeted one another without the aide of green or blue dots to identify Harley and Tyler. We made sure the donkey were comfortably installed, and putting all the scattered meteors back in the tote bag we followed the others indoors for a new term, a new class, and an' idea for an unlikely new show to work on.

Column de Fer

A unt Reema were a domestic goddess, and bending low to avoid the bunches of drying herbs, strings of onions and garlic plaits we followed our noses towards the promise of exceptional cooking. The fire were burning and Uncle Cole been lighting the hour glass candle lamps and "Come in, come in," Reema, invited in her low husky voice. She wiped her hands, tucked her shirt into her jeans and shut the Aga door with a deft movement of her hip. "Hiya," she beamed at Phoebe an' me, and directed a warm vague, "Hi, hi" towards Harley and Tyler. "Food will be up in a sec. We'll have to discuss our plans over dinner, the sunset's gone and delayed everything. A working supper…" Her voice trailed off as she disappeared into the larder. "Have you had a chance to look at the scripts yet?"

"Why yes, we have," I said when she reappeared again. "Take a seat."

"I'm here an' all ears." She perched on a kitchen stool and Tyler put a glass of wine in her hands.

I delved for the right words to kindle Reema's curiosity, then ventured, "I had this idea that the wordsmith and the blacksmith have much in common. They are both looking for the right way to shape things. Consonants, for instance, are hard as iron, an' the vowels is round an' burnished. Perhaps it's no coincidence you grew up in a forge an' became an' actress."

"Now that had never even occurred to me."

"An of course there is the power of the word, which some people like Stratford Bill has while others does not."

"Very true, and I wonder where is this leading. Pray do go on," she said.

"It's just we are all a little older now, and we've been wondering if you would be interested in guiding us through something a whole lot darker." Uncle Cole looked up with interest, so I went on. "And with this in mind, we came across 'The History of the Damnable Life and Deserved Death of Dr John Faust.'"

Reema giggled and said, " Since you put it like that, sure. I'd enjoy the challenge."

"And then of course there are the beguiling words of a Silver Tongue…" added Uncle Cole.

"O well, what if he is," answered Reema. "Besides, he has a point, they are older… You know, the story of Faust began life as a puppet-show, and very popular it was too, throughout the Middle Ages. Then it turned into a play and eventually it became an opera as well. I suppose you had the play in mind and not the opera?"

"Yeah the play, but with puppets. Sounds great, don't it?"

"This I have to see," muttered uncle Cole. "Faust the Puppet Show." Milo gave me the thumbs up and went to help Reema with the food while the rest of us sat down at the long table.

When we was all settled Ariel, who were a slight thing with a big voice, low and husky like her ma's, opened her script an' her reading been lively and good listening…

The History of the Damnable Life and Deserved Death of Dr John Faust (Part 1)

Trailing huge storm clouds of thunder and lightning, a Dark Angel flies over the city. Occasionally folding his wings and curling himself into a ball, he plummets earthwards, spinning and twisting until, casually unfurling his wings, he swoops up over the rooftops, predatory and powerful as a great bird of prey, and his passing is followed by a momentary absence like a black hole.

Hidden in the moonlight, the Angel of Light observes

him, and when the Dark Angel glides skyward once more, the Angel of Light swoops to join him. "Enjoying the thermals are we? How do you do it, I mean I could never get my wings closed so quickly. I'm amazed."

"Well you know, you've got to be cool, clever, handsome and all-powerful," replied the Dark Angel, somewhat embarrassed at being caught looping the loop and playing like Cupid or some daft young cherub.

"Such modesty. As always, an example to us all," the Angel of Light rejoined. Just then, their attention was caught by Dr John Faust, a man who had dedicated his life to self-development and acquiring the Ultimate Knowledge. Through the study of alchemy, Faust had dabbled in transmuting base metals into gold, but no longer in the first flush of youth and urgently pursuing a recipe for the Elixir of Life, he is up late, working on yet another formula.

"Eight pounds sugar of mercury, four rocks of sulphur, crushed through a sieve, seven drops of arsenic. Three full measures each of Calomel, Gentian, Cinnamon, Nard, Coral and Tarter, seven foils of copper and three of lead. Mix it up and make it nice, distil it slowly over a low flame, and hopefully pop goes the weasel."

Faust waits in patient expectation for the crystal-clear drops to form, but he doesn't have to wait long before his distillation forms into a toxic disaster. "Oh dolorous me, an Elixir of Eternal Death again. Useful perhaps for disposing of the bodies of victims of the plague…" John Faust clasps his head in bitter frustration, for as far as he knows the night had been another meaningless waste of time, an utter failure, and nothing has happened at all.

But something has happened, for he has attracted the attention of two powerful angels, who watch him curiously. After sometime, the Angel of Light says, "Thus far the alchemist has only succeeded in creating some fairly lethal spirits. Happily, the spirit he's after eludes him still. I dread to think what would happen if he ever succeeded in unravelling the mysteries of Heaven and Earth and thus somehow clambered into our world. What havoc would mankind wreak up here! See though, does not the good doctor pursue his work most earnestly?"

"Good doctor, say you?" replies the other. "I doubt it. Indeed, I will wager you his very soul that he is not, thus proving once and for all that I am easily more mightier then you."

"Is this not exactly why you got chucked out of heaven in the first place? I have nothing to prove, but if you really want to go another round, I'll take this wager on."

The fallen angel opened his wings widely in satisfaction, and in so doing obliterates the light of the distant moon. "Even the silver moon deserts me now!" Faust cries in desperation. "Hell and damnation, may the Devil help me."

"Right, fine, you can count on us, we are on our way," crows the Dark Angel, and plucking a black feather from his wing, he cups it between his hands, breaths on it briefly and lets it float to earth.

"And here was I thinking that you have to be invited three times," the Angel of Light comments, flexing his colours a little.

"And so we shall be. All in good time. Won't we, Mephisto?"

"Yes, meow… master," replies a skinny black cat, emerging from the fallen feather, with a fine long tail behind him…

A sudden tap, tap, tap on the window caused a collective gasp. Happily, though, it were not the Devil in disguise but a bird-worker from the Winged Messenger Service. Cole let the pigeon in, an' gently unrolling the tiny note banded around her scaly leg, he read, "Trouble on the river. Sleep over, sleep well, xx Liberty."

Ma's note was a relief. I weren't looking forward to the journey home. "Right, fine, you can count on us." Reema scribbled a hasty reply, and fixing it to the bird's leg, she released her into the moonlight. Gloria and Angelina begun to clear up the dishes, Milo and Eden collected up the scripts and Uncle Cole stole away to his study with his bag o' meteorites. "Come on," said Harley an' Tyler, "better make sure the animals is all inside. They'll be afraid if there's gunfire."

We went out to the stables but Solo, a long term resident of the garden, had been ahead of us, for everyone was all snug in fresh straw. Delilah lay on her side, half asleep with her legs stretched out in front of her, making it plain a return journey were out of the question. Kublai Khan the rooster stood on his cross beam, keeping a beady eye on his chicken wives who sat plumply in the nest-boxes, and the two red ponies lifted their heads from their stalls and whinnied a greeting, for Harley and Tyler was digging in their pockets for peppermints, something ponies is crazy for, an' just about every horse in the Big Smoke been on friendly terms with them. Once the twins done with patting an' feeding the ponies, we's all sidled off to join the others up on the wall and see if we couldn't catch a glimpse of exactly what sorta trouble were on the river tonight.

Gloria (age 16)

Gang culture can be a confusing thing. There is a lot of them about an' sometimes they is the all-happy, all-friendly, fun-loving, yo bro, dancing and drinking, have a nice day gangs, and then other times they is the all-buzzing-about like a angry swarm of killer-bees gangs, annihilating each other in conflicts that make Armageddon seem like a inviting party.

Tonight, even the Leggers are out-and-about on the water. Which is an unusual situation, for they was the most peaceable people, who was employed to push the narrow boats through the tunnels by lying on their backs and using their feet against the tunnel roof to propel the boat along. It were a niche market, exclusively cornered by them efficient Nippon punks who wore plaids and chains, ripped up jeans and spiked their florescent hair with Agar Agar.

The Leggers were big, big fans of Full Metal Racket. They was also mad for kite-flying, and often spent their time-out drifting along in little red-sailed Junks fishing, and although all their boats was fitted with lithium ion out-boards they never used them, for they was good with the winds and tides. Leggers were known to smoke poppy and protected themselves from raiders with home-made fireworks, which been sparked by magneto an' was deadly lethal. They spoke Japonica, a language that no native Japanese would have understood, an' any English were limited to short sentences. "You is fan of Full Metal Racket, yes?" Or pointing to their threads, "You dig me Westward Mangas?" ("What?")

The Smokes is mainly drifters, AWOLs an' ex-clinks – a different kettle of fish. Don't misunderestimate them, for they is canny an' obsessed with engines and the world of thermodynamics. A Smoke will parley poetically for hours on the subject of energy, force an' space/time, and bend his mind around the problems of mass, charge, matter and motion, so as he can buzz about on the river at night. Their makeshift Skimmers is powered by highly-charged an' volatile atoms called fizzballs, an invention of their own making, and when handling them ever-so-ready-to-blow-up river-craft they was agile as the Mongol hordes on horse back, leaning low over the water to balance while the flames come shooting out the exhaust pipes, an' poised to leap off in them meltdown moments. The Smokes is not employable.

The Hissy Boys is a nasty piece of work. They sharpens their teeth an' is partial to tattoos, which they earns through cage-fighting. They is part clone an' part nobody knows what, but they is better then dogs when it come to tracking, for once they picked up a trail they is blind to all obstacles, until the quarry is cornered. The Hissy Boys is vulnerable to cold weather and makes themselves scarce in the winters. Otherwise they works for whoever employs them, particularly the Mantle, an' they is rumoured to work for the Dark Elite, who patrols the outlands. Probably most the time a lot of filthy jobs came their way, for they has torched warehouses and been known to delete people at point-blank.

The Saracens too was out in force on the river. Though technically not a gang but a clan with their own ways, which generated a lot of mystique, their holt were way down river at the old Barrier, and usually theys kept to themselves. They was marvellous looking, swathed in black from head to foot, and it is said that some protection and magic comes from wearing their turbans, which they never do take off. Except for the one time, when they appeared bareheaded to salute Volco's final passing. I has no idea what it were that could have bought them out tonight, but I do know that their chief Topaz looked fantastic raffish beneath his pirate turban, and all gleaming in war-bling.

The gangs don't pose us no personal danger. Eden got shot once by a sniper, who were mortified apologetic even though the bullet had passed harmlessly through the Davy Crockett hat he wore non-stop as a boy. And when Milo were a nipper, a gang of drunken teenage girls stripped him bare and made him dance. An experience he now says he'd like to repeat, but at the time he danced an' hollered roundly with indignation, until Brother Sebastian happened along, which were a mixed blessing, for not above the odd snifter himself, he shouted, "Shameless infant, dancing naked for girls! Clothe thyself."

Besides them marauding tipsy girls, beware the Raggers, a gang of chilling vagrant kids who's armed to the gills with knives and shooters an' has an uncanny habit of always showing up were trouble was brewing.

Tonight it were all hell out on the river and there they was, swarming about on the bridge, lobbing clarts and rocks on the battle below. The Leggers was taking pot shots at them with rockets, howlers and Roman Candles an' such, which was mostly landing in the river an' forcing them Saracens, Smokes an' Hissy Boys into ducking and batting their arms about in an effort to protect themselves from catching fire. "I could do without the firework display," we heard Topaz say as he rallied his men just below our wall an' re-loaded. Catching sight of us, he shouted, "Get the hell down from there, it ain't safe."

"Respect," Column shouted back, gesturing downriver to where the Mantle had lined themselves up along the Projack Embankment with their water cannons and was waiting... for what? It were a mistake, cos once the Law were spotted every single sight been trained in their direction, and afore they knew what was what, they was under a hail of bullets, fireworks, rock salt and nails... Oh the Horse Hospital were gonna be a full-on place later.

It were cold an' having seen our fill we was ready to go when Phoebe says, " Hang on. Look, look at that... Be safe, be safe," she called to a white stork, who were flying down river through the gunfire an' smoke. We watched it apprehensively, till it were gone beyond the point of danger.

Milo de Fer

That night I been gently an' firmly persuaded awake by Uncle Cole, "Are you up for helping out in an urgent situation?" he asked.

"Yeah, yeah, course, absolutely," I mumbled.

"Good man," he says, "Wrap up warm." Eden were there, half-asleep, half-dressed but cheery enough, and soon we was all muffled up and slipping out into the night.

Man, it were intense outside, with a freezing smog wafting off the river that tasted acrid an' smelled of fireworks, and colder than the swamps of hell. "Grand night eh?" Uncle Cole remarked brightly, for he been one of them night-owl people who reached his zone roundabout midnight.

"Yeah Dad, I'm loving it," Eden replied through chattering teeth. We walked away, invisible men enveloped in the fog and dark, until we come to a high wall with a big old cast iron door in it. Cole checked the street cautiously an' unlocking the door, he ushered us through, then carefully locking up behind he lit a lamp and led us down a fire escape onto a derelict platform in the flooded underground. "Want something to eat while we're waiting?" he asked, an' reaching inside his jacket he pulled out a bag of currant buns, a welcome familiarity in existential circumstances. Eden an' I weren't exactly sure why we was here or what it were we been waiting for, but it weren't long afore a little wavering light appeared way down the blackness of the tunnel and come towards us with its reflections circling off the water.

An old-fashioned wooden boat drew along the platform, and the pilot was wearing a leather flying-cap. "Evening, Booker" said Uncle Cole.

"Evening Doc. Got company tonight, I see."

"My son Eden."

"Well I know's who they is, I've seen 'em around. Besides, I'm an old family friend." Booker's reply been puzzling, seeing as I'd never met him. "However, it's always nice to have a formal introduction. How you doing Eden? Respect, Milo," an' he shook our hands firmly.

"Respect," we returned.

"Well now," said Cole, "let us be gone from the land of the living."

"Tell you what," said Booker, casting off, "the land of the dead is exceptional lively tonight. I've been coming an' going like a ambulance."

"I guessed as much. It's good the interns agreed to come along." We interns settled into the faded red leather upholstery an' tuckered into our current buns, as the old pleasure boat bobbed off with the current.

It were a lost world down there, a archaeological surprise from the past, an' our laidback journey took us through places where the smog had crept right down deep into the tunnels, and parts where it lifted clear enough to see our travelling shadows looming large against the old brick walls. Now an' again our light dazzled a reflection in an old fish-eye mirror, and once or twice it were "Everybody down," when we passed beneath some low place where the roof had caved in. We travelled at the pace of the rippling tide, with Booker's guiding touch on the oar and our lamp swinging bravely upfront, lonesome as the North Star.

We docked at Russell Square, which were located somewhere in the deepest depths of Hades, for the long climb to the surface been never ending. But we did emerge eventually, an' walked around the corner to the Horse Hospital.

The Horse Hospital were indeed exceeding lively and busy with every variety of the people, and soon as we stepped through the door Uncle Cole hurried away with Dorcas to an emergency she were having with a birth.

It were a friendly place, brightly lit with torches set in sconces an' chandeliers made out of iron wheels all loaded with lighted candles. A corner by an iron stove were given over to "Help the Aged", and a couple of guys were shaving grizzled jowls, de-lousing hair and creating stylish wonders for them lank-locked gentleman of the road, while an older man were busy cheerfully chiropodising their gnarly used feet. A soup kitchen were dishing up pork-an-beans to a long line of the haunted hungry, an' volunteer nurses were checking folk in and telling them where all to go. "Next?"

"Me," said a tall, self-possessed women. She were pregnant and maybe about twenty-three years old. "Hi Abby," the nurse smiled, and placed her hand on Abby's stomach. "O my days, all engaged and ready to blow. Dorcas is busy with an emergency… But hurry on down to the labour-room, there should be someone there."

"Need a hand?" I offered, and escorted her through the hustle and bustle and opened the door for her. It was a quiet room. "Come in," said a couple of midwives, rising from warming their hands at the fire burning in the grate.

"Gees, I haven't had a bath in years," Abby smiled, eyeing the big round horse-trough all plumbed in with hot and cold taps. "Some other time maybe." She winced with pain and plonked herself down onto the bed.

"Are you the father?" one of the midwives asked me.

"Yes," said Abby, "yes he is."

"I am not, I'm a medic," I replied blushing, and reversed out hastily. I found Eden, who were making his way toward a bunch of hooded Raggers who was lolling about on a pile of bright bean-bags and making themselves at home on the rugs. "Mind if I sit here, Gertrude?" Eden asked.

"I is not Gertrude, I's Asbo, you plum," the boy growled.

"Respect, Asbo you plum. What's the problem?" Them murderous little boggarts sized Eden up with interest while Asbo uncovered the arm he was protecting, which hung like a broken wing an' looked dislocated at the shoulder. "I don't s'pose any of you lot has learned to count to ten yet?" At which the goblins bristled with outrage. "O well excuse I for thinking you was all bottom-feeding swamp-life." Eden bowed, and then helping Asbo onto his feet we manoeuvred him so his back was against the wall. "Well if you can count backwards with your eyes shut, you is a whole lot smarter than I thought. Alright, let me hear ten, nine, eight…"

Eden repositioned the joint firmly, which is likely to cause people to pass out with the brutal pain of it. Not Asbo, though, who winced, opened his eyes wide an' kept on counting "…three, two, one." We trussed up his shoulder in bandages, fitted him with a sling, and the war hero departed with his followers in the direction of the soup kitchen.

Pretty soon, all flushed with their victory over the Mantle, the wounded Leggers, Smokes an' injured perishing cold Hissy Boys come drifting in, all best friends now and sweetie boys together. For us it meant flushing out a lot of rock salt, nails to be dug out, burns to be treated an' fishing around for bullets. "Just prise it open an' dig it out boys. Don't worry, you'll get used to it." They refused the painblasters and flirted with the nurses, who ministered a round of tetanus shots in good humour. For the next few hours, Eden and I were engaged with stitching and sewing like a couple of old biddies at a quilting bee.

We was through by about six a.m. and just cleaning up when Dorcas come out of the operating theatre with a look about her that told us something awful had happened. Uncle Cole followed her, holding a baby all wrapped up and sleeping against him, while her uncomprehending daddy been left alone to say his last goodbye to his wife. The noise level dropped instantly to silence, a mark of respect for a mother who just bled out in childbirth.

Just before leaving, I checked on Abby, who had had a little boy. "Excuse me, I just come to make sure you was alright." I hovered at the door, for both mother and baby was in the tub, cosy and well.

"It's awful what happened, but we is fine. Come an' see us some time," Abby replied.

"Sorry, you know, unethical, the patient-medic thing." I waved, and closing the door, I heard her crooning to her baby, "Numbskull, I ain't a patient."

We went on our way then, friendly easy-going Eden raging inside about the loss of a life.

Mistral

E verything do come with strings attached like, "Beautiful tree," said God, "but no way be tempted to eat its lovely-looking, mouth-watering, delicious fruit." Or, "My sweet darling little shimmering princess daughter, you got the free range of the castle just so long as you never, ever go up dem intriguing stairs or through dat extraordinarily inviting door up there." I has a niggling feeling the Akashic Record is one of them outa bounds things. To read it do feel ever so slightly dightly like trespassing, but if yous is having a quiet read and you happen to come across Projack and a couple of names light up, you is bound to read on. One name, Nicky Nigredo, give me the heeby geebies and start ringing me alarm bells, flashing the internal warning lights, an' generally pressing me panic buttons. He is a do-not-approach kinda guy, while the other, Morgan Grey, is a more laidback, sitting-on-the-fence, I'm-dreaming-of-a-white-Christmas sorta fella. Neither of them is exactly status quo, probably numbers 8 an' 9 on the Weirdly Wonders of the World list, and either they musta spent a king's ransom on cosmetic surgery or maybe they was just getting their five a day, but whatever it were they is looking awful good for their age.

Morgan Grey do live on his ownsome, with about four thousand books for company, in one of them bijous style residences at the very top of the Projack Building. He spends a lot of time looking out the window, the rest is occupied in scholarly pursuit. Morgan's mind were proper way out there, for he'd gone through an eye of the needle and come out the other side of maths, chemistry and physics, well beyond hardcore science or the metaphysical an' all that jazz. Morgan Grey is the natural kahuna behind Projack, but he ain't been engaged in pulling the levers for a long long time, an' all that rarefied objective observing got Mr Morgan perfectly disconnected and out of touch with the nitty gritty. If he weren't he'd have blown a fuse at what his second-in-command Nicky Nigredo were up to, deep in the bowels of the Projack Building.

Things is looking up for Morgan, though, for lately his old heart been disturbed by love. It had come as a uninvited unexpected guest an' settled in. Love do be having a field day, colouring his vision, sweetening his mind and turning them ghastly grey skies into a heavenly blue. In all truthiness, most folks is not gazing out the window at the view, it is that challenging, but Morgan is a rare roast beef an' he do. What's more, he reckons hoptimistically that "It could be worse."

He may have a point, for along time ago the Projack Building itself were astonished as anyone to find itself rising brick by brick, out of the same sorta chaos we got today, 'cept with the added inconvenience of bombs which came whizzing down every night for a whole year. Howevers, with hobstinate defiance the power station did climb its way courageously out of the desolation of war an' helped return the stunned town into a city of light.

The Akashic Record don't predict who's about to come climbing out the rubble or who ain't, but Morgan could have a whole new chapter ahead... The fresh blue vellum is prepared and them stars is poised and waiting to be moved.

Morgan Grey

I was drawn to my window by the light of the moon. Far below, the river ran like quicksilver and for a moment, almost holy with intensity, our forlorn city looked majestic and proud to be illuminated in the moonwash. I nodded my head in acknowledgement. "I have seen you," I said. "You look beautiful tonight."

The moment fled, ruptured by a flickering explosion of gunfire and the fizzing of fireworks. A stream of lurid flares streaked across the tide towards the Mantle, on whom the woelorn lowlife had set their sights. The walls of Projack hardly registered the sound but my windows trembled with each blast, and looking at them anxiously, I caught sight of a white stork, winging her way through the smoke and air downriver. "And where are you going?" I wondered smiling, for her presence could only mean one thing. After all, a stork does have a duty to perform and a particular place in the world to be.

It took me a long time to understand that everything has a rightful place. Love and even war have their place too, for which there is no simple solution. Nor apparently for the psoriasis that has plagued my skin increasingly as time goes by, which may have its place too, for it was the psoriasis that obliged me to resort to alternative methods. Well, the irony of the Head of Projack ("Paving the Way to a Pain-Free Planet") lighting out to the Venus Man Trap for one of Liberty de Fer's natural products was not lost on anybody, but Liberty had been professional, graciously pretending that she was unaware of who I was (although I knew that she knew) and then, what with the radiance of her loveliness and the sympathy and genuine concern she showed over my ailment, my old heart skipped a beat and began to dance inside me.

I departed with a jar of her gentle skin cream ("The Peach, the Whole Peach and Nothing but the Peach"), warmed by this late waltz with love, and ever since then, feeling ever so slightly foolish, I have begun to watch the river.

I seldom catch a glimpse of Liberty, but have come to recognise her children and their friends from afar. Column appears regularly on the roof of the Winged Messenger Service, peacefully exercising the birds, and I have also seen him trading his fearsome knives for a ride on a skimmer with a Smoke. Once in a while I've caught sight of Milo, Eden, Angelina and Gloria wandering off to work or on their way to classes, enjoying each other's friendly company, and occasionally, Phoebe, Ariel, Harley and Tyler, all tucked away between the fresh green bundles on the herb barges where the twins, intense with concentration, demonstrate their sleight-of-hand, coin manipulation and the general re-arranging of the realm of time and space that magic requires. A realm that I could teach them a thing or two about...

All was silent outside now. The war had been abandoned, for a dense fog had thickened on the river, and rising in thick billowing blankets it obscured the light of the moon. 'I should know better. Of all people in the world, I should no better. What am I thinking of?' I retired from the window and returned to my books. 'Besides, she is married, very married, to the blacksmith Jean de Fer.'

Jean de Fer

I must have been very small when the army came marching home, for it is my first memory. They'd been recalled from defending the realm against the tides of marauding peoples who been left with no lands, for it were decided that it were more important to defend the realm against the sea afore we went the same way.

The shoring of the coast became a mainstay for the Wayland Forge, an' early one morning when I were sixteen, my father an' Luke an' Teddy, me younger brothers, made ready to journey down river with a cargo of iron to deliver up the east coast. Reema, who were a nine-year-old, made ready to hurl herself off the pontoon in protest, but always prepared for a dramatic gesture, my father Volco caught her in a bear-hug, an' wiping the tears from her eyes with them big rough sandpaper hands of his he consoled her, saying, "Cheer up, someone has to stay here to take care of things while I'm away. Do a good job and you can look forward to a really worth-it reward." They spat on their hands and shook on it, and turning to our Ma Amber, who just 'bout disappeared inside the embrace, he whispered something what made her blush. Then calling, "Keep the home fires burning!" he jumped aboard, saluted to one and all, an' took possession of the helm, solid as an oak. Reema stood in the threshold of the glowing forge and saluted back, but Ma looked like she'd seen a ghost as she waved us off on that cold December dawn.

The barges been daisy-chained together an' we was heavily armed with gunners against the Essex raiders. Me brothers an' I made sweet coffee and bacon sandwiches, which we took to the gunners afore settling down with Dad for breakfast. "Is we expecting trouble on the way up?" I asked.

"Not really on the way up," Volco replied. "Nobody 'cept the army wants a cargo of iron girders."

Sensing his reply were fishy, I thought a while an' says, "Seems a waste to make so many journeys up the coast and come back with empty barges all the time."

Dad took a long gulp of his coffee and replied, "My thinking exactly, son, and as a matter of fact we are coming back with a small load."

"Interesting." I said. "Like what?"

"Oh well, you know, one little red pony for Reema, some flint for the old-fashioned guns, plus about a hundred guns for reconditioning and as many sacks of apples as it takes to hide the lot. Oh, an' six Suffolk Punch horses."

"What the hell Dad, won't the gun-running make us a prime target?" exclaimed Luke. "And won't them huge horses kick up a fuss coming on board, six of 'em?" says Teddy.

"We are not gun running, it's army business! Calm yourselves lads, we are well armed and the horses will enjoy being at sea." Volco were jubilant and raised his coffee mug to clink a toast with us. It weren't that we weren't brave, but experience had taught us that either one had to have a lot of faith in God or some sort of death wish to be confident about some of Dad's projects, an' we were considerably jittery about his plan.

It takes one tide to bring a barge down to Southend and it were a matter of course that our progress were being charted through the hostile lenses of spy-glasses, telescopes and the naked eyes of cut-throats, causing them sharpshooting gunners fore an' aft to keep their peepers well wide until we was way out into the estuary, where we powered up the steam an' hoisted up the sails, and the combination allowed us enough speed to high-tail it out to sea an' out of sight.

You could never be far enough from Clacton, which operated along entirely different lines, it being the preferred place of residence for all kinds of villains and their nasty children, all living like a pack of happy families: Mr Beretta the shooter, Miss Blunderbuss the destroyer and Master Browning the semi-automatic, who never heard of codes of honour and was likely to board a boat, throw the crew overboard and divide the spoils, or just chuck 'em in an' all, for kicks. Saturday nights, some of them Clacton boyos rode around on armoured quads, torching the cobbledy Tinkerage caravans, robbing the outlying smallholdings and terrorizing the fishing settlements. The army were not eager to repair them flatland Essex sea defences, but invited the water in instead, and was leaving it to become a nature reserve. Or flush out the dross, it were all a matter of interpretations.

After years of negligence the coastline were a mighty disaster. People's homes been lost an' whole towns rubbed out by the rising tides, the level-lands were swamped out and up the coast, the fens had become shallows for hundreds of miles inland. The army was more-or-less building a new coastline wherever it were needed, an' taking no chances or short cuts. Mile upon mile of iron girders had been rammed in. They faced the sea in cliffs of iron that were all shored up at the back with rubble, boulders and landfill to a thick wideness which sloped off gradually to ground level and then overfilled with topsoil, where the grass took root and the whole thing slowly become part of a drier landscape.

We curved round an' put in by Felixstowe Ferry where, with a promise to bring back some lovely deep-fried clams an' chips for us, Dad and the gunners took off for the Victoria Inn, while my brothers and I were left to keep an eye on the boats and while away our time drinking beer, explaining to Teddy how to play poker and fleecing him of his unearned wages.

The clams and chips eventually showed up, and the next day we put out again but remained close in to the Suffolk coast-line, for it were all shored up safe and sorted as far as the eye could see. We passed by the Hollesley Bay prison colony, which is about fourteen hundred acres surrounded by fine high-wire prison security that no one could break into: a clink in reverse, settled by crims who'd seen off their Hissy Boy guards. But they'd kept up breeding cattle and them Suffolk Punch horses, some of which was soon to be ours. That evening we put in for the night at Psycho Charlottes Beach, and next day we caught up with the army where they was bivouacked along Kessingland.

We was welcomed ashore by Captain Dan, a friendly man who kept himself understated for someone on a mission, an' I been keen to help his army unload, for they was a rich mix of peoples working well together to shore up the lands. The Big Smoke were an each-man-for-hisself place, an' the army altruism were a whole new thing for me.

Later, over dinner, the spirit of camaraderie that sparked between my father and Captain Dan, affirmed to me the traditional link that lies between the war-mongers and the iron-mongers. Both was men who absolutely knew who they was and what they were about, no question.

The next day a fiery red pony and the six big beautiful chesnut horses was delivered. They had to be blindfolded to get them on the barges, two per barge an' the pony got one all to himself. Once on board they settled in no trouble, for they was the original gentle giants, and I been so pleased by them.

Captain Dan took care of loading the guns an' covering

everything up with apples, while each of us boys settled into the hold with a pair of horses to care for, the gunners took up their positions fore and aft, and we was off on the return journey.

It were sometime after midnight, an' I were sleeping in the straw by my horses, when I was woken by the creaking of the barges. The wind had picked up, the sea was choppy and the mercury had plummeted. I could hear my father moving about on deck, so I gone to help him tighten ropes and stow away any loose gear that been lying around. The wind come in freezing blasts, flinging a few icy snow-flakes out of the dark. "Put a life-jacket on and wake your brothers, an' light the storm lamps on your way."

I nodded to Dad and gone down the line of barges. "Teddy, get a life jacket on, untie your horses and come up front. Luke, wake up man, it's getting rough. Put on your life jacket, untie the horses." The barges lurched and rolled beneath me on my way back and checking on my horses I gave them some apples to calm them, for their ears was pointing back and the whites of their eyes were showing in fear.

When the storm hit, it come howling down the North sea like an iced-tooth wolf. The snow came thick and fast, an' our barges lumbered up the steep waves and slapped across the tops of them afore ploughing down into the troughs again. We was way too heavy an' shipping water, which took the apples floating everywhere. I were just untying my horses when a flock of Snow Geese came hurling out of the darkness with a rush of wings and outstretched feet that came to rest on the boats. The horses shied in alarm and amidst the confusion, I were caught by a rogue wave which rolled over the barge and put me in the gigantic snarling ocean. My breath were knocked out of me, the storm lights vanished into the whiteout an' I were sinking from one world into the next.

Milo de Fer (age 17)

A s someone who just come off their first shift in the Horse Hospital, I is in no doubt that my father were clinically a dead boy at that particular time in his life. There is a neither-here-nor-there department for them that's just passing through, but by the time my shift were over, a young woman called Lucy had died an' a couple of babies had been born. The Horse Hospital been the Big Smoke's portal through which some people come into life and others take their leave of it.

No good work we'd done there that night were gonna outweigh the reality of her death. Cole was all in, Eden were furious an' we descended down the long stairwell underground, sombre as a black cloud. We woke Booker, who were fast asleep in his boat, and set off home in a stony silence. After a while Booker give me a penetrating look, like the-atmosphere-is-doing-my-head-in kinda

48

look, and I been grateful for the cue to ask him something I been curious about. "How came you an' my parents to be friends?"

He seemed relieved. "Well, that's a good question. It's a long story, but we ain't in a hurry," an' he rowed into his story, his voice rising an' falling with the long slow strokes of the oars.

Booker

The news of the disaster came filtering through by way of the Winged Messenger Service, on tiny scraps of paper describing monumental events, and it were my job to ferry that news to little Reema and Amber at the Wayland Forge. I shined my shoes, put on my respectable clothes, a black silk scarf an' my flying cap and gone on my way. The door were wide open and an inviting sweet smell of cinnamon-spice Christmas cookies come wafting outside, and inside Reema, covered in coal smut, was doing a fine job of banking down the fires for the night. I hesitated, for it were Christmas Eve after all and a very hard thing to bring that news, but Amber seen me standing in the doorway and asked me in. "Hello Booker, what brings you here? " She asked, her eyes alert with cautions, apprehensions an' questions. Reema left off her shovelling and took a good look at me. I guess it wasn't every day a black man showed up at the door, I was supposing, until she shook my hand and says, "Good evening mister, what the hell is that you've got on your head?"

"Why, this here's a Spitfire flying cap. Don't they teach you anything?"

"No, not one damn thing, I'm afraid. Spitfire, cool." She smiled. Amber took the biscuits out the oven and made us all a mug of cocoa and then we sits down together by the fire, and I told them as best I could what I knew about the terrible storm, that not one single boat had survived, all were presumed dead an' perished in the freezing seas, but I had also heard that the Snow Geese had come white-winged in the darkness to carry their souls to heaven.

It was the hardest thing to tell and both of them slumped, broken-like, their eyes brimmed full of tears. I put my arms around them and we sat for a long while by the light of the fire. After some time Reema got up and began shovelling coal onto the fires and stoking up the embers again. "I sort of knew," cried Amber. "I had a presentiment when they left, you know. Volco suddenly said out of the blue, keep the home fires burning. It was strange because – you see – the forge fires never go out. Reema's been wearing herself to a shred, keeping them alight in hopes that it would bring them home soon."

Then Reema announced real quietly, "Ain't no crime without a body and if the sea committed a crime, it has to give my Daddy and my brothers back. It has to give the bodies back, don't you see? We don't know nothing till it does." Then I gone straightway to try and find them for her.

Far and wide across the land there still remains traces of little paths that used to run from the remoter settlements to the closest church with a graveyard. Them paths is worn away by a few thousand years of folk taking their dead to the church for burying. For the lonesome dead it were a good deal too, for they always knew the way back home and used them to visit their families and old friends, and if those left behind wanted to engage them a while in conversations, a stile or cross-roads was the traditional place to meet.

The Gitanes has done a fine job of keeping these paths safe by fuelling the local superstitions with tales of haunting, so I walked out through Canning Town and been able to make my way, undetected an' unmolested, towards the east coast. The walking were heavy going, for the country-side were knee-deep in snow from the storm. The woodland trees was creaking with the weight of it, and the streams petrified frozen still. A hungry horse followed along his side of the hedge for a while, and a robin made desperate by the cold came to share my bread. At night I found a sheltered dell and dared a fire against the wild dogs, and all the next day I walked unchallenged till I come to the frozen marshlands by the sea.

The murdering ocean broke deceptive peaceful with mild white waves of innocence on the snowy shore. The sandbanks were hidden by a fine sea mist, with the river Crouch somewhere down behind me and the salty Blackwater Estuary some ways up ahead. I made a fire in the hollow of a sand bank an' fell asleep to the sound of grumbling seals out on the icy mudflats.

A cold dawn broke but it warmed a little beneath a pale midwinter sun, when I set off slowly searching all along the empty shoreline. About mid-afternoon, I caught sight of a small pony far off in the low blue light. He didn't move as I came by but stood sentinel among heaps of bright red apples, which were scattered all over the snow. The pony were a bright red an' whinnied briefly, relieved to see another living soul had come at last to share his forlorn duty, for he was standing by the bodies of Volco with a boy at each side. It were incomprehensible to see them, whose natural element were fire, so cruelly frozen in their feather-bed of snow, and my heart contracted in misery an' sorrowfulness.

The pony were a spirited little thing, an' awful glad of his company I gone on to look for the others. Further up the beach we came across the bodies of the gunners, half-buried in the snow, but search as we may we found no sign of Jean the older son. The light fades quickly on them shortened winter days, and when the snow began to fall again we headed off in the direction of the sound of a bell which came ringing clearly up the Estuary.

Sometime after nightfall, we come to the gates of a monastery. Well, at first I thought I come across a mad-house, for a posse of beefy monks in tall black hats and long black robes were running around the torch-lit cloisters throwing snowballs at each other, but it turned out that St John the Baptist's Monastery were Orthodox, and the Muscovy brethren were just playing, enjoying the snow.

Our appearance brought an end to the snowballing an' a couple of Kalashnikovs come poking through the gates to greet us, for everyone do have a high level of security paranoia out in the sticks. Once they understood what our sorry mission were about, they opened up and let us in. Brother Pony were taken to the stables for a slow feed, and I were feasted and treated with generous cheer. As the night wore on, I been interested to note that there were one or two sisters amongst them brothers. Man, them Russkies is always a bundle of intrigues an' surprises. The next morning I was awesome hung-over, an' after a lot of coffee over breakfast my new friends offered to fetch the bodies and deliver them in dignity to the Black Friars, which I been grateful to accept. I bid them farewell, took the pony and returned by the ways I had come.

In the early hours of New Year's Day, true to their word, the monks set off along the Essex coast in a fishing boat with flaming torches set about the five open coffins on board. When they came up the river, the Thames Barrier was all draped in black banners and bristling with glinting swords, for the Saracens had swarmed up there and waited in bareheaded respect as Volco, Teddy, Luke and the gunners passed by on their last journey home.

Column de Fer

When I were about eight years old, I scarpered up the tunnel at the back of the forge so as to find out where the River Fleet were coming from. I never did find that out, but what I did find were that Grandpa Volco had left me a legacy. Inside that tunnel the water was knee deep, the rocks slippery as glass, and the rushing current were hell-bent on driving me down the chicanes and turning me outside in at the mill-pond. It were not looking good, until my fingers found handholds chiselled into the rock, onto which I fastened like the original limpet. After about a hundred yards of hauling myself along, I come across a cleft in the side of the tunnel and went inside. It was dry and quiet in there, which made me cautious about striking a light, in case it were an old powder room. Still, after a while of bumping about in the dark I chanced it and struck a flint, lit a torch, and saw that I were in a workshop – a lovely, perfectly circular place with all the hammers, anvil, furnace an' some fine tools for delicate work, all in their rightful places. I held my breath and listened to that place and it were definitely asking for someone to be working there again.

Everything that comes out of a forge is of an entirely practical nature, something my sister Phoebe's got the right touch for, but most of what comes out of my hands is entirely not practical, and that's how I is, something my father is trying to get his head around. Most of my creations is for trading or giving away, like the whale I made for Milo because he loves them, and the wolf for Uncle Cole, who's up all night, and I made Ma a silver rose. Dad were almost impressed.

First I model them out of wax and when they is just so, I set them in a cast and then pour in some melted pewter/copper/silver which melts away the wax and sets in its place. Last, I print my hallmark, a dove pierced by an arrow, on everything. Except for the knives I forge for trading, which are cold and razor-sharp just like knives are meant to be.

The discovery of my grandfather's workshop were epic. It were the perfect place for me to create in all the peace an' quiet I needed. Convenient too, on a number of fronts. Like Dad were unlikely to pay a visit, because ever since he drowned he ain't too keen on water. Fair enough.

It shown me that beneath all of Volco's thunder an' lightning there were subtlety, for his tools produced such fine work. An' I been inclined to share that with Phoebe, so she too could see there had been another side to Grandpa. Then it were only a matter of time afore Ariel were in on it too, for Volco were also her grandfather, an' wherever you has Phoebe an' Ariel, like spring follows winter, Harley an' Tyler is not far behind. An' they believes that this is the only place where they is totally safe from their "read all about it" Grandma-in-the-sky, and I believe they are right.

We puts our radio show together in the workshop, an' once a show is ready to air, it is my job to broadcast it far and wide from an old transmitter on top of the Winged Messenger Service, under the pretext of exercising the birds. It don't bear thinking about the consequences if the Mantle ever caught us at it. I have nightmares about that, and much of my night dreaming is spent running across miles of rooftops pursued by the Mantle, with baying dogs and them stinking Hissy Boy trackers… Them toothy dogs were still snarling in my ears when I awoke and been greatly relieved to remember that I were safe and sound at Aunt Reema's.

I dressed and shuffled off to see if any one else was up an' about, but the attic were empty of Milo and Eden. I passed on Gloria and Angelina, who were "Disturb us and die" types, and there were no evidence that Harley and Tyler had even slept in their beds. The house were a ghost ship, but I hoped that Phoebe and Ariel were in and maybe even stirring, which they was, busy giving themselves kohl black eyes and spiking their hair with Agar Agar. "Morning. Got your sackcloth and ashes on already I see. Coming out?"

"Yeah, in a mo. Come in. Want some eyeliner and your hair spiked?" they says, hopeful.

"Okay, why not?" I agreed, and when they finished turning me into a white boy Legger, we tipsy-toed down to the kitchen and made a big pot of cocoa, loaded a tray with some of them currant buns Aunt Reema makes for me, and stole out.

Inside its fortress walls, the garden were perfectly still. A little fog clung to the tree tops an' the damp come drip, drip, dripping off the leaves, the grass all wet with dew and dotted red with the last of the apples. We passed along the neatly labelled medicinal plants – Opium Poppy (painkillers, morphine, codeine), Liquorice (stomach ulcers), Broad Bean (L-Dopa for Parkinson's), Foxglove (digoxin to regulate the heart-beat) – making our way toward the more formal gardens down the left hand side, the right side being the "wild garden", mostly a wilderness intent on escaping over the wall to join forces with the jungle on the other side.

When we came here as children and stood small beneath the tall arching trees, we came to understand that someone else been living here long before Uncle Cole and Aunt Reema arrived. He were not a conversations man, but he was a good gardener who occasionally interfered with Uncle Cole's planting, for he were about protecting the spirit of the place which no big thick walls could ever do. He were solitary an' always elegant in white linen suits, and we seen him so rarely that he became known as Solo.

We set our tray down on the gravestone and tuckered into our cocoa and buns when Milo, Eden and Uncle Cole came along to join us.

"Now where on earth has you been?" asked Ariel.

"Helping out Uncle Cole. Got enough chai for us?" says Milo, pouring himself some of our cocoa. "Mmm, nothing quite like a stiff mug of chocolate sauce to start the day."

"Excuse me for asking," Eden says, peering at the makeup, "but are you guys on your ways to a funeral or something?"

"Not particularly. We is in character," I improvised.

"So you are Breakfast of the Goths, I take it," Uncle Cole said, helping himself to our cocoa. Eden looked perplexed but we were distracted when the rooster sprinted out of the stables pursued by his fussing harem an' followed by Harley and Tyler, who clattered outside with Delilah an' the little red ponies. "Cripes, if their Ma finds out where they've been sleeping," mumbled Milo, a thought that had us all removing straw from their hair and brushing down their clothes.

"Guys, guys, we loves you too!" They backed away slowly toward the house and into Reema, who finished straightening them up.

During our "proper" breakfast, Eden asked, " Mum, have you ever heard of a play called The Breakfast of the Goths?"

"Have you gone bonkers, or is it just that you've been up all night? Perhaps you and Milo should try and get some sleep now," Reema suggested. "The rest of you get a move on, or you'll be late for Liberty."

"If you is contemplating catching a ride down the Venus Man Trap with us," Gloria advanced on me looking difficult and dangerous, "pull the trousers up proper and get the makeup off."

"Okay, I'm on it." I pulled up my trousers an' wiped my face hastily.

"Big improvement, owl boy," she scowled, "big improvement."

Liberty de Fer

Not far from the rumbling thrum of the forge lay a lovely tranquil oasis, absolutely overwhelmed with Buddleia, Bulrushes an' Flag Irises, and choked with the luxuriant foliage of house-plants that had transmigrated outdoors, what with the increasing humidity in the Big Smoke.

I was often drawn there, perhaps at first because it was kinda boggy an' reminded me of home, but when I went rambling about an' exploring a bit, it seemed to me that something could be made of this overgrown wasteland, an' that the burned-out buildings had once been of a unique character. I weren't quite sure where I were going with this, until the day I come upon the dilapidated shell of a long low bar. It must once have welcomed so many people through its broken doors that it still retained a friendly atmosphere, an' appeared able-bodied enough to take on new life as a natural cosmetics studio.

The very idea of building something were a walk on the wild side. At the same time, I were keen to create something for myself. The place I'd found were that opportunity, so hoping that my artistry might see me through, I went for it.

The best thing about building the Venus Man Trap were the many friends I made along the way, starting with surly Mac who ran the city farm an' been very happy to parley ad infinitum with animals, but not with people. "My, what fantastic pigs. Saddle Backs, is it?" I enquired, smiling at them, for I had a soft spot for pigs. "Back home," I informed the dour an' massive farmer, "it's all Lincolnshire Curly."

"Is tha' reet? I believe Lincolnshire Curly 'bout the toughest pig on earth," he actually responded.

"Well, yeah," I squeaked back, "you has to be to survive the winters out there."

"Is tha' reet?" Farmer Mac loomed over his gate an' peered at me. "Hmm," he said, "wouldn't mind ta git me a couple of thems."

"Oh well, can't promise, but I'll see what I can do… Meantime, could I borrow your whole herd? Got some land that needs clearing, an' Saddle Backs is so good at it."

Farmer Mac's face crinkled into one of the few smiles I guess he'd ever made. "You women is all the same, init… Anyway, looks like you knows your pigs, an' if I might git a Curly or two out of it, a good deal all round," he answered, an' offered a mucky hand to shake an' seal the deal.

I got my land cleared an' in due course, three Saddle Back piglets set sail with Canada up the east coast to my Dad at Greene King Keep, and three Lincolnshire Curly came sailing back down again.

Once you stake a claim on land in the Big Smoke, you has one year to complete your project or your stake may be up for grabs again,

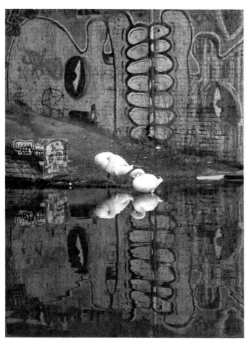

and harnessing up Axel an' Shadow (the smallest of the Forge's drays) we went to work in our own way. The horses an' I scoured the back streets an' alleys salvaging railway sleepers, doors and windows, some of which were stained a cool blue. It took a while, for I were picky about things an' came across a whole new Big Smoke while searching for things that was just so, because the one an' only philosophy I holds on construction is that a building should appeal to all of the many senses we has.

When I was a fourteen year old my father explained the concept of Phi to me, an' it sat well with me, it being a deeply satisfying thing to know there were some underlying order to the world, an anchor for a chaotic teenage mind to grasp.

It were also the single principle that opened a door on beauty for me, an' I been at great pains therefore to cut my stable doors, sash windows, the wooden steps and everything else I could in proportion with the Golden Ratio, as well as dividing the whole of the long rectangular Bar accordingly, which in actual practise were no joke.

I been very happy to work things by myself, but even happier when Reema, my sister-in-law, begun to help, partly because she was up for anything that whiffed of some sort of civilisation in the Big Smoke, but mostly because we had a hoot and then Mara, who were attracted by the element of free will she perceived in the project, come to join us too. An' thank heavens for that, for she had a quirky humour an' were down to earth an' practical. There's nothing more real than a friendship that's formed when wading around in cement an' firming up the foundations, while caulking out the timbers with oakum on the outside an' larch resin on the inside, with the laying of the large oblong tiles of terracotta upon the floor, insulating the walls with fleece and plastering up a place with gypsum. By all this a friendship moves onto the level of those that has survived a tsunami or worse, and our long low log-cabin took shape organically, even if rather unconventionally, for as yet it had no roof.

Jean had been quite content to stand back while we got on with it. Probably he was a whole lot more confident about my abilities than me. At any rate, it were not a feminist statement so I invited him on site to view the work in progress. "This is stunning. I thought you could do it. How very beautiful, an' a remarkable fine job." He looked at the details appreciatively and admired the whole thing, an' if he noted the long row of newly fashioned arching rafter timbers that vaulted skyward, kinda like a Celtic harp, kinda like the ribs of a

Viking ship, and the complete absence of the roof, Jean didn't mention it. Instead he said, light on, "Gees well, I'd love to be involved in someway. Anything I could do to help?"

"That's what I were hoping. See, I have this roof in my imagination, but haven't the foggiest idea how to go about building it…"

"Tell me about it. What exactly is you thinking of?"

So Jean and Canada Blanch (an excellent boat-builder) covered it all with a wide floating roof of copper that oversailed the walls to create a surrounding porch, and looked quite a lot like a marvellous protective upside-down boat.

I were very fit when Milo came into the world, who'd been considerate enough to wait till the roof were up before he were born, an' three weeks on Reema gave birth to Eden, and to celebrate their births we planted young birch trees all around the Venus Man Trap, a custom that we has maintained, for Big Smoke babies is few and far between.

Grandma Tookie
(the Akashic Record)

T he Venus Man Trap opened its doors at least half an' hour before her year was up, and right away there were people all over the Big Smoke, washing their hands, conditioning their hair, shaving, slapping on the moisturisers, painting on the lipstick, or lying in some old tin bath out in the yard, enjoying one of the Venus Man Trap's many products, and it was a small but fine thing to create a little comfort for people and take the edges off a harsh, harsh world.

Artisans of all kinds staked their claims nearby, walls sprung up, windows appeared, roofs were raised, stove pipes installed and an array of white-sailed wind-turbines began to twirl, and combing the river for driftwood they turned it into decking, tamed the Buddleia and trained exotic plants. Then the potter kicked up her wheel, the furniture maker set up shop, the glassblowers moved in and fired up the kiln, and "The Gossip Station" suffused the whole of Gabriel's Wharf with the lovely smell of fresh baked bread, cakes, muffins and coffee. And some years down the line, Linda Miscellaneous, a petite Brazilian seamstress, sat at her Singer stitching, binding and patching the tears and holes with a void in her heart that could never be mended, for it was her son Hope who'd been taken.

The trees grew tall an' the birds moved in: finches, parrots, house martins, a pair of red-winged starlings all the way from Africa, and during the night they'd been joined by a stork, who was busily engaged with making a nest on one of Liberty's chimneys.

"That's the stork we seen last night, I bet," said Phoebe. "Good she made it safe an' sound. Ma, Ma we're back! Come outside, take a look, we has a stork, we has a stork!" And Liberty, who had grown up in the land of a thousand storks, was very pleased this one had come to her.

Liberty greeted her class with a handshake, including her own children. "Good morning Column. Did you have a bad night or have you just smudged your eyeliner? Good morning, Phoebe…" which made it clear to them that Ma had temporarily transmogrified into Teach. "What a to-do on the river last night. Good to see you all, find yourselves a space.

"This term we are going to concentrate on basic soap-making. But first of all," Liberty looked around at her teenage pupils, "we are going to take a look at the unique properties of the Golden Ratio.

"Phi is a mathematical proportion that has been occupying the minds of people forever, because it crops up in all sorts of places. For example, our upper arms in relation to our forearms, or between the growing points of leaves spiralling up a plant stem, and I gather that even the moons of Saturn are divided in this way. I'm sure that if you take a measuring tape you will find many examples of your own, but now gather round and watch this… Take olive oil or beeswax, mix with this wood ash, or what we call lye, heat it up, collect the residue, and that's your basic soap. But what happens next is where the magic lies, for a soap-maker is always after a unique blend of their own. So today let's experiment with the Golden Ratio in liquid proportions. Add anything you fancy, rose, lemon, lavender… Have a go, enjoy yourselves."

Liberty had caught their imagination and work was well underway when kicking up a row, the nesting stork swooped down upon a man an' begun to mob him viciously. "Clear off, you egret!"

the man shouted, and defending himself with a leather bag, he made a dash for the sheltering porch. Dusting himself off, he clumped up the steps, opened the door and stood there surveying the scene, blocking out all the light and casting his long annoying shadow across the floor.

There were very few people (and storks) in heaven or earth who did not find the presence of Nicky Nigredo pretty disquieting, but not Liberty, who was mistress of her domain, and standing her ground, she surveyed him back coolly. He was a unusual-looking guy, with an edgy glitter to his green eyes. He had a mane of dark hair and was attired in a black smoking-jacket an' dark jeans that spilled over the top of his steel-capped boots. Altogether a bit of a hardcore puss-in-boots...

"Morning," he growled, under Liberty's scrutiny. " May I come in?"

"No, absolutely not," she replied with some disdain. "As you can see, we're closed for classes," a piece of news that the class affirmed with smiles and nods, but then the dangerous dude smiled and nodded back to them in a manner so chilling that the hair rose on the back of their necks. Liberty's eyes narrowed into two turquoise slits and squaring her shoulders, she advanced on him while unconsciously picking up one of the many pots that lay about the place. "Is there something specific that you're after?" she asked.

"Well yes," he said, raising an eyebrow at the pot in her hand. " Morgan Grey asked me to pick up some skin cream for him."

"Well, here you go then," Liberty said firmly, and removing the ointment from the shelf, she walked over to the door and handed it to him.

"Thank you," the stranger replied, and then fumbling about in his old Gladstone Bag he produced a bottle, saying, " Morgan asked me to deliver this by way of thanks. It's a bottle of rare Sour Grape wine."

How odd, thought Liberty, that's just not Morgan's style. Much too flash for a man who prefers anonymity. "Thanks, but no thanks," she said. "Now we really must be getting on here. Have a nice day."

"Suit yourself," the stranger shrugged, and depositing the wine on the outside table he left. A great "Hurray!" went up behind him.

Class came to an end, and hanging their mixing-pots back on the hooks in the rafters, stacking up the homely-smelling bricks of beeswax, wiping up spilt essential oils and washing out measuring cups, with a " May we borrow a measuring tape please?" and a "Have a nice day," Angelina and Gloria headed back home in the donkey cart while Column, Phoebe, Ariel, Harley and Tyler headed for the Bakery, and then trooped off the radar.

Liberty went outside, glared at the bottle of wine and rolling herself a rare cigarette, she sat down to smoke it with an extinguishing heart, for her fire always guttered a bit after a fight.

It was a relief when old Thor came trotting along with Jean in the iron wagon. "Everything all reet?" he asked, sensing she was down about something.

"A weird customer put the wind up me, that's all."

"And so you have been smoking an' drinking your sorrows away?"

"'Course. I'm quite bannered. Ever heard of Sour Grape wine? It's rare, apparently. A gift from Morgan Grey. It was the assistant who bought it over. He creeped me out. It felt suspicious, or like a bribe."

"Not that crop-eared creature? He's a nasty piece of work, that one. With friends in high places." Jean jumped off the wagon, hugged Liberty to him and said, "Still, absolutely, no point in looking a gift horse in the mouth."

"No," said Liberty. "I could use a drink."

Jean poured them both a glass and took a sip. "Tell you what, that's about the strangest wine I've ever tasted."

Taking a sip of hers, Liberty's face puckered up. "It's okay, though," she nodded her head approvingly. "Very smooth an' very sharp."

"Grows on you, though. Fancy a drop more?" Jean asked.

"Sure, why not?"

They sat, drank and relaxed together for a while, and when another glass reminded them of how much they loved one another they went inside and stepped into each others arms. Meanwhile, outside, old Thor chewed pony nuts appreciatively in his nose-bag while the white stork on the chimney waited patiently to deliver the soul of a new child for Jean and Liberty.

Mistral (the Akashic Record, Nicky Nigredo)

While Morgan been reacquainting himself with the kinder side of life, his second-in-command been free to explore that powerful darkly interior he got. Nicky were a prime meddling magpie who gone clumping down the Venus Man Trap in high spirits with a idea of checking out who Morgan had fallen for and maybe upset things a bit, but first he got attacked by a bird an' then that irksomely "Hurray" happened, and he had to concede that Liberty had not been fazed by him at all, at least for the moment. Man, I would definitely be worrying. Lawd, even an amoeba would be quivering in its socks, seeing as Nicky were not exactly a loving spoonful of forgiveness an' forgettingness. His people skills been mainly fear-based an' confined to conspiring, controlling and manipulating. He were an extraordinary clever geek who spent most of his time in his darkly lab beneath the Projack Building and he were absolutely not, not, not the out-in-broad-daylight, dizzy shopaholic kind, but there we is.

After the Venus Man Trap, Nicky stopped by the glassblowers' workshop, where he opened the door and waited like some big-shot theatre star for the whole world to notice theys here, until Leo the glassblower glowered at him an' said, "Come in quickly, sirrah, afore you let all the heat escape." Nicky went inside and waited while Leo trimmed a white-hot glass bulb into a bowl and set it aside to cool. He were not at all warming to Nicky, an' suspicious 'bout what he was seeing, he asked him what his business was in a most surly an' unfriendly voice that was actually meaning, "Get out of me shop."

But Nicky were used to this kinda reception by now and says, like he were coming from the most perfectly normal space, "I would like to order a crystal ball, please." Leo's face kinda wrinkled at that, for he were unsure if Nicky was kidding. But Nicky were dead serious an' gone on to explain, "Not a bauble. It must be solid right the way through and flawless, opaque in quality but transparent enough to let in the light."

Now Leo were a true glassman, with lungs nearly shot with all the long-blowing glassmaking required, and making a piece of work like that would be a challenge an' a satisfying thing to do. "Trouble is, the art of making a true scrying-glass was lost in the Middle Ages. I'd give my eye-teeth for some knowledge of the techniques they used."

"No need to lose your teeth, I have an old formula which may help," said Nicky, drawing a piece of paper out of his pocket. "See, the Venetians used equal quantities of Tin Oxide, Antimony and Arsenic to make a white opaque glass, but perhaps if we then add say about five grams of Manganese, it should become amethyst in colour. What do you reckon?"

Leo furrowed his brow, torn between the man and the project, but after scrutinizing the formula a while he said, "Sure, I'll give it a go, but don't hold your breath sir."

"That's all I'm asking. Give it a go, see you around." Nicky left, and continuing his excursion into the world of consumerism, he popped into "Linda Miscellaneous." Linda peered over her sewing machine, with her massive dark eyes and her lustrous black hair falling like the hanging gardens of Babylon, an' just because he looked a little like Beethoven she gave Nicky a friendly smile. Whatever – Nicky were so smitten by her looks, and that someone were actually smiling at him, he becomed momentarily brain-dead an' speechless, until she says, "Ahem, how can I help you?"

Recovering his cool, he enquired, " I need a new suit. Perhaps I could see some samples of cloth?"

Wondering what Beethoven would have worn exactly, Linda took her time, an' after looking him up and down carefully, she said, "I've had a roll of velvet indigo waiting around for the right person to carry it off. I think you'll agree it's perfect for you." She pulled out the cloth. "How about the jacket in velvet and the trousers in a dark grey moleskin?"

'Course he agreed, and while she were measuring him up she noticed his olive-green eyes an' mutilated ears, and he noticed the old poster with a picture of a little smiling boy. 'Hope. Missing without trace.' She say nothing 'bout his ears and he say not a word 'bout her son, and when she were all done, he thanked her and said a sotto voce goodbye and ducked out. That wickerdy old cat were not without his charms.

Nicky strolled along the cobblestone alleyways, feeling quite the man an' more at ease as darkness approached. His steel-toed boots sparked up the evening hollows, echoing beneath the arches as he passed round the back of Jabba the Sluts an' gone on his way to Borough Market.

Borough Market is one of them eggs-and-bacon by day and Thai by night joints, 'cept it's fruit an' vegetables by day and herbs and chemical substances by night, and popular with the international crowd. Man, there was Orientals with low-grade, high-grade an' mixed-grade opium cakes all securely stashed in ironbound wooden boxes, there were Raggers an' Hoodies ready to mule for a cut of the deal, leather-clad Smokes come for their skunk an' jittery junkies hollering for their crystal meth. There were slickly dealers come to cut them big fat lines for their yah, yah private clientele, an' East European smoothies, wheeling an' dealing left, right an' centre. An assassin come for his plug of hash an' gone unseen, while way back under the arches, warming their shivering selves by the oildrum fires, the hollow-eyed girls with loused-up hair is willing to do anything for a fix.

Here, too, come that Nicky, smiling and gliding and whispering up manna in the ears of them hopeless addicted cadavers, "Let Projack help you. We'll sort you out, food, excellent accommodation and top wages for all who volunteer for drug trials. Sign up here, you got nothing to lose." Which were a big fat lie.

It were a mighty convenient arrangement all round, a thing to which the chief of the Mantle, Mason Flint, been pleased to turn a bind eye, an' he were already waiting an' ever so helpful with transportation, because Nicky Nigredo had a most powerful useful gift.

There were one gentlewoman who volunteered herself up to Projack for drug trials, for she were terminal ill and a morphine addict for the pain. But while she bumped along with the other volunteers in the Mantle's Black Mariah, her time to die drew near and she whispered the name of her child. The story of her life started to unfold in a panorama of pictures before her eyes: the struggle of her recent illness, the birth of her child and all of the people an' events that had coloured her life, until she returned to the time when her family stood all around her, full of joy at the moment of her birth, which was also the moment of her death, an' her peaceful leaving of the world.

Now Nicky could see those pictures too, clear as I can read the Akashic script. Which were a source of great power to him an' also the Mantle, for it give them access to a whole lot of secrets in the world of crime an' power. Sometimes, on a need-to-know basis, the services of the assassin were called upon to delete a man or two for his pictures. "Anything useful to us?" enquired Mason Flint, as he and Nicky stopped the wagon to pitch that dead woman's body into the river.

"No, no, mate. Just another sideshow nobody," say Nicky, but as a matter of a fact he were really rattled, for she were once a lovely-looking women, someone with whom he'd kept company for a time, and Nicky'd just seen that he were the father to her child.

Soon as them addicts had been "safely" deposited through Projack's back door, Nicky slipped off to fetch that dead woman's child, but when he came by her home there been no sign that kid ever existed, for she were shipped out a long time ago. "One day" he says, "I'll catch up with that ten-year-old lambkin of mine. I wonder where she's got to, and I wonder why they called her Mistral?"

"What!" I slammed the book tight shut.

Phoebe De Fer (age 13)

When one door shuts, like if your Ma and Pa was detained at the Venus Man Trap for reasons which been unclear, trouble not, for another door do open up ahead. An' a highly inviting door at that, which had us wading up the tunnel of gushing water an' into Columns workshop, where we lit the stove, put the water on for a cuppa chai, and settled in to share some bits an' pieces we got together for our next radio broadcast.

Creating a show is a process whereby we's entered a time warp. The hours go by in minutes an' the minutes in seconds while we listened to something to make us laugh, or a piece of the best definitive knockout, earth-shattering scoop in the history of mumblecore radio. This time I'd come across a real hot potato which I been keeping to myself, for you has to consider well afore you allow your friends to get swallowed up by the ticking crocodile, which I knew it were. I been in a state of inner dithers an' procrastinated over boiling up the chai with plenty of milk an' lotsa sugar.

"Hurry up Phoebe, what is you doing?" grumbled Column.

"Well in the meantime, I have something," Ariel offered, plugging her Earport into the amp…

The familiar sound of the Black Friars' bell rang out, accompanied by the rhythmical swish, splat noise of wet plaster being smoothed onto walls an' the voices of Brothers Dominic an' Sebastian talking together…

"It won't be long before the renovations are over… Pass the plaster, Pasteur."

72

"Very droll, Dominic. Here you go. Only a couple more cells to do and the whole place will be like new."

"Chuck us a nail, Gail."

"Sorry Paul, I'm pointing the wall… Don't forget we still have to paint everything. Nice warm colours to make it bright and cheery, and we have to assemble the flat pack beds…Ted?"

"Quite right, Mike."

"Most likely they'll forget to include the alum keys again… Give us a brick, Nick."

"Seriously though, I reckon we will only just make it in time before they get here… Pass us the grout."

"Watch it, mate!"

"Sorry. Put on the kettle…Gretel," the Brothers said simultaneously, and collapsed into fits of laughter to which Ariel had added a great deal of bass an' echo that merged into the tolling of the Blackfriars Bell and the sound of their voices. "Give us a brick Nick, chuck up a nail Gail, put on the kettle Gretel, pass the plaster Pasteur, pass the plaster Pasteur, pass the…" faded out with the final toll of the bell.

We applauded, an' even in the unsteady light an' under all the makeup, Ariel's face gone bright red. "Brilliant! How did you do that?" asked Column.

"Thank you, thank you. I just got lucky passing by the window. Anybody else got something?"

" We does," Tyler smiled. "It's taken ages. It's comedy. Plug us in, Harley…"

Their piece opened with the sound of Miss Love, the ballroom dancing teacher, playing the piano in her customary sledgehammer style. "Good, now off you go again. One two three four five six seven eight, If you go down…" she trilled, and launched into The Teddy Bears Picnic, accompanied by a series of dog barks, howls an' growls that Harley an' Tyler had managed to arrange singing the tune, more-or-less, for a couple of verses, until the piano dropped out for a verse of unaccompanied howling and baying. Then the piano slowly came up again and Harley announces, "Ladies and Gentlemen, girls and boys, you has been listening to the lovely voices of the Hissy Boy Choir…" They let it play out to the end of the song, when Miss Love chimed in again, "Not bad my dears, not too bad at all…"

"You is very clever, you two." I handed round the chai an' asked, "Where did you get all them different barks?"

"Taking the barges up the canal to the City Road Basin. The Tinkerage have settled in the rubbish mounds up there and made themselves a dog track. You ain't anybody if you don't own a few coursers and fighting dogs," Harley explained. "There's loads of kids living rough, surviving in the junk, an' probably a dog is their only real true friend. I guess a courser will always bring you a hare or two, an' a fighting dog will protect you. Column, has you done the news and weather yet?"

"Not yet," says Column. "I'll get it together in the next couple of days."

"Okay," says Ariel, "anybody got a recipe of the month yet, or some culture or something 'bout entertainment?"

"Oi, ours is very extraordinary cultural. Got Miss Love in it, don't it?"

"Yup," said Column diplomatically. "Any chance you could help with getting a recipe in our next cooking class with Vatican Jack?"

"We'll have a go," the twins agreed and then it came to my turn.

"I, er, covered the entertainment slot by going along to hear Gloria and Angelina's band rehearsing, but when I listened back to it I found I'd forgotten to turn my Earport off, an' I has a whole lot more than I bargained for. Here goes then…"

"Every New Year's Day, in the maze of alleyways and tiny streets which radiate out from the Seven Dials, musicians, ballad-writers, poets and dancers come together to celebrate the Ceremony of the Winding of the Clocks, one of the Big Smoke's oldest festivals. It is only September but rehearsals are already underway, for each piece must be timed carefully to coincide with the sun's shadow passing across the dial. Today I have joined an impromptu audience that has gathered here and waits quietly for Father Time to begin the ceremony...

"Ladies and Gentlemen, Soft Sloth have been preparing a piece based on the Midsummer and Midwinter solstice and the Spring and Autumn equinox. It is called 'The Four Corners of the Earth', and goes something like this... One, two, three, four..." The cymbals gave a gentle roll an' a slow guitar slid evenly up the octaves, rising like the triumphant Sun on a Midsummer's Day, an' dazzled in the heights awhile with a little shimmering improvisation. The mingling voices of Angelina and Gloria called everyone down a little when the low resonant sound of a didgeridoo seemed to sound that first chill breath of Autumn and pan-pipes warned that the winds were on their way until, joined first by a sax, then a trombone that swelled into a hurricane (an also sounded a lot like dying elephants), they's resolved into the slow heart beat of winter drums, Beboom, beboom, beboom, beboom, joined by Angelina an' Gloria singing in thin pale unison, until a funky spring dance finale, had the audience clapping and dancing enthusiastically. Which led neatly into the next act, 'The Dance of The Seven Dials'...

"If you would like to join in the festivities on New Year's Day then all are welcome. The Seven Dials lies on the edge of Twilight Town and as rehearsals draw to an end, the donkey carts are free to pass through again. And the absinth drinkers reoccupy their favourite haunt..."

"Just keep on listening a sec. Pump up the volume, here it comes..."

The trit-trot of donkey carts continued, but then came the unmistakable voice of Mason Flint, Chief of the Mantle. "All set for Sunday night then?"

"Yes sir," the unmistakable cold voice of Turkish replied. "All dwellings suspected of harbouring Deviations have been staked out. The boys are at the ready, sir, an' expect to start the roundup Sunday midnight on the dot. We will rout 'em out, sir, from every little cave and hidey-hole they crawl into."

"Well Turkish, don't forget the Mantle are trying to present a new and kinder face around the neighbourhoods. So be firm but polite when removing these defective unsustainable children from their parents. Be a promotion in it for you, if all goes well."

They was as alarmed an' alert as if a green mamba had suddenly slithered into the room. "Come on, lets hear it again," Column broke the silence. It were a big relief to be listening to it among friends, and after we ran it through a second time, Harley shook his head in earnest an' said, "If we broadcast this, we will find ourselves top of the Number One to-be-deleted, rubbed-out-and-disposed of list."

"Well that's not gonna happen," says Ariel. "The compressor so distorts our voices, how is they ever going to know who done it? So far we managed to keep the show so anonymous even our own families don't have a clue who's behind it."

I don't think anyone were seriously considering not airing it, just taking on board the idea that we was raising the bar and the stakes were high. Ariel rolled us a couple of cigarettes to share and we puffed away in silence for a while. "Anyways," Tyler pointed out, "if it was Dad, he'd be shouting it from the rooftops. Only difference is, we is broadcasting it. Pirate radio is a communication weapon an' a responsibility. Many more lives than just our own is in danger if we don't air this."

"Well saving lives has been my family business for years. In for a penny in for pound," said Ariel and there were no arguing with that truth. "Okay, 'course, all right, yup, yeah and sweet." We all been of the same mind about it then, and raised our mugs.

We emerged out the tunnel into the friendly light of the Forge but the place were still deserted. We lit the lamps an' chucked some logs onto the fire. Column pulled a lump of driftwood out of the woodpile and settled down to drawing a puppet head on it. We left him to it. It weren't long afore the sound of Thor's hooves came rolling into the yard, and pulling the doors wide open I seen Mum and Dad up on the cart, looking a bit sheepish. And so they should, this late home. They was followed by Eden and Milo, who pulled in by boat an' moored up, an' afore Ariel could step on board, we's engaged in a parting hug between desperados. "Holy Moly, ain't I just arrived in the nick of time," said Canada, pulling in. "Break it up, break it up, tooty suity. I hate to see you all fighting like this. Get on board, boys. On board now."

But Column were hugging nobody. In fact he didn't even know they was leaving, for he had his work clamped up and was absorbed in bringing his block of wood to life with chisel an' mallet, rasp an' sandpaper. I could see the wickerdy face of Mephisto taking shape, an' that Column were making him in the image of that trash with no ears, who been in the Venus Man Trap earlier. Nice one, friendster, nice one.

Milo de Fer

If Uncle Cole were giving out awards for sleeping, I would have won hands down, no contest, the Big Smoke's clear favourite. Still, because I'd been sleeping the best part of the day, I couldn't even begin to invoke a sleep situation. So I gave up the tossing and turning, which were only stressing me out, got up and wound me way downstairs. The fires were banked down, glowing like sleeping dragons, and outside the river mist was up and doing its best to creep inside. I lit some lamps, fixed myself a chai and sat down by the fireside to drink it. "Hello, son," said my father. "Can't you sleep either?" And as he come down the stairs, I noticed he had taken on a slight limp.

"What's up with your leg Dad?"

"I don't know, could be a family thing. Volco developed a terrible limp as he got older."

I thought awhile an' wondered, "It may be you absorbed some arsenic after all these years working with iron. Ask Uncle Cole, I think there's a remedy might help you."

"I will next time I see him, thanks. Which reminds me, I understand you were up all night working at the Horse Hospital. Must have been kinda tough?"

"Oh no – no way Dad. It was very interesting. We spent most of the night stitching up big an' little gangsters, while a couple of babies was born…an' a young women lost her life. Also, I came across an old friend of yours called Booker."

"Booker?" My father's face lit up. "Did you? Now there's a rare soul, one of the best people I ever kept company with."

"Yeah, I liked him too. How came you to be friends, if you don't mind my asking?"

"Well, you know, the trial by water left everyone thinking I'd drowned, except Reema an' Booker. An' believing I were still alive, they been persistent enough to eventually find me an' our journeying home been about as unique as it comes."

"To be honest Dad, I don't know no more than a flock of snow geese come flying out the snow storm causing mayhem with the horses, and you was knocked overboard in the affray, but then what happened?"

"Oh lawd Milo, I'm no raconteur," Dad tried to object.

"Sure you are. Let me get us a beer. I really want to know what happened next."

My father is one of them lean types who got the power of an athlete lurking beneath his shirt. His word powers is similarly lurking inside, an' he paced his storytelling like a swimmer in the ocean, like a runner across the wide-open plains, an' intense as drawing iron out of the rock…

Jean de Fer's Story

Should you ever happen to fall off the solid-earth-safety of the world you know, and find yourself toppled into another, a whole mess of things do simultaneously occur. After the bitterly cold winter air, for a moment the sea that rolled over me felt most welcoming and warm, until, forced down by the invisible undertow I plunged forever through salty water into the strange calm that lay beneath the heaving sea. The sixteen years of my life so far come before my eyes, loosening out of me in a glimmering array of picture-cards that peeled away, dissolving into the phosphorescence of the water.

'No, you don't!' I called myself away from it. 'You ain't gonna wash the life out of me so easily, I intend to know what happens next.' That's when the cork in my life jacket finally remembered where it was supposed to be and hauled me back up towards the surface, an' up I come popping out the deep blue like a bubble, gasping for air in the icy needles of the wind. Buffeted by wave after wave, I heard my father calling, "Hang on to the horse son, hang on to the horse!" Then, fumbling a halter-rope around me wrist, I twisted my freezing fingers into Thor's mane an' clung on. We was a very small item out in those vast waves, and cursing the blizzard winds that whipped raving and roaring about us like an ocean banshee, I watched our storm lights vanishing into the distance and the very last thing I heard been the honking of the snow geese hurling by low overhead.

I washed out in the spindrift with the horses, alive but full of sea-water an' unconscious with hyperthermia, at the feet of your mother-to-be, who happened to be out walking on the snowy beach with her father, which were completely convenient. They both knew you has to act fast to save a lad from freezing, and stripped off my wet clothes that lowers the body temperature. They wrapped me up in his best coat and breathed warm air into me, to warm my insides. Even in a state of oblivion, it was perfectly clear that Lear, Liberty's father, were none too keen on a young man entering his daughter's hitherto isolated, unsullied an' well-protected life. However, he made an exception, because I come with the horses.

I was put to bed by a warming fire in a tack-room between the stables and the kitchen, where I burned up with fever while Liberty an' Lear burned with rage at one another. "He'll be fine in the tack room, between the kitchen an' the horses. He might be a horse thief, or a stable boy…"

"OR he could be a gentleman! IF you had any friends, would you put them up in the tack room? Well would you?"

"Come now, if he's a stable hand he will be very comfortable, and if he's a gentlemen he won't complain."

"Huh. If my mother was here she would be ashamed. He needs peace and quiet, not Uncle Ollie cooking an' klutzing around in the kitchen."

"Alas for all of us, your mother is gone. And be fair, Uncle Ollie is positively elf-like and no klutz. Liberty, surely you have something amongst the thousands of beauty products you've invented which would promote a bit of healing for him. Vitamin E or C, Aloe Vera or something? Have a go. We'll clean him up, wash the salt out of his hair, then see what you can do instead of shouting at me."

I'd left my memory slumbering somewhere deep on the ocean's bed, for when I did come round, I been wiped so blank I didn't even know my name. A lovely copper-haired girl with searching eyes of turquoise looked down at me an' said, "Hi, you're back. Take it easy, you ain't well. You're smouldered up with fever. I'm Liberty, who are you?"

I struggled with that, but could find no answer. "Respect," I ventured.

"Don't trouble yourself," she smiled. "I'm just gonna unbind your hands, they were shredded raw but they're on the mend now. It's great you've come round, but try an' sleep some more, you ain't out the woods yet." And I did fall back to sleep, contented in the knowledge that I would follow her to the ends of the earth. I knew that we were to be great friends.

We got to know each other in an unclouded freedom and honesty, for I had no memory and she had grown up isolated, which equalled us out. An' I, who never had a notion of destiny, seen it as an entity that delivered me to the feet of my soul-mate.

Liberty had been treating me with Copper Ointment, which is a very warming, lively thing, and after about ten days I began to feel my energy return, first in the tips of my fingers and toes and in the beat of my heart, and then as a lightning in my blood that ricocheted around my system like a fizzball, a mystical experience of a electrical nature which left me fully charged. I got up an' going outside, I seen I were on an island that rose out of the Fens. The Keep itself were on a low wooded hill and looking over its tiny kingdom, in extreme bad repair. The rest of the island were given over to ponies, cows, sheep, pigs and chickens who were free to roam, for we were surrounded by water and hundreds of miles of rattling reed-beds.

Everyday I took my horses across the drawbridge an' down a reedy track which wound beside a river to the beach. I watched the ocean and tried to remember how I'd got there, but I could not get my past from out this black hole of emptiness inside me.

"Are you thinking of moving on soon, now you're better?" Lear questioned politely.

" No sir, until I get my memory back I don't have anywhere to push off to," I explained, and kept myself out of his way an' busy by patching up the decaying Keep. I replaced the fallen stonework an' pointed up the gaps atween the windows, I's repaired the leaky roof with pine-pitch, timber and leading, and ransacking the stables I found seventeen cars, all in good nick. Removing the gears and dynamo from one, I hooked them up to the old tidal mill-wheel with strands of iron and copper wire. Once they were connected the lights

wavered on, the kitchen radio started talking in Nordic and an old CD player spun into action with "Lucy in the Sky with Diamonds". "Stone the crows," I said, "what the heck is that?" "Some sort of Norfolk trad, maybe?" Liberty suggested. After that we could play the CD's as much as we liked, have as many hot baths as we pleased and keep the place lit up night and day, all of which made Lear a lot more friendly. He taught me to play chess and I learned much by way of good manners an old-fashioned gentlemanly conviction.

About mid-August, Captain Dan were surveying the fenland coast an' convinced he'd seen a light shinning in the way off distance he came walking up the beach to check it out, same time as Booker who's searching for me had bought him to those parts. Their paths converged somewhere along the water margins where they's introduced themselves. "Guess you is the man in charge of those incredible iron cliffs…keep out the hungry sea for sure, along with any hungry raiders as might try to land. I don't suppose you ever come across the body of a boy, as you been working your way along the coast?"

"No, no bodies dead or alive for miles around. You ain't still searching for that de Fer boy? Six months, man, is a long time."

"Respect Captain, but no body, no death. Gives me hope. After all, he do have to be somewhere," replied Booker.

Even with the lights on, for most people Greene King Keep is perfectly hidden within its tree-cover, and you have to imagine those reeds are twelve-foot-high or more, but Booker and Captain Dan seemed to find their way alright, and arrived at the draw-bridge. "Blimey O Riley if the place ain't lit up like a Paris bordello. I can even hear music." Captain Dan been rather curious.

"Certainly looks to be fully civilized" said Booker.

"Of course we're civilized, greatly civilized. The question is, are you?" asked Lear, training a shotgun on them. Captain Dan and Booker was putting their hands up when "For goodness sake, put that stupid gun down and invite the gentleman in. Sorry. " said Liberty, raising her eyes skywards.

"My word, Jean de Fer. Is that you, lad, live and well?" And recognizing the sound of Captain Dan's voice, I started slowly across the bridge towards him. "We thought you'd been drowned with the rest, lad. Why did you not send word or go home?" I drew to a halt as my memories returned, like a flock of a thousand birds, and overwhelmed my heart with their roosting. "All of them, sir? Dad, Luke, Teddy, the gunners drowned?" I asked.

"Yes, son. You didn't know? I'm afraid so. Booker recovered them an' has been searching for you ever since."

Booker put both his hands on my shoulders. " I've come to take you home. Your little sister Reema is waiting for you, an' your ma Amber is close on despair," he related, kind an' quiet.

Although Liberty an' I been perfectly convinced of each other, it did not make it any easier when it came to parting in the early dawn. Booker an' I took the horses and left beneath a sky brimful of stars and the slow moon setting over the fens. The first night, we came upon a tiny fishing settlement of raft-like dwellings on stilts. We were welcomed in by the fisherman who gave us a decent meal and a bed for the night, and then heading on south steadily for four days, we walked out of the reed-lands and climbed a long slope into the great forest.

Booker is all about the journey and not particularly the destination. "The art of travel lies in the Zen of the road." He's the

Grand Master of wayfarers, and the closest I ever came to understanding religion were walking through those great trees with him. If you had just learned that your father and your brothers drowned, he is going walk you out of your awesome grief, sometimes in great silence, other times he's going to show you how to catch a trout, or quail, or lead you up an' up a secret gorge to a wide grassy outcrop, with a spectacular view over the rolling forest and a perfect place to pitch camp for the night. He is also gonna keep your mind busy by giving you the history of just about every tree, leaf an' stone you come across…

"The coastal countryside is pretty much the same as it has always been for thousands of years, with them sea breezes keeping the skies clear most of time. But inland, where we're headed, son, it's a survival-of-the-fittest situation. As you can see, it's been slowly won by the tallest trees, mainly migrants like Plane Trees, Eucalyptus and them antipodean Tree Ferns. There ain't too much sunshine that gets down here in summers, because this here heat creates all that there misty steam, which comes billowing off the forest canopy and eventually turns into the moist clouds which cover this part of the world…"

The six great horses moved surprisingly quiet through the bracken, and wrapped into the mists we travelled traceless an' listening, always listening acutely for the sounds of marauders or drifters. So far the only sentient beings we encountered was the shy descendents of zoo and circus escapees, or the odd monkey lab survivors who melted away between the trees on our approach. We also been followed by a big cat, an' caught glimpses of Ocelot an' tiny Muntjac Deer that rocketed away on dainty panicked feet. Sometimes we startled flocks of Macaws that rose like a blue-red cloud, squawking indignantly to circle away over the tree-tops, but we never did meet a human soul.

I been devastated and lonely for my brothers. Particularly Teddy, who was built square, a roly-poly teddy-bear boy who been entranced by animals and would have loved it there.

85

Once, we came to a place where the forest thinned out an' opened up a bit, and descending down a long bracken-covered incline, we came upon three long man-made mounds. The horses came to halt and refused to budge. I tried to persuade Thor to move on, but we were as unevenly matched as David and Goliath. "With respect, son, a horse like that, as saved your life, must have his reasons," cautioned Booker, and walked on up ahead to take a closer look. "We'll take a detour. I've come upon these before, they is mass graves full of the charred bones of animals," Booker explained as we circled round. "See, our ancestors didn't mix it up like we does. Some farms was all cattle, some poultry, some sheep and some pigs, and judging by the graves, thousands of them all been killed off after some infection affected the lot. The skies must have blackened an' reeked from funeral pyres that burned for weeks."

I reached up an' wound my fingers into Thor's mane, for I felt alone at sea again, an' wisely Booker took us by way of his invisible paths to an equally invisible settlement on a promontory in a big lake in the woods.

Every single dwelling and building was covered over with tropical plants that twisted an' trailed across walls an' hung like curtains over the plate-glass windows and sliding doors (which were a big feature there) that opened out onto paved walkways, duck-boarded verandas and a number of wooden skyways that spanned between the trees. All in all, with plenty of ropes for the grandkids to play on and some abundant allotments to grow their own vegetables, it looked a lot like a rest home for the retired Tarzan and Jane.

We arrived in the 'village square,' surrounded by tables an' a number of beat-up sun-umbrellas dotted about where a short, stout man, with a knotted handkerchief on his head and a beer belly that overflowed the waistband of his trousers, looked up from laying out a BBQ. "O, 'allo there Booker. 'Allo son, welcome to Elveden Forest… I see you found him, then?"

"Sure did. This here is Jean. Mind if we stop in for awhile?"

"Course not, always a pleasure, pull up a chair. How do, Jean? I's

Joe. Terrible about your family, your father were a lovely, lovely man."
A crowd of children came gathering round to say hello and been very
admiring of the horses. "Come on, give us some space. Gracie
sweetheart, put the kettle on will you? Tucker, go and find your mother
and tell her we has company. Scram scram scram, that's better."

My ears been glad to hear the Twilight Town accent, an'
wondering what all these folk was doing out here I says, " Pleased to
meet you. Are you on the run or something, if you don't mind my
asking?"

"You're quick. Sort of, in a manner of speaking. It's a long story.
'Ere, Ruby, Lewis, Smokey, Tillie, take the grys up the Pancake House
an' ask Jules to rub em down and give em a good feed."

"What where?"

" Yeah, I know. Why any one would want a build a bleeding great
Pancake House in the middle of a forest beats me. Still, that's exactly
what they did and now it makes a pukka stable." Joe turned to the
barbeque, piled on a lot of logs, and giving it a jolly good poke, he
exchanged a theatrical meaningful look with Booker, who nodded at
him. " See Jean, it's like this. We got six children, Ryan who's 12,
Grace 11, Tucker 10, then along comes Jules who's 9, Ruby 5 an' little
Lewis 4. Joe counted them off on his fingers. "But the birth of Jules
come with a change for all of us, because he has the Downs
Syndrome. No matter, he's one of us and we loved him to pieces
same as all the others. As you may know, Deviations is deemed
unsustainable and must be handed over. So we scarpered afore the
Mingers could take him off us and use him as lab fodder in horrible
experiments. Anyways, they is very wrong, he ain't even that
different. Just between you and me, Tucker got more problems
reading and writing than he do. Jules is capable an' also has an
uncanny feel for the horses. In the end the whole family came along
with us, which we couldn't have done without Booker, who ferried
us all out through the tunnels, 'cept Ruby an' Lewis, who was born
up here... O 'allo, light a BBQ an' the troops come marchin' in. This
is me wife Franny."

I got up to shake her long hand which she bypassed, giving me a warm hug instead an' saying, "Poor love, had a rough time of it I hear. This is me sister Sandy."

"Hello me dear," Sandy shook my hand.

"Now this is Slim Pickings, me father-in-law."

"Respect. I used to be a scrap dealer and knew your father very well."

"I remember, 'Pickings Scrap'. We used to come by your yard. My Dad been mystified by your disappearance." I brushed away some embarrassing tears with my sleeve.

"Oh gawd, Slim, now look what you's done," Joe tutted as Slim looked awkward. "This here is Sicily, the mother-in-law."

"There now, never mind. Time, lad, give it some time an' you'll be right as rain." She pecked my cheek and ruffled my hair.

"And this is me brother Gabriel, his poor long suffering wife Jesse and their kids Smoky and Tillie, who been born up here too."

"I'm never gonna remember all your names," I apologised, when Joe's oldest boy appeared with a tray full of steaks for the barbeque.

"Give us a hand mate, an' I'll explain it to yah."

"Sure," I said, an' while we's turned the steaks Ryan been kind enough to draw up a list of names in the earth. "See here…"

Slim + Sicily Pickings = Sandy and Franny
Franny + Joe = Ryan, Grace, Tucker, Jules, Ruby an' Lewis
Lorenz + Marie Mancini = Joe and Gabriel
Gabriel + Jesse = Smokey and Tillie

"Simple." Ryan looked up.

"Neatly done, Ryan. That's a fine family tree you has," Booker said, looking at Joe. " Shame if it gets rubbed out. You've all been here way too long. You're barely out of the Mantle's reach. They is employing Hissy Boy trackers in a big way these days, an' they has some way to find out every little thing that's going down. This ain't no place to settle. Go north! I been through the Big Empty to the very edge of the sea. There are high mountains and nothing but giant pine forests as far as the eye can see. It's beautiful up there, an' they will find you here sooner or later."

"Hear, hear," said Franny. "The point is, Joe, we is hiding out here, which shouldn't be confused with living. It would be nice to live freely and build something of our own. You an' Gabriel is builders, Sandy a school-teacher, Jesse a gardener. We has kids an' a future to provide for them. How about it Joe, Gabriel?"

"It's just the thought of moving all this lot on. And what about the older folk?"

Ryan nodded at his family tree, saying to me, "One side of the family is Gitanes. Which explains why one half is happy campers while the other half wants a roof over their heads."

"Oh reet," I grinned. The tiddlers came trooping back from the horses along with Jules, who plonked himself down next me and says, " Phew, I'd like to eat afore we goes anywhere. I's starving."

"So am I, mate. Thanks for rubbing down me horses."

"What's their names?"

"My girlfriend named them. Thor, Calliope, Axel, Spirit, Foxy an' Shadow."

"They is lovely, but not a patch on mine. See, they's over there." Jules waved toward the forest where a big herd of horses been picking their way to drink at the lake.

"Yeah, nice. What are their names?" I asked

"Gees," Jules gave a hearty guffaw. "Crazy coot, there's more then a hundred of them!"

Meeting Jules were a wide-eye-opener, an' his family was doing a good thing with a great injustice. "If you decides to travel north," I suggested, "make for Greene King Keep. My girlfriend will give you a warm welcome an' her father do respect a horseman. Just head northeast as far you can go."

We walked back into the forest with the dawn chorus.

All the parlari of building, picking up and starting anew set my own mind toward the future. "I is buzzing with ideas and grand designs for the Forge," I told Booker. "What were the old iron works like?"

"That was way before my time, but I believe the original Forge were at Bow Creek. That all got silted even before the extreme weather conditions washed away most of the bridges. Blackfriars seemed to have had three of them, one of which survived when the river Fleet burst out its pipe an' opened up again. The Forge were there a long time afore your father blasted out a lot of rock an' made it into what it is at present. But there's always room for improvements. Your Ma's an artist, ask her for some designs. You's all been sleeping in what amounts to caves. Arch them off with masonry, plaster them up or something, put in some warm wooden floors, get rid of them iron-staircases. The place could be state-of-the-art. There's a young boatman called Canada, 'bout your age, could supply you with wood, and he's good with dynamite. Besides, I is in no doubt that Liberty will be along to join you one day an' she may appreciate a more cosy situation than what you has now."

"You reckon? Let's get cracking. Thor, Calliope, no more coasting time to earn your keep. Let's ride!"

"I ain't too sure if these gry's is for riding." Booker been hesitant.

"Could be. My father told me they were bred to carry knights in armour."

"Which explains what all happened to them." But once I persuaded Booker onboard, Thor an' his girlfriend carried us along like it were the normal thing to do, and the other four horses been content to follow on.

Our time in the forest were nearing an end when we's cautiously approached a ramshackle field hospital. It been a couple of large square tents with faded red cross's on them, an' a wide canvas awning slung between a rock an' a donkey-cart. There was two people sat by a little fire. One was a bright birdie-women with a kindly open smile, the other were a rangy youth in a leather jacket who been good-looking as a wolf. " Respect, I'm Dr Clara Levet." The women jumped up to shake our hands. "And this creature is my son Cole." That was the first sighting I ever had of your Uncle Cole.

"Welcome," says he "to medicine sans frontier, sans tout, one of the world's most exclusive high-tech travelling institutions you'll ever happen upon, treating anything an' anybody who come our way. An' how mays we help you today?"

"Respect, I's charmed. How about some chai?" asked Booker.

Cole an' I was sixteen year olds, an' as happen sometimes, strangers who clicked, and we chatted open an' easy together as old friends. "Being the sole survivor of accident do come with a burden of guilt," I explained, "but I aim to honour my father an' brothers with my work an' I will not let them down with the future I intend to shape."

"I'm with you. I'd like to see this world a little brighter," Cole replied. He were studying to take his finals then. "Come an' stay when you're ready," I's invited him.

My father yawned, "But that's another story, ain't it?" an' he closed his eyes an' fell asleep.

Grandma Tookie (the Akashic Record, Eden)

Most people on the coalface of life were doing their level best to create some sort order out of the chaos, and working their way towards the small bang that would tilt the place into a more favourable spin. But not Eden, who was a hundred-and-fifty-percent at home in the world into which he had been born.

Eden navigated his way through the confusion with relish and ingenuity, not at the centre of life the universe and everything, but as part of the here-and-now of things. In short, he was a free spirit who wilted at any attempt to fix him down and was stifled by long-term exposure to order. From time to time, Eden felt compelled to bust out of the Chelsea Physic Garden and skedaddle, which certainly caused Cole and Reema to blow one gasket after another, my goodness me, until eventually, resigned, they came to occupy a more Buddhist headspace on the matter.

Eden came by it honestly, for not only was he a Levet, but Grandma Amber and Volco had been exactly the same. Their life together had been a trip-and-a-half, all marinated in romance, as it were, and fantastically unpredictable, bohemian, volatile and dynamic, crowned with a glory that all came to an abrupt end the day Volco drowned. Needless to say, Volco did not hang about reading the Akashic Record. "Grandma Tookie, how extraordinary! Where is all the action?"

"Here," I'd glared at him.

"Excuse me, ahem, here and where exactly?" And when I pointed out the way to seventh heaven off he shot, with his two sons tucked under his arms, all pale and sleeping soundly.

Meanwhile, back in the nitty-gritty of the Forge, it was all, "Out with the old an' in with the new, the future is a-coming in." Well, Jean's future, at any rate, for when he returned it was to rebuild, reboot and reshape the Wayland Forge into the kind of order we have now. Which was not Amber's cup of chai, and wilting big time, she felt obliged to fly the coop.

Amber was pitiably grieved and after three-hundred and sixty-five days of darkness, she found a way to fold the death of her husband and her two young sons into a fifth chamber of her heart, which was incredibly spiritual of her and certainly made her a top kind of creature. However, she never did come back, which got her on the blacklist and made her a taboo subject.

Eden (age 17)

As a kid, I were Robert Scott, I were Ernest Shackleton, I were Hernando Cortez. I were Roald Amundson, Captain Fitzroy, Captain Cook an' Dr Livingstone-I-presume, on my exploring expeditions.

I concentrated on the Boonies, that lay just beyond the garden wall an' spread to the west of the Big Smoke. an' a regular hanging gardens of Babylon it were too, a lost city all perfectly submerged beneath the weight of a countryside that had done a fine job of swallowing it whole. The river corridor blurred into enticing freshwater mangroves an' the flora exotica reached out from the homes it once adorned an' crept off on a world wide tour in search of their natural homelands. Unless, of course, it tumbled into the wilderness of Kensington Gardens, where the Community Paybacks was under orders to do something about keeping it tame.

The Boonies was inhabited by intriguing chary natives, marginals who'd withdrawn to live out of sight an' out of the Mantle's mind for a while. It were also overrun with a deal of skittish fauna, an' if the monkeys threw a mass panic attack an' fled clambering up and up into them rusting iron frames of tall buildings, I went with them so as to avoid the stalking of some big cat, or the hair-raising hyenas who came into the city in search of food in winter.

The Chelsea Physic Garden do house the biographies of all the explorers, for our history is linked to some of them. Perhaps there been days when the explorers got drunk, or occasions when they gone native, for there is places, times, dates an' days missing from their Logs an' Diaries, indicating they's only wrote what they wants us to know. They hid a lot, an' held secrets that they didn't care to share. That happened to me too, for I uncovered a secret during my explorations, which I been bound to keep throughout my childhood days.

Grandma Tookie (the Akashic record, Morgan Grey)

Morgan closed his book and looking through the window, he glimpsed Nicky setting off along the embankment with a very long ladder over his shoulder. He appeared ant-like with his load so much bigger then himself. Morgan regarded him with unease, for though Nicky was undoubtedly very clever indeed and right up there with the elite of scientists, with whom he also shared a fair dollop of wacko peculiar eccentricities, his assistant had become more than that, and it had begun to dawn on Morgan how naïve he'd been in leaving Nicky to run Projack for so long, because it had given him some power and Nicky had become positively sinister.

A few days ago, when he'd summoned Nicky up from the labs with the progress reports, Morgan had been suspicious, alarmed by the sudden rise in people volunteering for drug trials and signing up for organ donations. But when he commented on the ethics of this, Nicky had blackened and launched into a lecture. "Ethics are a thing of the past. Everybody is unethical, the whole world is unethical, God is unethical! Naturally I'm unethical, ethics are standing in the way of progress…" and curling his hand about a rare bottle of sour grape wine and raising it to Morgan, "Just you wait, just you wait and see," he'd purred smugly and stalked out, leaving a sepulchral silence behind him.

Morgan bathed himself and shaved, and putting on his finest clothes, he summoned to his mind's eye an' imaginary gathering of hand-picked historical figures with whom he was in the habit of conversing, whenever he needed to clarify his thoughts. "Thank you for joining me today, most venerable and trusted friends. Let us not 'just wait and see' but go and see for ourselves. I look forward to hearing your opinions." Morgan looked over his shoulder and led his invisible delegation down the long wood-paneled corridor towards the heavy doors that opened onto his empire. "I really do hope that none of you suffer from altitude sickness," he smiled, unlocked the doors and stepped into the marvel of Art Deco that was the Projack Building.

The view plummeted away some three hundred metres to the floor below, the centre of which was denoted by a simple eight-pointed star-like compass floor-inlay, modestly implying that Projack was the centre of the world, and directing the eye towards the series of elegant white-tiled pillars that rose, floor by floor, to support the cast-iron walkways upon which the laboratories were set. A glass dome winged its way across the entire central atrium, and Morgan paused beneath its dizzying heights to make sure that every one was on board. 'What would they think, what would they say?' he wondered, and ushered his respected allies into the empty pharmacology labs.

There were many new drugs under investigation, but most of the department was given over to the study of genes and chromosomes, and the mapping and manipulation of the genome. "The genome," Morgan explained, "contains the entire hereditary history of the organism." He peered down microscopes and contemplated the models. "This is a wonderful biological system, elegant and complex as the solar system itself." One of his delegates exclaimed, and asked, "Does its medical potential outweigh the irreverence of interfering with it?"

On the way down to Level Three, one or two of his party sneaked off, not interested perhaps in the Protein Engineering Department, which was dedicated to the production of enzymes for industry, medicines and genetic engineering. It was a lively place, generally buzzing with quirky young people as busy and bright as enzymes themselves, who were often the creative catalysts of all sorts of new and novel ones. "What for?" Morgan heard a mutter.

"That's just what they do. They're good at it," he replied.

They descended down to Level Two, Animal Experimentation. "Here, much of what is created upstairs is tried out in a number of ways. For example, the cloned mice are infected with strains of human diseases and then injected with new cures to see what happens next."

"An animal is not just a piece of biology," someone challenged him, "that can be used for experimentation because they have a corresponding part to that of the human being. You are using rabbits for eye irritation trials, for rabbit eyes react similarly to those of human beings. Cats for neurological studies, dogs for cardiology, bone and joint studies, macaques, spider monkeys, squirrel monkeys, baboons, chimpanzees and marmosets for toxicology, neurology, reproduction and grafting and transplanting involuntary donated organs from one animal to another, in order to experiment with anti-rejection treatments... And not a single one of these creatures will outlive their usefulness, will they?"

The speaker was challenged by someone else. "Lighten up," he was told. "All in the cause of science... Look at all these freezers! What I could have achieved with access to such incredible research facilities. At least I might not have died as a result of my own scientific experiment."

"What did he die of, then?" somebody asked.

"He caught pneumonia after stuffing a chicken with snow to see if he could preserve it."

"He should've pickled it. I pickle everything," commented an artist.

"No great loss. He was a social climber who shopped one of his best friends." A furious row broke out between the delegates. Dante drew Morgan aside. "The alternative is to use human guinea pigs."

"Well, we do that too."

"I know," said Dante with enthusiasm. "Love it to pieces, let's carry on down! It's exactly like descending round the Circles of Hell."

"That's it, that's what I was looking for," Morgan exclaimed. "Thank you, you've put it in a nutshell." And politely ushering his few remaining guests down to the Palm Court Canteen, he dismissed them. "Goodbye Francis, Alighieri, your Eminence Rouge. Always good to include a few plotters and schemers. Thanks so much for joining me today. And good luck Damian, bless you Johannes… Madam Blavatsky? I don't remember inviting you."

"No, but I tagged along with Bulwer Lytton for the hell of it."

"How like her," thought Morgan, and continued his tour alone.

Right to the very bottom, the Projack Building remained true to the spirit of Art Deco, and even below sea-level the long hushed corridors and closed wards of Basement 1 were wide-striped in a black-and-white marble which gave the Department of Human Engineering a touch of Egyptian tombiness. The rows of occupants lay in their cream pajamas tucked between white sheets, shaven-headed, identical and held in sleep, until thoroughly de-toxed and healthy enough to be used for drug trials or the organ donations they'd signed up for. All destined for somewhere: the Cristiaan Barnard Ward (organ transplant), Aldous Huxley Ward (drug trials), Watson Crick & Wilkins Ward (genetics), Ian Wilmut Ward (cloning) or Gunter Von Hagen Theatre (dissection and autopsy). Reading the signs overhead, Morgan passed by the supply rooms which ran along the length of the back of the building, and then turning the corner at the eastern end, he came upon a modest wooden door set in a dark recess with the words "Vacanti Ward" written on it. Which was more then weird, for he had always assumed it was a cleaning cupboard.

"My word," Morgan murmured, "what a beautiful place." For the door opened onto a small circular library with a walkway that lead passed the books and spiralled down to the floor. On his way down Morgan noted the dark teak shelves were delicately inlayed with the words, *Let them have dominion over the fish of the sea, and over the fowl of the air and over every living thing that moveth upon the earth,*" all interspersed with highly stylised roebucks and fishes of gold leaf. And looking from the bottom, he could see that the domed ceiling was awhirl with the fishes of the sea and the creatures of the earth, and crowned by the golden disc of the sun that shone down with the words, "The Bucks Club" scrolled across it in heavenly writing.

The Bucks Club, Morgan recalled, was a tasteful low-key hunting club out in Buckinghamshire, with a powerful membership that included politicians, judges, Masons, Bilderbergers, bankers, Yankee Pirates, you name it, all hunting, shooting and fishing together while manipulating and plotting a New World Order. One, moreover, that drove the planet into the ditch. He peered into their dining-room, a room of cold opulence. In those days, he remembered, shooting had been a sport. 'These days even the likes of me can handle a gun. It would be foolish not to.'

He tried another door and walked through a small comfortable sitting-room. 'They must have enjoyed the symbolism of having their secret headquarters within a powerhouse," Morgan thought, as he entered a lavish bedroom with a grand old four-poster bed surrounded by velvet curtains of a deep red. A fearsome Polar Bear skin lay spread across the floor, its jaws gaping open and its beady glass eyes alive with reflections from a fire that burned in the grate. Realizing someone must have lit that fire, he tiptoed towards the bed, drew aside the curtains a crack, and stepped back in horror at what he saw.

The boy looked to be about ten or eleven years old, and lay curled up on his side. His head was shaven, his body emaciated, and he was clothed in fisherman's trousers of white linen. A pair of white ears had been seeded onto his shoulder-blades. Obviously sedated, he lay oddly still inside an antibacterial bubble, looking for all the world like a homunculus. "Hope," his clipboard read. "Nil by Mouth."

Morgan sat down gingerly on the edge of the bed, and pushing his hands through the vents, he took the boy's chilly hands in his, saying, "You need human contact. Let me see, a story about a boy, perhaps?"

A Story for Hope

"There was once a boy who was the last of his kind, and fearing that his world would be lost and forgotten forever, he knew he had to gather as much of it as he could inside him.

"Thus when he was happy and felt his spirits soar, he gathered the birds of the air inside himself, and when his hopes and dreams were pulled like the tides, he drew the watery moon inside him. He absorbed the frozen earth into his bones and the wildfire to run in his blood, and when he was burdened down with sorrow he tempered it with bravery and courage. Now when that boy looked at the silvery Moon, he saw that her light was reflective and mirrored the Sun. And when he looked at Sun, he saw that its light radiated from inside itself, and he hoped that one day he too would have a heart of gold.

"The boy's parents were cloth merchants and when they discovered that their son was gifted with numbers, they pulled him out of the fields and thickets and packed him off to university. At university the youth continued to gather all of his world inside himself. He was interested in astronomy, but he also investigated nature, philosophy, spiritual discipline and apothecary, the study of herbal and chemical ingredients for medicine. And he was the last of his times to study alchemy, the transmutation of base metals into precious metals.

"Through his endeavour, the young man became learned and powerful. Indeed, he understood the natural world so well that he was able to call up a storm of such magnitude as to sink the Spanish Armada, and from then on people believed him to be a Magus.

"Whatever people believed of him, the young man continued to

101

pursue his task in all peace, and to further his understanding of the world he sought to talk to the angels. In those days, many people claimed to be able to talk to the angels, but one man in particular stood out as a gifted scryer, who never failed to call a white-winged angel into his crystal ball.

"The Angel and the Magus got on like a house on fire. The angel taught him much: for instance, how unprepared and flabbergasted God had been by man's liking for comfort. The Angel also revealed that he had sought sanctuary on earth from a terrible war that raged in heaven and while they fought it out, the Earth below had lost its cohesion, disintegrated and changed forever. From then on, people felt themselves quite separate from the world, and looked out on it as though through a window, for all the world had become a stage.

"The young Scryer had been the first to be born in that new age, and the Magus was the last man on earth who believed that heaven and earth and man were all in it together. The Scryer and the Magus became good friends. They shared fame, and some misfortune, until the Scryer said that the Angel had instructed them to share each other's wives. After that, the Magus felt he no longer needed the Scryer, as his research into angels was completed. And the Angel himself said that while he had enjoyed their conversations, strictly speaking humans were out of bounds for him, and he had received orders from on high to return.

"'On high?' the Scryer fumed. 'Not so, you treacherous creature. Oh no, my fine feathered friend, you are subject to me and my summoning.' And so saying, he trapped the Angel inside the crystal ball.

"Sitting crossed-legged with his wing tips folded over his head, the Angel calmly blew up the crystal ball. It exploded into a thousand shards of glass and feathers that flew everywhere while the Angel walked calmly away, and gathering a white linen suit about him, he vanished over the horizon. But from that day on, the Angel remained trapped on earth.

"With the Angel gone, the light dimmed a little for the Magus and the Scryer, and they half-heartedly turned their attentions to making the elixir of life, with which they had an unexpected, unrepeatable and unexplained break through. And thus raising their glasses to eternal life, they downed the cocktail.

"The Scryer became horribly intoxicated, but the Magus realised instantly that he too was to remain trapped on the earth forever. He lived on, in fitness and in health, while his dear wife faded into old age and died in his youthful arms, and his son grew grizzled and grey, puzzling over his fathers longevity to the last. And when his old enemies and dear friends, the fine noblemen, turbulent kings, magnificent queens and their petulant children had all gradually faded from his life, he lived, lonely as the Angel in the crystal ball, or you in your plastic bubble…

Morgan released Hope's chilly hand and looked at the boy, with ears on his shoulders where there could have been wings. "Piteous little creature, I'm going to get you and everyone else out here."

But Hope turned over painfully, and opening his very serious eyes, he said, "Don't call me a piteous creature, I is a boy with a task to do. I too has been secretly gathering in my world. Give us a helping hand and we may earn ourselves a heart of gold an' all. Come on, let me show you what's going on down in Basement 2."

"Are you sure you can manage it?" Morgan asked.

"Oh sure," said Hope, "do it all the time."

"In that case, while the cat's away, the mice will play," said Morgan, and they set off together.

Column de Fer

"Hello, 'ello, 'ello. I is Mephisto, the peerless nasty of nastiness." My puppet looked fittingly terrifying, with an earless likeness to the spooky man at the Venus Man Trap good enough to scare the living daylights out of anyone, an' giving him a final sanding, he were finished.

I'd earned a break an' set off along the river. I stuck out my thumb, with the idea of exchanging a knife for a ride on the back of skimmer, but been a bit fazed when Topaz, chief of the Saracens, pulled up alongside me and growled, " Looking for a ride? I's heading up stream." It were more of a order than a question, an' I climbed on behind him in obliging trepidation.

Taking a couple of fizz balls out of an ornate powder horn and feeding them down the fuel line, we was off. No surprise, but Topaz's skimmer were a cut above: smooth, almost silent an' exceeding fast, an' it were only about three-quarters of an hour before we was pulling up on the shingle of one of them little upstream eyots. Topaz cut the engine and making his way over to a fat swamp cypress, he sat down on one of its long gnarled roots.

I got to say that while this unexpected joy-ride had all the correct components for a terrific afternoon on the river, keeping company with Topaz was like being with a fighting bull. All the time, I had a uncomfortable feeling that this were more agenda then coincidence an' been a little afraid of the purpose behind it, so I's just hung about waiting for him to talk. " I been meaning to catch up with you for sometime, Column, so as we can have a little chat. See, my father were good friends with your grandfather. There was a lot of respect and understanding going on between the Saracens and your

Grandfather Volco. Matter of fact, we had an alliance, because it seems to make sense that those of us that can has got to stick together.

"Now listen up. If you ever make another knife for a Hissy Boy or Smoke, your father is going to hear about it, because I got a lot of respect for him an' all. What's more, sooner or later your brother Milo or Dr Cole or his boy Eden is going to be stitching up some terrible wound caused by one of your knives. Think on it."

A whole lot of briny tears come pouring out my eyes as I apologised. "I got it. Pax, never happen again. I understand, it were a mistake... What kind of an alliance would that be?" I snuffled.

"The sort of alliance that will tumble the corruption of the Mantle," he rumbled, offering me his bandana so's I could wipe my face.

"Well, if old Volco were friendly with the Saracens, we is all on the same side, and I reckon you would be interested in listening to this." I pulled out me Earport an' gave him an ear-piece for listening.

Topaz switched it on and paid a lot of attention to what he were hearing. Then he says, " Thank you, tar very much. I believe we is going to be friends after all. Vital piece of information you has here. What was you planning to do with it?"

"Broadcast it loud and clear across the land, save a lot of lives and end up as top Number One to be rubbed out by the Mantle."

He scratched his head, "Could be, but I's had an eye on you for sometime and had no idea you was behind that show. Your slot's got popular, perks folk up an' makes 'em smile... I's been wondering who got the recklessness to air it. Where do you broadcast it from?"

"I could tell you but then I'd have to kill you. Anyways, I's just the news an' weather fairy."

"Don't fancy been killed by the weather fairy," he guffawed. "Still, keep your head down. Go ahead broadcast it but try not to lose your life while you're about it. In the meantime, I got a few things to be getting on with. Now hand over that 'orrible knife you has stashed in your boot. After all, you owe me for the ride. Hop on."

Topaz dropped me off beneath Chelsea Bridge. The tide were

very low, so I walked all along the bottom of the river wall until I passed Projack and climbed the stairs at Tideway to join the towpath. Which I never did do, on account of hearing the sound of steel-toed boots coming toward me. There were only one person who could be wearing them boots, and very afraid to be alone with that particular nightmare, I's slipped inside a kinda air shaft just afore he gone clumping by with a big old metal ladder over his shoulder. Once he were out of earshot, I found myself in a marvellous interesting place, which were definitely in need of exploring...

Mistral (the Akashic Record, Linda Miscellaneous)

The revelation of my Daddy's ID been an extreme naked truth moment, totally lacking all the usual grace an' romantics that's s'posed to accompany these discoveries. Altogether, I were hit on the head with a overwhelming disappointment that put me in the Psychic Trauma Department. My old man, Nicky? A sweet name for the worst of the worst, who been fond of people like cats is fond of mices an' sooner or later were bound to come hunting for me.

Well, a safe house is only safe for so long, so I's packed up my bag an' gone out on the road to recovery. I been walking an' walking ever since then, slowly getting my life back together, coming to terms with things, picking up the pieces an' checking the starry writing for signs of the biological papa.

Now Shad Thames is about the worst place one could ever hope to live, but them Raggers lived there happy as a ball of nesting vipers. The river were free to roam through the ground floor while them tykes ran free-range about the rest of the place. They had contributed generously to the decrepitation an' dereliction of the warehouse apartments by bunging just about everything they could get their thieving mitts on into the old fire-places, an' in them long hollow lonely nights the little darlin's bedded down with the high-odour ferrets they loved and cherished so deeply. Everything else that moved were in danger of being rubbed out. Still, at least it were a cockroach-free zone.

As Shad Thames were mostly in the river the only approach were by boat, and any unwanted visitors was seen off with a ferocious amount of volatile projectiles that come hurling down from off the over-head gangways. But when Linda Miscellaneous first arrived, she come with a big umbrella an' said "Hi", totally failing to be afraid of them kids, who was speechless an' exasperated beyond belief. She did have a convincing, don't-even-think-of-messing-with-me, back-off, I-means-business air about her.

Linda took a good look around, apparently blissfully obliviato to the threat they was attempting to impress upon her, an' all they could do was shadow her indignantly while she climbed up and downstairs, until she says, "Thanks for showing me around. I'll take the penthouse." "No you isn't," them Raggers replied.

"Sure I is. Think this is bad? You should see where I come from." Which took the wind outa their sails.

"Where is you from, then?" a sniffy kid called Rickers asked.

"Rio de Janeiro, of course. A favela."

The Raggers looked at each other like a line of blanks. "What you saying?"

Linda moved into the remains of a big apartment on the top floor, and hooked up about a hundred roof-flags to generate electrics for herself. The Raggers got over it. Well, they did get hot water and lights. She treated them like they was normal dignified humanity and everything become sweet between 'em all. Though not between them abandonees and nobody else, mind.

Linda were working into the evening on Nicky's new suit, her old sewing-machine whirring along the fancy paisley lining, when Asbo an' Rickers poked their hooded heads inside her door to say, "Some weirdo been paddling around outside up to his waist in water. He got a big ladder across his shoulder and he's looking for you." Just then a voice come drifting up from below, "Linda, are you there? Open your window, I want to pay you a visit."

"Want us to kill him?"

"No, no I don't think so. I'm making him a suit, too bad to waste it. Let me see what he wants."

"Shame. We knows a bleeding psycho when we sees one." Then come the noise of a ladder scraping up against the window and them steel-toed boots rattling up it. "We is right outside the door, when you need us."

"I'll be fine. Now scat," says Linda, an' opens her window. "Come in. What's with the ladder?" Nicky clambered through the window an' tumbled all wet and dripping onto her sofa.

"Ah well, it's a darn sight better than having one's throat slit coming through the front door. Get many visitors, do you?" He smiled and cast his eye about the lovely place she made for herself, passing quickly over her photo of Hope. "Is that my suit?"

"Yes. I just started lining the jacket. You're all wet. Still, put the trousers on." Linda chucked him a towel and made them some coffee while Nicky changed an' stuck his boots in front of the fire. "To what else do I owe the pleasure of this visit, then?" she enquired.

"Nothing much, just thought I'd stop by."

"Oh, like on your way to fire practice? Or do you always walk about with a ladder?"

Nicky give her his best mournful smile. "No. You know, I get a bit lonely. My wife died sometime ago."

"Oh dear, I'm so sorry…" They kept company well into them small hours. and when Nicky finally made a move to leave, it were only to find that "Those bleeding little psycho's have stolen my ladder!"

Linda laughed and said, "No big deal. Rickers and Asbo will escort you down." And, hey presto, her door sprung open like a jack in the box and there they was, voila, at your service, ready and waiting.

Dorcas Vine

No matter what colour or size a kid is when they arrive in the world, they has a way of landing in the best family for them. Chances are the potter's kid can throw a pot and ain't no bars or locks the burglar's girl cannot undo. I chose to be born in a family of mid-wives, an' picked up where my mother and grandmother left off. an' if you is gonna be a singer, then you better make sure you choose a father who goes rolling down them empty rail-tracks, warming up the sullen lands with a voice to eat your heart out.

My partner Tobias bestowed his love of words on everything. "You all sit tight in the earth over winter, you'll be amazed at your appearance in the spring," he said, spreading earth over the seeds he was planting, an' "Ain't you looking good?" as he admired the Rainbow Chard and checked the Silver Beets for weevils. "Bring it on, do your worst! We is ready for you now," he challenged the wind…

Autumn were a highly charged season for Tobias, who were at home a lot more due to the leaves-on-the-track situation. The first heavy winds threatened to wipe out his winter crops, no matter how much he tied them up and staked them down, when "For crying out loud!" somehow or other them well-ordered patchwork water-gardens the Orientals maintained out on Hackney Marshes remained intack an' producing luxurious, pristine vegetables no matter what.

Angelina and Gloria were rehearsing in the basement with some of the Soft Sloth crew, for they had a support-act booking at Jabba the Sluts, and I was making an onion, actually a French onion soup with dumplings, so we could all have a meal together. Which turned out to be a piece of easy-going normality that was never seen again before the day was out.

After lunch, Tobias set my midwifery bag and baby scales next to me in the Donkey cart and I said goodbye, took up the reins and trotted away on my rounds, the support act for when the babies get home.

I understand that the behaviour of animals change before an earthquake. The difference can be subtle but it is there, like a change in the breathing pattern of a new born baby. Listen up, pay attention, it means something.

Delilah may be quirky but we has communication, an' the moment we left Embankment Gardens an uneasiness come over the both of us. Her ears flicked back an' forth, which meant something was amiss and something weren't right. There was a fine mist hazing up the roof-tops, but otherwise everything looked just about the same as usual when we skirted around Charred Cross Station and headed up St Martins towards the maze of Soho's Oriental markets.

The Oriental Quarter is closed at night-time and better-guarded than the walled city of Kowloon itself, but by daylight it is a colourful place to be, where life takes place out on the streets. The narrow alleys are crowded with traders and some streets is piled sky-high with bolts of silk of vibrant hues. The flower market greets you, bright as a sunrise an' all spread out beneath the yellow canopy of trees in Soho Square. Herbalist stalls sit side-by-side along the length of Brewer Street, and cheery Chinese masseurs enthusiastically work away the knots and tensions from out the weary backs of Leggers. A cobbled courtyard provides a place where folk can take a burning Moxa treatment and beneath the shade of wide umbrellas made of parchment, inscrutable acupuncturists ply their trade. I always love it there, but all that gaiety an' the sweet enticing aromas of the Berwick street food-stalls failed to banish the disquiet that stalked us through those streets, and parking up Delilah with the other donkeys I cut behind the smoking grills of seafood, found Abby's front door and knocked.

I seen right away that Abby was a confident new mother by the way she held her baby, relaxed and sure. I left my troubles at the door and followed her upstairs into their tidy home, and we parlaried a bit while I weighed and measured Mica, who was not all that thrilled about it. "How's he doing, putting on the pounds? Is he alright?" Abby asked me

"Fine, absolutely fine. You might soak a muslin cloth in water with a few drops of eucalyptus or pine essence and hang it over the window to keep the air fresh… The smog is thickening out there," I suggested, handing her a phial of eucalyptus oil. One out of three of our babies contracted a respiratory problem in their first few weeks of life. "It's kind of curious, you two living here," I remarked.

" I suppose. I've been here most of my life. My Dad was a watch-maker, who were keen for people to be in perfect time with the cosmos. He insisted on setting his watches by the Sun, which meant waiting around for the Sun's occasional appearance. He also created these incredible intricate security-systems, works of art really, that used the forces of gravity and levity in order to trigger a chain of lightning events that bought about a lockdown He refused to work for the Mantle so we moved into the Oriental District, where he been immediately employed to set up warning systems. Some of them were over a mile long."

"Ain't that something? It's amazing what people can do."

"Yeah, he was a great father an' I miss him. Life goes on, time goes by… Now that I have Mica, I'd love to move to someplace where we could see the Sun more often." Abby frowned a little.

"My partner is a railroad man," I said. "He once took me way outta town to see the stars. It were unbelievable peaceful. You takes your chances out in the sticks, but he says there are pockets of decent folk out there. Well Abby, it's been nice talking but I has food to pick up and I must see how that baby who lost her mum and her poor father are coping on their own."

"Riley? He ain't even twenty-one yet. Lucy were a good five years older than him, I don't know what he'll do without her . Tell him to drop by if he wants company. See you next week, Dorcas, thanks."

My uneasiness returned the moment I stepped outside into all the racket of Berwick Street but I made for the fruit-and-vegetable stalls, all overloaded with fresh produce that came in everyday. There was such a variety to choose from I was having trouble deciding what to pick, when I found myself next to one of the world's best gardeners, dressed in his usual white linen suit. " Five leaves of pickled radish and a tub of wasabi, please. Hello Dorcas. Don't react in any way but you are being followed on your rounds. Best not to visit the ailing ones, I should say."

"Thank you Solo. Who by?"

"Turkish. Obviously the best the Mantle have to offer by way of an average white man." He smiled and walked away.

"One large bag of wild rice, a big bunch of those green leaves over there, a couple of Ginger roots and two big handfuls of Shitake. That'll be it, thanks." On the way back up the market, my unease turned to down-righteous anger. I stopped at Peeking Ducky for one of his delicious pancakes, and chucking my purchases into the back of the cart, I said "Hello Delilah. Been a slight change of plan."

Turkish were lurking behind a tank of crayfish and lobsters when I set off through the thickening smog, just slow enough for him to follow. I nibbled on my pancake an' ambled along Brewer Street.

There was a big funeral processing down Glasshouse Street, with people playing a wide range of traditional instruments, letting off fire-crackers and generally doing their very best to chase that dead person's ghost away. Those Orientals are a very superstitious people.

We left China Town an' went round Piccadilly twice, then up one lane, down another and wended the most exasperating route I could think of toward Shepherds Market. I hoped Turkish was keeping up. I popped in on a family whose children were long out of my care and spent the rest of the afternoon visiting as many old friends as I could remember. "Hiya, I was in area on my baby rounds, thought I find out how you're all doing…" I even visited my mother for a spot of chai. "Hi Ma, how are ya, it's been ages…" Ma gave me a terrible reproachful look over her glasses. "I won't be around forever you know," she threatened while I peeked out the window at Turkish, who was refreshing himself at the "Stop an' Retox" across the road.

I'd intended to spend my afternoon helping Riley out with his babe. I'd no idea he were that young, what a load he were carrying, but I dared not visit them with Turkish on my tail. It was time to make our getaway, so we set off at a furious pace and lost him in the twilight smog when Delilah fled pell-mell for the sanctuary of the Chelsea Physic Garden, which was the kind of genius idea she sometimes came up with. "You're a good old girl, you is the best," I told her, and burst into tears. But then there was Ariel by my side, calmly taking hold of the situation. "Mum, make Dorcas a cup of chai. Eden, poor Delilah needs some food an' attention. I'll fetch the Arnica and set another place for dinner, you come inside now and sit by the fire. Dad, how about a shoulder massage for Dorcas?" Ariel was self-assured in a crisis, kinda of confirming my theory that children contrive to arrive in the best family for them. an' as Dr Cole laid his warm hands on my shoulders, my tension begun to ease away.

Grandma Tookie (the Akashic Record, Cole Levet)

Sometime after they'd bid farewell to Booker, Jean de Fer an' all his huge horses, the nights drew in and the days grew colder, and Clara and Cole Levet knew it was time to pack their field-hospital up and head on to an old railway tunnel where they'd often overwintered. They harnessed up Tuppence and were just having a last cuppa before setting off when a posse of Hissy Boy trackers darted between the trees and surrounded their dell.

"What's the whereabouts of the mutant kid Jules?" the Hissy Boys asked, and slithering down the slope they closed in a tight circle round Cole and Clara. They wore jeans of shiny black leather and peered out from beneath their hoodies with the dead eyes of those that are either GM's or the soulless descendants of early cloning experiments.

"What are you talking about?" Clara asked, shrugging her shoulders.

"The kid named Jules. 'Course you knows him, you's doctors init?"

"Yes, but the only people we've seen is woodsmen an' Gitanes, no kids."

Cole kept his cool, but the Hissy Boys spoke menacingly low as they weaved about their work with the smooth economic body-language of hunters. One placed a machete to heat in the fire while the others wound their vice-tight arms around Cole and Clara. "Better start talking, or we'll squeeze it out of you. Nope? 'Ave it your own way then," and they tightened their grip. Cole and Clara gasped for air but had nothing to say. "Well, perhaps the lad might remember a bit more when we squeeze the living daylight out of his mother?" And with the increasing pressure, Clara's ribs begun to bend and break audibly until she collapsed.

Cole held his tormentors gaze stoically until turning shifty, the Hissy Boy veiled his eyes and pulling the machete out of the fire, he struck at Cole like lightning. "Stitch yourself up, Doc." A haze of colour filled Cole's eyes and sinking to his knees, he howled with the pain that seared through his thigh. "That's more like it," the Hissy Boy leered. "Come on lads, let's git," and grinding Cole's hand into the dirt, he turned on his heel and left.

Using the cart to haul himself upright, Cole struggled over to his mother, and helping her into the back of the cart, he thought how fragile and tiny she seemed, her bright spirit diminished with pain, as he tenderly packed her in with their bedding. "How about you, Cole? You must be in terrible pain. And it's not over yet, we have to move… Hissy Boys so far from town can only mean the Dark Elite are not far behind."

"Don't say a word Ma, I'm on it," Cole replied and checking his wound, he found the red-hot blade had cleanly cauterised it. Fumbling a rough splint onto his broken fingers, he struggled onto the cart, took hold of the reigns and said, "Tuppence, Tuppence, let's go boy, let's fly."

Tuppence came flying into Elveden Forest just before midnight, his hooves clattering through the dreams of the sleeping denizens. "Joe, Franny," Cole yelled, "you've got to get out of this place! The Hissy Boys are onto Jules."

"What's up?" Joe came running outside. "Steady on lad, you're safe," Gabriel told him.

"No, no we are not safe," said Cole, "and Mum's in a very bad way. Help her…"

" I hear ya. Take it easy, we'll take it from here. Come on, bring them inside. The rest of you get lively. It's code red, we're leaving now." Franny doused Cole's wound with colloidal silver and stitched it up with button thread, while her sister Sandy eased his broken fingers back into their joints, reset the bones and splinted them firmly together, assisted by Ryan, who poured knockout doses of Moonshine down his throat. Which was the first and last drink Cole ever had, for ever after the taste of alcohol reminded him of pain.

"Were you hurt on our account?"

"It's nothing. You've got to go now."

"Don't fret, the cold will slow the Hissy Boys down a great deal an' we was leaving tomorrow anyway. Just gotta sort out a place for the both of you and we're outta here."

The wagons drew up beneath the torchlight, and muffling up the harnesses, Slim Pickings and Sicily settled Cole and Dr Levet comfortably in the back of their wagon amongst a pile of bedding. Then, with a mixture of dread an' adrenalin, a quick pat on the back and a quiet embrace, they mounted the wagons and made to leave when Jules planted his feet firmly on the ground and stubbornly refused to budge. "What about me ponies?" he cried loud enough to wake the dead.

"Here Jules, ride with us," Grace and Tucker tried to persuade him.

"Come on son, don't muck about." Joe was impatient.

"I isn't mucking about, I ain't coming," Jules began to cry.

" It's okay, Jules." Little Lewis took his hand. "They will follow you, an' everybody knows it. Come on, get in here with us. We is responsible for the doctors' donkey ambulance."

"You sure?" Jules asked, wiping his snotty nose on his sleeve.

"Yeah, course. Your horses love you an' they loves keeping people company. Come on man."

Ryan walked ahead with a dim blue lantern to light the way. Gabriel and Jesse's wagon fell in behind him, then the little kids Smokey, Tillie, Ruby, Lewis and Jules pulled the ambulance in behind them, followed by Joe, Franny and Sandy, her sister, in their wagon. Eleven-year-old Grace and ten-year-old Tucker fell in behind them in charge of their own wagon, and Slim Pickings and Sicily bought up the rear with Dr Levet and Cole, who was temporarily pain-free under a haze of alcohol, gazing out of the back of the wagon at the wild horses, who razed the vegetable garden before following behind at a distance, their dark shadows glistening in the moonlight and their many hooves eradicating any traces of the tracks the wagons left behind.

Dr Levet was out for the count, either unconscious or sleeping, and covering her with as many rugs and coats as he could muster, Cole watched the ponies for a long, long time, until at last he too drifted off to sleep.

They kept those wagons rolling along the earthy forest floor throughout the night and all the next day, only stopping every so often to change shifts. The late afternoon found them on the banks of a wide river and finding no immediate fording, they splashed along the shingley shallows for an hour or so before a crossing could be chanced. Grandma Sicily was at the reins, and checking first for signs of pursuit, she expertly headed the wagons across the river towards a spit of shingle on the opposite shore.

They passed safely under the cover of the trees and a few miles on, drew to a halt in a small clearing, sitting a while in an exhausted hush, for every one was bushed. Joe was the first to jump off his wagon. "Phaw, I ain't half knackered after that little jaunt."

"That's the trouble with the youth of today. No staying power."

"Right you are Slim," says Gabriel. "How about you fix us all something to eat then?"

"Don't mind if do," replied Slim. "Look at all these mushrooms! Come on kids, give your old granddad a hand. Whoever picks the most gets a swig of cider."

Cole woke up with the pain to greet him. He winced and carefully shifted position so as not to disturb his sleeping mother, then gently checking her broken ribs. His hands began to warm, to blaze and tingle with heat. Clara's eyes crinkled into a smile. "Your father could do that sometimes. Being a man of science, it used to annoy the hell out of him." Had her ribs not been broken her son's disbelieving face would have made her laugh. "Resistance is useless. Healing hands are a gift, takes the power out of the pain. That's much better, thanks," she wheezed, and closed her eyes again.

Tuppence pushed his shaggy head through the awning and begun to nuzzle Cole earnestly. "Hello mate. Hm, I smell fresh mushrooms." Cole eased his broken fingers around the donkey's neck and hauled himself gingerly out of the wagon, wiped a couple of tears out of his eyes and hobbled off with Tuppence to support him.

Cole was greeted by a round of applause and treated with a hero's respect. The kids made a space for him to sit with them beside the fire while Ryan and Gracie heaped up a plate of food for him, and offering them a battered wolfy smile he tucked hungrily into his rice, wild mushrooms and bacon, which was about as delicious as it comes.

They stowed everything into the belly-boxes and stuck them under the wagons, then stretched out by the fireside and kipped beneath the open sky. Overhead a few early stars came out, while Jules's ponies slowly streamed into camp and began to crop the long damp grass.

At about four in the morning, Gabriel woke them all up. "We've slept too long," he said. "We ain't safe yet."

"Quite right," said Joe, sitting bolt upright, and while Sandy brewed a hasty mug of chai for everyone the bleary-eyed lads hitched up the wagons. "Which way from here, Dad?" Ryan asked.

"North-east, straight as we can towards the marshes," Joe replied. Ryan took up his post as pathfinder, and they up and followed the light of his blue lantern until the break of day, when it begun to rain.

They journeyed steadily through the rain for a couple more days. The going became increasingly heavy, for the forest climbed steadily and the ground became rough and stony, until at last the rain eased off and they came to a high rocky outcrop. Some five or six hundred feet below, the marshes spread away for as far and wide as the eye could see. Not a single one of those children had ever seen so much open land or sky, and they were taken aback by it. A pair of Peregrine

120

Falcons wheeled and turned high overhead and a gentle breeze billowed over the flatlands, bending the reeds into silver grey-green waves. A few small wooded islands scattered away towards the horizon and one or two green ribbon paths wound into the broad terrain.

"Come on," said Tucker, climbing back into his wagon with Gracie and Ryan. "That's enough gawping, let's get in it," and set off.

"Oi, wait for us!" Smokey shouted, leaping into the donkey-cart with all the little ones piling in behind. But Tuppence was in no hurry, and took his precious cargo down the long slippery track at state funeral pace, and ambling out of the forest, he waited responsibly until the grown-up's caught up.

Flanked beneath the willows, a mossy towpath meandered through a tunnel of reeds, drawing them into the wide green embrace of the wetlands. The restless company begun to feel a little safer, and as the afternoon wore into evening they felt their troubles begin to lift from their shoulders. They made camp on the shore of a wide lake into which Slim Pickings, the grandfather of them all, gratefully plunged. "Oh it's great! Very refreshing," he gasped. "Wash the grimy journey off you. Here Jules, I'll give you a hand." And while they swam, Cole doused his wound with colloidal silver to keep it clean and Franny, Sandy and Jesse, lit a fire and prepared a meal of pasta and a sauce of tomato and basil.

The swimmers came out shivering and sat by the fire to dry, Gabriel cracked open a few beers, and Slim Pickings pulled at his pipe while Jesse and Sicily rolled themselves cigarettes. Easing herself carefully into a deck-chair, Clara Levet seemed much brighter. "I'd forgotten how lovely it is here. My sister and I were raised here. Ouch," she winced. "Never mind, a bit of real pain is bound to make a better doctor of me."

"You is my very good doctor already," said Jules, taking her hand and kissing it, when a lonesome noise came floating over the reed beds. At first it was eerie and unnerving, conjuring visions of Death riding a rusty old bicycle towards them, a scythe across his skeletal shoulder and rattling his chains behind. Nobody knew what to expect, but with its rapid approach the sound became the rise and fall of a haunting singing voice, fit to tear the soul out of you. Their mouths fell open when a hand-car came flying through the reed beds, pumped by a young man who interrupted his singing to say, "Hello, you all," and bought the hand-car to a screaming halt. "Respect. Does I smell pasta by any chance?" He raised his eyebrows expectantly. "You on holiday or something?"

"Respect. Not exactly, darlin'," said Jesse. "We is desperado fugi's, escaping the Dark Elite,." explained Tillie.

"You could have fooled me. Anyways, chill out. Ain't no Dark Elite nor no one else for a million miles… 'Cepting me, of course. I is very dark an' real elite."

The kids started giggling. "Reckon, you is," Gabriel nodded and offered him a beer. "Sit down an' join us, won't you? 'Ave a bite to eat. I's Joe, by the way."

"And I's Gracie. I'm a dancer," and she executed a neat back flip. "I been knocked out by your singing. Speaks to the insides."

"Well thank you, Gracie. I's Tobias."

"What's you pumping about in the middle of nowhere for?"

"Grace, leave the poor man alone," Sicily scolded her.

"It don't matter. I's working for the railroads."

During supper, they watched the scores of geese return, in an exuberant commotion of honking and calling, tipping their wings and steadying their unstable splash-landings with outstretched feet of orange, pink and blue, and settling into their rounded wakes they paddled about in long flotillas on the darkening waters of the lake.

Five days later, blindfolded by fog and quite unexpectedly, they rode onto the drawbridge of Greene King Keep. Lear came striding out and raised his shotgun. "One more step and I'll start firing!"

To which Dr Levet firmly responded, "Come now Lear, technically this is more my home then yours."

"Clara! Good heavens, say no more. You and your friends had

better all come in." And Lear lowered his gun, but he remained guarded.

"Are you Aunt Clara?" Liberty beamed. "Come in and most welcome. Plenty of room for one and all. Stay forever, no problem."

"Tar love, don't mind if I do." Gabriel tipped her a wink.

There was a moment's struggle when Lear tried to raise the drawbridge behind them. "No guv, we ain't doing that till everyone's in." Jules was desperate.

"My name is Lear, as in Shakespeare's King Lear. How many more of you are there?"

"Oh beg your pardon, Shakespeare Your Majesty. Lots," Jules replied, "an here they comes."

"Look at them all! How extraordinary." Lear stood back to admire the wild horses streaming in over the bridge. Then, putting a friendly hand on Jule's shoulder, he asked, "Do they all belong to you, lad?"

"Sort of. More I belongs to all of them... Does you want a hand with the bridge now, guv?"

They had only meant to stay for a few days on their way up North. "But it's a journey of two months or more, and winter will overtake you sooner rather than later. Jules isn't up to that," said Dr Levet. "Far better you stay put with us."

It seems the fenland winter is notorious. The Akashic record is littered with entries the gist of which suggest that the weather comes roaring out of the North-east direct from Siberia, with bitter winds which harry across thousands of miles of land and sea solely to encase the Fens in ice and bury the marshes in as much snow as possible.

At Greene King Keep, Ryan discovered the library. Tucker took a shine to Ollie the cook, an ex-dancer who was not averse to sampling Liberty's beauty products or making helpful suggestions about them. "A little bit sickly sweet for my taste, darling, but Tucker seems to like it..." Jesse vanished into the old greenhouses to sort them out, while Sandy found everything she needed to make a classroom, so school was in. Cole, whose wound was slow to mend, sat studying for his medicals by the fireside, while Dr Clara Levet hobbled cautiously through the Keep consulting with Gabriel, Joe and Slim Pickings as to repairing it. "Well, courtesy of Jean de Fer, who done a good job on the water-wheel, we does have heat an' light. Still, I could spend a lifetime putting things to rights," Slim thought out loud. "Now, I happened across seventeen cars in one of the barns, some of which we could trade with Captain Dan in exchange for the building supplies we needs."

Gabriel, Joe, Slim Pickings and the kids set about fixing up the inside of the place. Their work was entirely about re-wiring, replacing, re-plumbing and re-plastering, and under Lear's watchful eye, carefully restoring and painstakingly preserving the past. And the perishing army were only too glad to come inside and use their expert shoring skills to pump a mix of fine shingle and cement into the towering cavity-walls, which made it watertight, forever draught-free and solid as a rock. And like the Hoover Dam, the cement is still curing to this very day.

Winter crept south, the snow falling thick over forest, muffling the outlands and sending the Hissy Boys into semi-hibernation. The Big Smoke became the Big White, where no such careful preservation or reconstruction of the past was taking place at The Wayland Forge. Indeed, their building was about leaving the past behind them where it belonged, and purposefully trying to lay it to rest. Jean, Reema, Amber de Fer and Canada Blanch worked hard together, pushing barriers, breaking moulds and asking an awful lot of rock and iron in order to create a whole new genre of architecture that looked ahead optimistically. and seemed to suggest, "Hang on to your hats now, the future is a-comin' in." But not for Amber, who up and left with no warning. She was not alone, though, for the settling of the dust and the melting of snows saw the parting of many ways, mostly between the past and the future.

Dr Clara Levet spoke affably with Lear. "I know my sister couldn't stand it here, and it is inevitable that Liberty will go too, but when she does perhaps you'll accept to remain here as Seneschal? Show some respect to those who happen to come upon Greene King

Keep and even if nobody ever does, it is a dark world, Lear and a comfort to know that some humanity exists in the loneliest of places. Slim Pickings and Sicily have decided to remain here when the others head North, and I'll go with them, for they'll need a doctor."

"You always were dedicated to the open road. I suppose it would leave Cole free to choose a life of his own?" Lear smiled at her.

"Of course it's good timing for me, but I have hopes that the far North will become home to another pocket of humanity. It's my intuition that things will get a lot worse before they get better."

"I see. Then I will man the fort and willingly. Besides, I have come to belong to this place over time. I live in dread of Liberty's departure. She is my daughter whom I was left to hold," and the tears begun to roll down Lear's noble face, "but who am I to interfere when fate washes a handsome boy like Jean to a girl's feet?"

Down in the Big Smoke, much to Jean's relief, Canada offered to deliver the shoring iron up the east coast. He recruited Albin and Tobin as gunners and they made the maiden voyage without a hitch, returning safely a couple of weeks later on the spring tide with one old car, a bag of flints, a couple of boxes of kippers and Liberty on board.

And sixteen-year-old Cole Levet set off on foot for the Big Smoke. But it took him three years to get there, because in the forest the wide river was raging an' swollen with snow melt, forcing Cole to head west for many a mile, until he found shelter with a herb gatherer, a master of significance, who took him on.

Franny (the Far North)

I t's been eighteen short years since we first come up here, an' how right Booker been about the North. With nothing up ahead clear to the North Pole an' no fear at our backs, we been free to live in the wild an' lovely landscape. When we first come upon this place, the small fishing cove been weather-wasted skeletal, but it were the place for us and it come together, piece by piece in its own time. Now the smoking-chimney crofts straggling higgledy-piggledy up and down the cliffs, fruit trees that somehow or other green-fingered Jesse has managed to grow, an' cottage gardens that overflow the dry stone walls to flower along the rocky ledges, have raised the spirits of the place an' brought it back to life.

Jesse, Gabriel, Joe and I climbed up a path that wound through the sweet-smelling pines to our bench on top of the hill. It were a very steep climb, which we made without actually collapsing or having a heart attack, and sitting down together, grateful for the rest and comfortable old friends in a familiar spot, we engaged in our familiar vigil of watching the ocean, searching the waters and scanning the horizon, for a sign, any sign at all, of our children Grace, Tucker and Smokey, who was somewhere out there bringing the fish back home.

The evening light were a deep shade of lapis and the sea satin-flat, a sign we has learned to read as meaning the fine autumn day were only holding its breath afore exhaling a gosh-almighty storm. A pair of Mute Swans headed inland with the strong wide wingbeats of blue angels, and a flock of Arctic Terns skittered a quick fish snack on the wing, for they were long-distance travelling, but of the boats there was no sign.

A big red squirrel come pattering down the branches an' sidling up hopefully. Jesse told him, "We is panicking not picnicking."

"We is not, here you go," said Joe, scattering a handful of pine nuts.

"Now we's up here, strikes me pr'aps we'd be more use down there, lighting the harbour lamps." Gabriel had a point. None of us moved, though.

"They'll put in on a island if it gets too rough."

"'Course, love." Gabriel folded Jesse's rough hands between his. "They'll be fine." Their son Smokey were the youngest out there. We watched the ocean till the light began to fail, afore plodding back down the pine-needled path.

Everyone were scurrying about down town. Jules were shooing the cattle into the barns, Ryan, Sandy and Corbin her husband were ramming home the shutters on their school-house, where due to the books donated from Greene King Keep, the local nippers come in by boat, or trotting out from their far-flung farms for a remarkable highfalutin education.

Everybody were happy at school, 'cept perhaps Tucker. Indeed, it were likely that the best teacher in world could not have taught him a single thing, but he always been very kind to Jules, keeping him company and giving his time to him. Ruby an' Lewis, who is on the wild side, took themselves off into the forest and built themselves a small holding in a clearing, right plum in the middle of a territory belonging to a pack of Timber Wolves, who they was learning to get along with and joked was excellent security. "Against what?" I asked them, seeing as the only security you might ever need out here is against wolves. They has a few head of the most mournful-looking cattle you ever did see, with long horns, shaggy coats an' reproachful eyes, which is even distained by the wolves, and they survives off trapping, exchanging their pelts for goods down at the Altnaharra Clothes Exchange and Trading Post. But they has also taken up distilling a very dark whiskey, and "Smoky Old Peat" do seem to be making quite a name for itself around the logging and trapping community.

Jules's Downs Syndrome do come with a number of sides, an' Dr Levet has hung on to him through several bouts of pneumonia that had him knocking on death's door. She keeps herself lively with learning, an' her rounds includes way-out hill farms an' solitary trappers all the way up to the grizzled herders on Cape Wrath, accompanied by Tuppence who were now about twenty-five years old, and Tillie, who were her practical an' capable assistant and perfectly happy to drive the doctor, come rain or shine or snow or howling hurricanes, provided she had her Rook-an-Rabbit rifle across her knee.

Gabriel, Jesse, Joe an' I lit all the coloured lamps around the cove, the string of green lights to mark the right side of the harbour and the big red mirrored light on the left side of the pier head. "That should do it. S'pect we is visible from outer space now." Joe seemed satisfied, and then with nothing more we could do, an' without no sight of sails coming over the dark horizon, we went to batten down the hatches of our homes afore the storm come hurrying down on us.

Tobias (the Big Smoke)

I t's Dorcas herself who's gonna tell you to pay attention to all the little things an' listen real carefully to the truth of what you is feeling, then you is bound to perceive the appropriate response. I knowed something were up as the day gone on and by night fall I became so full on anxious about her whereabouts, the only appropriate response were to go look for her.

I climbed into our Lighter an' lit the green navigation light on the starboard, the red larboard light an' all the many other lights that hung onboard courtesy of Angelina an' Gloria, and the very splendid array of multicolours that come shimmering off the fog give the impression that the King of Elfland were heading up the search-and-rescue tonight.

There were no need to see the moon to know that she were full, for the tide were right high and the current so strong that I knew the upstream wetlands were already closing over with dark waters and all the little eyots disappearing in the drink. I could have been in the lost world of Atlantis, everything were that vague and muffled in the smog, but when I drew abreast the Wayland Forge it were glowing like a dragon's cave through the dark arch-mouth of its doors, an' Jean an' Liberty came hastening out at the sight of my wavering lanterns in the fog. "Is that you Tobias? Have you got Column with you?"

"No, I do not," I answered, an' chucked a painter to Liberty. She wrapped it around one of them outsize double-bit iron bollards that Jean's so fond of casting. "Is something up, Tobias? Even the Smokes and Hissy Boys are giving it a rest tonight."

Jean give me a keen look. "I don't know exactly, it's more a feeling.

Lawd knows but Dorcas is often out all night. I just thought I'd have a look for her, that's all."

"I know what you mean," said Liberty, "I'm feeling that way about Column. Nobody's seen hide nor hair of him since midday, an' he'd never normally be out in this."

"Yeah, he don't like the fog," added Jean. "Panics if he can't see or hear clearly."

"Well he's in the wrong city then, but I'll look out for him on my way up river. You is welcome to come along. I'd thought to go as far as the Chelsea Physic."

"Just let me put on another layer or two," and Liberty made to go inside.

"That's okay, I'll go. What sort of a father would I be if I didn't?"

"Reet ho," Liberty responded cautiously, but Jean the water-phobic untied the painter, pushed the boat out into the late night current, leapt in and settling himself into the bow, saying, "You'll be fine Tobias, I shall keep a good eye out for sharks."

"Much obliged, Jean." And though some say that being a man means facing fear alone, there is much to be said for sharing it. That's just what friends is about.

Once in a while, Jean hollered, "Column, Column!" over the water, an' when we was well nigh Projack, a answering call finally come. "I'm here Dad, over here." We picked Column up off the river wall and he were very agitated to see his father in a boat. "What's happened Dad, what's wrong?"

"It's all right son, we were worried about you."

"Sorry Dad, I got spooked by a dodgy dude and hid in a pipe. Then it were dark and foggy an' I were trying to make my way to Uncle Cole and Aunt Reema's…" His words faltered when it dawned on him that his Dad had probably thought he'd drowned. "I'm so sorry. Thank you for coming to find me." The boy reached his arm across his father's shoulder. "Lucky you come with Tobias. His boat is a very friendly distinguishable and recognizable item."

"Well that's because Dorcas is missing too, and Tobias and I are out looking for her an' all. Don't suppose you've seen her have you?"

"No, no I haven't. I'm sure she's just been marooned somewhere by the weather." And indeed we found her hauled up at the Chelsea Physic Garden, where the welcome was generous and warm, and while Reema put on the kettle an' made us some toast, I took Dorcas aside and held her close in my arms. She felt comfortable an' easygoing on the outside, but turbulent an' real thoughtful on the inside, and later she told me that Turkish been stalking her all day.

Topaz, Chief of the Saracen Clan

Jabba the Sluts were a wingding establishment an' in many ways, the Therapeutics Anonymous of the underground, as all men were equal there. It were the only place in the Big Smoke where a bargeman, assassin, Gitane, gangster, bankster and all the world could rub shoulders with each other and even sit down peaceably side-by-side to enjoy a show, total free from the angst of being eliminated.

There were no need for a dress code. Folks came in their best threads, nobody would've dreamed of showing up in

anything less. They tipped their hats and gave up their intriguing arsenal at the door and I has speculated how Jabba acquired her big blond blue-eyed bouncers, but assumes someone cloned them up for her as a favour.

Even the ice-cool bouncers couldn't help but raise a eyebrow at the sight of Column's knife when I gave it up on the door. Still, they managed a polite, "Good evening sir?" hoping perhaps to discuss the blade, but I says "Respect," gave them a polite nod an' sailed on down the stairs with a plan I been hatching with the information the boy trusted to me. And some of it included a little co-operation from Jabba, an old friendster of mine.

"Respect me darlings, an' good evening me dear," I says to Jabba, who were sitting in a booth of Zebra skins and glitter, doing a fine job of lighting up a hookah, and I kissed her hand as were right for a women of charm and chutzpah.

She indicated for me to park myself next to her. "Respect sweetheart, long time no see," says she, exhaling a lungful of apple wood tobacco. I called a waiter over and ordered a round of the fire-an-ice cocktails the girls loved so much. "Don't spoil em," Jabba's eyes twinkled. "They've got to be fit for their dancing later."

"No big deal, just a treat. Some of these girls is a long way from home."

"How's you been keeping?" She paused an' rested her shrewd Gitane eyes on me, and after a moments scrutiny she asked, "What's up love? Something wrong?"

"There is, but we has the head start, an' I's wondering if your girls could do me a little bit of a favour tomorrow?"

Jabba beckoned them over, remarking, "Might do them some good to see a little daylight... What exactly is it you want them to do?"

Most of the time Jabba's girls is obliged to assume the personas of a bunch of flapping dipsticks from La La land, whereas in fact they were good sorts an' daredevils, with the kind of discipline and va va voom it do take to achieve a very classy, dangerous an' highly skilled act. The task I had in mind were not exactly gonna stretch them, so they says "Sure, no problem, don't worry about a thing. Could be a laugh in it," an' agrees to help me out.

Jabba an' I swopped news and parlaried a bit about old times, while they gone about their Go Go business, slapping on the makeup, wrestling into leather outfits, ramming home studs, clipping up buckles, slipping on the stilettoes and checking their equipment. They cracked whips, stacked hula hoops, stuck the fire clubs in paraffin to soak and draped Horace and Hilda, the resident boas, over them buff and shiny shoulders of theirs. Then they was gone, up the ropes an' poles into the iron cages which hung from the ceiling, or tucking themselves away on the trapezes hidden under the eves, all ready and waiting for the show.

"'Ello big boy." Emil the MC minced his way across the dance floor, an' giving me a exaggerated wink, he arranged himself in his red leather "electric chair". The bar staff polished glasses, the bouncers took up their positions at the entrance an' the lively clientele start to come down the red carpet in their dribs and drabs to find their preferred tables an' places, light up the bubbling hookahs and set the dazzling smiling waitresses to flitting about taking orders.

Jabba's filled up thick and fast. A small floodlight come on directly over Emil's head and his electric chair begin to blink on and off in shades of pink, lilac and orange, which caused an expectant hush to fall over the place. Then, through the wisps of smoke curling up around him, Emil lisped, "Tonight, ladies and gentlemen, is my very last night on earth." "His very last night on earth, how sad," chorused the girls. "But I have travelled far and wide and before I die, let me conjure before your eyes, before your very eyes, some of the many fabulous wonders I have seen." There were total silence, "But first," he paused dramatically, "welcome to the champagne of entertainment, the shining Swarovski of the Big Smoke, the incredible, incandescent, incomprehensible, irrepressible and iridescent world of Jabba the Sluts! Welcome, my friends, welcome." The crowd responded with enthusiastic applause as Emil waved dismissively with both hands, an' once the audience calmed down again he says, "Our story begins with the distant memories of my boyhood, in the far reaches of the mysterious East." "East End, you mean!" someone heckled. "The nerve," simpered Emil, "And now ladies and gentlemen, without further ado, I give you the sensational, the sinuous and sensual snake dancers of Siam!"

Emil were no tink. Indeed, he had a couple of youngsters to provide for and a sweet wife. But he came out of Reema's acting classes, a pretty decent compère who knew how to control his audience. Although a murderous clientele do go a long way to give a show a bit of edge and ba-da-bing.

With a clan to preside over an' mountains to move I were no regular at the club, but when I were there I was always discreetly looking an' checking sidelong, in an anticipatory way, for a lady, perhaps in a magenta dress, who looked like she might not mind too much living in a old damp and rusting fortress with a big fella like me. But as no-one like that appeared to be coming in tonight, I said, 'Never minds, all in good time," philosophically. And besides, it were time for me to go. There were one more person I were keen to hook up with afore the night was out.

Then, on me way down the long fogbound alleyways, I come across a bright oil-drum fire, abandoned by a crowd of absinth drinkers who gone shuffling off under some arches at my approach. "I ain't nothing to be afraid of," I called to them. It were such a sorry bunch of creatures who come cautiously out the foggy shadows and held out their trembling hands to warm by the fire, all convincing scared and shifty about something, "Who did you think I was?" I asked.

"Department of darkness." "'Orrible click-clack stalker." "Big boots." "Stealthy needles." "No ears." "You's got a turnip on your head."

"It's a turban, you humpty." Absinth so fugs up the mind, I couldn't make head nor tail of what they was saying. "You're all right now." I left them to it and carried on me way toward the public baths.

Booker

No matter whether they is the Buddha, Zarathustra or Christly Jesus hisself, they is all going to suggest that an attachment to the creature-comforts of life is to be avoided and a very bad thing indeed. What is more, they is going to back this up ferociously with a number of annoying arguments and platitudes. For example, them Brothers Sebastian and Dominic is awful fond of saying, "You can't take it with you when you die." How do they know? Not that I is planning on taking it with me when I walk up that great hill towards death, but I do have a fond attachment to the public bath-house.

The front of the building is lit by two modest cressets, an' their quiet low-light flickering suggest a gateway to the inner sanctum of a sacred order. You will needs to be a mystic or a Rosicrucian at least to come inside. The old oak-panelled portico and uncomplaining swing doors has opened and shut on a hundred generations of people walking through, through the years, through their life. Push them open, step right up and

you is welcomed by the amazing opulence of yester-yore, and the uncompromising majestic shabbiness of the present. Even the receptionist has gently faded with the passage of time, and smoothed away by the constant rising steam, acquired a pasty look like a creature made of clay, a Golem who whiles away the time playing chess against himself an' against the clock, moving his pieces across the length of the black-and-white chequered entrance-hall towards an inevitable stalemate. "Who's winning?" I'd ask him and his reply, "You're having a laugh, mate," followed me all the way down the sandstone staircase that swept grandly around the baroque cooling bath, and out of earshot.

I like to have the place to myself, and generally roll up real late on Thursdays, which is Women Only Day, because they do leave the place so very neat and tidy, with all the deck chairs and massage beds arranged nicely about the chill-out room, the schmeiss buckets and long raffia bazen brushes stacked up properly along the length of the tiled corridor.

There is a particular procedure to follow. I's picked up a towel, disrobed, an' passed through the temple vale of transparent curtains into the mellowing heat of the steam room, settling down to the age-old ritual of purifying the body and soul. I hadn't been there long when the Saracen Chief, who were a large man but delicate on the feet, came in calmly, sat down beside me fully clothed except for his turban and says, "Respect, Booker. I knows this is space invading an' all, but I hoped to find you here alone." Which were a curious situation, seeing as so far, Topaz and I never had crossed paths nor was we ever acquainted. As a matter of fact, I thought my existence where little-known, let alone my name and location, but there you is.

I confirmed we was alone and then he says, "That's all right then. See, what I have learned is big-time dismaying, for the Mantle is planning a raid Sunday midnight on all those who's got them so-called Deviations or unsustainable kids in hiding... Now I don't know what you is going to do with this information, but I'm sure you does."

"What terrible thing is you telling me? An awful treachery... I'm extraordinary grateful. Thank you, Chief."

"Sure man." Topaz started to wind his turban about his head thoughtfully. "On me way here, I come across some itinerants that been terrified by something overwhelming sinister. I is looking forward to giving the Mantle and their ilk their comeuppance some day. I never could fathom how trash like that got so much power."

"Respect, why not fetch a towel and stay awhile to steam? I can explain some of it."

"I'd be very interested. I'll be right back," says Topaz, and a little while later returned with a towel around his waist an' a towel turban, looking like the prince of orient. Which of course he were, in his own way.

"I am with you 'bout routing the Mantle," I said. Now far as I understand it, and pardon me if you've heard some of this before, the Mantle first come into power with the departing of the bees. And it's my opinion that if anybody had noticed the bees was leaving, they would have understood the Earth were gearing up for something big. Perhaps it were preparing to adorn itself with a whole lot of water, or psyching up for the tectonic plates to clash, or contemplating a big volcanic spectacular, or maybe thinking an ice age would be nice. Some of them bees inexplicably died and others caught the mite, but most of them just up and vanished.

"They done their disappearing at a time when everyone were on the take. The banksters shafted the people for their money, and when the government became so corrupt there was nobody left to vote for, Parliament dissolved. The police became an unaccountable entity, and surreptitiously dismantling their own surveillance, so as to make their liquidations without being photographed on the job, same time they enlisted a number of volunteers out the local communities to help patrol the streets. So the Community Police come whistling through the rye, real cheerful, real helpful, real understanding, real effective, very of-the-people, by-the-people and for-the-people. And they became known as the Mantle, 'cause for a while that is just what they were, a big protective cloak over the people, that didn't take long to organise themselves into a protection racket. By which time the bees had all gone and three-quarters of the Earth's population lost their lives in the destruction that followed. You know, floods, war, diseases, famine an' all that four horses stuff. Rode roughshod over the earth.

"It were a long time before the bees come back and the Earth settled down to what we has now. A council were pulled together out of the dust an' the army dispatched to repair the infrastructure, but the Mantle was now basically an' organised crime dynasty and in the hands of one family, Mason Flint's ancestors, who came creeping out the chaos, exploited the post-disaster situation and begun to pursue a ruthless style of policing. They invented a really way-out-there ceremony, mainly cribbed from ancient Egypt an' a secret society of Shooters an' Fishers, to swear in new members. The rest we all knows, clear as a bell... Tell me something, Chief. Who told you about the raid they is planning?"

"Well," said Topaz, flashing a lightning smile, "I coulds tell you, but then I'd have to kill you." A statement that rendered the pair of us hopeless paralytic with laughter.

Grandma Tookie
(the Akashic Record)

The Akashic Record takes some getting used to. For example, when Booker mentions ancient Egypt, there it is in all its sandy glory. Or if the lovies are reading Faust, one may get the front row first-hand account from the muddy medieval times, for the Akashic does not distinguish between past and present. It's all there simultaneously and appears in real time. One learns to edit and ignore, and piece together a Friday Flyer, for example, from all the events of the following day.

"I don't suppose you has any idea as to who's responsible for broadcasting that bleeding radio show?" Mason Flint enquired.

"Nah, not a clue sir. But I's instructed the assassin to keep a sharp eye out."

"I weren't planning on deleting nobody, just putting a stop to it."

"Nor me neither sir, I just ask him to report anything suspicious."

Heaving a hefty sigh, Mason furrowed his brow and said, " I don't know if that was such a bright idea, Turkish my man. Observing ain't an assassin's thing. He won't be able to stop himself from killing the culprits. Furthermore, I reckon he's a clone."

"What? I had no idea, sir." Turkish was genuinely astonished.

"No matter, can't be helped. Oh look, here we are already." At the end of the Friday afternoon shift, the Mantle's top brass would pull up in their horse-drawn Mantle Wagons (a.k.a. Black Mariahs) at the public baths to sweat away the cares of the working week, socialise and discuss the latest from the mutter line. On this particular Friday they couldn't believe their luck, to be greeted by the young ladies from Jabba the Sluts! Especially the bloodless-lipped old patriarchs, who removed their shades (all the better to see them with) and taking a girly on each arm, gamefully escorted them downstairs, where the usual burly black Froth-Master had been replaced by a lovely woman who stood over the wooden washtub, whipping up the soapy water into a thick froth with some allure.

The Mantle had an enjoyable time of it. The girls wielding bazen brushes schmeissed them in the steam-room, swam with them in the cool pools, massaged them, and squeezed lime-juice over pineapple for them to eat, enthusiastically putting their hearts and souls into keeping the Mantle busy for a couple of hours. Eventually, though, Mason Flint and Turkish became suspicious and smelling a rat, they made themselves very unpopular by asking, "Who sent you lot down here?"

"No one, we done it for a laugh."

"You hear that Flint? They done it for a laugh," the retired chief protested hoarsely.

"Party's over now, girls. We has got business of a very sensitive nature to discuss." Mason ousted them.

"Well that's young Mason for you. Sure knows how to sour up the atmosphere," the old boys grumbled amiably to each other. "Ta ra, then." The girls gave a cheerful wave and filed out, having kept the Mantle off the streets while the broadcast was aired.

Phoebe, Ariel, Harley, Tyler and Column set off to fly the birds, so to speak, with a great sense of purpose – bloody-minded, devil-may-care, foolhardy, wired and lively, which helped to override the underlying fear that was pattering away in their hearts – only to find that the way to the pigeon loft was bared by Solo. 'Well, this is a fine conundrum and a turn-up for the books,' thought Ariel. She was intrigued, having only ever caught glimpses of Solo the shy gardener within the landscape of the Physic Garden, and within the landscape of her childhood, a childhood she had so recently and rather reluctantly tumbled out of. She was very glad to meet Solo here on the other side of childhood and larger then life, with his fading blond hair flowing over his shoulders and what's more, speaking to them.

"I'm here to help you out. Keep moving." Solo smiled reassuringly and remained seated squarely in the middle of the bottom step. "Secret's safe with me, just tuck it into my pocket, then go up and fly the birds as usual." They squeezed passed him and Column let his Earport go with some relief and some regret. "Mum's the word. Now let those birds enjoy their wings awhile and then head for your rehearsal." He stood up and was gone by the time they'd reached the top of the water-tower.

Over the river in his eerie, Morgan Grey saw the commotion as the children released the birds into the air, and watched charmed as the Winged Messengers flew away on their circuit, including the lazy birds who were obliged into flight by being tossed into the early evening air. And when the birds returned and settled peacefully into their cots, the kids closed the doors and departed.

A moment later, Morgan gasped as a shadow rose up on the rooftop, swathed in the black garb of a Hashshashin. "What the blazes is he doing up there? Have we descended to murdering innocent children now? I don't think so, over my dead body!" he railed, and removing his Winchester Repeater from the cabinet, he loaded up, took careful aim and fired three rapid shots – bang, bang, bang. The first two drove into the assassin's murderous hands and the last, adding insult to injury, hit him in the behind and took him down. "Ha," thought Morgan ducking out of sight, "gotcha." Then pouring himself a drink, he wiped off his gun, re-loaded it and put it back in its cabinet. "Eat your heart out, Bucks Club." He raised his glass heavenward, took a good long drink and settled down to listen to the radio.

Mistral (the Broadcast)

Solo were a smart cookie when it come to broadcasting, for he had a great deal of hands-on experience of the airy element, an' being on intimate terms with the air waves his know-how were a powerful thing. Solo brung back to life ancient radios that been long-gone-dead for years, causing Booker to wonder "What the?", as them underground tannoys howled aloud in his water-world. Solo activated all them rusted-up old speakers in overgrown warehouses, an' even way up North an old boat transmitter come crackling into action for Gracie, Tucker an' Smokey who was riding out the wild weather.

After some ear-busting feedback, it also come eddying round the Black Friar's refectory, where their holinesses Brother Dominic and Brother Sebastian turned an almost psychedelic shade of pink at the sound of themselves larking about at work... "Pass the plaster Pasteur" and "Put on the kettle Gretel," and a heavily distorted voice, which sound like someone had half-inched the captain's megaphone, announced, "In the meantime, with no job too big or too small for the Black Friars' construction team, try them first for all your building needs... Pass us a brick Nick, chuck up a nail Gail, pass the plaster Pasteur, pass..." faded away with the tolling of the Blackfriar's bell. Which bring a smile to Sicily, Slim Pickings, Ollie the cook and Lear, who was all ever so cosy an' draught-free in the spanking new kitchen up at Greene King Keep. "Pass us a beer, me dear," Slim Pickings said with a wink...

"Find your pencils and keep 'em poised, while we try a live link-up with our team who are sweating it out in the cavernous kitchens and gritty atmosphere of the Hell Fire Cooking Club. And here we go, keep as cool as you can, it's Recipe of the Month Time!", which been announced by the crashing of pots an' pans in the background. There were also some kid in that class that kept up a running muttering commentary throughout. "Good morning children. How nice to see so many of you today!" (Not for us it ain't)

"Good morning, Vatican Jack."

"Come gather round my little cherubs. Close your eyes an' count to three…" (Pervert) "…a one, a two, a three an' abracadabra! Now who wants to see what I have in my big tall hat today?" (Nobody) "That's right, a big white fluffy bunny. Hand him round, give him a good stroke and kiss him goodbye…for today we are going to learn how to make Bunny Burgers." Which cause a chorus of disapproval both from the class an' all the folk up and down the land who got their ears glued to the radio. "First of all we have to kill it. No sense in mucking about, so I suggest we use this big gun here. Any volunteers?" (Someone alert the animal liberation front) "Dear oh dear oh dear, what a row of cross little faces. Want to know what your problem is?" (Nope) "No sense of humour. Cheer up, just a little joke of mine… For here's one I prepared earlier, all skinned an' cleaned up nice" (Hilarious) "which you is gonna learn to stuff. Now put that little fluffy bunny back in his cage, wash your hands and let's get busy." (Child an' bunny abuse in the name of education) "You two, chop up a couple of good handfuls of walnuts and you, chop up a couple of handfuls of those dried apricots. You two can pound this old toast into breadcrumbs, and you boys squeeze the juice out a couple of oranges and you, young lady, can add four tablespoons of red wine." (Five, I's gonna add five or six) "That's good, that's very good indeed." (Go ahead, patronise the work force) "Now we are going to mix all the ingredients together. Add some salt and some pepper and stuff it all well into the cavity with our hands, like so," (A horrifying satanic ritual) "then pop it in the roasting dish, cover it well with the bacon rashers, put a lid on it" (You put a lid on it) "and then let it roast slowly for about a hour-and-a-half. Meanwhile, we are all going to make a lovely lemon meringue pie for pudding.

144

Except Sabrina, who's going to wash up, because she's done nothing but mutter and moan the whole time." (Sonofabitch…)

"Quite right. You naughty girl, Sabrina." Morgan Grey waged a finger at his radio. Jabba, chuckling away at the show, dried the tears from her eyes and said, "Jeez, that kid's got talent, give her a job." "That kid happen to be me eldest daughter," said Emil, looking like fifty swarms of killer bees, which only made Jabba laugh even more.

Up on the east coast Captain Dan and his men sat atop the sea defences, taking time out to listen the transmission. "I'm always agog at their version of the news and weather. Their intelligence is often more accurate then ours!"

"…And now lets join our news teams for tonight's main story… Over the course of time, our old river musta seen just about everything, meandering through the Big Smoke down to the sea. It's a highway for a hundred boats and sometimes all choked up with logjams or wild with the churnings of gang war-fare, and once or twice it has even caught fire with pollution. However, it ain't seen nothing yet, for the rumours is rife and spreading like wildfire that a deal has been struck, a soul has been sold and an agreement has been reached that will bring Full Metal Racket sailing up the river as part of their world tour. Those flying Dutchmen of the hardcore metal world appear to be planning a spectacular event to top them all, right here deep in the heart of the Big Smoke next summer. You heard it here first, and that concludes the news…" A piece of news that had the Leggers swooning with joy and bring a smile to Dr Cole, who liked to let his hair down from time to time.

"And now let us hear what the Weather Fairy has to report." The Weather Fairy were very chaotic and delivered the weather in a breathless falsetto, as though she were sharing a scandal… "Today's high could well turn into tomorrow's low. You never can tell. One thing for certain, there's a whole lot of weather whooshing around out there. My oh my, we got troughs, we got rising, we got falling, we got them undulating isobars, we has dampened spirits, we has jet streams, we has our depressions and sooner or later them autumn winds will be along to scare the bejasus out of us, rip the leaves from off the trees and flatten your lovingly planted home-growns. Alas," she heaved a dainty sigh, "Big Smoke by name and Big Smoke by nature. Quite frankly, shut the curtains, pick up a book, it looks ghastly horrible out there and most likely the worst since records begun. Them Asperatus Clouds is filling the skies with menace and foreboding, while black smoke piles up beneath them and fires continue to ravage the northern reaches of the city which, combined with our daily dose of toxic waste what come billowing out the chimney-pots of all the usual suspects, altogether do rather make for a overwhelmingly depressing outlook. Today, a spokesman from the College of General Practitioners offered this advice. 'We lives in post-Armageddon times for which there is no reference points. Sit tight and try not to breath until we has had an inquiry and is in full possession of the facts.' And this," sobbed the Weather Fairy, "concludes the news and weather report," and blew her nose very loudly several times.

Returning home along the Thames, Canada Blanch paid attention to the unmistakable sound of the enthusiastic piano of the Ballroom Dancing teacher Miss Love. "Good. Now off you go again, one, two, three, four," and she whacked out The Teddy Bears Picnic, accompanied by a number of dogs who done a very good job with the tune for a couple of verses, until they was given their own solo for a few bars of frantic howling, barking and growling. Then the piano picked up again and a voice said, "Ladies and Gentlemen, girls and boys, you has been listening to the unforgettable and lovely voices of the Hissy Boy Choir." After that, the piece faded away and Miss Love said, "Not bad, my dears, not bad at all." Down at the dog tracks, the sound of all them dog barks did bring a big cheer of delight from the Tinkerage. "Well there you have it, the Hissy Boy Choir, going from strength to strength. Good luck guys, good luck…" But Canada sat in his boat considering. 'I ain't one for speculating, but I has a feeling that me own flesh an' blood had a hand in that. They goes to Ballroom Dancing an' they's up an' down the Union Canal all the time…'

"…Our final piece for this evening's show is for all you highbrow culture-vultures out there, and we leave you with this sneak preview of some of the preparations already underway for New Year.

"Every New Year's day, in the maze of alleys and tiny streets which radiate out from the Seven Dials, musicians, ballad-writers, poets and dancers come together to celebrate one of our oldest festivals, the Ceremony of The Winding of the Clocks…"

"Interesting perception of highbrow they have down south," Dr Levet remarked to Tillie, as they patiently worked their way through a backlog of grizzled herders, beneath a billowing canvas tent up on Cape Wrath.

"This year we have been working on a piece based on the Midsummer and Midwinter Solstice and the Spring and Autumn Equinox. It's called 'The Four Corners of the Earth.'" ('Hey, it's us, we're on the show! Awesome.' Angelina and Gloria were taken by surprise.) "If you would like to hear more of Soft Sloth, they has the opening set at Jabba the Sluts, 8 to10 next Thursday. Be there or be square, for they is the next Big Thing…" Phoebe's piece faded out with the low-level rumble of street sounds … "And that's the way it is, on Friday the seventh of October."

And that were over and out for a great deal of folk. But there was others who was told, "Stay tuned. There now follows a severe warning for some of you… 'All set for Sunday night then?' came the gravely voice of Mason Flint.

'Yes sir,' Turkish replied coldly. 'My boys have staked out all the homes suspected of harbouring them unsustainable Deviations. We start the round-up at Sunday midnight.'

'Excellent, Turkish. There will be a promotion in it if all goes well…' Which were repeated two more times and broadcast North, South, East and West, but only to those that needed help and to them that could help out. Which were one of them astounding mysteries of transmitting that only Solo could explain.

147

Eden Levet (Theatre Studies)

There been a pause after that piece of news, like the one just before the Big Bang, and sensing that the cast was about to disintegrate into disarray, my mother says, "What we have just heard is appalling news, and in time I have no doubt that we shall be hearing a lot more about it, but for now we are here for Theatre Studies and as you know, come what may, death, flood, war or famine, The Show Must Go On. Because we actors always keep the curtain raised and footlights on. It's what we have to offer in a crisis. So Phoebe, perhaps you'd be kind enough to read for us this week?"

The History of the Damnable Life and Deserved Death
of Dr John Faust (Part 2)

No Sun nor Moon illuminated the Angel of Light, for he was of a sheen that glimmers of itself, quite imperceptible to the human eye. Cloaked in moonlight, he stood beside the Angel of Darkness, a princely velvet shadow among the shadows of the night. They watched together, treading the light and dark of a single moon-shaft that shone down through a high Gothic window, lighting a path into the alchemist's laboratory.

Dr Faust's lab was in keeping with every other alchemist's lab of the times, littered by an uncommon amount of blackened and blown-out retorts, victims of the ongoing, highly competitive and hotly pursued formula for the elixir of life and/or turning lead into gold. The rest was given over to the art of brewing beer and lined with sacks of barley malt,

148

baskets of hops, and some quantities of yeast to convert the malt sugars into alcohol.

A flame flickered beneath a tall cylindrical crucible of simmering water, as the steam rose up a funnelled lid and along a shiny metallic pipe that looped into a glass demijohn where the distilled water collects, to be analysed. For Dr Faust and Edward his student had been trying to fathom why it was that those who drank the local water were condemned to an untimely death, while those who stuck to beer were far more healthy and often in good spirits too.

Faust and Edward were working, the air crackling with scholarly focus. Edward sat at a long worktable with a skinny black cat sleeping across his knees, busily restocking jars and labelling them. "Animal, Mineral, Vegetable... Ginger root, leaves of Sage... Which reminds me, Dr Faust, some people recommend adding Ginger to the beer, as it might help against the plague."

"Let us put it to the test, then," replied Faust, who stood over a crucible of porcelain heating some shimmering Antimony, for it was rumoured to have near-miraculous healing powers. "Come quickly, my dear fellow, and observe this," Faust called as the Antimony began to collapse and melt, and removing the cat from his knees, Edward approached thoughtfully.

"To be honest sir, so far we appear to have killed more patients than cured with Antimony."

"Well, I know, but that is the nature of research. Win a few, lose a few! Besides, I bet those Parisian Puffers have killed a lot more. They stick it in just about every remedy they make."

"Perhaps the key lies in the strength of the dilution?" Edward suggested.

"Now that is a very interesting notion..." began Faust, when an unexpected explosion of beer sent the molten Antimony hurling across the room, scalding the cat who skittered away uncannily on his hind legs with his ears and tail aflame. Dodging the falling debris, Edward lunged for him and plunged the burning creature into a vat of water, which was not well received. "Hellfire and damnation," Faust shouted, with his ears ringing. He picked himself up from the dust and railed, "What on earth possessed you to bring your cat along, anyway?"

"Beg your pardon sir, it's not my cat. I thought it was yours, so I let him in with me," Edward explained.

"Ah no, he isn't. A clever hungry stray, I expect." Edward began to restore a little order. " Never mind my friend, no real harm done," said Faust. "You have worked hard all day. Go you and join the other students in the alehouses where surely they are drinking now."

"Thank you sir, and goodnight," said Edward gratefully, and departed.

"Goodnight, young man. Rejoice in your youth. For me, the sands of time slip through the hourglass and I grow older day by day," Faust said after him, and sitting down amongst the disorder, he began to weave his hand in and out of the moon-shaft streaming through his window. "I have been true to the study of Alchemy throughout my life and most earnestly believed to find the truth therein. Have I not put my faith in these good books and learned all there is to know therein? Yet all my endeavours end in failure, and the mysteries of true knowledge elude me still." Faust withdrew his hand from the moonlight into the shadows. "Poor scalded cat, bide you here and keep me company, and let us see what a blacker alchemy may reveal."

Unfolding his wings in the moonlight, the Angel of Light spoke quietly. "Ah Faust, do not from disappointment stray off the goodly path on which you tread. The fountain of eternal youth that you pursue so doggedly lies in the grace of Heaven."

"Nobody wants to wait for Heaven," the dark Angel said scornfully. "Come to me, Faust. Come to me now and your powers will be instant, your knowledge know no bounds."

The Moon went on her way, withdrawing her face from the window and leaving the long, long night to fill Faust's soul with darkness. When the grey light of dawn touched the skies, a poisonous miasma coiled through the laboratory, where Faust was acquainting himself with the fundamentals of the Black Arts.

Book in hand, Faust stood over a crucible. "Four level spoons of Sulphur, three of Mercury, two of ground Chalcedony and one of Spirits of Salt…this had better work," he scowled, emptying the entire contents into the fire. It flared momentarily, releasing a cloud of sulphurous vapour and sweating a flow of molten coal that seeped over the floor towards the cat, who took to his hind legs and remained standing, gradually growing taller until with a yowl of pain and loud bang, he burst out of his singed tail and coat and stood in a puff of smoke, transmuted into Mephistopheles.

"Dr John Faust? Your servant." He bowed and rose, patting his ears gingerly, for they were still burned. "I will perform all that you ask for the space of twenty-four years, in exchange for your soul. What say you? A bargain, I'm sure."

"For twenty-four years of your service, my soul is yours," Faust agreed with relish.

"Here then. Sign here, on the dotted line, in your own blood," and Mephistopheles whipped out a parchment.

"Blood," said Faust, "is a very special fluid. If I sign away my soul in blood, I'll sign away my self," and he drew back alarmed. "Don't you trust me?"

"Come now," insisted Mephisto, ripping a cruel fingernail across Faust's palm, "'tis but part of the bargain. Your name in blood, for power beyond your wildest dreams." But when Faust dipped his pen to sign his soul away, the words 'Fly Man' appeared upon his arm. Thus Faust crossed the final T, the point of no return, crazed with terror and trembling in dread and fear.

Then double-quick and hey-pell-mell, Mephisto called up the Dance of the Seven Devils, and with their whirling, turning and tumbling, Faust's fears dissolved into astonishment at this first taste of the marvels he had signed up for...

Phoebe's reading came to a standstill, for Harley and Tyler were writing, "Fly Man" in big red letters along their arms. "Fantastic spooky in it?" they said with relish, and truth to tell we were all enthusiastic for her to continue reading, for it were an' engrossing story. But Mum said, "Thanks Phoebe. How about we get some food together now?" And after Dad gone off to answer the clanging bell, he came back to ask if Milo and I could help him with a patient.

Man, somebody had dumped a bloody cadaver at our gates and hightailed it, and going down on his knees to take a closer look, my father appeared very conflicted about what he was seeing. "An Assassin... Thanks but no thanks," he says, deeply conundrumed. "If I were not a doctor, I'd chuck him in the river, glug glug, bye bye." He sucked on his teeth awhile, struggling with his conscience, which were something I never seen him do before. However, 'the goodly path which leads to heaven' apparently won the day, for he says, "We need Mandrake and Opium to render him unconscious for a good long time. Let's get him to the teaching lab. Hopefully Reema is keeping the others occupied preparing a meal."

"Well, so long as it ain't bunny burgers," says Milo, which caused the paramedics a moment of hilarity and my father to lighten up enough to confide, "Just between you an' me, I'm quite fond of bunny burgers. And the sooner we get this creature fixed up, the sooner we can be rid of him." The body moaned a bit when we picked him up, and while we were carrying him along I wanted to know, "What are we gonna do about that severe weather warning on the radio, and the rounding up of all them."

"Hush up son. We have a very dangerous piece of work here, and who knows who he works for."

Milo de Fer

O f course, it is always mighty troubling to find a body all shot up and left on your doorstep, but there been something about this particular body that was causing Uncle Cole a great deal of uneasiness. The patient were losing an uncommon amount of blood but afore I could do anything to stop him from bleeding out, Cole administered him about enough Knockout Pops to zonk out a mammoth. "Are you angry, or something?" I ask him.

"No, no, but you don't treat a wounded hyena until he's out cold. On top of which, I believe the creature is a clone."

"What? What are you saying?" says Eden, taking a good close look. "How do you know?"

"I don't know. One just gets a feel for it as the years go by." Uncle Cole cut away his bloody clothes. "But his perfection is the giveaway. He's so lean, so uncompromisingly hard as iron and altogether flawless. No doubt about it, he was designed to be a killer." He prized the bullet wounds open for us to staunch and clean. " On my count now, one, two, three." We rolled him over, removed the bullet from his backside, and swabbed the wound which Eden then began to stitch up with a cautious deliberation.

"Why's he dressed like a Ninja?"

"Camouflage, I suppose," Cole speculated and rummaging around in the pile of clothes he found a big lump of hash. "Ah, he's a Hashshashin clone."

"What's that?" Eden asked.

"They were a secret religious brotherhood that appeared in Libya or Syria during the Middle Ages," Cole explained. "Its members underwent all the usual rigorous training and education that such cults demand, until they were deemed ready to be initiated into the holy art of assassination. This one, though, has been wrongly instilled with the idea that smoking hashish is part of their ritual before killing."

"I see. Just remind us again why we is helping him out?" I asked.

"For one thing, whoever shot him through the hands knew exactly what they were about, because he will never work again. And for another, a doctor is bound to treat all who come by... After all, everybody has some good in them, and one has to allow for the possibility that people change."

"Oh yeah, well, quiety righty Uncle Cole, but some people might have a hard time believing there's a sunny side to the angel of death."

"The real problem now is, just exactly what can we do for these hands? The bones is so shattered an' the tendons torn." said Eden

"Stitch and sew as best we can and set his hands in splints," I replied. "You do one, I'll do the other." An' we done our level best to sort his hands out, until Cole says, "You can't do more for him than that. I'll set his splints and plaster him up. You go on now an' join the others. They must be having supper by now." An' taking them freezing murdering hands into his warm and healing hands, he looked up and says, "Thanks. Silver Gilt certificate, perhaps? I'll be along soon…"

Ariel Levet

I had been extraordinary relieved when Solo took the show off our hands. I's even assumed it were more a confiscation thing an' the chances he'd broadcast it were zilch. How wrong was that? Our show had gone national. Hard to believe that the world of muffin mumblecore media could be so astonishing effectual, but it were.

After rehearsals, we hardly had time to tuck into our food afore the parents began arriving two by two, saying, "Thought we might come an' pick you up today." But as they didn't appear to be leaving, we became increasingly crowded, and between the chit-chat and the buzz, the radio underground was obliged into communicating our relief an' surprise with raised eyebrows and silent speaking eyes.

"I don't suppose you all could see your way to a couple of grilled cheese sandwiches for a old dog just in off the high seas?" Canada asked, and when Harley and Tyler delivered them to him he says, "Woof, woof," by way of thanks.

"Woof, woof yourself, Dad... He knows something," whispered Harley. "Nope, he's fishing," Tyler whispered back. "Here you go, Ma," and they handed a lemon, lime and bitters to Mara.

"Your health, boys," she toasted them mid-conversation with Dorcas.

"Did you hear us, Dad? We were on the radio?" Angelina and Gloria asked Tobias.

"I did! It was astonishing. How about that, eh? Celeb daughters, here's to you." He raised his glass.

"What's going to happen to those children?" they asked.

"I guess," said Tobias thoughtfully, "that's why we all came here at the same time. See if we can't organise some way to help them out."

156

"I hope so," said Phoebe, who were keeping a very low an' helpful profile, an' handing out the drinks ever so demurely.

"This wine is delicious. Cheers, Phoebes," said Jean.

"Not for me, darling," said Liberty, "I feel a bit queasy."

"Queasy, eh? Is that right Liberty. My oh my."

"My oh my nothing, Dorcas," Liberty shrugged it off.

There were a hint of the frazzled about my Mum when the bell rang once again, but when Column came back with Topaz and a big guy wearing a flying cap, her face brightened into the kinda misty smile of romantic proportions that indicated she could have had a past that spells Old Flame. "Ah Booker," she hugged him rather freely, "it's been a long time. Come in, come in."

"Well, I know, my dear. Far too long, but if I may say so you ain't changed, you ain't changed one bit," Booker flirted, an' removing his flying cap with a flourish he settled in.

Column ambled over with Topaz, and handing him a beer he introduced us all. "This is my cousin Ariel, our friends Harley an' Tyler, and Phoebe my sister."

"Respect," rumbled Topaz, grasping our hands in his massive mitt. "Good to know we is all on the same side ain't it? Come on, let's sit down an' see what happens next eh?"

"Respect." We sat down, wondering how Column and he come to be such close bosom buddies.

Then Eden and Milo came in from their medical emergency, and after a while my father joined us too, but when the bell rung once again the room went real quiet, because everyone was already here. "I'll go," offered Jean, and after a while he came limping back with Brothers Sebastian and Dominic in tow. "Evening all," said they. "Mind if we join you?"

"Of course not," my father replied politely, and in they sailed.

The sudden manifestation of the Black Friars certainly sent the mercury plummeting, particularly in Liberty and Mara's location, where conditions became positively polar, because they was free spirits an' claustrophobic around dogmas and doctrines. Unfazed, an'

157

predictably, Brother Sebastian plonked himself down right between them, saying, "Evening your graces. Better the devil you know, eh what?"

"Chin, chin," Liberty and Mara responded frostily, and raised their glasses.

"Don't mind him," said Brother Dominic, joining in. "Have you ever noticed how all the books are full of history being made in great halls by wise councils and gatherings of powerful men?" Brother Dominic were a study of shrewd churchy diplomacy. "It is my belief, however, that history was more likely shaped just like this, far more quietly, far more modestly, here an' there and often in the homely warmth of a woman's sitting room, and through the earnest endeavours of ordinary folk intent upon righting a wrong." He had everyone's attention now. "Under the excellent cover of collecting their young folk from theatre studies, we are here to offer the services of the Black Friars."

Tobias looked up brightly and said, " Well that's okay then. Put on the kettle Gretel!" Which raised a smile from everyone except Dorcas, who flashed him an' extreme look.

"Never mind the kettle, I fished something truly remarkable out the water," said Canada, producing a bottle with Smokey Old Peat written on it. "Down the hatch," he toasted and after sinking a large measure, he shared it round.

We settled down to parley 'bout things, when my father suggested, "Perhaps for their own safety the young folk should leave now."

"What?" We was incredulous.

"Dr Cole, with respect," Canada came to our defence, "I believe the young folk have every right to participate in this." We nodded our agreement. "And I was counting on them for me plan. I mean, the best place to hide youngsters is amongst other youngsters, isn't it?"

"Plus they knows the water maze inside out, which could be useful," Topaz said.

"They aren't that young, eh Cole?" Jean spoke quietly. "You weren't much older when you were willing to sustain a wound to protect Jules."

"Who's Jules, Dad?" asked Phoebe.

"It's a long story, but through meeting him, I understood that dehumanizing terminology like 'Deviations' or 'unsustainable' implies that some folk is an alien aberration that's best off in the lab, for our safety an' theirs. They don't, nobody does. They's just a little different, that's all. They's innocent and vulnerable, an' their situation is a thorn in all our sides. So Dorcas, tell us what we need to know, so we can try and formulate an appropriate plan."

"Yes, of course. First of all, we have two kids with the Brittle Bones and a young man with Leukaemia who are way too sick to travel."

"Then we must find a way for them to come to us," Brother Sebastian offered.

"Thank you very much indeed. That way, they could continue to be under my care," my father said.

"Something else," Dorcas continued. "A few days ago, I been shadowed by Turkish on my rounds. I laid a false trail visiting my mother an' folk I haven't seen in years. But I'm concerned for Abby an' Riley, who may be in danger of losing their kids, for the Mantle has cooked up the authority to remove children from lone parents without explanation an' put them into 'care'."

"Better count them in too, then..."

Deciding that small amounts of folk trickling out of town by different ways was less conspicuous than about thirty-five people hopping in an' out of darkened doorways, we come up with a decent set of plans to vanish them kids out of their already invisible lives.

"Any problems now, head for Elveden Forest. It lies exactly midway between North and Northeast on your compass points. We is perfectly capable of pulling this off, no doubt about it," Booker concluded reassuringly.

Hope (age 10)

They say "No man is a island," but I felt like one until the black-an-white radio came winking to life. The show came to my ears like a message in a bottle that washed up on my shore, with astonishing singing dogs, a recipe of the month with a mutinous critic to remind me I could laugh, an' a severe weather warning to give me hope.

Basement Two was an icing-on-the-cake, top-of-the-range Hell Fire Cooking Club too, where the head chef was working from an alternative recipe book, and far from turning out those mouthwatering lemon meringue pies, had successfully transmuted Uranium into chaotic and unstable radioactive elements. It lacked only one ingredient, the extra neutron to initiate the fissile process, that would force the Uranium to transmute into Neptunium. Which in turn would transmute into Plutonium and create energy, in a perpetual chain reaction, by destroying its mutating self. And if that ain't the recipe for the elixir of eternal death, I'll be darned.

Nicky's 'baby' had been a fast developer, accelerating from one stage to the next at such a rate it appeared to be inventing itself and using Nicky to help it along, like a knitting machine where someone is required to set the pattern until off it goes, clickerty-clack, clickerty-clack, clickerty-clack and then whooee, hey ho, one nuclear reactor prêt-a-porter…

I showed Morgan everything there was to see down there. It was a recce, a clear-headed fact-finding mission about illicit activities on his own territory, but we were jittery. "Perhaps Nicky has a secret death-wish. A nuclear explosion might just do the job," Morgan speculated quietly.

"More like a secret wish to rule the world," I whispered.

"But without control rods?"

"There will be," I put him right. "The Mantle are colluding with him to procure some from their East European counterparts."

Morgan eyed the reconditioned turbine that sat gleaming idly an' looking uncannily impatient for action. "Even so," he said, "this nuclear power station would be on such a small scale as to power the Projack Building only."

"The journey of a thousand miles starts with one small step."

"Don't I know it," Morgan reflected.

"Can we get out of here now?" I hissed. We made it back without mishap and climbing into my plastic bubble, I asked, "Who's Mistral? Nicky is always muttering about a Mistral." I settled into bed.

"The Mistral," Morgan replied, hooking me up to my drip feed, "is the name of a wind, not a person."

Sicily (Greene King Keep)

The departure of the family had happened with a natural amount of heartache an' a great deal of pandemonium, an' right in the middle of it all, Jules turned to Lear and said, "Thanks for having us. I's leaving the pregnant mares for you to keep." Lear responded with a bow and Jules responded with a nod. More than a thank you, it was a gesture between kings, an' there were a finality to it that allowed them to ride away in dignity.

Eighteen years on, an' herds of their offspring grazes all along the back of Captain Dan's defences. Every sundown brings the old mares home like clockwork, but one evening a kid came hiking in behind them.

"A result at last. Ain't this the only road-stop in the middle of one-thousand square miles of alligator territory, an' just 'bout as difficult to locate as the Holy Grail itself? Don't bother shooting me," she glanced at Lear, "shame to waste a good bullet, I is fantastic overwhelmed with unbelievable fatigue of the long walk up here an' ready to drop dead anyway. Respect, how do, I's Mistral. Didn't know where else to head."

"Well that's all right, kid," said Slim, who'd come out with the commotion. "You has headed for exactly the right place. How did you hear about us anyway?"

"Hear 'bout ya? I didn't hear 'bout you, I's been dreaming 'bout this place, all total tinted in the colours of the rainbow. I's just been pursuing the dream."

"Well in that case, you're very welcome." Lear looked at her kindly. "I'm very glad to meet you, Mistral. How old are you?"

"Twelve."

"One day you will be, I expect," Slim chortled. "Are you hungry? Fancy a bite to eat?"

My guess is she were somewhere around nine years old, but it were hard to tell, for she were gaunt as a castaway. Her head were framed by a shock of unruly black hair, an' her sage green eyes peered out of big dark hollows with the intensity of a Raggedy Rawney. Mistral had all the symptoms of them who's been toughing it alone for too long. She were stunned by the plate of food that Ollie rustled up for her, an' contemplated it a long while afore allowing herself to eat. Any normal kindness were an overwhelming thing that bought the tears welling in her eyes, an' she slept outside a good month afore she were ready to come inside.

She were unusual knowledgeable for a feral kid, a library rat who turned out to be a sharp reader, an' when Lear offered her a game of draughts, she turned out to be pretty hot at that too. It don't do to pry into the past, an' it'd be a romantic notion to think a kid like that could recover a childhood. What's done is done. But there were a future, an' if she belonged anywhere it were here, poling her way about the marshes, checking out what the army were up to an' living in the undemanding company we older folk could offer her.

One evening, Mistral an' I spotted a homing pigeon flying across the wide green landscape. The little bird already looked exhausted when a Marsh Harrier began to mob her. "Come on little darlin', come on babe." I willed her in, an' as the Harrier's big yellow claws closed on her for a sec, Mistral murmured, "Let her go you big bustard," an' shaking loose the pigeon gained a little height, while the hefty Harrier gave up the chase an' flapped away.

The pigeon flew in an' fluttered onto my outstretched hand with her heart trembling. I unrolled the scroll from around her leg, an' seeing Liberty's tiny hand writing, cupping the little bird in my hand Mistral an' I went to find Lear. Lear peered at the note through his large magnifying glass and said, "Ahem. Suffer little children to come unto me and forbid them not... Well that's a first, Liberty quoting the Bible."

"She must mean the wandering tribes of Israel is on the move an' wending their ways up here."

"Oh," said Lear "is they? I mean, are they? How many? We are not a hotel."

"Not yet we isn't," Mistral replied cheerily.

"I been wondering." said Slim, "If they heard the radio show up North, maybe some of them is coming too."

"That show gone to everyone who were meant to hear it. Of course they did, of course they's coming," Mistral insisted.

Grace (the Far North)

Soon as we heard the radio show, Smokey, Tucker and I turned our boats about unanimously and headed for home. It was sometime after midnight when our cove came to view on the horizon looking like a Christmas party, for some kind soul been thoughtful enough to light all the harbour lights. It looked more friendly than anything, and we come chasing in off the gale with the big ocean swell beneath us, which gave rise to one of them moments of hectic multi-tasking the world of sailing frequently has on offer – drop them sails, loose the anchors, hove to at right angles, let fly – and we washed into the harbour, aiming to draw our boats alongside the wall with some sort of aplomb and a whole lot of modesty, for we salty dogs is rock steady and very understated about everything except other people's sailing, when we's allowed a slight frown and a quiet "'Ello, what's he playing at?"

It were late an' horrible out. Nevertheless, a number of lanterns was bobbing through town in the dark, an' a little while on Dad, Ma, Jules, Gabriel an' Jesse dashed along the corniche beneath the lashing rain and scooted onto Smokey's rig, disappearing into his very comfortable custom-made (by him) wheelhouse.

Ryan appeared beside me. "Lovely weather. How were the fishing?" he asked, helping wrap up the sails.

"Thanks, the hold's almost full," I answered.

"Yo," called Tucker, an' clambering across the abyss rising and falling between our boats, he says, "Fancy going down south, see if we can't help them kids out in some way?"

"Fancy? I's hell bent on it," I nodded.

165

"Me too," says Ryan. "Better keep your gloves on. We is gonna have to go a couple of rounds with the old man about it, I expect."

The gale outside were nothing compared to gale in Smokey's wheelhouse. "My guess is they'll all head for Greene King Keep," Dad were declaring. "It's my plan to go down with Jules and Gabriel to see if anyone wants to come up here and join us."

" I don't think so, Dad. Why should you go?" asked Tucker.

"Don't talk to me like that, son," Dad glowered.

"Look at that, they's locked horns already," Jules scowled, and helped himself to some rolling tobacco.

"I wish you wouldn't do that, Jules," Dad snapped at him.

"Leave it out, he's twenty-seven. It's up to him," I defended him.

"Yup, I like a puff from time-to-time, calms the nerves." Jules lit up an' exhaled a lot of smoke everywhere.

"The reality is, you has a dodgy ticker, so it may not be such a bright idea for you to go," Mum said matter-of-factly.

"I have not got a dodgy ticker, me girl, and for gawd's sake can someone open the bleeding window?" he fumed. Smokey got up and flung open all the cabin windows, inviting in the blast and clearing the air. "Right, that's settled then. Gabriel, Jules and I…"

"No way, Dad," Jules interrupted. "I'm far too slow, you's far too cross, an' I can't leave Mam or me horses. Then there's the cows, chickens, couple of wild cats an' what about me Pine Martins?"

"Ah now Joe, I put me travelling days behind me long ago." Uncle Gabriel were emphatic. "Anyway mate, why can't the young folk deal with this? You want to go, Smokey?"

"Not much, Dad," said Smokey, shutting the windows." I'd like to stay here do me fishing and help build something for them."

"So would I," Jules agreed. "Building is what we do best, Dad. You, me, Gabriel and Smokey."

"It hadn't occurred to me they is gonna need homes." Dad simmered down a bit thinking it over.

Mum looked relieved that her Jules were not about to be whisked away, an' turning to me an' Tucker, she said, "You must be exhausted.

You go on home now. You don't half pong of fish! If you don't want the wolves to follow you down South, may I suggest you pour about a half gallon of Pine essence or Eucalyptus oil into a bath and have a good long soak tonight."

Then I gave me Dad a big warm loving embrace. "Gerroff," he growled. "It ain't funny, you pong to high heaven."

"Oh, daddy, daddy, so do you now." I let him go.

"Phaw, I'll be gutted to see you go." Dad rolled his eyes. "Where was I? Oh yeah. Tucker lad, would you be so kind as to blast us out a couple of plots before you goes?"

"Sure. 'Course I will, after a bath and bit of shut-eye." Tucker replied with some dignity, for he was proud of his blasting skills.

Mistral (the Akashic Record, Tucker)

Tucker was the spit of his Grandma Sicily. His eyes were a gentle grey and his hair were somewhere atween brown an' blond. He also shared her easy, go-with-the-flow, roll-with-the-punches, in-it-for the ride disposition, an' although he'd been seriously back-burnered when Jules come along, he didn't mind too much. He loved Jules an' they was close. What Tucker did mind were the three R's, which were worse than climbing mount Everest. Particularly the maths, which don't even have an R. His folks consoled him by saying, "Never minds sweetheart, takes all sorts," and Tucker would smile politely, for he knew he weren't all sorts.

Luckily, it weren't all school, an' he liked cliff-hanging for gulls eggs, which meant a whole lot of solitary scrambling an' wriggling along a network of ledges an' burrows that the gulls had worn out over thousands of years of group activities on the cliff face.

Then one time, when Tucker were crawling along a ledge that been a dizzying height above the ocean, he come upon the entrance of a walled-up cave, and after working away at it with his fingers and kicking at it with his heels for about half the morning, he loosened enough stones to make a hole. In he crawled, out of the wind and into the sudden silence of a cave, an' soon as his eyes was adjusted to the dim light, he seen that it were very enormous an' ram-jam stuffed full of army supplies.

"Geronimo and boy, oh boy," he says, "what has we got here Tucker?" an' he gone to take a closer look. There was guns, rocket-launchers, ammunition, rope, leather jackets, trousers, boots, sunglasses, goggles, wet suits, a couple of bikes and lotsa tools, as well as what looked like a inexhaustible supply of cigars, case upon case full of shiny rows of tin cigar cylinders. Which was not containing cigars at all, but very entrancingly, was containing individual sticks of dynamite with the name 'Libya' printed on them.

Tucker were a very happy Aladdin. He also come across five ornate cedar boxes which he expected might be full of grenades but were terrible disappointed to find they only contained a quantity of illegal substances of the Class A variety an' about a thousand and one layers of cannabis resin neatly spread between leaves of silver paper. "Oh well," he said, slamming the lids down again.

Tucker were over the Moon with the dynamite discovery an' he decided his destiny lay in dynamite: an unusual career choice, seeing as it were generally foisted off on some poor critter by their place of work. Whatevers, it gave him a identity an' were a move that tumbled the walls of Jericho, opened the iron curtains and blew the lid right off the mysteries of learning, for very soon he were calculating depth of charges, densities of rocks, lengths of fuse and quantities of powder, for his very life depended upon it.

Tucker shared most the booty with his family, lowering down them handy supplies of shooters, ammunition, ropes, nails, chains, pulleys an' useful tools to Joe and Gabriel, who was waiting in the boats below. But he also kept a good deal of it under his hat, in the safety of the weather-free cave.

"And if," thought Tucker, letting himself slowly down the long rope, in the early morning, "and if you just happens to be gay, ain't nobody, no way, ever gonna suspect the dynamite man." Then he helped himself to what he calculated were a reasonable supply of cannabis and dynamite for trading on the long journey South, said "So long" to his cave, and went to level out some building plots for those that was staying behind.

Jules

"So long Jules," said Tucker, an' his farewell hug smelled fresh with Eucalyptus an' dynamite.

"Bye bye, Tucker," I said, tears clouding me eyes. "And you, Gracie. I love you. Look after me horses."

" I love you wide as this," she said, flinging her arms out. "Look after me dogs," and her hug smelled of Pine essences.

"G'bye Ryan. Come back soon, an' bring us a wife."

"I'll do me very best, mate," and he gave me a hug too, and Mum said to Ryan, "You is in charge. You is the oldest, take care of them."

"I will." Ryan give Mum a hug, then Corbin gave him a couple of books for the road and Sandy told Gracie, "Don't take any guff from the lads, sweetheart." "As if," muttered Jesse, an' they mounted their horses, buttoned their sheepskins against the cold, tilted their hats an' trotted off into the damp morning.

We waved till they was out of sight, when Dad said," Huh, rescue mission my foot. Nothing but a raiding party in search of mates. "

"It's both things, Joe. They haven't had much luck so far, sitting in the middle of the sea in a fishing boat or blowing things up," Mum replied.

"Well hello, Tucker wants a wife like a fish needs a bicycle." Jesse were sometimes hard to follow.

"'Course he does, what you on about girl?" Dad seemed peeved.

"Well then, let's hope he finds one," Gabriel replied evenly.

"Hang on a sec," said Dad. "Now tell me just exactly what you mean by that, Jesse?"

"Well Joe, perhaps Tucker just rode out of here wondering if you would have been as eager to save him from the lab as you was to save Jules."

"Now why in the world would he be wondering that?" Then Dad were rather quiet for Dad. "Oh, what? You sure? Nobody tells me anything…"

"Well you knows now," said Mum. I hadn't the foggiest what they been on about, but decided to smile and nod at Dad along with the others.

And then I were very sad for they was gone away and suddenly the cloud burst and I were crying a great deal, and Mum said, "Now Jules, why don't you show us what you are planning on building?" She were being kindly, but it were a glass-half-empty day.

Ryan

Establishing a safe haven were not top of the bill for Ruby an' Lewis, who were born in a forest with no fear at their backs. They was unruly, but also refreshing an' kinda unspoilt, and while they was perfectly happy during all the chaotic years of renovating an' manic building, soon as things resembled any kind of normality, the wild things had moved out.

Ruby an' Lewis was only a days ride away though an' we came by their place just as they was closing the barn for the night. "Wow, 'ello! Had a feeling you'd be passing through. We ain't half glad see you." They seemed unusually pleased an' appreciative to see us, possibly about the most friendly I've ever seen them, an' leaving our horses in the barn alongside theirs, we went inside together, where there was a big haunch of venison on the roast. "I put it on just in case you came." Ruby's brown eyes settled quietly on us.

We ate, drank a lot of their Smokey Old Peat, an' poured over their copy of *A Trapper's Rough Guide to the Wilderness*, which is like a ordinance survey map, but illustrated with detailed landmarks, such as Shaking Rider Ridge an' the Rumpled Rock. "See, we's here at Endless Larches," Lewis explained, "an ain't nothing but miles of forest an' mountain with scant trails atween here an' Lairg, a right rough trash logging camp, well worth avoiding. But pick up the Old Train Trail on the other side of town, which go all the way to the Moray Firth, about seventy miles. I ain't been further than there, but looks about another hundred an' sixty an' a few high mountains before the Forth. Follow the pipeline to the coast."

"It's gonna be awful tough." Ruby looked at us bleakly. "You has

172

a good hard couple of months of travelling ahead, with winter at your backs all the way."

"We'll be alright kid," said Tucker, "but if the winter do get as bad as they say it might, I'd like to think that my younger sister an' brother was safe and sound in my place."

"Thanks," said Lewis humbly. "Truth to tell, taking care of your place do sound extraordinary inviting compared to another winter out here... But what about our still?"

"Set it up in me shed, why not?" Tucker replied. Lewis an' Ruby heaved a sigh of relief an' begun laughing at themselves. "They's lost it, gone mental, the life of wild an' free been all too much for them."

"Go on home. You has been greatly missed," smiled Gracie, and curling up in a sheepskin fleece, she drifted off to sleep by the fireside.

I were rather hung over in the morning, but Lewis were bright an' busily stuffing as many bottles of Smokey Old Peat as he could into our saddle-bags. "It would be ever so fine," he prattled away cheerily, "if a few more people came to live up here, wouldn't it? Keep a eye out for a petite, upbeat, foreign girl for me, and maybe some old blind deaf git for Ruby."

"Oh yes please," she said. "Get going now. Be safe, so long, love you... Tucker, you is a diamond." Tucker raised his hat and away we rode.

Grandma Tookie
(the Akashic Record, Solo)

Solo concluded the broadcast with a bow to the elements, North, South, East and West, to thank them for carrying the transmission so far and so wide, and he walked home to the Chelsea Physic Garden in the quiet company of the closing twilight.

The main house was full of conspirators whose lamplight shadows fell across the lawn, but he also perceived another presence on the premises and roamed around until he found the anaesthetised body of the assassin in the teaching lab. Solo noted that the emergency services had given him their full attention, but an assassin is all about death and a garden is all about life, and the sooner he were gone the better.

An assassin's hair is never cut but Solo, an excellent pruner of trees, cut it very short, and removing some of Eden's clothes from the washing line, set about dressing the creature and writing a Get Well note on his plaster cast: "Do not remove plaster for six weeks approx. Morphine for pain, Colloidal Silver for infection. Phials in top pocket," and wheelbarrowing the assassin over the damp lawn and down to the river, Solo laid him in a long skiff which was half-full of Mint cuttings and set him adrift, leaving him to his fate.

Solo returned to wipe away all traces of his presence in the garden. "Say no more." He left a note for Cole, pocketed the hash, and burned the Ninja outfit and hair.

Harley an' Tyler

"Grandma," I says, "we wilfully goes into the world of purpose an' danger today. Put on your spiritual glasses an' watch the stars, there maybe something worth the reading afore this day is done."

It been barely first light when Column, Harley an' I took our Lighter into the disused Snow Hill tunnel, a wired environment, full of creaks an' groans caused by the subterranean wind racking along the iron girders. Still, it took us all the way to Smithfield Market without collapsing, and to Topaz, who were a rather formidable sight at the end of tunnel.

"'Ello Column, here you go. Harley, put these on. You too, Tyler," he said, handing us some Saracen clothes to wear, in no doubt as to which twin were who. Which reminded me that a Saracen only comes of age when he has "The Knowledge" down pat, which do give them an eye for details. He were also a less-haste-more-speed man, which been good for our jangling nerves. We changed into Saracen gear, making a terrible mess of the turbans, which proved challenging. "I ain't expecting any trouble at all. We is after all thirty-six hours ahead of the Mantle," Topaz offered, adjusting our head-gear patiently. "You look fine, although a Saracen with turquoise eyes is a rarity." He squinted at Column. "Still, you'll do. Are you ready?" he enquired, an' leaning over our Lighter he tugged it out of the water easy-peasy.

We was obliged to portage the boat about halfway round Smithfield to a conduit which bought us floating out into the open air an' the water-maze. There were a bit of early-morning traffic about by way of a few boats punting into town, overladen with produce for the market, but we were swift to get off the beaten track, paddling north through the deserted ramshackle shanties of Twilight Town.

I sensed our passing did not go unnoticed, though. Perhaps a man, perhaps a stalking cat, perhaps a Ragger, but an hour or so later we pulled into a lock, and while we waited for the waters to rise, three kids been handed down to Topaz, followed by a big basket of food. "Be safe, you all," and the woman blew a quick kiss over the parapet before winding the lock gates open. While the water level slowly rose we scrambled the kids into Saracen clothes an' passed out of the lock with Topaz sorting out the last of them pernickety turbans.

The oldest of our three passengers were not strong. He had a curving spine an' drooping eyes, but he smiled very friendly an' says, "I's much obliged, Sahibs. Much obliged indeed, way to go."

"Sure, no trouble at all," we assured him. Then there were a younger boy of about eight, who sat quietly regarding us in apprehensive curiosity. "I'm Dylan. I can't believe these clothes." He flashed a shy smile.

"Well you hang on to them then," Topaz told him.

"Really? Hear that Willa, the Sultan says we can keep 'em." Dylan

176

looked up. "Thanks. This is me sister Willa, but she don't talk."
Dylan's sister were older. She looked numbed, like she seen too
much, an' hid beneath her turban, afraid of being out in the open.

"Once you has been wearing one of them for a while, you
can understand why a Saracen never takes it off. They makes you feel
safe an' even a little magic, alright Willa?" Column extended a open-
palm hand, to which she offered a small nod and a tentative high-five.

We relaxed soon as we crossed into the Empty Quarter. The
feeling we was been watched lifted, Topaz fired up the little outboard
an' we's enjoyed an hour's straight run up the lovely River Lee, where
we's waited to rendezvous with Booker an' his all charges.

Angelina (and Gloria)

There were a calm underlay to the early morning, an' a flat light softening the harsh city edges. It was still enough to hear the faraway lowing of the cows on the city farm, and from time to time a smell of freshly roasting coffee beans come wafting through the air. If Gloria an' I had come trotting up here on a weekday, we would have been bamboozled with the heads-down haring of people from A to B, the A to B that don't exist at weekends and distinguishes them from the week.

For once, Delilah were behaving like a almost normal donkey an' the ride been a momentary interlude, with time to reflect on the outrageous plight of these children…our Ma's secret role out on front line…our opening to shake a stick at the Mantle…until we rattled through the bottleneck into Neals Yard.

Dr Cole led Delilah into the granary an' Eden gently pulled the doors closed behind us. "Thoughtful of you to arrive a little ahead of time, thank you," said Dr Cole, and led us through to the grain store. "Well, this here is Lily." Eden introduced us to a little girl an' I got to say, Gloria and I both been taken aback by the sight of her, all cushioned-up between the sacks of flour with a leg an' a arm in plaster.

"Ain't as bad as it looks, I has bones of porcelain an' eyes of china blue," Lily smiled bravely.

"And this is Jamie," he gestured towards a skinny boy, who were grey with sickness. "'Ello, are you the wheels?" Jamie asked.

"Got it in one. That's the getaway cart an' Delilah, a donkey faster then the speed of light. I's Angelina an' this is Gloria, me sister."

"Reet then, wicked," said Jamie.

"How do, I's Jerome." A young man about our age came slowly down the grain loft stairs. "Jeez, ain't you something." He give us a shy hug. "Ain't met too many girls so far," an' all of a sudden tears start rolling down his face.

"Oh lord," said Dr Cole, "this is deeply touching guys, but no time for flirting."

"Doctors is so very caring an' total callous all at once," Jerome remarked, wiping his eyes.

"Cripes Jerome, I didn't have you down for a moon fruit," says Jamie.

"Neither did I," Lily rolled her eyes.

"No," said Eden, "neither did I," an' rolled his.

We wrapped Lily up in sheepskin fleece an' laid her on a roll of Sea Sponge under the cart seat, an' then did the same for Jamie. "All right in there?" asked Dr Cole.

"Yes, we is, but where is we going?"

"Nice try, Lily. You can't know that till you get there," Dr Cole replied, placing some flour sacks an' our musical instruments in front of them. Then Gloria an' I climbed up front, an' pulling their hoodies well over the heads, Jerome an' Eden climbed in the back, posing as the band. "All righty-dighty Delilah, walk on, walk on, walk on."

We went through Seven Dials, for it were not a tale of the unexpected for a band to be checking out a venue where they was gonna have a gig. We drove slowly round it an' low an' behold, there were Turkish blended in amongst the absinth drinkers. You'd have to have been blind not to spot him. Still, we kept our cool an' departed sedately down the lane with Turkish sleuthing along behind us, an' he followed us a long way, until he probably twigged that we was on our way to the Blackfriars for music, because Saturday morning is always music an' the entirely usual place for us to go.

Milo de Fer

They says "truth is stranger than fiction," an' they maybe has a point. The Down Street Tube Station, for example, do not exist, nor has it ever been on any map, an' we don't see it when it is perfectly plain for all to see. What's more, this total dilapidated ghost station also housed a piece of living accommodation that some patient craftsman with fine taste had restored in the clean-lined minimal style that I admired most, an' I happen to believe that Booker were headquartered there.

One entrance is concealed in a burned-out alleyway full of rubble, an' families that has something to hide do not arrive together, but has learned to operate in ones an' twos that reassembles into the family unit once they come inside. "Well done, Christiana. Hello, here comes your father an' Felix…" But that way, every single one made it safely, an' the empty ticket hall been filled with quite a crowd.

"Ladies an' Gentlemen, girls an' boys, my name is Milo an' I's your tour guide for today." I waved a torch. "It's easy to get lost down here, best follow me." Well, it ain't the best place to take a lot of high-anxiety people, their kids, their gear and their dogs, with its crumbling bottomless pit where the lift shaft used to be an' the all-pervasive smell of mustiness, its long winding stairwell into the void all rusted through in numerous places, an' the various black-hole corridors where I thought I heard the flat-footed scuffling of goblins or perhaps a little Ragger. "Are you with me, are we all here?" I made sure they was before negotiating the final flaky bridge that spanned uncertainly across the underworld and down, down, down the claustrophobic set of stairs that run to Platform One, where my father an' Booker was waiting beside a fleet of torch-lit pleasure-boats.

"Wow," my charges breathed a little freer at the sight.

"How do, glad you made it alright. I's Booker. Time is on our side for now, so let's get going an' make our introductions on the way." Soon as all the brothers, sisters, fathers, mothers, dogs an' clobber was in the boats, Booker put out into the swift current. "So long Jean, see you around Milo," an' with a hasty "Take care" an' a humble "Thanks so much," the boats departed one by one. 'Don't look back, don't look back, you all,' I thought. "Come on, son," my father said. "The day has only just begun."

Phoebe de Fer and Ariel Levet

It been our task to inform Abby and Riley of the situation, an' armed with a couple of boxes of Venus Man Trap baby products, Ariel an' me went to Chinatown.

"Ladies, massage for you?" wheedled Madame Solarium.

"Not today thanks."

"Pity, pity, you look stressed. Meridians out of whack." She wagged a threatening finger at us. "You'll regret it. Here today gone tomorrow, you could be dead very fast…"

"Help!" We backed into the tattoo parlour, where the glyphs maestro was at work. "Hi," he said and looked up, "check out the new transfers. Special offer for you two."

"Oh, these are marvellous. You is a very clever man."

"I is a very poor man."

"You is not," and I offered him a bagful of studs an' spikes I'd found in our scrap iron. "Alright? See you later."

"Okee cokee, hope not," he grumbled when we left.

"Nut bag," remarked Ariel, an' we moved along with the browsing market crowds till we reached the "Fresh Today, Live Crayfish, Cheapest Crazy Deals" of Berwick Street. "Maybe later," we replied, an' sidled behind the grilling fish to knock on Abby's door.

Abby opened her door with her baby draped like a bag of flour over her shoulder. "How do, respect," she smiled friendly.

"Some natural baby products, a freebee courtesy of the Venus Man Trap," Ariel announced, an' held out the gift pack cheerily.

"What a surprise, thanks!" Abby replied.

"Beautiful baby," said Ariel, peering around Abby's shoulder at him. "I don't s'pose," she lowered her voice, "you happened to catch that severe weather warning on the radio?"

"I did, as a matter of fact…" Abby looked round, anxious and alert.

"Stay cool," I smiled a warning. "Each product is labelled with a clear set of instructions for the long-term well-being of mother an' child. You has choices, so be sure to read them carefully."

"Thanks, I will. It's very kind of you, thanks so much." Abby took the box inside and closed the door quietly behind her.

You'd have to be pretty self-developed to walk down Berwick Street an' avoid the temptations of Peeking Ducky's. Ariel were already searching her pockets for bartering objects. "I don't think these'll quite cut the mustard," she said, pulling out of few dusty old pony peppermints.

"It's okay. I've been feeling guilty about the bits an' bobs we offer him, so I made him something special." We queued at his stall an' when it were our turn, I handed him a copper puzzle-ring. Peeking Ducky were definitely pleased. "Ah," he said, admiring it. "Result, my daughter's birthday sorted. Good idea!" Then he filled a couple of takeaway baskets to overflowing an' gave us a bag of prawn crackers each.

We schlepped on to Masons Yard, where Dorcas had explained that Riley lived "in a big cube come bunker thingy of concrete, plate glass an' steel, bursting with plants an' some serious trees."

It were hard to miss an' not my cup of chai. Anyway, we banged roundly on the iron door an' when a distant voice called "Just a mo," we sat down on the cement doorstep to wait an' munch our chicken wings. The door were eventually opened by a man with spiky hair, who was clasping a tiny spiky-haired baby gingerly an' awkwardly in his arms. "'Ello girls, is this some kind of brunch do?" Riley peered at us rightly bemused.

"Ah, not exactly," I said standing up. "Good morning! Some natural baby products for the long term well-being and safety of father and daughter, courtesy of the Venus Man Trap."

"Oh right," said Riley, totally not getting it. "That's very kind of you girls, but I'm not sure I'd know what to do with that stuff. My wife would've, but …" His voice trailed off.

"The point is," said Ariel, laying a warm hand on him, "did you happen to catch that severe weather warning on the radio?"

"Yeah." We had his full attention now. "It might affect you. Now each product is very carefully labelled. Just read the instructions and then you'll understand what to do," said Ariel.

"Oh, right," Riley repeated himself, and then he rolled his eyes. "I get ya. "Just for a moment there, I thought you was speaking in tongues." He hugged his little girl very close then. "Hear that, darlin'? Help's at hand, the rescue services is on their way, the cavalry is coming." The baby opened her eyes in alarm.

"Shush! Keep it down, fruit cake," Phoebe whispered.

"Who?" he whispered, leaning over our takeaway an' inhaling furiously. "Smells fantastic. Give us a chicken wing, ain't had a proper meal since she was born."

"Sure, we has way too much. Take it easy." We left him the lot and departed.

Liberty de Fer

t was D-Day, and I awoke with a jolt. 'Jeepers, that's the last time I ever drink Smokey Old Peat.' My head were muzzy, I felt queasy, an' while folks stole out of town by their different routes, I was struck by the alarming thought that should any of them make it through to Greene King Keep, my father were liable to shot the lot on sight. Now (I crawled out of bed) seemed like a perfect time to visit. Some people may even suggest that after eighteen years, a visit were slightly overdue.

There were a hangover to work through, an' never having seen the virtue in travelling light, there was an awful lot of packing an' flying about to do, for Canada's boat were leaving at midnight.

Column an' Phoebe were not best pleased when we stood on the foggy quay to say goodbye. "Here's a present for Grandfather Lear, who we've never met," hissed Column. "Oh yes, sure do hope to meet him sometime soon, afore it's too late," added Phoebe.

"Of course you will. I'll be back soon an' love you both very much."

"Be safe," they scowled accusingly.

"Ignore them," Milo said encouragingly. "We'll be fine, won't we dad?"

"Alright for you to say. But I'll miss you. What am I gonna do without you?" Jean gave me a hug.

"Everything, of course. You're gonna have to do everything." I returned his embrace. 'Stupid me,' I thought, realising he were anxious of losing me to the sea. "One piece of breaking news," I whispered, to keep his mind off things. "How do you feel about a new addition to the family?"

"What? I thought you had a hangover?" he whispered back.

"I did, and I am."

"Now you tell me?"

"Ahem, we has the midnight tide to catch," Canada reminded us quietly.

"Aye aye, Captain," I replied, an' hopped onboard. Pulling in the ropes, Albin an' Tobin took up their positions with the guns fore and aft, and the blackout barge slipped off into the turning tide.

We dared not shine a light on deck, but down below Abby and Riley were playing a round of cards by candlelight, their babies settled in the kiddie hammocks for the night. "Any idea where we're headed? asked Riley.

"Yes, I'll tell you when we're safely down the river," I replied.

"It doesn't matter. Anywhere out of the Big Smoke is fine with me," said Abby.

"Yeah, well quite. Can't believe the Mantle can remove a child from a single parent, without explanation. I just lost me wife and I isn't about to lose me daughter. She don't even have a name yet."

" No no, of course not. You know what, you'll probably find a name for her on the way… How about some Chai?" I offered.

" How about a nice big mug of coffee with a lot of sugar?" Canada's voice came down the hatch, about loud enough to wake the dead, or worse, the babies.

Tobias

There is a danger element to falling asleep, for the soul takes off, leaving the body to fend for itself, and some of the most turbulent times of your life can happen in that moment. My dreams was veering into the miracle of disappearances and successful vanishings of the Rope Trick as performed by one terrifying evil-looking Indian fakir. Bang, bang, bang, his staff smote the dusty ground. Bang, bang, bang... "Wake up man, someone at the door." Dorcas shook me back to Earth.

"Okay," I says. "It's probably someone needs a midwife." I climbed out of bed.

"Or it could be Turkish," Dorcas replied, full of fear.

I opened the door to find an older gentleman with a fine head of silver hair accompanied by a young lady swathed in a snood. "Is this the midwives' house?" asked the gentleman. "We thought we might find help here." I pulled them inside pretty sharpish, with both my hands. "We heard it on the radio an' headed here fast as we could. Marley here has the Downs, you see."

"You've done the right thing. Well done and welcome, I'm Tobias," I said, my mind working furiously as to what to do. At the sound of the voices, Dorcas came hurrying downstairs. "Otto? My lawd, been a long, long time." She gave them her warm wide smile. "You must be Marley. I bought you into the world, just look at you now. Sit down, have some toast an' chai while we sort something out for you... Where's your wife?"

"Long story, but not around," Otto replied.

"Okay then, let's think."

"Oh hello, what's going on?" asked Angelina an' Gloria, who'd come to join us. "any Cocoa about, want some?" they offered Marley, "I should cocoa," she replied, chortling at her own joke.

"We can get you out of town on the new handcar a friend an' I just built," I said. "Should give us a chance of catching the others up. If not, we'll find them somewhere in the forest. I know the way, been there afore."

"With respect, we didn't mean to be any trouble."

"No, you're no trouble at all. Perfect timing for the maiden voyage I's been meaning to make. Put on everything warm you has, we must be well clear of the city before first light."

It ain't clever to wing it in the wilds, an' packing up a thoughtful amount of provisions we's loaded up Delilah an' legged it to Charred Cross Station. "You're a good man. Be careful babe," says Dorcas, an' she put her arms around me an' give me a kiss of unusual tenderness. "I love you," she said. "So long."

"I love you too," I replied sincerely. "So do I," said Marley taking my hand and clambering onto the handcar. But Otto, who had a particularly intense pair of blue observing eyes, looked about ready to cut an' run soon as he seen the car were named "Shock and Awe," but I steered him firmly into his seat, pulled down our over-shoulder restraints, an' rammed home the lap-bar. "Chocks away, if you don't mind ladies please," I says nonchalantly, an' locking a couple of fizz balls into the ignition rod, Pow! We was away like a flying man out a cannon, with blue flames playing about the wheels an' the G-forces wobbling our faces an' pinning us well back in our seats. Marley gurgled like a drain, grabbed our hands in a death grip an' clung on, till we settled down to humming along the gleaming miles of steely tracks, with the Empty Quarter spread out before us and the clouds above opening up into a starry night. "First come the Shock and then comes the Awe," said Otto, happily resting his eyes on the wide an' beautiful sky.

Asbo (age 12)

A in't a single Ragger not been nabbed an' done time in the lab. Some is missing a kidney, some's had their brains fried, Rickers even had her bone-marrow swiped, an' no-one were particular anxious to relive the rush.

It been a matter of personal interest to witness an amount of Deviations being slipped out of town, in a now-you-see-thems-now-you-don't operation what included boats, a donkey cart an' some kind of technological breakthrough by way of hand-cars, a white knuckle ride that come streaking out of Charred Cross Station an' gone rocketing away over the Empty Quarter with blue flames playing lovely about the wheels.

Next day it been all very calm, business-as-usual an' going about their lives like a bunch of Holy Innocents, but we Raggers stayed vigilant. We kept our ears on the rails an' we was right to do that, for what do ya know? Twenty-four hours after it were all long gone, done an' over, the Mantle come breezing through the city and cooler than a icy winter wind, them Dark Elite gone loping through the hollow spaces an' fanning out along the empty darksome streets.

The Mantle had their visors closed for maximum intimidation-value an' kept their guttering torches cowled against the rain, an' them stinking scum Hissy Boys had sharpened their teeth, tarred their braids an' decked themselves out in spikes an' war paint. Their detail been to slink around the back to cover all the exits while the Mantle takes the home front. Knock, knock, knock, they wakes indignant families, fuming furious with the invasion an' the whirlwind searching of their homes, while their kids looked on in boiling

189

loathing as sniffer dogs gone slouching through their rooms an' burrowing about with filthy paws inside the cupboards.

To their astounding mystification, the search revealed no moaning Deviations in the attic, nor no raving loonies lurking down the cellar, but they shouts "All clear" undaunted, an' carries on the same charade at the next place on the list.

The Mantle hit on places where them families had just abandoned ship, scarpered off an' flitted out of town, leaving closed their shutters, the pots an' pans all stacked up nicely, the beds all neatly made and ready for a kip, an' also thoughtfully laced the lot with frankincense an' pepper-dust, which do so confuse a hunting dog an' tracking clone.

All baffled out, "Probably we have a mole," suspicions Turkish. "Probably you're a complete idiot. Who'd dare grass up the Mantle ? Crack on, crack on," Mason brushed him off, incredulous.

"You is entitled to your opinion sir, an' may believe what you like, but this ain't right. Them kids was there, I's telling you, an' now they's gone, so someone must have tipped them off." They drove on, brooding moody, in their Paddy Wagon.

The next place they stopped, the lights was on an' the door been opened by a little old lady in a brightly-quilted housecoat. "Uh oh," says Turkish. "Begging your pardon, but is the midwife here, or have I just confused it with another place?"

"No, yes, well maybe. That's me daughter. She drops by sometimes on her rounds. If you has an emergency, take your missus," and she gave Mason a funny look, "to the Horse Hospital."

"Tar ducks, will do," said Turkish an' backed out hurriedly with Mason Flint. "Well sir, I think we should arrest that midwife."

"What for, visiting her mother?" Mason laughed out loud.

"No sir, for questioning sir. She's set us up. Somehow she knew an' must have tipped them off."

"Well with your tailing abilities it's hardly surprising."

Ignoring him, Turkish gone on, " If it was the midwife, she'd know that lone parents' kids could be on our list as well. We have to know if they is at home. How about we call it a night an' try again tomorrow?"

"We has the whole Force out and you want to try again tomorrow? What's up with you?"

Turkish plainly got the hump as he explained, "Well, for starters, one of 'em lives in the middle of the Oriental Quarter, which is fine by day but not by night."

"We'll be fine, Turkish. We is the Mantle, you prannet," Mason assured him.

"All right sir, may I suggest we begin with Mr Riley? an' if he's in there'll be no need to go to China Town…"

We Raggers remained absolute concealed, relishing the night's events, but when Rickers hissed, "We has to get them bleeders into China Town," we bristled up alert.

"Yeah, that should sort 'em."

"Nice one Rickers."

I thought a moment. "Tell you what, I's an idea. Come on, lets git down to Riley's."

Then the weather gone ballistic an' the rain come peltering down in rivers. It come down forcefully an' it come chucking out the sky, in one of 'em big emptying events that bring the autumn on.

The Mantle soldiered on, almost invisible inside the walls of rain, while beneath their squelching boots the waters come rising up an' gushing out through all the broken drains. The streets was awash with water an' scores of scuttling half-drowned rats when, Oh happy day, a band of paralytic binge babes come splashing out the dark an' lurched into the Mantle ranks, all shivering, soaked an' screaming hysterical about the rat situation. Which delays the Mantle a good deal, as theys attempt to shake 'em off an' retrieve the tracking dogs, who was swimming around, chasing the girls, snapping at the rats an' barking in such as state of doggy disarray as to be beyond useless.

There weren't a great deal of time to admire Riley's place, but the trees which we climbed was mostly on the inside, an' with plenty of potted bushy stuff to hide behind we was well outta sight when the Mantle rolled up an' barged inside.

The ambush were a big surprise an' a blinding success. We's jumped em an' inflicted a deal of damage of the slash-an-burn variety, creating a lot of disorder, until I got caught by Turkish (all part of me plan), who hung on to me ear with his girly pincer fingers like a working ferret, while the dogs pursued me mates into the night.

"Well if it ain't Asbo." Turkish breathed his sewer breath all over me an' struggling me into the Paddy Wagon, he rammed his arm across me throat. "If you has any knowledge of Mr Riley's whereabouts, we might be kind enough to overlook deleting you."

I lay struggling for air an' thumping me heels on the floor, an' when he give me a bit of air to breath I yelled, "Help, get the paedo cretin offa me! Help, help, he's molesting me, who's in charge?"

"Varmint," spat Turkish, an' increased the pressure.

"Ease up, easy does it, we need him alive. Now my boy, I am Commissioner Mason Flint of the Mantle an' Head of the Metropolis. What have you to say? Ain't nothing to be afraid off," I rolled me eyes, shook me head an' remained mute.

"Start talking, or I break your fingers, one by one, till you squeal," said Turkish, falling into the old 'good Mantle, bad Mantle' routine.

"No, no, pleease… Alright, 's not exactly classified nor nuffink though."

"We're listening," says Mason, an' snivelling credible, I sniffs, "Riley gawn an' moved in with some broad called Tabby or Abby or something up in China Town."

"And so the Raggers was looting his house?"

"Perish the thought sir, absolutely not sir, never we wasn't."

"Course you was, don't you know better? Ain't you seen enough of the inside of a lab by now, little grassing snitch?" Turkish looked like Mr Happy. He slammed shut the doors an' I give him the finger through the bars.

Mason dismissed most his men, who give him a half-hearted "G'night sir," an' schleps off, nursing their puncture wounds, while we lights out for China Town along with a couple of Hissy Boys, four dogs an' a few hard men. "Right lads," says Mason, drawing up beneath the walls. "Keep stealthy. We're going in, by gum."

Keeping stealthy were not gonna do it. For one thing, them Orientals can fly over the rooftops, an' two, just passing through the Lion Gates triggers one of them warning systems that Abby's father was so total genius at installing. You can bet our presence were already being relayed by way of a whirligig, gliding magnetic ball-bearings, a wind-chime, the thud of the water-powered deer-scarer, a spinner, a cue ball rolling down the guttering, a swinging pendulum, a widget, a sack of falling rice, a compressed coil, a rotating flywheel, a pivoting winch, a gee-haw an' a high-speed foofy slide that gone unseen in a domino effect, to alert Zero Tolerance, the Wushu master, and them full-contact barehanded fighters of the Shaolin Tutorial, Sami Ling the Tibetan, who's also known as Buddha's Fist, as well as Kim, a Lone Women of Combat, an' all the other members of the Rung Tung. Not forgetting the Yakuza, which is a bunch of Nippon gangsters who was easily upset an' ever so nifty with knives an' shooters.

I ain't no psychic, nor is I a seventh son sixth-senser off the fells. Nor did I have to be to sense the shift, when the empty alleyways seemed to lean a little closer, like they was listening an' watching, silent as a hungry cat, while we's the tiny little mice gone by. The Mantle's teeth was set on edge an' their nerves was uptight jangling, but we's made it in one piece all the way to Abby's door.

The door were opened by some sleepy Nipponese females who was just moving in an' looked to be setting up some weaving shop in Abby's home. Their faces dropped like a ton of lead balloons at the sight of all them menaces on their doorstep. Seeing the house were occupied by unexpected strangers, Turkish an' Mason understood they'd been set up and backed away slowly when a Hissy Boy snapped, an' grabbing one of the ladies, dragged her outside, dropped her onto the wet cobbles an' start ripping away at her clothes. The women set up a horrifying caterwauling which strung out into a long silence, as the Hissy Boy keeled over an' gone buckling into the gutter, a knife in his back an' the blood all spurting an' oozing an' streaming away in the rivers of rain. Mason pick up that fainting female an' holding her in front of him, he turned full circle checking the roof-tops for the invisible knife thrower.

Too late. "Let go the girl." He was total immobilized in an iron grip with a Stanley up against his throat. "How about," says the Lone Women of Combat, "you take your lady-boys and scram, before we slits your throats and eats your dogs for breakfast?" an' with the rest of the Force similarly up against the wall, the Rung Tung come an' sprung me out of the Paddy Wagon, saying, "You done good. Smart brat pack." I nodded politely an' swopped places with Mason Flint, Turkish, his men an' their dogs, who was locked away inside the Paddy Wagon an' told, "You come back, you is dead Mantle walking."

It ain't a easy thing to translate their pigeon, but I think Zero Tolerance an' Buddha's Fist was going to drive 'em to Projack, park up at the door and leave 'em there for someone else to find.

The Shaolin Tutorial gone inside to help them Japanese weavers put their place to rights, an' Kim, the Lone Women of Combat herself, asked me, "You hollow hungry, young chavvi?"

"Tar, I's starvin."

"Come on in, so am I." I ate well but gone on me way soon, through the rain which were falling more normal, called down by gravity an' gentle, so as to make sure me crew was alright. Which they was, in their variables.

Grandma Tookie (the Akashic Record, Dorcas)

A great deal of rehearsing, combined with their stars being on the rise and favourably aspected, the night Soft Sloth took on the happy hour at Jabba the Sluts they achieved a spellbinding gig that few will ever forget.

Even the dodgiest members of the club were aware they were witnessing a one-off quality event and Dorcas, who sat proudly in a booth amongst her companions, Reema, Cole, Eden, Mara Blanch, Milo, Jean de Fer, Brothers Sebastian an' Dominic, raised a silent toast to Tobias her partner, not yet returned from the evacuation, and a delighted glass in support of her daughters Angelina and Gloria, then relaxed into a rare evening amongst friends and the wholly enjoyable music. The youngsters, who were thought to be keeping each other company in the Forge, were in fact in the ladies' toilet, recording a bootleg.

In the early hours of the following morning, Dorcas was taken hostage on her way to work. Her assailants were professionals who left nothing to chance, and slipping onto the back of her cart, they quietly overpowered her. They taped up her mouth, put a muslin sack over her head, trussed her up firmly and folding her silently into the back of the cart, drove away through the dark dawn.

Shaking with shock an' shivering with the cold, Dorcas tested her restraints but finding no way to ease herself out of them, she resigned herself to the situation and drew courage from the thought that it had all been worth it, for right now, somewhere out of town, the children were waking up and struggling bravely on their own journey into the unknown, and passing a procession of each and every one of their faces through her soul, she let them go with a 'Be safe, so long you all.'

When they drove Delilah unwillingly over the river, a light rain began to fall, and a wind picked up which blustered disconcertingly through the endless dereliction of Rotherhithe. And when first light came filtering through Dorcas's hood, they drew to a halt, waited briefly while some heavy doors were rolled open, and clattered into the empty shell of a warehouse.

No old wharf-side building had been built to accommodate a staircase, rather people rode the goods lifts between floors, and when Dorcas was being shuffled onto one of these, Delilah took off and galloped away with the cart careening behind her. Ignoring the unfortunate slip-up, her captors climbed onto the lift on either side of her and began the long winch upwards by means of a squeaking hand-pulley.

They came out at the top into a vast roof space and led Dorcas across a wooden floor, disturbing a great many doves who rose fluttering to safer perches, and although not a word had been spoken she was aware that there were a number of other people in the room. Someone reached under the sack to rip the tape off her mouth and force a rag bung between her teeth, others hastened to manoeuvre her onto a long inclining board with her feet raised and her head lowered. Her hands were bound at the back of the board with soft bindings and Dorcas, summoning up the calm she used when assisting a woman through a long and difficult labour, said to herself, 'You're doing fine, take deep breaths, you can do this...'

Water poured over her head. It ran through the muslin sack, up her nose and into her airways, forcing her to retch. "This is how it works. You answer our questions and we stop pouring water. Otherwise, you drown and die," a quiet voice purred. At the same time, Dorcas had the creepy sensation that her mind was being probed, but well used to keeping secrets she focused her thoughts and feelings on Tobias and a journey they'd once taken down the tracks to see the stars rise over the ocean...

Again the water splashed down on her. "Who told you about the round up?" Gushing down her throat, it entered her lungs. She choked, gagged and struggled to draw breath, but still the water came, and just when Dorcas was beginning to hope she'd hurry up and drown, "That's enough," the voice said, and the water stopped. "Who else was involved? Where is your partner now, and above all where have the Deviations gone?" Dorcas did not answer, but filled her heart and soul with the music of Soft Sloth and the mellow singing of her daughters Angelina and Gloria...

When the water came again, Dorcas knew her lungs were all but submerged in water, and fought in vain to catch her breath. "No sense in a heroic drowning, me dear."

'Makes all the sense in the world to me,' thought Dorcas, and the water stopped abruptly, her torturer stalled. Sensing that Dorcas had decided that there were some things well-worth dying for, he was unprepared for her sacrifice.

'No, nothing is worth dying for' – he struggled with his thoughts for a moment – 'but do not seek to turn the tables on me, or I will reap whatever information your pitiful panorama yields up in death.' But detaching from the long cascade of water that gushed over her, Dorcas heard only the cooing of the doves in the rafters and with the restless fluttering of their wings, an image of Solo passed briefly through her mind before a white-winged angel came to ease her pain.

"Untie her hands, remove the hood and chuck her in the river," Nicky gasped, in holy terror of the powerful angel that the lowly midwife's panorama had revealed.

Brother Dominic

So tenuous was the body that came to rest on the shingle, I had the overwhelming impression of one of those rare people who are born retaining a memory of their heavenly home. They harbour a deep-seated yearning for the light, and are liable to seek it through gnosis or mysticism… That was my first impression, as the rising tide threatened to pull her away, and stooping to lift her, Brother Sebastian found her to be light as a feather. But not until the sound of Delilah's terrible braying came to our ears, as she galloped our way with an empty cart behind her, did the realization dawn that the battered and muddied form might be Dorcas. Horrified, wonderingly, we laid her upon some old sacks in the donkey cart and took her to the Priory. "Hold on Dorcas, Dorcas hold on…" We prayed out loud, for she was neither dead nor alive.

We sent for Doctor Cole, who came straightaway, while Reema went in search of Angelina and Gloria to tell them what had befallen their mother. She found them at the Venus Man Trap, and they arrived soon after with a bar of rose soap to cleanse the violence off her skin, and apple shampoo to wash the river from her hair.

Phoebe de Fer

My brother and I combined forces to make an angel for our show. While we worked, we also attempted to come to grips with what had happened to Dorcas. Which was no easy thing when all things was on hold with her, as she lay in a coma and the outcome so unsure.

Column had a rare piece of golden-barked ash to carve the angel's head from, while I engaged in some pragmatic research into the world of angelic armour, for ever since I read the passage in Faust that states, "No Sun nor Moon illuminates the Angel of Light, for he is of a 'sheen that glimmers of itself,' that is quite imperceptible to the human eye," I'd been wondering what in the world could possibly be the composition of a unearthly metal like that?

I hoped it were going to include some meteorite, seeing as it comes out of the sky, an' noting that Faust himself been partial to a five-four-three-two-one recipe, maybe, just maybe, if I tried five fist-sized meteorites, four tin coins, three copper nuggets, two old silver teaspoons, one vial of mercury and perhaps a sprinkle or two of some unspecified minerals that old Grandpa Volco left behind, packed it all into his little furnace with some lime to absorb the impurities, I might extract something with a glimmering sheen in an alchemy all of my own. (If you is trying this at home be very careful with the heat, meteor iron has a low melting point.)

We worked away until, satisfied with the way things was shaping up, we downed tools more or less simultaneous, with the common idea that it were chai time, an' going to fill up the kettle, I been pleased to see the silhouettes of Ariel, Harley and Tyler splashing up the long dark tunnel towards us.

They came sloshing into the workshop sober as pikes, an' brushing away her tears, Ariel informed us, "Nobody's saying if she's going to make it."

"Nobody's saying she ain't gonna make it either." Column gave her a hug, Harley cluttered about making chai while Tyler stood thoughtfully, rolling up his rabbit tobacco, an' said, "We should try an' think of a way to get the Mantle back. Something subtle, that undermines them to the very core."

"Not too subtle, or they won't get it," Ariel giggled through her tears.

"What makes you think it were the Mantle?" asked Column.

"Dad found evidence her hands had been tied," Ariel said quietly.

"You know what?" Column turned to Ariel. "I've been meaning to play you the story I got when I were hiding out under Projack. I don't know who's telling it or who it were being told to, but whoever it may be is one of the best storytellers I's ever heard."

"I'd like to hear it." Tyler looked relieved. " Right now, I couldn't think of anything better then a roll-up, a steaming hot cup of chai an' a good story."

"Me neither," I replied. "Let's have it then."

"There was once a boy who believed that he contained a little piece of Heaven and Earth inside him. He was peaceful and at one with the world…"

"I know that voice! Turn it off for a sec, Column. It's a man called Morgan Grey. He comes into the Venus Man Trap occasionally for skin cream," said Ariel. "He fancies your mum."

"Oh, him… I know who you mean," I said.

"Don't he own Projack?" Harley wondered.

"You want to hear the rest of it or what?"

Morgan told his story skilfully, unfolding it slowly and drawing you into the warp and weft of it, until there we were shivering a little beneath the night sky.

"When this boy looked up at the elegant Moon in the dark of the sky, he saw with delight how the light of the Moon had the same reflective quality as the silvered glass of the mirror. And when that boy looked up at the Sun, he saw that its light was not reflective but radiated from inside it…"

And we too hoped that we too might earn ourselves a heart of gold.

"Through his endeavours, the young man became learned and powerful. Indeed, he came to understand the natural world so well that he was able to call up a storm of such magnitude as to sink the Spanish Armada, and from then on people believed him to be a Magus…"

Harley and Tyler looked up startled. "Our grandfather believed it was perfectly possible to do that. He said that all magic begun with weather-workers."

"How he longed to talk to the angels in order to further his understanding!…"

"Who wouldn't? Who wouldn't want an angel to talk to from time to time?" Ariel sighed.

"By and by, he met a young Scryer, who became furious and used a ritual to trap an Angel inside the crystal ball…"

"What?" It seemed outrageous.

"Well now, the Angel sat crossed-legged, with his wingtips folded over his head, and calmly blew up the crystal ball. It shattered and exploded into a thousand shards of glass, feathers and dust, from which the Angel emerged in a white linen suit, and calmly walking away, he disappeared. But from then on, he was trapped on Earth. The Magus and the Scryer turned their attentions to making solid gold and the elixir of life, with which they had an unexpected breakthrough, and one night, raising their glasses, they drank a toast to eternal life and downed their cocktail. And when all had departed and gone, how broken was his heart, and how lonely the Magus became, more often longing for friendly death than dreaming of a heart of gold…"

"It's like Faust, but more intimate," Harley said, "and instead of going to Hell, they all get trapped on Earth. I think it might be the inside story."

"That feels right to me, Harley," I said. "And I'd really like to know who Morgan Grey were telling it to, anyway."

"Me too," said Ariel.

"Perhaps when things have settled down a bit,' suggested Column, "we should go back and find out." An' the idea of sneaking into the Projack basement to see if we couldn't find out a bit more 'bout what was what, and who were the mystery listener, been a thing to discuss all the way to the Venus Man Trap, where we were on duty for the afternoon, because my mum Liberty, the beauty queen, had gone to sea. an' thus were not even in the running for a heart of gold.

Grandma Tookie (the Akashic Record, Linda Miscellaneous)

inda Miscellaneous was more of an "in here" person than an "out there" one. She worked hard, and while going about her daily life, she kept up an interior dialogue that rose – unedited and uninhibited reams of it – in a sloping hand of baroque loops and chains with rings above the I's instead of dots, and all of Linda's stars burned pale with the unbearable pain of her son's disappearance.

'There we go. Gee wiz, can't fathom that one out. Anyway, perhaps I won't need to, once he's got his suit,' thought Linda, and prizing it out from beneath the foot of the sewing-machine, she began to sew the button-holes in tiny invisible stitches. Pausing every so often to re-thread the needle, she'd look up at a faded picture of Hope, who smiled down on her with his merry eyes of cinnamon and his hair so startlingly blond... 'A real surprise, considering I'm a Latin girl.'

On the other hand she didn't know who his father was, for practically the day she'd been confirmed barren and catapulted into a vortex of despair, Hope had been conceived with a mysterious lover who showed up, in her blackest moments and only ever under the cover of darkness. "And he doesn't appear to need any goddamn ladders, either," she mused. "I just fall asleep and there he is beside me, the great comforter to sweeten the night." There were times when she questioned the reality of him, for he was gone in the morning as mysteriously as he'd arrived. 'Except, of course, the proof was in Hope, the pudding.'

Whoever he was, was pretty much to her liking in every way.

There was nothing edgy about him, nor was he jealous, for Linda had the warmth of the Brazilian sun in her heart and there had been one or two other lovers. Nonetheless, her man returned without fail in her darkest hours, and over the years the complete experience of love that he'd bestowed upon her had smoothed her troubled brow and helped to shoulder the load of her vanished child. 'And how perfect is that?' she sighed. Linda was not hung up with commitment issues or remotely interested in discovering his identity. Indeed, erring on the superstitious side, she was rather afraid that if she did find it out, a spell might be broken and her mysterious lover would be unable to return.

Linda's reverie came to an end with the sound of Nicky's steel-toed boots clumping along the Gabriel Wharf decking, and returning to her everyday world with rather a bump, she finished off the last button-holes.

"Come in," she invited when Nicky arrived at the door. "Your suit's ready," she smiled.

"Fast work, thank you." Nicky's icy green eyes glinted at her appreciatively.

"I think," said Linda, keeping it professional, "you'd better try it on. There could be some minor adjustments to be made." When Nicky emerged, Linda saw the suit was perfect, 'except perhaps for this,' she thought, handing him a red foulard to complete the Beethoven look and complement the dark velvet suit.

Nicky took a few turns in front of the mirror, and after regarding his reflection appreciatively for a while, he turned his attention to the invisible stitching of the buttonholes. "This is exquisite. Such beautiful work." He certainly seemed happy, and giving her a bashful look of great charm, he bowed and said, "Thank you."

"You're welcome," Linda replied.

"Em, just out of curiosity, I don't suppose you have any experience in stitching wounds and the like?"

'Bit random, oh weird one,' thought Linda, and noticing how stifling hot the place had become she opened the door, letting in some cooler air before she replied. "No, I'm a seamstress. But it can't be that different from stitching cloth, I suppose. Why?"

"I don't know, just crossed my mind you'd be good at it." Nicky shrugged.

But Linda was not to be put off, suspecting that some kind of alternative agenda lay within the question. "What are you getting at? What's on your mind?" And disarming Linda with a calculated look of great vulnerability, Nicky replied as pathetically as he could, "It's just… You know, I lost my ears… A fire many years ago. I don't want to seem vain or anything, but I've managed to create a new pair from seeded cartilage… I just thought you might have the skill and kindness to sew them on."

"Oh," said Linda, completely taken aback, but at the same time feeling very sorry for him and understanding how sensitive the subject must be. "I could give it a go," she offered, with a great deal of misgiving.

"That's very kind of you, and a bit unexpected. Thanks," he said humbly. "Now let me give you something for this wonderful suit." He drew out a snuff box and handed it to Linda, who exclaimed "Good heavens!" when she opened for it, for it was full of little gold coins. Something warned her that he thought she could be bought, so she declined as graciously as possible. "Thank you, Nicky. That's very generous of you, but there's a possessive quality to gold… It's a gift, a thing to be owned, and as such I can't trade it on. Brass now, I really like brass. But any small fare will do," and she handed it back to him, adding lightly, "Keep the suit on, you look tremendous. Pay me later."

"Oh, all right then," Nicky replied nonchalantly, but smiled darkly.

Ariel Levet

Saturday afternoons at the Venus Man Trap were always a bit of a workout, what with the horde of weird an' slightly wonderful customers the place attracted. Amongst whom today were a bunch of lively Leggers, looking for fluorescents to enhance their Manga look, one disenfranchised Banga hip-hop for his kohl, a couple of swish ballroom dancers for their rouge and powder, multiples of exotica from Jabba's swanning about looking for lipsticks or something from the Eye-Lure range, browsers for the feelgood factor a bath bomb or a sweet perfume provides, and tricky customers with personal colour charts, whose mixing an' matching of assorted ingredients is continuously contributing to the periodic table (as if it ain't long enough). An' I been intrigued to observe that each of our customers, in their own particular uniqueness an' individual ways, were in hot pursuit of transforming themselves into the vision of loveliness that is eternal youth, which do appear to be one of mankind's primary ongoing preoccupations.

When the last of the costumers had trudged off into the late autumn afternoon a lull descended, when Harley and Tyler settled down to practise some magic, while Column busied himself with stoking the stove an' sticking on the kettle. Phoebes and I were playing a few rounds of Stone-Paper-Scissors, the loser of which was gonna sweep up, when I spotted someone coming through the yellowing birches. "Customer!" I called out. "Looks like Morgan Grey. Let's see if we can't engage him in some way an' find out a little more about him."

"That's not gonna be easy with Mum gone. He'll be disappointed the main attraction's out of town." Phoebe rolled her eyes.

The door opened, an' bestowing a quick smile all round Morgan entered. "Good afternoon, ladies and gentlemen. My, it's very warm and cosy in here." His firm voice left us in no doubt that he were indeed the storyteller.

"How may we help you?" Phoebe enquired.

"Oh, I've just popped in to pick up…" He left his sentence unfinished, distracted by the simple coin manipulation that Harley and Tyler were weaving about their fingers.

"Gosh," he exclaimed, "I used to be able to do that." An' fishing a coin out of his pocket, Morgan rolled it expertly over his knuckles and around his fingers. "Is Liberty about anywhere?" he casually enquired.

"Er nope, she's away herb hunting or something at the moment. But I think she keeps the cream over there."

"Thank you, my dear," he replied, keeping a close eye on the twins. "You boys are pretty good at that."

"You're not so bad yourself. How about a cup of chai and a Magicians' Duel?"

"Oh," he said, "how delightful. Why not?"

It was hard to know who were charming who. They sipped chai and bent the spoons, eyes were discreetly misdirected, an' coins disappeared afore they reappeared out of thin air. The atmosphere thickened, densified by the concentration required to bend the boundaries of perception. Tyler were more skilful with the coins and disappearances an' Harley more a showman, better with a pack of cards. "Pick a card, any card," he invited gleefully, his cards appearing to levitate momentarily before settling into a neat fan.

For every trick the twins performed, Morgan met them with a suave an' different one, until with a "That's all folks, you win," the boys conceded their defeat.

"So soon? I was just getting started. But what have I won, I wonder?" asked Morgan, looking around expectantly.

"Congratulations, you've won another delicious cup of chai," Column said, hastily pouring him one.

Harley and Tyler Blanch

We sat an' drank our chai together amiably, an' veering the parlari in the magic direction, Morgan Grey did his best to answer the many questions we'd been harbouring.

"Mr Morgan sir, is there something more to magic than misdirection and trickery? We is asking because our grandfather told us a true magician inherits his magic an' can work the weather. Can you explain for us what did he mean?"

Looking pensive for a moment, he replied, "I'll try. I imagine he meant that while most people are bound to absorb a certain knowhow from what their parents do, there are also gifts that run in families, and magic is one of them. As to misdirection and trickery, they have their place, because they manipulate the space that lies between things and that is where the realm of magic begins. A very lively space it is too, filled with air and sound for example. But it's also the space where the colours of yellow and blue can meet to perform the magic of creating green.

And like the colour green, the natural home of the ancient weather-workers was in the in-betweens. From there, they were able to call upon the wind to sweeten the souring grapes and persuade the snow to force an advancing enemy into retreat, or conjure down the lightning to strike a fire. Even today, a few rainmakers still exist."

"Oh, I know what you mean." Tyler were all innocence. "We heard once that someone called upon the wind to sink a thousand Spanish ships."

"Heavens to mergatroid, that old rumour's been going around for years. You can't believe everything you hear!" Morgan exclaimed, an' carried on unfazed. "One thing I do know, though – if you pay

208

attention to the natural world, it will certainly pay attention to you. But be warned, the elements are not to be tamed. They can be wild, hostile and forbidding. For although our world now lies exhausted, it is by no means all spent."

"Don't worry, rest assured. Only puzzling over what the grandfather said." We smiled at him, our minds buzzing with information.

"Well, perhaps I should be on my way now. Thank you so much. I haven't had such a good time in years." Morgan returned our smiles. "Goodbye now," he said, and picking up his skin cream, he left.

Mistral (the Akashic Record)

Talk about paying attention, Morgan's smile took a big downturn when he were struck with the disambiguating notion that although he gone about quite deliberately to find out a little more about them, it seemed more like a total distinct possibility that he himself had been subtly manipulated and controlled by the little devils instead. "Ah well, what a naïve old goat I can be sometimes," thought he, which were a great truth. Sighing to himself, he walked along the Gabriel Wharf decking an' bumps straight into Nicky, who come out the glass blowers workshop, looking fantastic dapper in a blinding new suit and cautiously holding a fancy square box in front of him. "Oh, hello. I'm just heading back. Would you like a lift?" Morgan enquired.

"Yes, sure I do. That'd be great." They gone climbing into Morgan's flashy boat and lit out for Projack.

"Nice suit. What's in the box, a red hat to match the foulard?" Morgan cajoled.

"Yeah, yeah, a hat," Nicky replied, which were a great lie.

"Why not put it on then? Let's have a look," said Morgan, who were paying attention now and not about to be caught out twice in the same afternoon.

"Oh lord, but it's all wrapped up nicely," Nicky were explaining when Morgan unexpectedly lunged for the box and deftly flipped the lid up. "Oh dear," said Morgan, "you must have picked up the wrong box. This looks very like a scrying ball. Thank you very much," he scowled, "I'll have that," an' dropped it into Father Thames. "Nothing but trouble in your hands, those things."

"Bloody hell, Morgan!"

"Language Nicky, language." And they cracked on up river, bristling with hostilities under the big black umbrella of bad temper.

Grandma Tookie (the Akashic Record, Nicky Nigredo)

The day came when Nicky went purposefully into Hope's chambers and finding them freezing cold, he stocked up the fire and checked out the boy. Worried by the boy's declining condition, Nicky lost no time in administering a dose of local anaesthetic into Hope's shoulder blades. The room warmed up while the anaesthetic kicked in. Then, taking a scalpel, Nicky meticulously and painlessly removed the ears from off Hope's back, placed them in an ice-filled medicine box and clipped it shut, all ready for transport. "All's well that ends well," Nicky sighed in relief. But when he set about cleaning the small crescent wounds, he discovered that a couple of bony protrusions had developed beneath the areas where the seeded ears had been. "Well, well, well, what have we here?" he breathed. "Bless me if I haven't caught these right on time."

Nicky dug cruelly deep, and quickly removing them with his surgical bone shears, he swabbed the bleeding wounds with adrenaline and sewed Hope's wounds up hastily, slapped a couple of large sterile plasters over them, and zoomed off pell-mell, extremely concerned that his ears might start to perish before Linda Miscellaneous could stitch them on and restore the circulation.

Linda couldn't know that the ears she was sewing had been seeded on her own son's back, but she knew she was being exploited in some perverted way, and 'on top of it all, s'about as disgusting an' totally kinky as it gets. Yuck.' Her thoughts came thick an' fast. 'It don't exactly take a clairvoyant state of mind to know this ain't right. Nor any special powers to turn the tables,' and she plotted her

212

revenge while sewing her tiny stitches. "Hold still while I wipe away the blood. Okay, turn around please," and one ear off and one ear on, Nicky spun around in a kind of quick step. 'A death dance. Nice. Just you wait.' Linda's thoughts rose in heat.

When at last the gruesome job was done, he asked, "How do I look?"

'Like the malicious psycho you is, creep,' she thought, but said, while winding the bandage around his head, "Not too bad. It'll be fine once the swelling goes down." Then, summoning her dignity, she quietly commanded, "Out you go now, and don't ever come back." And opening her front door, she called out, "Asbo, Rickers, kindly escort this thing off the premises."

Nicky left under a hail of spit, bricks, live rats, dead fish, you name it, which rained down on him from the overhead walkways, and Linda filled her bath with steaming water and essences of apricot to sooth her frazzled heart and stem the tide of flowing tears. Later, deep in the night, when Linda's lover came to lie beside her, just for a moment she was tempted to open her eyes, but she dared not lest he lose his power.

Hope

A local anaesthetic is a fine an' dandy thing, an' it does a wonderful job by way of pain relief, but I been so shocked an' flabbergasted by the unexpected pain that hit me, my soul escaped an' I passed out. Who knows how long I were gone for, and when I did hear the sound of angels' voices calling, I came to the bittersweet conclusion that I were dead.

I drifted in an' out until I thought, 'Hang on a sec, I'm breathing.' My fire were still crackling an' also it seemed to me that the angelic voices were coming out of the filigree iron grill, which were a highly unusual port of entry for the heavenly host. Still, all things is possible. But when one of them said, "Shut up," it seemed encouraging. 'Gods sake, it's kids down there!' I been so excited I's got up, which were wincing painful, an' shuffling over to the grill I called, "Wait, wait, please don't go," creating a great scuffling an' crawling in the basement below.

"Where are ya?"

"Up here," I says, an' pulling the lamp off the table I shone its beam down the grill.

"Gotcha," a voice called up the stack. "Weren't there a ladder back there somewhere?"

While they's gone to fetch the ladder, I grabbed some old coins off the mantlepiece an' tried with trembling, fumbling fingers to unwind the screws that held the grill in place. While two come out easily enough, I struggled with the third until it began to shift an' turn at last. "Look out," they says, an' pivoting the grill around on the fourth screw, we's opened a space large enough for five big kids, two of them identicals, to crawl through. "Respect," I says, "I'm Hope Nil by Mouth. An' who are you?"

Column de Fer

I don't know what we was expecting exactly but not Hope, an' we met him in silence, for he were an emaciated shaven-headed spectre, an' the sight of him been so awful shocking. There were no resemblance to the little kid we once knew, except perhaps his cinnamon eyes, which was bright as a lion's an' how I remember them.

"Hi, I'm Column," I recovered an' introduced myself.

"Column?" He gave me a really quirky look. "I can tell you ain't by the timbre of your voice. You is the weather fairy."

" Huh, really?" I says. "You get our show here?"

"You bet I do. Makes me laugh an' reminds me how to talk. I's honoured you celebs is visiting me."

The twins hid their smiles. "The honours all ours. We're Harley and Tyler. And your name ain't Nil by Mouth, it's Hope Miscellaneous."

"Hope Miscellaneous... I love it! Got a ring to it, like a DJ. Random bit of uselessness, total appropriate, very me." Hope gave us a pitiful lopsided grin.

"I'm Ariel, an' with respect you don't look that well. Perhaps we could sit on your bed an' parley a bit?"

"I'm okay. Had some minor surgery on my back, that's all," he replied lightly, pulling his heavy bed-curtains aside an' shoving his plastic bubble out of the way. But when he climbed into bed we seen the back of his shirt were blood-stained.

"Ah," said Phoebe giving him a big hug. Then finding him a fresh shirt, she said, "Here you go, let me help you get this one on." Gees, when he took off his shirt I been very hard-pressed to see what kept Hope alive.

215

"Get comfortable, relax a bit," said Ariel, plumping up his pillows, "while I try something." For a moment he looked overwhelmed. He'd been alone a long long time.

Ariel worked on his back an' parlarying gently to an' fro, we told him how everybody been searching for him up an' down, an' how his Mum had never ever given up on the idea he were still alive. But when we suggested we'd like to get him home to her, he said, "I can't come just now, you see," indicating his plastic bubble an' the myriad of drips. "Maybe soon as I'm drug free. I has stitches in my back an' of course there's my skin. Terrible raw, but it's improving with Morgan's skin cream."

"That won't be a problem," says Tyler. "Ariel's Dad is the finest doctor in the world."

"A lab rat," Hope replied thoughtfully, "is likely to perish, for they forgets who they is, but I always clung to the notion that I is a boy who has purposes an' reasons to be. Ain't no question that I has a job to do here, an' cannot come home till it's been done."

"What sort of job?" I asked him.

"S'pect I'll know when it comes along. It's a calling, a sense-of-destiny thing."

I never met a ten-year-old with a vocation afore, but he been so absolutely intentional it seemed better to go with the flow an' not argue the point. "That's okay," said Phoebe, who must have felt the same, for she took his hand reassuringly. "Whenever you're ready kid, we'll help you."

"Thanks a lot," he replied, relieved, an' after a quiet pause, he added, "There is something you could help me with right now. See, it's Sunday night an' the place is deserted. Please, I've been wanting to do it for ages."

"Of course, sure, anything," Phoebe volunteered us.

"Well I'll be, don't I feel a whole lot better? I am healed, it's a miracle, halleluiah, praise the Lawd!" Hope jumped out of bed, an' flinging his skin-an-bone arms around Ariel, he asked, "How did you do that?"

" Ah well now, she has healing hands. It's inherited magic, runs in her family," Harley explained. Hope's eyes opened wide then, an' touching Ariel gently, he murmured, " Wow, how deep is that?"

"Where are we going?" asked Tyler.

"Well first," said Hope reaching into a box by his bedside an' pulling out a whole pile of surgical gloves, "put these on, to avoid finger print issues. Coming?" An' following him through a comfortable sitting room, we went into a beautiful circular library.

"Oh my God." Ariel were over the moon. "Look at all these books!"

"These books," Hope beamed at Ariel, his goddess, "have been good friends to me. Everything I know comes out of them."

"What, you've read all of these?" Tyler asked him, amazed.

"No man, is you bonkers? First, I had to crack the code that A is for Alpha, and so on. Then I read a few."

"You done that all by your self?" Hope nodded modestly. "I could never do that. You is really something, Hope," Phoebe told him.

" Come on," he said, an' making for the walkway, we started at the bottom by the books on the Big Bang theory an' spiralling up the library, passed early man slugging it out with the dinosaurs an' the ice ages. Then we moved through mythological times into ancient history, Chaldea, Mesopotamia, Egypt, Greece and Rome, which took us neatly to religion an' then, circling around the top shelves with God, we arrived at a little Gothic door an' went out into Projack. "Follow me, follow me, follow me," Hope chirruped, hobbling along in his bare feet.

Opening all the doors an' windows on the way, Hope lead us up to Animal Research (Level Two), where together we opened the cages an' released all the animals, who did not have to be told twice afore they made for fresh air an' freedom. I don't know who were more relieved or grateful, once they all was gone an' we'd got the cages locked behind them.

Mistral (the Akashic Record, Nicky Nigredo)

ain't out the 'You EARNS yourself a heart of gold' stable. I believes everybody already do got one, they just takes it or leaves it, is all. Well, some with hearts more murky turbid, then the skies above was settled beneath the great glass dome of Projack's atrium an' taking their coffees in the Palm Court canteen. Serene it were not, though, for Mason an' Turkish been displaying all the classic symptoms of the attention deficit disorders, lapsing in-an-out of concentration, rooted, riveted an' flabbergasted by Nicky's brand new ears. Which been an' improvement, even if – did he know, did he know, did he know? – the ears been sewn on upside-down.

All about them The Projack machine were abuzz with acute consternations at all them locked an' empty cages, an' while smoke come curling up from the fat cigars that Turkish had extortionated off some poor critter, he were liberally splashing Smokey Old Peat into the coffee, it being a crisis situation.

"First an' entire batch of kids vanishes without a trace, gone, poof, into nowhere. Now the Animal Liberation Front has snitched the animals from under our very noses, and as of this morning half my staff are twiddling their thumbs an' out of a job. an' all with no signs of a break-in nor any finger prints to go by. What if anything are you going to do about it?" Nicky enquired, tolerably resigned, for he were not one to cry over spilt milk.

"Infiltrate and Eliminate," Mason suggested.

"Yes, but who?"

"Well the pineapple workers, of course." Mason's an' Nicky's jaw fell open. "Turkish you nonce, what is you on about?"

"They don't have finger prints sir, do they?"

"An seeing as only you know that, how likely is it, I ask you, that the ALF is actually a couple of elderly pineapples workers down in Canning Town?"

"Ahem gentlemen," Nicky broke in, ever so diplomatic. "Whoever they are, we can't afford to have them breaking in and snooping around again. Not at the moment, not with our other project coming along so splendidly."

"I see," said Mason. "How about we offer a reward for information and post a few guards about the place?"

"We already have a reward out for the Deviations," Nicky pointed out. "Perhaps now the others have made their point they'll leave the place alone for a while," an' taking a sip of coffee, added, "This tastes delicious. Where's the whiskey from?"

"No idea, sir. Fell off the back of a wagon."

"Wherever it came from, Turkish, you've had quite enough of it," Mason growled.

"Would either of you be interested in coming along to see how well it's all progressing in Basement Two?" Nicky invited pleasantly, an' picking up their coffees they trooped off down the stairs. "Soon as the Russians come up with the control rods, we're in business, you know."

"Oh," Mason replied. "A law unto themselves them boyos, but I expect they'll be along eventually."

"I hope you don't mind my asking but I was just wondering," says Turkish, bursting with curiosity, "who's your cosmetic surgeon?"

"Not at all. Thank you, Turkish. I was beginning to think no-one had noticed. I went private as a matter of fact. But if you're considering getting your nose straightened out, Projack is brim-full of top people who could help you out,' Nicky offered, by ways of keeping things sweet till them control rods showed up. "On the house, of course."

Turkish ran one of his delicate fingers along the craggy ridge of his conk, remembering sadly, "Used to be aquiline like a Roman emperor. Been broken so many times I doubt there's much can be done about it."

"Not at all, go an' have a chat with Dr Fleming. He's our rhinoplasty man."

"It's a generous offer, I'll think on it," Turkish politely replied, not total over-the-moon ballistic enthusiastic 'bout having a upside-down nose installed.

Down an' down they gone, until arriving at Basement Two, Nicky paused for a moment's reverence before unlocking the doors to his lab, like he was opening the holy door of true love for the first time. How delightful alluring the ice-blue light, an' how soft its deadly hum… Nicky folded his paws together, prayer-like, an' purring inwardly, 'Whoever owns the Power is the Power,' he took them inside.

Tyler Blanch

Y ou never knows who's in the fog an' you never can tell what's in the shadows. You lives in the Big Smoke you watches your back, an' all the time you want to fly, but you's obliged to keep your wings well-pinioned. So any little bit of anarchy do go a long way and Big Smoke people is subversives, bolshie an' bloody-minded, an' the sudden influx of sorry lab creatures been treated as a personal victory an' greeted with overt delight. It were loaves an' fishes all round.

Forty or so Chimps been taken into people's homes, for they been too poorly for the great outdoors, an dear old, kind old, sweet old ladies sat in doorways fussing lovingly over nervous cats an' treating the Mantle to acerbic smiles. Our Ma also been particular keen to welcome a couple of crotchety dogs to our home, most of all because she always liked them. She justified it by saying dogs is sacred to the Zoroastrians and handily, our dad were up the east coast somewhere and unable to object.

Them animals did not look back. The tiny Ring-tailed Marmosets divided into groups an' settled in the canopy, the Spider Monkeys remained in one big troop, the white clone mice vanished an' blind rabbits been left to roam the vegetable patch in peace, an' it were all rewarding. Like Morgan said, "Pay attention to the natural world and it will certainly pay attention to you."

Harley Blanch

When our ancestors washed up in the Big Smoke they's invested in one Clipper an' began trading across the world. One Clipper led to another an' soon it were boom times all round. Now they is all long gone, cleared off by degrees, some maybe peeking over the shoulders of Grandma Tookie an' reading the Akashic, but most I expect has moved on up into the sunlight.

All that remains of the Cama & Company building is a green grass floor surrounded by massive walls that reach for the open sky, like a forest of Redwoods, and an archway with a time-blasted engraving of a Farahavar, the winged symbol of duality which belong to the Zoroastrians. An' us, of course. Mara Blanch & Sons we remains. It is one of them quiet-as-the-grave an' rest-in-peace sort of places, a fine one for Tyler an' me to light a little fire in an' apply ourselves to "Paying Attention," like Morgan said. Weather-working were not a blind swipe thing. It could be done, we had a key, for what Morgan said had been confirmed by Hope knowing Column by the timbre of his voice, despite it's multiple distortions.

Listening ain't all that far out there. It's kinda pleasing, as sound do have a friendly tone, all full of familiar voices. How you listens do count for a lot, an' with the damping down of our own grey noise, we been able to divine three very distinguishable qualities within the multitude of random sounds.

Our first come from the natural world, whose sounds is of a assuring continuity, like the blackbird's song that do seem to say there's always been a blackbird singing, an' the voice of the river that do seem to suggest it will be flowing forever.

Our second came from the world of people, whose scattering

footsteps speak of their bearing on the earth, an' whose voice is of communication.

Our third come from the world of machines, whose sounds is all groaning, moaning, grumbling or shrieking out in constant complaint about the burden of service they's pressed into.

There were nothing more to be heard. It were suddenly so acutely quiet, an' the silence were so alive an' overwhelming, I wondered who exactly were listening back? an' I been so uneasy I got close to the fire for its warmth an' protection, when Tyler opened his eyes wide an' whispered, "Bim Saladin, Abracadabra an' Alcasan... Now we has caught each other's attention, ain't no harm in trying whisper up a gentle wind."

Canada Blanch (the East Coast)

The wind picked up an' come scudding over the waves like a blind man on a crazy horse. It drew to a halt, pawed at the waves for a moment, churning up the spume, then slammed through the rigging, causing us to duck smartly as the sails swung about, click clack, before it bolted off westward ho over the wide horizon to round up the buffalo. Least I had a feeling that were not the end of it, more like the beginning.

I don't suggest that the weather is a personal friend. We both has our agendas, but it had been good so far, our progress been stately but it were progress, an' the trawl up the East Coast been more a cruise than a flit, a easy number, with ideal conditions for them like Abby who was keen to learn how to handle a boat. Naturally with Liberty on board, my dirty old luger begun to smell like a regular floating perfume palace, but then it were shipshape for the first time in a long time an' the food were sensational. She were also extra mindful of Riley, who were lost to grief an' fixed his baby onto his front with a sling, for he didn't like to let go of her.

That freak wind had shook things up a little. The babies was caterwauling in the hold and Liberty chundering overboard, an' who could blame her. An' if things weren't exciting enough, Albin an' Tobin our gunners, who been hand-line fishing, suddenly sprung into action an' trained their guns upon the water. In my innocence I's assumed they'd caught a shark, but no, there were a boat drifting towards us, hosting a crowd of beady-eyed gulls an' steely-beaked Frigate Birds perched along its gunwales, which turned out to be full of herbs with a individual of unknown origins moaning inside it.

"Bon voyage," I sent the wildfowl packing with a boat hook. Then grabbing his boat, I said, "I'm Canada Blanch, an' who are you?"

"John Dory," the body mumbled back. "'Course you are," I says, releasing his boat again, "an back into the water you go."

"Wait… My name is Serco Tagging. Now go ahead an' shoot me, I could always use a few more bullet holes," he says, looking awful vulnerable an' astonishingly dark all at the same time. Then putting up his bandaged fists, he says, "I surrender," an' his eyes slipped heavenwards as he passed out cold.

"Pretty lippy for a stiff, ain't he?" guffawed Albin an' Tobin.

I imagined from the unmistakable funeral look of his vessel that this clone been embalmed in mint an' cast away to take his chances for some reason, an' I very much hoped we was not gonna regret hauling Serco Tagging aboard.

While our backs was turned, the clouds had been sneakily gathering up, an' way out on the dark horizon the menacing sky were drawing low enough over the ocean to form a twister. "What is you playing at?" I asked the wind. "This late in the year, it's beyond out-of-order, you know," an' perhaps if there weren't babies an' what-not on board, I might have gone storm chasing, but oh well there it were, a captain is never laissez-faire with his crew.

"Albin, stay with the guns, Tobin take the wheel. Abby," I hollered down the hatch, "help me reef the mainsail. We gotta put in an' toutey suitey."

"Aye aye Captain," she called back, an' hushing up the mewling offspring she parked him on Riley an' come to join the mammoth struggle of furling up the straining carmine sail. Tobin, a man with nerves of steel, ran before the wind toward the harbour of Psycho Charlottes Beach. We lowered our sails just as the Harbour Master raised the grilled portcullis, an' we was in an' docked behind the iron-clad wall, super, with no less then two tornados bringing up the rear.

Serco Tagging (age 29)

I don't know how I came to be adrift on the wide ocean, but it felt as though the land had shed me and the life I'd known had discarded me, much as an old snakeskin rids itself of the snake.

I was in the hands of others now, and things could be worse. I came round on a camp bed in the hold. My clothes were drying out by an iron stove and a high wind howled overhead, but my pain, which ought to have been raging too, was dulled by an overwhelming urge to hug the women who was thoughtfully reading some instructions written along my plaster cast.

"'3 bullet wounds. Check regularly for infection. Shattered bones + torn ligaments. Do not remove splints until fully healed/6 weeks approx. Top pocket. Colloidal Silver for infection + Morphine for pain…' Hm, been in the wars." She seemed concerned, and dosing me up with morphine she saw to my wounds and redressed them thoroughly. "Respect," I said, rather lamely for a man who'd fallen in love for the first time.

"How do, I'm Liberty," she returned, floating in an' out of focus. "I am without skin," I told her, sliding into the disturbingly dark fields of a morphine sleep.

"You'll grow a new one, trust me. I'm a retrieving-bodies-out-of-the-ocean specialist." She seemed confident I would, as she graciously stretched herself out alongside me with the laidback maternal languor of a grown-up women. Which was a reassuring gesture an' helpful by way of banishing the rigor mortis from my limbs.

When I awoke again, she had gone and the storm was blowing itself out. Feeling somewhat recovered, I ventured over to the mirror an' sat down gingerly on my shot behind. 'This ain't right… Perhaps it's the morphine,' I thought, staring at the reflection in front of me. The Racoon of Doom came to mind, the eyes were so muddied and the hair short, and raising a bandaged hand to touch my head, I had to accept that it was my hair, my hair that never had been cut before, as spiky as a hedgepig. It was dumbfounding. 'And who are you now, so very humbled and starkly denuded?' I sat stunned and, I'll own, on the verge of tears. 'Nothing and nobody at all,' was the obvious reply. But not quite, for the stranger who had treated my injuries to a fiery and meticulous healing had left his handprints edged lightly across my chest, with a meticulousness moreover that my own hands had once paralleled so coldly with death. I who never was intended for love appeared nonetheless to have gained it.

Abby

The twisters hit land due north of Psycho Charlottes before we had time to disembark, an' in twenty-five nerve-wracking seconds, while we was quaking in our boots on a seesaw boat, they's removed all the tin roofs an' made off with all the stacks of new-cut timber. Apart from that the place was more or less intact an' the dispersing ragged clouds revealed a distant moon with a silver ring around her.

"Mind if I join you?" Serco Tagging asked, an' coming out on deck an' checking the stars, he said, "Three-fifteen a.m. and people are still around?"

"Well you see, you got the morphine while we got the storm. No peace for the wicked," Liberty explained, making a space for him to sit beside her. "My dad could do that."

"What's that?" asked Riley.

"Tell the time by the movement of the planets an' the constellations. He spent a lifetime making clocks an' setting his times by them. Then just before he died, he said, 'Cripes, better late than never. Been staring me in the face all along. Our lives aren't guided by the stars at all, it's us and what we do that moves the stars and sets them into motion!"

"Really?" said Canada. "He weren't the only one to come to that conclusion. My old mother-in-law believed much the same, an' just before she died she were very keen for my boys to understand that everything they do gets written in the stars."

"I like that idea," Riley said, hugging his tiny daughter to him. "I like it a lot. Her mother was called Lucy, I think it means light. Are there any names that mean Star?"

"Oh sure," said Canada. "My wife's called Mara, which mean star of the sea."

"Then there's Maria, Hester, Esther, Estelle, Astra, Stella, Celine.." Serco reeled off unexpectedly.

"Stop right there," interrupted Riley. "How'd you like to be called Celine," he asked his child. "Sounds full of promise, don't it? See if you don't set a few things in motion on your way through life, eh?" And everyone agreed that Celine was a very fine name indeed. Except Canada, who disappeared into the wheelhouse, saying "Sure you wouldn't rather call her Psycho Charlotte?" an' reappeared waving a bottle. "Now this 'ere is Smoky Old Peat, an' a remarkable fine whiskey for to wet a baby's head."

"Here's to Celine!"

The last thing I remember was curling up to sleep beside my baby an' watching Albin an' Tobin giving a plaid donkey jacket, a tinderbox an' a poacher's knife to Serco Tagging before he limped down the gangplank an' set off painfully along the towpath inland.

Booker (the Forest)

Our journey were a day-by-day procedure an' without no hindrance nor yet no sign of hostiles in pursuit, I slowed my pace to that of children, who were not to be hurried. But with the passing of each dignified mile, they walked a little further from their loads an' caution, an' brightening up a bit they become more like children oughta be, open an' inquisitive about the forest they was in.

This vast forest do have a Grimm's fairytale quality to it. Because of its reserved perpendicular hush, it seems to be listening to you. It is home to an array of wild creatures and sometimes a hideout for brigands, and it is very much bigger than you, so you are constantly reminded of who you really are an' the amount of damage it can cause you. But more then this, just as in any tale that's worth its salt, this forest can also hold you, provide for you, shelter, protect and watch over you.

"Hush up now for a just a second. Can you hear that?" I stood still an' asked, for it seemed to be suddenly awful quiet. "No bird song, no wind, no constant pattering of leaf-fall…in fact, no sound of nothing at all. Which means that every little thing has taken cover, and so should we. Come on, now is the time to hurry."

There were at least three old railway tunnels in the area, an' I made for the closest one. I'd been afraid it might have been a home for Timber Wolves or Coyotes, but it were not. Instead, to my great delight, my friend Tobias were there, in the company of an older man an' a young lady, who stood behind a crackling fire, pointing farmer rifles at us. "Tobias, I am so glad to see you!" I exclaimed, my heart lifting to see him, an' my ears warming to the unique line of his familiar patter.

"Oh man, thank heavens it's you. an' how do, you all?" He lowered his gun an' embraced me. "I were hoping beyond hope we'd hook up with you somehow, an' now here you is just like, er, just like a pied piper. You couldn't have shown up at a better time, Booker. The forest is spooking me out and I is experiencing a terrible unprecedented sense of foreboding."

"It's just the quiet afore a storm, Tobias."

"Yeah, that, bro," he said, "an something else, but I can't put my finger on it… Oh, have I forgotten my manners or what? These are my friends Marley an' Otto, her father." Marley lowered her crow gun, a relief all round, I can tell you, an' "Respect, it's good to meet you," I says. "A great deal of kindness an' some extraordinary timing has led us to you. Respect, it's good to meet you too. No meeting comes about by chance alone I think, but let me not forgot my manners either – Otto, Marley, Tobias, these here are my friends."

"How do, I'm Romola an' that's my kids Unity, Dale an' Joel over there…"

"How do," piped up Dale, an' casting a admiring eye over the vehicle that were parked some ways up the tunnel, he says, "Tell me, you didn't come all the ways up here on that?"

"What that? No way, you'd have to be crazy to ride in that thing. We come by way of seven-league boots an' a flying carpet," said Marley, with a cackle. The kids cracked up with her, which were a great ice-breaker an' about the best thing to hear in the oppressive gloom.

"Hi, good to meet you, we're Annie an' Fionn, an' our kids is Kieran an' Misty…"

"Respect. Tom an' Hanna, these are Nimh an' Hal…"

"How do Otto, pleased to meet you Marley. I'm Jamie an' this is Lara, our two Christiana an' Felix is over there…"

Otto were doing his politest best to remember all them names when Jai, a lad of perception, came to the rescue. "Don't worry Otto sir, it's a lot of people to take on all of a sudden. I'm Jai, an' these is my friends Willa, who don't talk, an' her brother Dylan, who talks an awful lot. We's on our tod, independents. Do you fancy helping us roasting up these coneys?"

"Thanks Jai, let's get to it. Now tell me who are all these dogs. Do they have names too?"

"Sure they do. The Deerhounds is Blue an' Lobo – they's the ones who supplies the Coney – an' the little one is Heinz…"

The youngsters unloaded their rucksacks an' bedrolls an' set about creating a comfy sleeping space for themselves, while Tom an' Jamie, both practical men, fetched in a good store of firewood. But there were some who was very young an' fragile, like Nimh, who were seven, an' his little brother Hal, who were only five, settled down with the dogs in the tunnel entrance, an' licked their lips while the Coneys slowly roasted. Romola sent her three to fetch water from the brook, and Fionn, who was fantastic imaginative when it come to turning anything into a meal, discovered that we was all out of fresh verdure. "Oh what a shame," "That's just awful," "What are we gonna do?" the kids sang out, delighted.

"Ain't that typical?" remarked Tobias, "No matter what kind of kid you has, or where you is or where you is from or even how hungry they may be, kids has enough vegetables issues as to keep a shrink in business over several lifetimes… Too bad!" he raised his voice. "We has in our possession one ton of rice, two of oat groats, flour for damper-bread an' enough homegrown squash of all shapes an' sizes to last for years, plus at least four huge cabbages an' a massive bag of super leeks."

"Are you kidding?"

"Nope, we's bought enough to feed the world."

"What a dote! What we can't do with all that ain't worth mentioning," said Fionn happily, rolling his sleeves up.

The wind catapulted weirdly about the treetops an' a flash of sheet-lighting lit up the forest gloom when a couple of Gitanes came tearing through the trees towards us, broadsiding their wagon to a halt (a manoeuvre I'd never seen afore). "Evening cobbers. Mind if we sit the storm out with yous?"

"Yeah, ok boys," replied Otto. Then jumping off the wagon, they hastily unhitched the ponies an' the mule they had in tow. "We heard something about *a massive bag of super mega leeks* from about ten miles orf. Seemed like too good an' opportunity to miss," they grinned.

"You're welcome, 'course," says Fionn. "Plenty of food to go round."

"Thank you, sir. Here you go, a keg of poteen for the quartermaster," and handing him a small wooden barrel, they led their animals away deep inside the tunnel.

We just about finished eating when the storm came roaring, whistling, crashing and shrieking over the forest, an' the forest collapsed before it like a house of cards: old trees, friends who had been standing over my paths for hundreds of years, was ripped up from their roots and tossed into the air like feathers.

"Things is getting rather existential out there, ain't they?" said Tobias, referring to the unquestionable quality of the eerie uncanny when not just one but two tornados were out an' about at the wrong time an' in the wrong place.

"Maybe so," Otto replied from his perch on the Shock an' Awe, "but ain't it the surprising and unpredictable things of life that make it so great an' worth living?"

"Here's to that," toasted the Gitanes.

Somehow or other during all that overwhelming noise, the youngest children had all dropped off to sleep, happy with a good meal inside them an' exhausted with the bravery of their long days walking. And for a while we played whist with Unity, Dale, Christiana, Kieran an' Jai, probably worse cheats than the Gitanes. The fire were fantastic smoky, the coffee were full of grounds, an' every now an' again the wind came blustering through the tunnel threatening to take our cards away, yet despite the unusual gambling conditions, at the final score I'd made the most tricks.

When all had become severely quiet, Marley an' I went outside, where we remained rooted at the sight of sky, because the wind had swept it quite clean an' there were about a million stars to see. A distant moon with a silvery ring around her rose over the trees that was left, and although I understands that Mother Nature's state of continuity relies upon the constant changes that she makes, I could not help but feel downhearted to see the forest so revealed in all its stunned an' uprooted trauma, painful sad as a elephant graveyard.

Slim Pickings (the Marsh)

ain't one to over-romanticize the event of an Unsustainable being born into one's midst. The arrival of me grandson Jules, for instance, come with love an' also a lot of confusion, guilt, blame, shame and fear. But as a scrap merchant, I can tell you that there ain't nothing that is unsustainable or without its place in this world, and that's why every broken piece is worth the salvage.

The time came when Mistral and I could no longer abide just hanging around an' waiting, an' when she pointed out, "How the heck's them poor critters ever gonna be able to find their ways through them miles an' miles of rushes? Ain't they the needles in the haystack that we has a duty to find an' fetch back here? Is I right, is I right or is I right?" we lost no time in packing up a Reed

Lighter, an' set off into the Fens on a search-an-rescue mission of our own.

Perhaps if you grows up in the Big Smoke with everything looming over you, you is going to find the wide open spaces overwhelming an' pretty nerve-wracking. Once you're acclimatised, though, you is going to like it very much an' come to realise that there is no better place to be about than here, here in the endless marshes in the late autumn.

The marshes is the only place I've ever been where you paddle all day an' it seems like you is still in the same place. But you is not, an' in the apparent motionlessness, you has become a hunter scanning the reeds for water deer or the overwintering ducks for the perfect one for supper. an' careful about keeping your tinderbox dry, for there's nothing like a fire in a soft fog at the end of the day.

After a full day's travelling we nudged our boat out into open water, and paddling beneath the row of Asian-style fishing-nets that hung suspended from the riverbank, we fetched up for the night with some fisher boys.

Teo, Ricky an' Fisk were all that remained of a small fishing hamlet that had faded an' gradually died out. The brothers eked a living from everything that come out the marches an' lived in cabins raised on stilts, surrounded by a network of duckboards, platforms, rope ladders and sling bridges. They had about a half dozen ring-necked fishing Cormorants, who stood on their posts like a row of pterodactyls, drying their wings in the last of the sunlight, and our approach were announced by the barking of their swimming dogs, Spaniels and Labradors, clever mutts whose job it were to carry the cast-nets floats in their mouths and swim the haul back to shore.

The drying racks were always full an' the smoke houses constantly on the go, for they sent their wares into the Big Smoke via Canada Blanch, who picked up their catch along the coast in exchange for whatever they fancied or needed. That's how all their windows got shining panes of glass, lined with good thick-weave curtains, an' a few coloured-glass lanterns glowed along the wooden piers with canvas hammocks slung beneath their porches, and why, in general their homes had come creeping out from under the mud and was beginning to look like a bower bird's nest, a place perhaps, that might one day attract a woman, one of the few things that was unavailable in the marshes.

They hailed us cheerily, an' just like me they were immediately protective of Mistral, because you knew she come with a price on her head, even if she kept mum about it. In return Mistral, who were entranced by their setup and not shy, give them her best toothy grin and says, "My words, I just love what you've done to the place, some fabulous residence you has out here an' no mucking about. Need a hand with scrubbing up the tatties and cleaning them mouthwatering crayfish?" An' over dinner she gone out of her way to cheer and entertain the Lonely Hearts Club.

The following morning Fisk, the youngest brother, showed us a thin river that run due south, and after making us promise to return on our way back, he waited an' watched us till we were out of sight.

We were on our own from then but had each other's company an' the foghorn boom of the bittern's call, an' occasionally we was both jump-startled by the squeaks, hissings an' piercing squeals of water rails. Mostly, though, we paddled in a time-warp, an' disturbed nothing until the water no longer rose and fell with the tides an' we was well beyond the boundaries of our local explorations.

There come an evening when the reeds glowed warm in the sunset, but the eastern horizon were covered with long dark storm-clouds. The droves of geese that usually came into land passed overhead instead, an' flew inland with a honking an' beating of their wings. Deciding by that we might be in a great deal of trouble, we made for a large wooded island, which turned out to be a lot further away than it first appeared.

It were practically dark by the time we hauled our boat onto the solid shore, an' finding a sheltered hollow near the top, we's pitched our camp, lit a fire, put the kettle on for chai an' then made haste to prepare the catch of the day.

The lip of the dell were the perfect spot to settle down, eat our deep-fried clams an' chips an' watch the mighty storm roll by. We only really caught the tail of it, which was quite enough, with back-to-back lightening flickering through the skies, rolling thunder an' a powerful wind that whirled through the dark reeds, upending a big old Willow right on top of our boat with a crash. "Right, that's it Slim," Mistral hollered over the noise. "We's shipwrecked, one hundred percent marooned in a typhoon. However's, in these extraordinary busy shipping-lanes, search-and-rescue is bound to be along shortly. More chai me dear, to calm the nerves?" she shouted, sharing out the last of the chai.

"We *is* the search-and-rescue, actually, an' it could be better but it could be a whole lot worse. Any rate, show's over, so unless you is planning on an all-nighter, let's get under cover for a bit of shuteye."

I woke in the cold light of a full moon with a wide ring of silver around it an' remained still, fully alert an' listening, for something were out in the reeds and stealing through them in our direction. The fire was almost out an' instinctively finding my knife, I covered the kid with me pelts. "Forget it, Slim," Mistral whispered. "They is many an' we is but a few." an' slipping her rough little hand into mine, we waited.

All skinny and wet-legged, the horses came out of the water an' striking the pebbles with glistening hooves, they shook out their manes and tails in the moonlight an' began to crop the grass. "Ten out of ten for scaring the living daylights out of us an' for the total romantic entrance, but boy, ain't I glad to see you all," says Mistral, jumping up to stroke them.

The storm'd pulled the chilly weather in behind it, an' the daylight showed us a marsh that was straightening out its ruffled feathers. We also seen that we come as close to the southerly edge as we dared go, for the line of forested hills that marked its borders were only a few miles on, an' setting out some lines for fishing, we salvaged the shipwreck an' made a raft out of it. And it were a luxurious comfort to have the Greene Keep herd for company, during them days we spent waiting for a sign of the fugitives.

Ryan (the Northern Territories)

The first seventeen days of our journey been one long battle of wills, for Grace, Tucker an' I was in the hands of the environment an' all that it did download on us. The raw wilderness of the Northern Territories done its best to block our way with rocks, wind, rain, fallen trees an' plagues of mosquitoes, an' all the way we was shadowed by a threadbare Wolverine who moved in on our game every time we shot something to eat. He dined on venison while we's settled for fish, fish, fish.

We kept to the tracks as best we could, an' followed rivers whose banks was temporary an' whose waters overwhelmed the forest in swiftly flowing muddy waters. The resistance were so formidable some souls may even have questioned the wisdom of pushing on, but we did not an' carried on, one step forward an' two steps back, until finally we was spat out on the shores of the Kyle of Sutherland, up by Bonar Bridge.

I could never have made that journey without Tucker, who met all obstacles with a good-humoured "Outta of my way or I may have to blow you up," an' Grace, who ignored danger, for she were fearless an' sure of herself. They was my brother an' sister an' friends, an' it felt good to be together in conversation, in silence an' in a fix. Man, we sat on our horses taking stock of the situation, which were that Bonar Bridge don't actually have a bridge to cross the great water, but it did have a tumbled-down church through which the loch been free to flow, and a small fleet of old Herring Bus that were moored up around it.

"Hello," a man hailed us off the boats. "Friend or foe?"

"Friend, excellent friends... Totally your absolute new best friends," called Gracie, which bought about a guffaw an' a "I'll be right over, my total amicus bonus meus."

"Wow." Tucker sucked in his breath when a man built like a Viking lowered himself into a tiny little round coracle an' began a slow an' perilous paddle towards us. A number of his mates stood on deck following his progress in doubtful silence, as indeed was we. He made it safely an' stepping carefully out of the coracle he announced, "Hi, I'm Brother Thomas. Thomas by name an' Thomas by nature, mind if I just check out the reality of you?" An' then, shaking hands vigorously with each of us in turn, he proclaimed us "Real enough, what a surprise. We've never seen anyone come out of the North before and bless you, bless you for just being here."

"More like bless you for just being here." Tucker removed his hat an' bestowing his quiet shy smile on Brother Thomas, he went on, "We ain't seen a soul for days an' days an' days."

"Nor have we my boy. Even so, some of the brothers are hell-bent on setting up shop here."

"More power to them," said Grace, looking about approvingly. "It's beautiful here an' it could be done. No doubt about it, this place do have potential," she concluded enthusiastically and with a dazzling smile. I guess it's just one of them things, when your brother an' sister both take a shine to the same man.

Our journey became a whole lot kinder then, for the Brothers took to us an' boarding our horses onto their fat boats, we headed down to the open ocean an' sailed across the choppy Moray Firth.

The next day found us anchored in the wide mouth of the Spey, an' a part of that dignified river do remain in my heart forever, the gentle sound of water rippling beneath our bows, the constant wind in our sails an' the easy companionship that arose between us an' the Brothers, and as we sailed a hundred miles or more inland, all down through the hush of the wilds toward the mountains. It been so perfect, I did wish it would last forever.

But of course we parted ways, for our route lay south through

Glen Feshie, the mountains and on into the Big Empty, while they's gone on to Loch Insh an' their monastery.

You ride through them mountains an' you ride into the past, the past our parents left behind, retracing a journey we once made long ago and a past that were barely buried an' still scars the land, an' it did not feel good. The Big Empty is just that and the further south we rode, the more we came across the remains of settlements where people once lived, farmed an' thrived. The towns was proper eerie with desertion, with empty streets all silted up an' overgrown that ran between the hollow shells of burned-out houses.

Sometimes we'd happen upon a ruin where some poor white trash had staked a claim. "Keep moving, Pikey vermin," they'd warn, harsh with hostility, an' train their shotguns on us until we was well gone. But there was some friendliness too along the way, and them with nothing that'd greet us with the weathered faces an' cracked tooth smiles of folks that's gathering no moss an' always moving on.

"Evening cobbers, is you hungry? Come an' join us, plenty in the pot for one an' all," an' nights of long good cheer, exchanges of news, ghost-story-telling over a couple of rounds of Smokey Old Peat an' perhaps a little music, when even the hardest of the hard would lighten up at the sight of Gracie's dancing.

Most the time my sister were clear an' held herself very straight to face the world. Then there were her dancing, which were the kind of thing that would have our dear old dad blushing an' shouting, "For gawd's sake Jezebel, stop that at once, where do you pick up that stuff?" But her body been made for it an' her style a unique blend of top-rocking, body-popping, dropping, dipping an' corkscrewing, in a routine that could include capoeira or something from the further reaches of flamenco, which she done all very controlled, very tight, very minimal. Some people may have found it alluring, but to me it were all just about being alive.

Grandma Tookie (the Akashic Record, Gracie, Tucker and Ryan)

O ne night Grace, Tucker and Ryan pitched up in an' old barn, and while they slept, winter stole down from the north and covered the hills with drifting snow. They awoke to a bleak dawn and struggling to fan up the flames of last night's fire, they finally got it going again, made some damper bread and a breakfast of last night's pork and beans. Then saddling up the horses and belting their sheepskins closely about them, they pulled their hats down and rode out into the beating snow.

The horses were nervous, for they had caught wind of something and went at good speed with their nostrils flared, their heads up and their tails pluming out behind them. After a good hour's hard riding they topped the moors, and out of the worst of the weather, Ryan, Grace and Tucker heaved a sigh of relief an' began to descend a long slow incline toward the coast and toward the lights of a small walled town they could just about make out in the distance.

"Here's to you, Lady Luck!" Tucker whooped and waved his hat to the sky, but turning around to return his whoop of good cheer, Grace caught sight of three marauders just topping the hill behind them on their quads. "Fly!" she yelled, "Ride for your lives!"

How could they have known that these were Clones, and to run from them is to be hunted down? The hail of bullets was immediate. Ryan caught a bullet in his shoulder but zigzagged on, galloping out of range, but Tucker exploded into death with the dynamite that was in his bag, and pulling her bolting horse to a halt, Grace slipped off his back and walked back towards the flames of the explosion.

The firing stopped and Grace knelt down in the burning snow but there was no trace of Tucker. She paused a moment, doffed her hat, and then walked on quietly towards the marauders. It was a wholly unexpected thing to do and truly baffled, they shifted uneasily on their quads but lowered their guns and warily watched her approach. "Respect," Gracie called, and raising her hands she stepped right up to them. "You has your choices," she said and stood on tiptoe.

"What?" they returned.

"This is your head, it is for you to think with," and she touched each one on the forehead. "And this is your heart," Grace pushed her hand inside their leathers, "it is for you to feel with. And these," she opened her hands palms upward, "these are your hands, they is for doing great deeds with. This is the human condition."

No hail of bullets followed Grace when she turned her back on them and rode away. The good people of Berwick opened wide their wrought-iron gates for Ryan and Gracie and took them in. The doctor there removed the bullet from Ryan's shoulder. They sent the only homing pigeon they had on the long flight back with the news of Tucker's death, and in time the local mason carved a stone to mark the spot where Tucker had fallen. "Tucker Woz Here," it read. Tucker woz here.

Kim, the Lone Woman
of Combat

For them's that have eyes to see, Solo were around, but discreetly woven into the Big Smoke's fabric. My home is like that too, an' its entrance by rooftop only. Still, Solo found it. Just one of them things. There he were, tapping on my door, an' when I pulled him inside, I seen that up front an' personal, he been blessed with refined blond looks, tawny eyes and ageless: in short, an' incredibly lucky guy.

"How do, Kim?" He smiled apologetically. "Sorry to break in on you like this, but I'm here to ask your help." \

"Okay, what's it about?"

"It's about Dorcas, who is not doing well. I'm not sure if she is going to survive. Someone fleet of foot needs to go up-country to find her partner Tobias and fetch him back. I am hoping this could be you. Only the very best of trackers will find him, for he is wayfaring with the man called Booker."

"Sure," I agreed immediately. "'Course I'll go for Tobias. No problem." This should be interesting, I thought, seeing as Booker were a mythological rumour around Chinatown whose actual existence were a whole piece of curious news to me.

"Thank you Kim. Just head northeast, an' keep safe."

Well ain't the Shaolin Tutorial fond of trotting out the old maxims like, "Know the man by the paths he walks"? Sounds great, very Zen an' all bull, but it assumes you can finds the paths he walks in the first place. The reality is, you is knowing all about yourself an' your tracking inadequacies, an' has a lot of questions to ask. What kind of man is it that passes unseen with an entire tourist party an' leaves no trace? How come paths that been so resistant to being found had opened up for him? There were mystery to the way he used the forest boundaries, an' when I did find them, his paths turned out to be so old they ran straight through a lot of trees, rivers, rocks and up all the impossible slopes that had appeared since they was first laid down. The paths also turned out to be the A-to-Z of ancient graveyards, for sooner or later they was bound to pass through some old pile of broken tombstones. "How about that?" I thought, realising I were following a man who used the Paths of the Dead. An' what kind of man is that? Well, one at least to take your hat off to, for a change.

While my route were silent an' dappled by autumn's flame, the rest of the Forest was restless with traffic, for an' unbelievable amount of folk were sneaking about in it. The Dark Elite Corps were loping along up ahead of me somewhere, an' the forest were rank with Hissy Boy tracking clones an' any number of privateers an' bounty-hunting independents, all eager to find them kids and claim a reward the Mantle had on offer. But so far off the reality of the scent was they that I were not inclined to delete a single one of them.

I almost did delete the three Nippon weavers when I happened upon them, lost an' on the verge of a nervous breakdown. "Hi Kimmy," they said tearfully, an' explained, that they'd headed for the hills after their recent ordeal in Chinatown. Plainly the young ladies were looking to enhance the Nippon reputation for suicidal tendencies, or alternatively perhaps they'd recently been released from Cranksville. At any rate, I stuck them under my protection until further notice, for their own good. They been lucky to survive this far, solely because of the weaving they wore that blended into the autumnal surroundings.

Tobias

The inner atmosphere were of an inexplicable foreboding, a feeling that I did not care to brush aside, for feelings has their reasons an' don't just come out of nowhere. The outer atmosphere was a very different place too, for the mad storm had made its changes. It bought the end of autumn an' the forest were going to ground. There were a great earthiness to it, smelling of damp an' sweet sap. Puddles of water collected in the hollow tree boles, mushrooms had pushed their heads above the fallen leaves, an' the colder air bought a rising mist between the trees.

I set off with Otto, Marley, Booker an' all, for I wanted to see them safe to the marshes, an' eight days on we came to a high escarpment that do mark the very end of the sheltering forest an' the beginning of the wide open fens. It were a view-an-a-half but peering down the plummeting distance of the cliff face, we also been afforded a breathtaking birds-eye view of the Dark Elite Corp, cleverly camouflaged amongst the reeds an' lacing up the entrance of the old marsh road, like poison in a drink.

It were disappointing, but after quietly withdrawing into the trees, I explained to Booker, "I once found a old railroad line, no more than six or seven miles east of here, I can't imagine that anyone knows about it. It leaves the forest between two hills an' then traverses the marsh, just below the waterline."

"All right! A second chance, let's go," Booker said, highly relieved. "Slowly now, no running. Keep as cool as you can, our lives depend on it." An' leaving the Dark Elite to overwinter with the birds, we headed east on eggshell footfalls, my underlying angst moving right along with me.

As if we weren't already quite wired enough, her appearance were exceptional dramatic, for she stepped out of nowhere right onto the path in front of us, an the sight of a China girl, in them baggy pants the Shaolin Tutorial favour with a cross-bow on her back, seemed to do it for Booker, for he became temporarily out-of-order. Meanwhile, very understandably, about every weapon we had was drawn an' aimed upon her. "Respect, you all," she said, an' clasping her hands together she gave a Buddhist bow, which bought Booker back to Earth, for removing his flying cap, he returned the bow and, giving her a very frank once over, said, " The Lone Woman of Combat, I presume?"

"Robin Hood and his Merry Men, I presume? Kim to my friends, an' by the way your paths are a total nightmare," Kim were replying when, "Hi, hi, hello," some of her charming friends materialized out of the woods too.

"Well hello, let me be the first to welcome you," Otto said enthusiastically, an' strolled over to greet them accompanied by the dogs, who was equally thrilled about the newcomers. Indeed, there followed a great deal of the intense introducing an' parlari that do happen when partisans collide, but "Excuse me," I's interrupted, "while it is lovely to have half of Chinatown for company, if we is to make the tracks by nightfall, best to walk and talk."

I was thinking how highly unlikely a chance encounter with Kim were, when she asked, "Which one of you is Tobias?"

"I am," I replied.

"Well now Tobias, I am the bearer of bad news. You an' I should walk together a while."

My heart sank. We waited while the others proceeded down the path. Then she said, "There ain't no way to soften the blow of the news I bring. Dorcas was tortured, probably water-boarded."

"What?" I whispered in disbelief.

"Brothers Sebastian and Dominic found her…" I felt myself going out, like a hurricane lamp in a fog. "Tell me she's alive," I asked, realising that Dorcas had been hovering in my mind for days, asking for help.

"Yes she is, but she's in a coma. Dorcas is with the Black Friars, and Gloria and Angelina is with her…" The Lone Women of Combat were kind in her telling but when we came to the railroad tracks an' she offered to accompany me home, "It's okay," I told her, "I have transport not too far away."

I don't remember saying farewell, for I were reeling with horror an' walked down the tracks into the well of the night. One days, two days, three days, four maybe, I don't know, but when the echo of my footsteps told me I were in the railroad tunnel again, I found the Shock an' Awe, curled up on it an' began to snarl an' howl, mad as rabid dog.

Not many creatures would have had the guts to come into that tunnel but one did, an' after laying a pair of heavy paws on me, the act of getting a fire together were a cumbersome task for him. He were very klutzy-clumsy with his flint, and once his tinder caught, he used his feet to manoeuvre the branches an' logs into place. Finally the fire flared up, an' checking him out through my teary fingers, I seen that my baying had attracted some sort of post-mortem vampire creature. He were harmless, though, for despite both of his hands being plastered up to the elbow, he were doing his very darndest best to set some water on for chai. "How do, that's kind of you." I pulled myself together and gave him a hand. "But what has happened to you?" I ventured.

"Love," he said. "I fell in love and nothing's been the same since."

"Wow, some relationship. She broke your arms and shot you in the butt?"

"Er nope, I fell in love after that happened," he grinned. "I'm John Dory, by the way." I almost laughed. "You is not, that's a type of fish. You has to think of something better."

"Thank you. Old habit. People in the sticks are more savvy than I reckoned on. Respect, I'm Serco Tagging. What's up with you anyway?" he enquired.

"I's Tobias an' thanks for the chai. What's up with me is that someone has gone tortured my partner and I has to get back to her."

Serco Tagging were taken aback by that and after a long while of quiet, he says, "You may be able to call her home, by talk, talk, talking to her… Sooner or later we have to put an end to all this, grab the wolf by the ears an' shake it down."

"I know son, I know. You is not alone with that idea."

There were enough provisions onboard the Shock an' Awe to help the man survive until his hands was mended. "Here," I said, gifting him my farmers rifle. "I won't be needing it. Stand back an' stay safe," an' ramming a couple of fizzballs into the ignition, I gone home.

Tucker

The pictures came slowly. They began with the blinding confusion of my end an' finished in the bright peacefulness of me beginning. To see my family an' friends so clear an' lovely vivid bring about this awesome longing to be with them. Same way as the living gets numbed out an' misses their dead, the dead too is missing the living so very much, an' I's very lonely amongst the stars.

"There now Tucker my dear, you are not alone and you are not without your folks. My name is Grandma Tookie. Come now, draw up a chair. Let me show how to read the stars."

'Reading, oh no,' thought I. 'Is there no escape?'

"You won't exactly have any trouble reading this. It's the real thing and an absolute blast."

"A blast, eh? You sure about that?" I were beginning to warm to Grandma Tookie.

"Check it out," she replied.

"I will, just give us a sec," I said, for it had all been a wrench an' shock, an' I weren't expecting this.

"I know," she read my thoughts. "On the other hand you must have been expecting some kind of afterlife or you'd never have landed up here."

"How come you seems to know me?" I wondered.

"Well you see Tucker, when people say, 'It's written in the stars,' it is. Not before it happens but *as* it happens. And because our families are all heading for the same place at the same time, they appear in the same chapters of the book known as The Akashic Record."

I drew up a chair and sat beside her then. "Ah, show me, show me how this works?" An' the old lady turned to the dark vellum vault of the sky. "Let us focus our attention on all those heading for Greene King Keep. See over there? Now that is Captain Canada, my erstwhile son-in-law, sailing his passengers to safety up the east coast... Oh yes, look. Follow my finger forty miles or so inland, and this is Booker, who has taken his group up through the forest unseen. And here's Kim, the iron-fist-in-a-velvet glove, who has fallen for Booker because of the paths he walks. I ask you."

"What happened to me. Was it clones?"

"I don't really know Tucker, but perhaps, for the doings of clones don't find their way here, because no stork has ever waited patiently to deliver them a soul, so they have no panorama to yield up in death. And I suppose that until they inhabit their own lives, they are not actually doing anything. However, nothing is written in stone up here, and once in a while a whole chapter lights up for them, such as this one over here, which is headed 'Serco Tagging'.

Well now Tucker, see this little island in the middle of the reeds? That there is your grandfather Slim Pickings, with the child Mistral, who is often leafing through the Akashic Record with her grubby little fingers. Do you know, I once caught her trying to rub her father out?" And there, I found Gracie an' Ryan, laying a stone which read, 'Tucker Woz Here'. "I still am! I still am, I always will be."

"Come away now Tucker, we'll get chucked out," said Grandma Tookie. "You're disturbing the other readers."

Mistral

And I woz here, with their grandfather Slim Pickings, an' knowing something he didn't, I hugged him tight an' says, "Slim, I loves ya utterly, an' is totally enraptured by this bonding exercise we is on."

"Well then," he replied, "that makes two of us." The horses pricked up their ears then an' started to leave, an' heading single file into the water, they's waited impatiently for us to join 'em. "Come on," says Slim, "they knows something we don't. On the raft, kid, we'll follow them."

We's punted after them horses, like forever, through the Big Green. Eventually they's all clambered onto a flooded old railway track by the edge of the marsh. Perhaps the sight of us two an' forty or fifty horses been unnerving for the fugis or something, for there weren't half a lot of shooters pointing in our direction. "Booker, it's me, Slim Pickings."

"Slim? Slim, jeez man!" They's embraced each other, stately and bear-like. "I thought the savages had come to slit our throats."

"Oi," I hissed at the Lone Women of Combat, "you can lower your bow now. Just ain't polite to shoot the search-and-rescue."

"Thanks for the tip, pond life," she hissed back.

Them first four days were lovely juvely, an easy sociable outward-bound event through Shangri La for the over-nineties, all blessed with the harmonious quacking of ducks, crispy winter days an' mystical starry nights to die for. The next twenty-four hours, howevers, seen us defining the exact nature of an exodus, ticking all the boxes admirably.

Some kids rode pillion, some was well at home on a horse, some was towed through the briny water on the raft, but we was all shivering beneath our pelts an' rig-welded to our mounts. We was so dog-tired an' flat-line exhausted, we kept drifting off to sleep, while them hearty mother- and father-figures tried cheerfully to keep us going with handfuls of horse food, or 'trail mix' as they called it, while stoically reminding each other, through their loudly castanetting teeth, that "The last few weeks been far better than all the years of furtive living in the Big Smoke, even if it is a bit nippy." Nippy? That were like understatement of the year, for the powers that be brung down the snow upon us – not your soft, fluffy, cotton, lacy, delicate snow we knows an' loves, but shed-loads of your hardcore stinging grapple snow. Never minds, eh? Bring it on, for an exodus wouldn't be nothing much at all unless a few of you's cark it along the way.

We gone northeast, with a north-easterly wind against us, until all them coloured lamps and Asian fishing nets come looming out the snow. And not a moment's too soon, for Marley gone a permanent shade of eggshell-blue with cold, an' our legs was so outta circulation we had to be prized off the ponies. "I see you made it back then, darlin."

"I done me best to see ya just one more time afore I popped me clogs." Fisk smiled, give me a hug and set me down by the Aga.

The thawing-out were right up there in the pain department. Everyone were mullered, huddled in front of the iron stoves reclaiming fingers and toes, inspecting the chaffs an' chillblains, draped with sheepskins an' rugs but coming alive an' very chuffed about being under a roof, an' by the unexpected design of the place. But for them three Nippon's soaking in the hot tub, it were the Wabi-Sabi that caught their attention and make it feel just like home for them.

It were the first place any of them ever been truly safe, and for some time the whiteout marsh lay astonished by the sound of the rising and falling of carefree conversations, a few snatches of song and the lovely smell of cooking.

I never ever did meet a single one of them kids afore, but I come through that battering bamboozling journey like a high-end socialite with a enviable list of real proper friends. We's all gone to crash out on a mountain of sheepskins in the warmth of the big round loft. Howevers, looking out the window, there were no mistaking that Booker were sitting steaming in the outdoors hot tub, without his flying cap, in the company of the Lone Women of Combat, surrounded by coloured lanterns with the snow whirling down around them, just totally enjoying one of them absolutely gorgeous romantic events that's all part of the exodus package…and an open invitation to yell out the window, "Oi Kim, now who's the pond life, eh?"

"Yeah, who is the pond life now?" All those kids – Unity, Dale, Joel, Christiana, Felix, Kieran, Misty, Nimh, Hal, Jai, Dylan an' even Willa, who don't talk – been ever so interested to know.

Romance were also in the air for Teo, Ricky an' Fisk. Golly, them poor fisherboys lay awake, hardly daring to breath lest they disturb the three Nippon girls who lay snuggled up against them.

I too been wide awake. The marsh were blanketed from end to end, but with their chances of survival being zilch, I knowed the Dark Elite was still out there waiting in ambush for us, for their kind follows orders even if it do mean freezing to death.

Mistral (the Akashic Record, the Dark Elite)

They was perishing in their freezing hidey-holes, but rather then dying lonely one by one, the Dark Elite came crawling out, and standing in a wide circle, they laid their arms across each other's shoulders, leaned forward towards one another and bent their heads close, so as to share their last remaining warmth and keep each other company as they slowly froze. They waits and waits, bowing to their fate until the snow which were carrying Gracie's words come flurrying by. "This is your heart, it is for you to feel with… This is your head, it is for you to think with… These is your hands, they is for you to do great deeds with…" There were no two ways about that. Them clones exchanged some sideways glances an' Loco Vance, their captain, finally said, "Heads up, lads. You heard, find some way to make a fire."

Most remained with Loco, a few shouldered their belongings and gone off singly into the hinterlands, and one or two gone slinking back to the Mantle. But wherever they did go, them clones was as individual now as the snowflakes that fell upon them… Which is the condition of man.

Liberty

Sailing toward my father came with its pensiveness, an' while there are many metaphors for life, the one I love best is waves. An ocean wave arises from the interplay of energy between the wind and the water. Like us, a wave has a life, an' a single wave travels from one shore across a whole wide ocean to another. They start out small but they grow, an' they draws energy to themselves. Some go calmly on their way, others become colossal power-houses and there are rogue waves too. They all has their adventures an' can easily deliver a boy to your feet or just as easily swallow you up. That all depends on the conditions, an' just like our physical bodies are in a process of constant renewal. A wave borrows the water through which it moves, until the time comes when it runs out of ocean, and at its journey's end, the energy of a wave is taken by the land.

We hove to under the great swell that rose an' fell along the sea defences where the wall was subtly overlapped, allowing the tides to flow freely in an' out of the marshes. Then, riding the tide between the walls, Canada took us through into wide white lands that lay beyond. The peace of the marsh was instant, its unique fragrance immediate.

How perfectly preserved lay Greene King Island, all safely sealed within a great liminal timelessness. Freezing fog wreathed the long lake, all but concealing the North, South, East and West watch-towers of the Keep, while Jean's great millwheel still steadily turned. Everything temporarily enchanted by the snow. "Wow" said Riley at my side. "Wow, this is something else." And then, with a "Stand by… All hands on deck… Brace yourselves… The captains word is Bible", Canada sounded the foghorn loud and long enough to make the mountains to lie down, or at least give us all a heart attack and startle every little duck for miles around. "I has to do that, I has no choice. Naval law," he shrugged.

"Hmm," I replied, "I bet. Just wait till I tell Mara you said that."

I stepped ashore an' into Sicily's gentle arms. "Lawd love you Liberty, welcome home. Angsty times, eh? Welcome you all, thank heavens you made it safe an' sound." She nodded somewhat tearfully to Abby an' Mica, an' to Riley an' Celine.

"'Course we made it safe an' sound. What's up with you?" asked Canada.

"Nothing, what counts is you's all here. Come on in afore we freeze to death."

I has some experience in building, but the restoration of Greene King Keep was amazing. The transformation were extraordinary an' the transformation were unbelievable. The honeystone walls had been softened by sandblasting, the floors were stripped and covered with long carpets of sea grass an' the dour old windows had been re-curtained, their sills overflowing with herbs an' house plants. "This is incredible, it's so friendly an' lovely an' warm."

"Thank you," Sicily replied modestly. "Once the army had finished, Slim an' I done it together, bit by bit." She stopped to blow her nose. "Slim an' Mistral is out there somewhere looking for any folks as may have made it through. They's been gone a long time an' it got so very bitter cold."

"Now don't you fret about them," said Canada reassuringly. "They'll make it, every single one of them, I promise."

"They'll be okay, you know. The Captain's always right," offered Abby with a kind smile.

"Thank you," said Sicily, wiping her eyes.

"Now you've gone an' set me off," said Riley, brushing the tears from his eyes. "Never mind, get a grip," he told himself, an' sniffed. "Look at this big old friendly place! You's done an amazing job round here," he said, popping an arm through Sicily's. "Could you show us about a bit?"

"Love to. Lets find somewhere to put the babies down an' sort you out some accommodation…"

I tiptoed along to the sitting room where the senior members of the household had conked out in front of a dying fire, ancient dainty Uncle Ollie snoring faintly with a tray of half-eaten breakfast beside him, while my father slept moulded into his favourite armchair, with a little pig moulded into his lap.

Dad looked amazing, not like the marsh had perfectly preserved him or anything, but rather that he'd finally reached an age to suit his noble bones. His dark-storm hair had turned a smoky blue roan, which made him look a whole lot less an unpredictable Poseidon and a more refined aristocrat, arty even. There were a softness to his edges, as though Slim had inadvertently sandblasted him along with the rest of the place, an' smoothed him down to reveal the more subtle grain that lay beneath. The castle and its keeper were at one. Although perhaps on closer inspection, he could have used a little moisturiser.

It were typical of Dad to have a pigling on his lap, for he loved the company of animals an' kept bees, chickens, a few cows an' salt-marsh sheep. When Jean arrived, his only redeeming feature had been that he came with horses. An' the boy Jules an' Dad both found their dignity in the company of horses, which is perhaps why Jules had left some behind for him.

"Hello Dad," I ventured quietly, trying not to disturb the piglet.

"Liberty?" He opened an eye.

"Yes," I said, an' leaned over to embrace him. "Beautiful baby, if I may say so." He looked down. "Isn't he just? Bites a bit I'm afraid, eh Hypo? I hardly dared to hope you might be coming. It's so good to see you Liberty, I've missed you so very much. Missed laughing with you and even missed fighting with you." He smiled widely and looked me up and down.

"So have I Dad, so have I."

I drew up a chair an' gave him the little packet from Column and Phoebe. "Oh, how very timely," he said, on seeing a little pair of dice, one of silver, one of gold. "Ollie and I have quite worn the corners off the old wooden ones. Did they really make these?"

"Oh yes absolutely, that's them all right," I said, wondering where they'd got the gold. "And here's a letter from Milo."

"Well bless my soul, how very thoughtful indeed. It says a lot about them. Perhaps they'll be allowed to make the journey up here, you know, before too long?"

The wave of Dad's life did not look about to break upon the shore. "They were very put out I came without them, but if I made it safely I'm sure that they could too, sometime."

"Well for the time being, I shall make the most of you being here. And may I just say how absolutely radiant you are in your old age."

"Huh!"

Riley

Greene King Keep gave me cause to hope that there was a life beyond my grief, for there is something heroic about a place that remains so total solid, within the instability of surroundings that is neither land nor sea, and I come to love it, particularly for holding its own against the odds, which seemed like a very fine an' hopeful thing to me.

I made up beds with Sicily, I learned to make pastry in the kitchen, I laid fires in the bedrooms an' I helped Liberty distributing her fantastic soaps and bubble bath in all the bathrooms, and a funny thing about her was she were still seasick even though we been on dry land for a good few days. But she been thoughtful enough to dig up an old CD for me. "Here you go," she said. "You need to hear this. It's called 'Lucy in the Sky with Diamonds'." I did, an' it been a mind-expanding thing.

I also got covered in grease with Abby, who were drawn to all things clock-and-lock like, and were buried away in a freezing dungeon, refining the mechanism of the Millwheel that powered the place. I manned up, and helped Canada to haul in brick after brick of turf, and I even gone hunting with Albin an' Tobin and bagged a couple of Water deer. Which been a revelation, 'cos once you realize you can provide food, you know you is okay and gonna be a good enough father.

Then I gone to the Library, and sat down for the first time in ever so long to ply my trade an' write a letter to my wife.

Dear Lucy,
    I were so lost without you, I didn't know where to begin, until I

called our daughter Celine after a star, a little link to your name that does mean light an' when I heard a song called 'Lucy in the Sky with Diamonds'. That's you, I thought – written right across the sky in stars, an' where you are for me forever, now…

"My word lad, you are blessed with a very fine hand," Lear remarked, peering over me shoulder.

"Tar, tar very much. I really like writing, it's the thing that I do best."

"I can see that. It's an uncommon trade."

"Me dad worked at the printing press, and I earned a living from traditional sign-writing (some forgeries), an' as local scribe penning letters for them's that couldn't."

"Well then, make yourself at home in the Library. How would you feel about penning a letter to my grandchildren for me?"

"Yeah, love to, any time." And then scratching his pet piglet fondly atween the ears, he said, "It isn't easy bringing up a baby girl on your own, you know. Liberty's mother just up and left one day…"

He were about to expand on that when we was very interrupted by a half-pint swamp-creature who come squelching along, saying, "Your honour, 'tis me. I's home and back from the frozen wastes, an' what's more, I's alive."

I were touched with how very pleased they was to see each other, and how tolerant he were of her clarty status. "So you are my dear, all safe and sound. We were beginning to worry about you… Now then, let me introduce you to Riley. I believe you two will get along splendidly. First of all, you speak the same argot, and then he's a writer and you're a reader. This is Mistral."

"Respect," she give me a toothy grin.

"High five," I smiled back at her.

"Oh 'ello, Hypo," she kissed the piglet an' gone on, "Come on guv, the others ain't that far behind… You'll never guess what, the horses come and helped out."

"My word, did they really? I rather wondered where they had got to…"

"Nah, put the bleeding shooter down. It ain't no way to welcome weary guests."

Otto

For a while, when we were trekking through the blizzard, my senses became numbed and muffled enough to allow a fleeting glimpse of the children as a band of knights from some really way-out-there order, snow-blurred kings of the road, in it together and up for the long campaign. The perception was brief, but it stayed with me.

The morning saw them rested and chivalrously sorting their mounts for the day according to the time honoured Stone, Paper, Scissors code. "Stone, paper, scissors, stone paper scissors, stone… All reet, Marley, you gets the big spotted horse again…" And things had happened in the night, for when we rode out, the Japanese weavers remained behind with Teo, Ricky and Fisk (the fisherman of no resistance). "Sure gonna miss them, like a hole in the head," the Lone Women of Combat dismissed them, but I would miss them. They were gentle souls and had been good company.

For so long Marley an' I had existed in our most reclusive of modest burrows, our friendly companionship like those living in a hard shell, but with the journeying came the slow uncurling of our spines and a lengthening and widening of our backs, until crawling into uprightness, we rode together side-by-side, splish splash through the freezing fog, no longer away from something but towards a life with a world of possibilities ahead.

In our common flight, I have made more friends than in all the sixty years of my life so far. I have become friends with the sun, with rain, high winds and freezing days, I have made friends with the unbearable fear at my back and the mighty overload upon my shoulders, and far from saving their lives, I am indebted to the children for saving mine an' I acknowledge them for that. Even if they do call me Auto.

Sicily

When they rode in off the marsh they was all in, well beyond normal levels of tiredness. They'd been living on will-power alone, an' without an ounce of strength to spare, they was very quiet an' self contained.

"Respect to you." It were not entirely obvious if Lear were speaking to the dogs or to them, but there were a warm dignity to his words. "What you have achieved is no mean feat in any way shape or form, but it's all over now. Come inside, please make yourselves at home."

The kids followed Mistral to the long apple store above the stables which they was to share, while Abby, Riley an' Liberty showed the parents to their rooms, and Lear took Otto an' Marley under his wing an' showed them to some rooms in the South Tower. Slim directed Booker and Kim, who seemed like a item, to a romantic room at the top of the East Tower, and I made friends with a relaxing individual called Romola, who turned out to be a hairdresser, alone with her three children. "Jeez," she said, eyeing the bed an' bright fire in her room, "this is about the most heavenly thing I've ever seen." The house were made for many people. It took them in with ease, and it felt right that way.

Some moved in but Canada moved out. "Just in case, darlin'," he explained, bolting for his boat, "some woman decides to stick me in a tub and hose me down." For a while every bathtub were overflowing with kids an' bubbles, scrubbing up or being de-loused with Borax which, to quote Marley, were "No dream ticket, but bye-bye lice, hello happiness." Romola an' Liberty gone to town on the hairstyling, plaiting up corn rolls, rolling up the rag wraps, shaving in the rails an' spiking up hair. Well, Big Smoke kids always was obsessed with their hair.

The late afternoon seen the winter marsh close in around us. The dogs slept with half an eye on the kitchen door, where Ollie were overwhelmed with helpers, and while Otto an' Romola played cribbage in the library, Booker an' Kim sat with the young uns by a roaring fire in the sitting room, all ever so busy cutting up cane, snipping up paper an' gluing it together. A minty clean Mistral, with four or five colourful wraps sticking out of her hair, looked up at me an' explained, "We's making lanterns, it's a Chinese thing. Once they's dried out, we's gonna put candles inside an' let them float away with all our wishes an' messages."

"That's a brilliant idea, mind if I join you? Don't I have a long list of suggestions to send skywards." And while we sat an' worked away together, the smell of slow-roast pork began to fill the house, an' one of those rare moments come along when everything were perfect an' how it oughta be.

Gloria's Litany (the Big Smoke)

L ife goes on out there/ timeless the tide rises an' falls/ the daylight comes/ another day goes by/ a lonely man/ leans his frame into the slanting rain/ on the foreshore/ the single women walks their loyal protecting dogs/ at night the Smokes/ come out to churn the steady river/ them bored stray kids/ burn out the worn-out buildings/ some keeps their heads/ above the water/ an' some do keep/ their heads well down/ some is successful/ an' some is on the way/ some is found/ an' then some is not/ an' all of it/ a world away from here/ the days pass by like everlasting evenings/ my mother lies/ quite still beside me now/ her breathing rises/ an' her breathing falls/ she sleeps serene/ her life poised in the invariable dusk. Amen.

My father returned from the outlands a determined man of many words, who sat by her bedside conversing with my Ma's shadow in a never-ending flow of talking blues that reached for her mind with memories, that sought to kindle her heart with love, that spun for her soul with lyricism an' tried to win her back with dreams they once had shared.

My sister Angelina were angry with the world, an' she blamed heaven for allowing this all to happen. "Come on, come on, come on now you archangels," she shouted, "where the heck is you when you's needed? Where has you gone, what is you doin', when is you coming to fix this thing for us?"

"In their own time, in their own way. And Angelina, you interact with angels through prayer and meditation, they aren't to be summoned by shouting," brave Brother Dominic advised.

"Oh excuse me." Angelina looked him fiercely in the eyes. "I did, it don't work. They's out of earshot, one's obliged to shout."

"You're quite right, heaven is a long way off. And I suppose you aren't the first to bellow at a unresponsive cosmos." Brother Sebastian intervened with some authority.

Most everyone we knowed came up to the Priory to speak their lifeline of words, trying to coax her back across the light years, but I were afraid my Ma liked her wings too much an' hovered nearby with her hands over her ears, waiting until our words was all dried up and we was ready to let her go.

Jean de Fer

The winter dawn came in by stealth, just one shy grey line that hovered on nights edge an' took its time to push the dark into day. The restless forge, banked down, kept one eye open an' flared an' hissed in its sleep, an' while my slumbering children lay safely wrapped in night-time's gravity, I slipped out to sit by the river for that quiet moment of idle time, afore ever a word gets spoken an' a whole new day begins.

I were ready for the new day when Milo came out with a plate of toast an' mug of chai for each of us an' sat down beside me. He didn't break the silence, nor did I, although I knew he had something worrisome on his mind, but he were one of those that liked to sort things for himself, an' he were fantastic fiercely if he reckoned you was interfering with his life.

I sat tight, until he offered me a slice of toast an' asked, "Are ya missing Mum?"

"Yes, a good deal, son. But then I has also been enjoying the quality time with you."

"Of course, yup, me an' all," he replied, an' retreated. We remained on hold a long, long time, drank our chai an' munched our toast. The sweet river flowed by, an' the seagulls came to polish off the crumbs between our toes, afore he asked, "Are you busy, Dad?"

"Eh?" I shrugged.

"Good, there's something I need your advice about."

"What's that then?" I replied evenly.

"Reet then." He steeled himself. "I ain't sure. See the thing is, I mean, well you knows how it is, ahem. Point is, I has been tending them sick kids the Black Friars is hiding, an' doing me best for Dorcas. I is all right at it, in fact I enjoys it a lot. I knows the blacksmith trade but my heart is with the medicine, an' I was thinking of taking the exams. What would you do if you was me?"

I didn't reply right away, for it's so important to be earnest with the eldest son. So I didn't say I'm awful glad you decided to give the blacksmithing a miss, but leaving a respectable time of furrowed-brow deliberating, I says, "Follow your heart son, I've always done that, it's the only way to be." But then, so as not to undermine his older brother status, I adds, "However, son, I still need you to take charge of the forge on those days when I is out on business."

Milo were not the hugging kind so I shook his hand, which all but disappeared within me grasp, just like his mother's. "Go ahead, son. You'll make a fine doctor."

"I hope so, Dad. Thanks… Also, I'll need a spot away from it all for studying. How about over the wagon room?"

"Yes, of course." I been afraid for a moment he'd meant farther afield. "That's a decent space but it'll need fixing it up."

"I know, I thought about it. I like them clean cubist lines an' them iron floors the Russians has, an' I like mirror an' long glass skylights. Perhaps a big black desk to study on, an' a platform bed."

"Sure you wouldn't rather study architecture?"

"Nope, I like a bit of style. I get's it from you, like that death-trap hand-car you and Tobias put together for example. I's gonna get Column to help out. Everything he makes is very stylish, he has a good eye."

"Well, he's an artist I suppose like…"

"Like Amber, your mum and our grandma who gone and vanished and we don't talk about?"

"She didn't vanish, she upped sticks an' left to pursue a career as an artist. The point is, I were your age an' been left with Reema to care for an' a forge to run. I were so angry with her, I let her go."

"An my point is, that Column is upping sticks an' pursuing a

271

career as an artist up his tunnel. You needs to include him more, or you'll be letting him go an' all, Dad," Milo said firmly.

"All right, I hear you. I'll bear that in mind. I'll be interested in what you two come up with. I can't talk for Liberty, but I expect she'll be pleased with your decision." And with Milo's wishes all come true at once, he been quite a light in the gloomy dawn.

"Yo Mr Happy, hallo Dad," Phoebe yawned. "Something we can share?" She emerged sleepy an' catlike from the Forge.

"Why yes, we has cold toast an' Milo's going to take his medicals."

"That's good, free drugs for all the family," said Column, staggering out behind Phoebe. "Boy," he said with a smile, "Love the alfresco breakfast thing. Nothing beats the enticing aroma of snow upon the air an' the prospect of catching pneumonia. Absolute magic." He looked about an' shivered a little, when a messenger bird came winging out the murk, stalled midflight an' settled onto Phoebe's outstretched hand. "Who's it from?" she asked.

"Lemme see, lemme see. Ahem, well now," said Column, unwinding the note, "It's from a mouse, in tiny, tiny writing. My darling, handsome, lovely Column, I is lost without you, I miss you soooo much an' I can't wait to be home cooking an' cleaning for you again," Column squeaked in a tiny, tiny voice.

"Thank you," I retrieved the note an' read, "Jean, everything's gone to plan. All live an' well. Lotsa new herbs. Love yous, miss yous. an' would you mind blasting out another room?"

"Sure, couldn't be more delighted," I said laughing, while my kids did stare at me like a row of dogs at a butcher's window. "In the meantime," I stared back, "could you two have a good long swim in the cool pool, wash your hair and put on some clean clothes, why not?" Total lost cause if ever there were one, for no matters how long they took in cleaning up an' studying what togs it was to be, they was still gonna finish up looking like a dogs dinner, but what the hell. "Off you go. Milo lad, we has everything to celebrate. Let's make some coffee an' pancakes for breakfast."

"And some bacon an' eggs. Is there any maple syrup? an' there'll be no need to blow the place up, you'll have my space very soon."

"Very true, if slightly disappointing…" An' while we was making breakfast an' they was floating about in the pool, I heard Phoebe remark to Column, "Reckon Mum's up the duff."

Eden

The only time I ever asked about Grandma Amber, my Ma said to me, "I've ceased to wonder why she abandoned us and I no longer speculate as to what became of her. She could've sent word, she could've come back anytime she wanted, but she didn't, you know." I never raised the subject again.

I first came across Grandma Amber when I were 'bout twelve an' surveying the Boonies from the top of a tall building. She were rather hard to miss, as she made her way across a rooftop garden some way below me. "Jeez," I thought, knowing her immediately for who she were, "how about that?" The missing Grandma were in a league of her own, a dramatic production, like Mum only a whole lot more Queen of the Outback.

Amber were wrapped in a winter kaftan of powder-blue an' her hair were wild an' tawny. Likely it didn't respond to combing, like mine, an' then when she settled herself into the cushions of a old steamer chair an' began covering herself with rugs, I sensed that she were unwell an' gone to see what if anything I could do about it.

"Hi. I's a medic. Not feeling too right, are we. Mind if I check you out?" I tried to sound professional. "Oh sure," come her laidback response. Well, her forehead were so burning up with fever she might have thought I were a hallucination, so I set about my work in the breezy offhanded way of doctors, so as to let her know I were a reality. "Got any vinegar, or mustard perhaps? How about some Belladonna?" to which she waved vaguely in the direction of the kitchen.

Inside, the place were ram-jam full of her artwork, an' while I prepared her remedies I had a jolly good nose around. Grandma's creativity were an accurate an' quirky mixed-media account of life on earth. There was pots depicting Aardwolves chasing their tails an' rows of Dockers marching around mugs, drawings of plants swallowing up buildings, befuddled Hissy Boys standing under moonbeam spotlights, shoeless gangs of empty-eyed Raggers an' burly Smokes on skimmers an' four or five lovely clay models of an angel perched on the shelves. But I been particularly drawn to some surreal family portraits, like a very little portrait of massive Volco bursting out onto the frame, an uncle Jean hurling meteors into outer space. My mum Reema, portrayed as Pierrot, was bearing a wheat-sheaf over her shoulder, an' Liberty the mermaid floated down the river on a scallop shell. There were a lot of art but what were really interesting about it were that whatever Amber chose to paint – clone, man or angel – she gave them all an equal humanity an' a equal dignity. Which made perfect sense to me.

I took my remedies an' went back outside, and I couldn't help thinking, 'Oh grandma, what great big clodhoppers you've got,' when I removed her socks an' put her feet in the mustard-bath to draw down the fever. Then I begun to cool her brow with the vinegar compress, rinsing it out an' replacing it every time it got tepid. After a while I washed off her feet an' stuck em back in her socks, an' pretty soon she give me a easy smile and dropped off to sleep.

Come the late afternoon a big old man appeared at the kitchen window an started shouting at me. "Hey, what the hell is you doing here?" 'Man' thought I, 'did Grandma Amber have a thing for the outsize fella or what?'" But I said, 'Keep it down," and put up my hands. "I's a medic. She's none too well."

The man came bowling over remarkable quick for someone built like a mammoth. "Bit small for a medic, inchya?" He loomed over me.

"Not particularly," I returned, not to be intimated.

"Why is you here, an' what's it got to do with you, lad?"

"My intentions are good, how about yours?" An' with the sincerest of man-to-man looks I been able to summon, I says, "We have a lady to take care of. She needs Belladonna every hour, if you knows where it is. Keep her cool with this compress, but don't let her get cold. Now let's get her inside."

He calmed down an' after checking me out one more time, he rumbled, "Ok boss, whatever you say. I's George by the way."

"How do. I's Eden." Then, picking up me grandma, he carried her inside an' tucked her into bed quite tenderly. Afterwards, a cup of chai and piece of cake brought about a truce. "How did you happen to find us?"

"Evading coyotes."

"Those stinkers come slinking into town along the old Piccadilly Line. Listen boy, you done good. Thanks for helping her out."

"No trouble, but with respect George, I'd better hit the road."

"Busy bird eh?"

"Yes, an' flighty. They say I is flighty, can you imagine!"

"That's no bad thing, take it as a compliment. It's everything that won't be stuffed in the box what makes life interesting." His face crinkled into a smile. "See you around then, kid."

That night, I woke up with a start. 'Oh my god, Big George is a clone! No wonder Grandma never came home.'

I kept Grandma well tucked-up my sleeve, while she enlisted me as sometime first-aider for clones, fugi's, itinerants, black-boy charcoal burners, thieves, vagabonds and all them forlorn outlaws who haunts the Boonies.

Over the years I may have become a passable medic but to my mind Ariel could be exceptional, an' I put it to my Dad, saying, "Ariel's the one with real possibilities. She ain't too young to go along to the Horse Hospital with you either. Don't let Ma baby her to death, give her a equal status to me."

He gave me a big hug then an' replied, "Eden, you are far more than a passable medic, you are you own man and a man of the people. But that's very generous of you an' I'll bear it in mind. Come now," he added, "You and I must go up to the Priory and work our considerable charms on Angelina and Gloria. I think Theatre Studies would do them a power of good…"

Gloria and Angelina was stranded in that big logjam that do exist between duty and recreation, an' were understandably relieved when we come to fetch 'em out of it, but I been so sad at the sight of Delilah, who'd got skinny with pining for Dorcas, she hadn't even touched the tempting selection of carrots, apples, onions, thistles, oats or even the hay the Black Friars an' Vatican Jack had bought to tempt her. "Buck up, we's taking you up to the Chelsea Physic, your favourite place," Gloria consoled her. "See if you don't feel better up there."

There were no question of harnessing her up, so we walked and led Delilah between us. "Seems ages since we last did any Theatre Studies," remarked Angelina.

"I know. Does any one have the foggiest idea why it is that when Faust signs his soul away, them creepy words 'Flyman' appear on his arm?" asked Gloria.

"Oh yes," said my Dad. "It is a warning from the Angel of Light against signing his soul away to Mephistopheles. Not 'Flyman' but 'Fly, man'. As in flee, run for your life, split this joint, remove yourself, buzz off, vamoose!"

"I see. Better explain that to the others, I mean they wrote 'Flyman' on their arms, you know." Gloria begun to laugh.

"They would, wouldn't they? But could someone just remind me who exactly is Mephistopheles when he's at home?" Angelina asked.

"Hang on," I said, "I know. Mephisto is the servant of the Fallen Angel."

"Alright, I see. And now he's Faust's servant for twenty-four years."

"That's the deal. It's a sell-out. Faust sold his soul for personal advancement."

"Are you all sitting comfortably? Now we'll begin…"

The History of the Damnable Life and Deserved Death of Dr John Faust (Part 3)

There was only one cloud in the perfect summer sky, and the cloud wherein the Dark Angel soared could not have been more of a blemish in a sky of light ham-blue, nor its racing shadow more of a stain on the golden fields below. The Dark Angel glided, open-winged in the billowing dampness, and looked down, a wet-winged sea-eagle, brooding over the magnificent curvature of the earth. "Hell," he proclaimed, "lies everywhere upon the earth, incomprehensible in its might, far-flung across the realms of space its glorious power, and Hell has no circumference."

"LOVE, you mean Love lies everywhere upon the earth." The Angel of Light settled beside him. "Love is incomprehensible in its might and love has no circumference."

"Boring, boring, boring. So banal and gauche, so mind-numbingly humdrum, so entirely predictable and irrationally pathetic. Love? No, I mean Hell. But come, let us see where now the fortunes of your Dr John Faustus and my Mephisto lie."

Gretchen, a radiant young girl, walked lightly down a dappled path, innocent as a forest flower and carefree as the sparkling brook she followed. The little town where she was headed lay muffled in a bank of fog and shadowed by a single cloud.

Faust and Mephisto sat drinking. The tavern was stale-aired and crammed with rowdy soldiers who, proudly patched and stitched, had hobbled home from war to celebrate their victory in a downpour of dedicated drinking and a constant round of crude ribaldry, while Mephisto entertained himself and them with cheap tricks, and teased them with base charms.

"Enough," said Faust, frustrated. "I have not sold my soul for this uncouth vulgarity." But catching sight of Gretchen through the filth-smeared window, the world stood still for Faust.

"Now show me your power, Mephisto my slave. Make me so dazzling and comely that she will fall in love with me, for I do desire this maiden above all things."

"Hellfire and brimstone," Mephisto cursed his luck. "Trust him to fall for Gretchen, who is so pure of heart. Great cunning must be used if I'm to sway her off the path. Come Faust, let us away."

Conducting Faust to the crooked house of a witch, Mephisto persuaded her to brew an elixir that would make Faust appear young and irresistibly handsome. Raising his glass to the brief vision of Gretchen he held, Faust downed the drink, and the illusion had barely taken hold before he hastened back to town with Mephisto, in search of Gretchen.

"Alone and unprotected, a child so fair?" said they. "Let us accompany you home…"

Gretchen (age 14)

"And I agreed, although until that moment I never felt myself to be alone or unprotected. But Faust stroked my hair and leading me gently by the hand, we walked along beside the little brook.

"How different and how strange those gentlemen seemed to me! One who made my heart feel glad, so did he shimmer and glitter with youthful vigour. But the other, silent as a prowling cat, I did not like at all, he was too dark an' caused my heart to shrink."

"Oh you shiver. Here, let me put my coat about you," Faust said to me. " How close he stood to wrap the coat about me, how warm his breath upon my face, how delicately his arms encircled me, and how confused I felt when we walked on together side-by-side.

When we came to my home, I thanked them for escorting me back and my dear mother invited them in for cake and tea, and while she delighted in Faust's company, I was amazed at the sweet quiet words he kept for me. I did not think to see them anymore, but from then on they often came to visit. Then my best friend Marta took to leering and flirting most persistently with Faust's friend. "Come 'ere, you old devil you," she would say, and I wondered what had come over her, and how she could not see the man was shady and reeked of fireworks, while his breath was vile and smelled of fish.

When my good brother returned from the war, he did not warm to our new friends. He was suspicious and resenting of them both, and straightway showed them to the door."

Banished from the house, Mephistopheles gave Faust a golden

necklace to send to Gretchen, saying "Thus Gretchen's love will be assured for you, if she wears this."

"Mean you Mephisto, bound together as with some golden wedding ring?"

"Faustus, you are a naïf. I mean, bound well beyond the powerful subtlety the witches brew affords you."

"Ten days later – yes, I begun to count the days – Faust sent me a necklace of gold. I was bemused, for it was a beguiling thing but not a fitting gift for me. Why had he not sent flowers? But Marta, bad Marta, encouraged me to try it on. 'After all,' she persisted, 'it is beautiful, and what harm could it do?'"

"Fly sweet child, fly away as fast as you can!" The Angel of Light did his best to warn, but the Dark Angel guided Marta's hands as she did firmly clasp it around Gretchen's neck.

"Faust gave me a sleeping draught to give to my mother, so that we might be alone together, and while my mother lay poisoned and dying in her sleep, he charmed and whispered to me to lay in love with him. But when the first birds began to call, he left and never did return again."

The Dark Angel drew the remnants of the night into the shadow of his wings, and clothed in silence, the Angel of Light opened his wings to release dawn to the skies.

Returning home in the early morn, Gretchen's brother challenged Faust as he was leaving. "What do you here? My sister is but fourteen! Put up your sword, man, so I may run you through and thus protect my sister's honour." But Faust, a man of middle-age and powerful with the witch's brew, ran his sword through Gretchen's brother and killed him in the duel.

"I sank with the weight of my mother's death, and lost in grief for my dead brother, I drifted through the long months, the weeks and days, until the lonely hour arrived when my babe was born. And I took her to the sparkling brook where first I'd walked with Faust. Lullay, lullay my little tiny child, I sang to her, there now my sweet baby, I said and I laid her down to rest forever. Sleep you now, here within the still waters of this pool, so you will know no shame, nor suffer the blame of being born to an unwed mother. Hushabye, lullay, I sang to her again…"

"That's enough, she's drowning her baby!" Tyler burst out. An' he were right, that were enough. We sat very quiet for a long moment. "Faust's gonna rot in hell for it." Harley wiped his eyes.

"That don't really make it okay though, does it?" Angelina put her arms around Harley an' Tyler's shoulders.

"In some stories he goes to Hell," Ma explained, "and in others Faust is redeemed by Gretchen's love and saved from Mephisto's grasp."

"I don't think redemption makes it okay either. We're talking about the suffering of an innocent girl."

"I agree with Milo about that. An' besides," Phoebe added, "Love's so banal, so gauche. We want justice! He has to burn slowly in hell forever."

"Er Reema, I fear there's something burning slowly in your kitchen."

"Oh no, our dinner! Thanks, Gloria." Ma got up and made for the kitchen.

"Hey, guess what? Our Mum's up the duff an' all," Column whispered. "What're you saying?" The tearful cast cheered up. "I knows. Extraordinary goings-on at their age…"

Captain Dan of The Wall

You stand on Hunstanton Cliffs and you is stepping into the long-lost shoes of all them many people who stood here once before. The water-levelled ruins of their little villages lie down along the low-tide mark, an' beyond that, the petrified remains of Noah's Woods spreads out to sea along the ocean floor. Their cow byres, fertile fields and flowers rest in peace beneath the swamps, and their quiet old ghosts are with me now, watching the long slow sun sink into the West to flood the Wash with fire.

Hunstanton represents the end of the road for us, save for a pylon bridge I do intend to built out of the Wash and into the Lincolnshire fens: a road to nowhere, but an open line to the Big Empty that lies beyond, just in case anyone should wish to enjoy the sunsets an' come to populate these parts again.

That evening a boat come out of the North, which were a highly unique event, for nothing not ever had come out the North before. But there it were, charting a course across the Wash, which in my experience is most liable to take you out to sea in more-or-less a straight line until the tide turns and brings you back again. Not this boat though, which hauled in her sails close to breaking-point, and drove across the current, dodging seals and lifting the keel to plane across them grounding bars. Youngsters, I decided, it had to be youngsters, daring the sea to try and stop 'em, and using the water like a bird in thermals.

A number of my men gathered beside me on the cliff path beside me, and when that boat come in an' hove to, thoroughly drenching the pier with spray, 'course, why not? We burst into spontaneous applause, an' they gave us a wave an' we gone to help them with the mooring up.

"Ain't had so much fun, since…since Tucker." The young lady's eyes began to cloud, but pulling it together she looked at me enquiringly an' asked, "Respect, but don't I know you. Is you Captain Dan, by some stroke of good luck?"

"Yes Mam, I is, an' at your service. An' who might you's be?" I returned.

"Well I's Grace an' this is Ryan. Most likely you'll remember our brother Jules. We come through here a long time ago."

"Jules, why yes, who could forget? All the horses grazing down the sea defences, they're all offspring of the ones he left behind." Their eyes opened wide at the amount of them, "Ain't our Jules a card," Ryan chuckled fondly. "We's exchanged ours for a boat in Berwick to get down here a bit faster. We come due to a severe weather warning we heard on the radio, to see if we couldn't help out somehow, but, but then we was attacked by marauders an' our brother got killed on the way."

"That's awful, I'm reet sorry to hear that. See now, we heard that warning too, and aim to do something about it an' all. Still, you might like to know, all of 'em is safe an' overwintering down at Greene King Keep."

Grace an' Ryan was very harrowed an' overshadowed by their brother's death, but to me their appearance was remarkable, an' as hopeful as a rainbow in the rain.

The next morning we set out for Greene King Keep, which were a couple of freezing days' ride down the coast. "Now Berwick, where 'bouts is that now?"

"On the borders. It's a fortified coastal settlement, real friendly, took us in and were very decent."

"And you say that between here and there lies Robin Hood Bay?"

"Yeah. It's all reet, bit of a pirate station. Lotsa booze, sheep an' fish." I questioned them greatly about their lives up North an been very interested by the long journey South they's had made, until we came by Greene King Keep, where their grandparents was waiting to take care of them.

Tucker and Grandma Tookie (the Akashic Record, Greene King Keep)

See now Tucker, if you want to follow them inside Greene King Keep, a prism is required, or you won't see anything at all, for the place is not exactly an open book. Many a traveller has passed it by. For one thing, the reeds around the lake are up to twelve foot high, and for another, it is liable to shroud itself in mist and simply disappear, poof, gone, like a gap year. But a prism will show it's still there, in all the colours of the rainbow, quite firmly rooted in the foundations of Old World civility, although not an old Norman Keep, as Lear believes, but an ancient brewery, with a millwheel for grinding grain and four tall towers for drying hops.

Greene King Keep has proved more powerful than all of the conquests, wars, famines, weather and whatnot put together, because it survived them all without its peacefulness ever really being shattered, and that's what makes it so awesome, and even slightly holy. It is a time-out house to heal the wounds of Gracie and Ryan, as well as one of the most ideal venues around to hatch a plan to save the world.

For one night only, the rare constellation of Captain Dan, Booker, the Lone Women of Combat and Canada Blanch sat around the same table, at which no less then three bottles of Smokey Old Peat was produced. "Ain't half bad, is it? Captain Dan, can't the army establish trading routes, tootie suitie? This stuff is moving at sky-rocket prices," asked Canada.

"All in good time. You wouldn't want to flood the market."

"Why not?"

The house became the isolated headquarters of the revolution, for when dinner was over, the children relieved Riley of his Ear Port and left with plans of their own, while everyone else remained around the table, explaining the situation in the Big Smoke to Captain Dan.

"The Mantle has linked up with Projack. God only knows what they is all up to, but no good, I should think."

"Well," said Liberty, "Morgan Grey is a customer of mine, an' he's a affable scholarly man who lives in a world of his own. However, he's left the running of Projack to his assistant, who's a terrifying piece of work. I should know, I had a showdown with him, and there's something about him that don't add up. The point is, I bet he's the one quietly orchestrating things behind the scenes."

"The Mantle has scaled down their protection rackets, extortion business an' enforcing 'law-an-order' where it suits them, in favour of human trafficking for Projack. They has to be getting something out of it."

"That's a very good point, Otto," said Romola. "Meanwhile, the gangs feel free to roam and some clients of mine, good hard-working people who pulled their lives together piece-by-piece, has simply disappeared."

"An more than anything though, Captain," Jamie explained, "the streets is paved with a ambiguous fear that's crippling, an' folks is feeling impotent an' helpless."

"But they aren't, the army is there to protect and support the people."

"Of course, Captain," said Riley, "but the army been gone for so long they's become vague in people's minds, an' no one knows who they can trust anymore."

"I see," sighed Captain Dan. "They should know that we are here to stand and fight beside them."

"Beware though, Captain. As Jamie suggests, there is something very dark at work. The Mantle has some creepy way of knowing what's going to happen. I don't understand how, but I believes it is related to a trail of mutilated bodies I's found floating in the underground. Every single one of them poor critters been the victims of a long slow death," said Booker. "I fear Dorcas was in their hands on account of our activities. Whatever we come to agree here tonight must remain within these walls. Not a single word until the time is right."

They were not the only ones conspiring together that night, for the children sat together, recording their histories on Riley's Ear Port.

"How about we start with Mistral?"

"Ah no," she declined. "It's me fate, destiny an' karma to remain under the radar. Just one whiff of me an' I's history. Total downer, but you goes ahead an' I'll think of some way to get it to the kids behind the radio show. They might like to know whose lives they saved."

"Ok, does I talk now? Ahem. We is alive an' extraordinary well, which is miraculous considering all what gone down. Tar, tar very much for what you done, your show's a lifeline, a knockout wonderment. We is reaching out a friendly handshake across the air waves, by sending you this in return. Sit tight, stay cool, be happy, here we goes now, one, two, three…"

"My name is Unity, I is the daughter of Romola the hairdresser. I is a fourteen-year-old an' me brothers is called Dale an' Shane. I were born in the Horse Hospital but after that I been hidden away, quiet as mouse, nobody knew about me…"

"My name is Kieran. I am thirteen. I has me sister Misty an' me Ma an' Pa, Marie an' Fionn .."

"I is Felix and I am ten year old…

"Well hi there, I is Jai. I's fourteen an' on me tod…"

"I is Dylan and is eight, and I speaks for me sister Willa…"

"My name is Nimh…"

"And I is Hal and I's with him…"

The night wore on, the council of war concluded, and having completed their recordings the youngsters trooped down to the kitchen in the early hours. "Oops," said Slim, looking up, "I'd completely forgotten about you lot."

"Never mind that now, hot chocolate all round then, is it?" offered Jai.

"Yes, thank you, don't mind if I do," said Abby.

"Hold your horses, what is you lot up to?" asked Riley.

"Huh, Riley, a suspicious mind is a terrible thing. But we still has all the Chinese lanterns we made, an' ain't it a perfect night to light them up an' send them off? What is we waiting for?"

"What indeed?" asked Lear.

There was a lantern for simply everybody, and with a smile from Captain Dan and a "On your marks, get ready, get set… Go!" the flickering red lanterns floated off on their long journey to the sky.

Phoebe de Fer

Our Ma were raised in the marshes, an' being at home with all things watery, she came back fresher an' with the afterglow of her long sea voyage upon her. She hugged us greatly an' when we all sat down for breakfast, she shared the baby news an' it were smiles all round.

"No kidding, a baby!" We drunk our chai an' tried to look surprised. "Well I'll be... Ain't that something?" "If it's a girl," Column said brightly, "we could call her Columbine."

"Or Libertine," Ma smiled, an' then giving Milo a long letter from Grandfather Lear to read, she told us how very touched he been by the little dice. "And by the way," she enquired, "I did rather wonder where you got the gold to make them."

"What gold?" Dad looked at me.

"Oh that, I can explain it," I said. "See, like, a while back I were trying to find out what kind of mix of metals would make an armour that glowed of itself, like the Angel of Light wears, an' I reckoned it could be meteor iron, mercury, tin an' some other stuff which I smelted down slowly, and lo, if it didn't come out pure gold, just like what the alchemists was trying to achieve. Anyways, here it is, see." I pulled the egg-sized nugget out of my pocket an' passed it round. "Don't get your hopes up. I did make it once, but I has not been able to make it again, which don't matter... Like Gretchen, I been disappointed to get gold."

"What are you talking about? Who's Gretchen?" Dad looked pretty exasperated.

"It's astonishing, why didn't you tell me?" asked Mum.

"I forgot. See, gold ain't the king after all. The other stuff I was trying to make is."

"Oh, I get you." Milo came to my rescue. "Still, it ain't nothing either."

"I guess not," I admitted.

"But," he said encouragingly, "I'm quite certain that if you keep at it, you'll come up with a formula for the Angel's armour."

"Thanks, Milo, I'm on it. Matter of fact, if we is all done here, I needs to go an' check out what I has this time around."

"No, no, totally. Go an' check right away, take as long as you want," my Dad said, messing up my hair. "What Angel's armour?" he asked as I was leaving.

Column de Fer

Our mother been the reluctant bearer of new instructions from Captain Dan. They was hush-hush, an' I been a bit surprised when Dad asked me to look them over with him.

I seen we had plans for two separate projects. "One's for some sort of bridge he's constructing. An' no pussyfooting about," I said, "but when you put all these bits together, this 'ere is some sort of ironclad boat."

"Shhh, so it is," Dad retorted, like a gun with a silencer, then taking a cautious look round, he began whispering rapidly, "Look, he means to rivet it together along here and here, an' weld it across the top. It's armour for a boat he already has."

"Well it's none too suave, awful rough, got all the style of a skip." I studied the distasteful drawings. "Improvements could be made, the whole thing needs streamlining, fewer pieces to rivet, an' it needs to lie a whole lot lower on the water for better manoeuvrability. I am thinking twin-engines. Dad, your hour has come: the fizz-ball engine comes of age."

Dad laughed, "Not at all, your hour has come. You're the draftsman around here. Draw up some new plans an' I'll, well, I'll put the kettle on."

I been quite high with the change in dynamics, an' went to it with all dynamos charged. Iron do have its benefits. For all its dead weight, there is a rock-an-roll to iron, it has purpose and an innate enthusiasm, which do lend itself very well to the rightful design, and when I was done, Dad looked at my drawings an' after scrutinising the dimensions an' carefully checking my maths, he said, "Captain Dan ain't gonna know himself by the time we're done an' dusted.

Helluva fine boat we has got here, great stingray shape. Gives it menace an' a touch of the dreadnought. You've sorted his bridge out as well, that's good. We'll get the apprentices to work on that and I'll get the cladding cast, quietly on the side like."

"What's that you're casting quietly on the side?" Phoebe asked as she reappeared.

"Spells," answered Dad empathetically, "sunny spells. How did your alchemy turn out this time around?"

"Almost but not quite," she replied. "It do not glow of itself, but it do reflect its surroundings truer then a mirror. Very space-age, light-weight, almost titanium tough."

"I'm reet sorry to hear that… But tell me, if we dip our iron cladding in it, would a boat be camouflaged into the surroundings?"

"Yeah Dad, practically invisibilized. An' I has a formula this time an' all."

"You is a genius, kid."

"I is aware of that, what I is not aware of is, what's Captain Dan want it for anyway?"

"Lumme if I knows." But Dad were not vague enough.

"Dad, you has been indulging in a lot of criminal activity recently, spiriting kids away, that secret Shock-and-Awe contraption, now this boat of mass destruction. What's more an' on top of it all, you has got our mum up the duff. Where will it all end, one wonders?"

"Good question. I often wonder the same meself."

Liberty de Fer

A forge is a forge an' war is a fact of life, but it ain't a backseat subject and does not come in half-measures or watered down by temperance, an' once sullied there is no washing your hands of it. Like love, war is a very full-on thing and the cause of more turn, turn, turning then anything else. Particularly if you is expecting.

But the Venus Man Trap is the Venus Man Trap, a bastion of peace, an' thank heavens I also came home with bundles of herbs, infused with all the subtleties of the landscape I'd grown up in.

The bright coloured soaps and hefty essential oils we delighted in producing so far were fun, if you likes an in-your-face statement for the brash and bold, or a sometime necessary defence against the Big Smoke's fug, but I'd decided to put together a whole new line for those who liked to get to know each other slowly, and them who enjoyed a anticipatory state of mind, an' those that can wait for a secret to be revealed.

Harley and Tyler

Our Papa returned, a man who once again just about made it off the high seas against all the odds an' in the face of some particularly trying circumstances, such as the mystery of the stiff in a skiff, an' a close encounter with a couple of rogue tornados. "Why? No way," we said. "This time of year, what the…?" Then the local weather got colder than the mesosphere. But though the journey been touch-an-go, fatally flawed even, from beginning to end, the whole baby crusade been safely delivered to the port of their destination, an' that were a total miracle.

Papa came home with a mega-earthenware jar-o'-honey, with its lid all sealed with beeswax, to sweeten Ma's life. An' informing us that a helluva winter were on its way, he said, "It's a ill wind, but you an' me, Mara, will be amongst them first romantics out dancing on the icy river," waggling his eyebrows up and down at her expectantly.

An' she responded, a sea of charm, "You bet, love. The very first, I can't wait. By the way, did you know that while you was away, all the poor animals were liberated out of Projack? An' one or two dogs has come to live with us." She done a great waggling-eyebrow routine back at him, an' opening the back door the dogs came in.

You didn't have to pay too much attention to catch their drift. 'Best behaviour, no barking, don't knock anything over, don't stare at their food, man's best friend.' They was a modest pair of black Schipperke, who was recovering well an' whose friendly fox's faces followed Ma's every move, an' gently wagged their tails of loving gratitude every time that she came by. "How do," said Papa. "You has been through the mill a bit." They responded with bowed heads. "These are boating dogs. What are you calling them?"

"Foxy and Bear."

"You could use them on your barges," says Dad. "They's fantastic guards an' good ratters. Some of these critters spend their whole lives on boats. We'll bring 'em along fine."

'He seems safe,' they thought. 'I had no idea we was boating dogs. How about that, eh?' And they curled up at Ma's feet.

"Boys, your Ma and I is going to see Tobias an' sit with Dorcas for a while. We could give you a lift to the forge." An' when our Ma were getting ready to leave, our Pa took us aside an' said, "I has an interesting something for you, too. This kid I met said to me, 'Captain I is sure that ifs you pass this on to them twins of yours, they is almost certainly, maybe, perhaps, gonna know just possibly exactly who is behind the radio show, an' who to pass it on to next. Nah if you don'ts, I is gonna know about it. Catch me drift, needs I say more?'"

"Boy kid, girl kid, what kid?" But Dad weren't telling. He just shrugged an' handed us a little Ear-Port disc.

Ariel Levet

O nce we understood what was in our hands, our next broadcast came together with a vibe of true professionalism. We downed a lot of chai an' coffee, and smoked a constant round of rolling baccy, but we knew what we were about and kept out hands firmly on the tiller. It took time an' it took patience to give the show the measured justice it were due.

On Christmas Eve we set out for the Winged Messenger Service, so very terrified of the random stop-an-searches our hearts pumped out a lurching cha cha cha all the way, but we got to the stairs with no mishaps, where once again Solo were waiting. "Respect," he greeted us, and "Respect" we returned. "Fly the birds, enjoy the snow, why not let me handle that for you." It were not a question, it were a demand, an' we handed our show over to him. He said  "Cool Yule" to us an' left. We traipsed on up to the pigeon loft, only to find the entire, twenty-four-seven, whatever-the-weather Winged Messenger Service on unanimous strike over flexing their wings in the first few flecks of falling snow.

Mistral (the Akashic Record, Yuletide)

Y uletide come in every colour, shape an' size. It come with Asbo herding a flock of geese down the empty snowy streets, it come with the lighting of sacred flames for Zarathustra an' the heating of rocks in the White Eagle Sweat Lodge, an' of course it come with the pealing of the Priory's silver bells, which is fine fine fine. People's free to believe what they likes. Howevers, the Mantle's heart were with all things Roman, an' they celebrated Saturnalia down the Bath House. Just like the Romans, they also gave the whole shebang the day off, an' the savvy proletariat been philosophical about that, considering what a

extraordinarily helluva ironical coincidence it was more-or-less the shortest day of the year.

With a jingle bells, jingle bells, the Mantle's finest come trotting down the street an' parked up at the Bath House. Theys alighted an' flowing through them swinging doors, they come to a full stop, stacked up ever so respectfully behind the boss.

Mason Flint only had two modes: one, deranged cruel scary psycho nutter, and the other, extreme sentimental scary nutter. An' being a total sucker for

Saturnalia, Mason were taking a moment to look at all the ever so lovely burning torches as filled the place with smoke an' festive flame, an' cast his misting eyes over the long table that twinkled in the polished candelabra light an' down the rows of glinting dark-red wine bottles an' piles of scrumptious grub. 'Ahhh,' he sighed, deeply moved. There were even a Christmas cracker for everyone. Then happy as Larry, happy as Sand-boy an' happy as a clam, he swept his long sable-trimmed mantle over his shoulder to 'Hail Mason!' an' sallied down the crumbling marble staircase.

Meanwhile, the rest of the empire were in the grip of a cooking marathon. Even the clones was giving it a go. Reema'd been slaving away over a hot stove since crack of dawn, while good old Linda Miscellaneous had four geese, well plucked and gutted, already roasting in the oven while the rest of the flock, by the ways, was counting their lucky stars an' sneaking out of Shad Thames, fast as they could. Liberty's Duck a L'Orange been well an' truly drowned in Grand Marnier, an' down in China Town, Peeking Ducky too were doing a roaring trade. Canada Blanch were advancing on the turkey with a blow torch, a speciality thing of his to brown it up, an' Vatican Jack, that skinny racing demon, had hurled himself into a creative frenzy, "to give all them Brothers a religious experience." Back in the Bath House the Mantle, all done with their ritual bathing an' feeling splendid close to godliness in cleanliness, took their seats, uncorked the wine, and pulled their crackers, pop, pop, pop.

Easy as one two three, the entire nation was off, the Yuletide feast were underway an' La Grande Bouffe were on, yum, yum. The aftermath, however's, left no man standing. Quite frankly the people were done in, an' sinking into one of them mother-of-all-slumps that only a decent cup of chai might remedy, they's stuck the kettles on an' up an' down the country, they's put their radios on...

298

The Yuletide Special

"Ding, dong, ding, the time now is three-o'-clock. Hello and welcome to the Yuletide Special! This broadcast is for you snowbound herders of the north, it is for you loggers on the icy rivers, it is for you trappers an' them forest wolves that's prowling at your doors. This to them excellent distillers of Smokey Old Peat an' for you fisherman on your one day off from the rolling seas, it is for you homesteaders in the heartlands and for you lonesome cobbers in the wilderness, you woodsmen, you teachers, you soldiers an' you lamplighters. It is for one an' for all, because no matter where you is, or who you are, fact is, we all come into this world the same way, an' no time better to celebrate this event than Yule. So come, why not join us now an' raise your glasses to the Big Smoke's longest serving midwife, Dorcas Vine. Sit back, chillax, and listen well…"

They's opened their broadcast with the bootleg recording they got of Soft Sloth, playing down at Jabba the Sluts the night afore Dorcas were nabbed. And the music faded into the unmistakable wail of a newborn baby announcing its arrival to a nation that was pulling up their chairs an' turning up the volume on their radios.

"…There you goes now, a very healthy girl. Ah look, she's settling down already, happy to be here at last." The baby were relegated to low-level background snuffling position, while the midwives talked together. "They says there used to be a new one born every minute, now they is so few an' far between. I knows that whatever's keeping Dorcas must be serious, she'd hate to miss a birth." "I heard that she's been interrogated…" "I heard someone chucked her in the river, an' her body washed up with the tide…" "Drowning a midwife, what kind of world is we bringing these poor babies into…?"

The Bath House were so still, nobody dared move a muscle except Mason Flint, who pulled off his party hat an' fixed his very cold grey eyes on Turkish and hissed, " You're about as useless as a two-legged squirrel. I thought you sent the assassin to take care of whoever's doing these bleeding broadcasts?"

"I did, an' I never set eyes on him again!"

"What?"

"I said I did, an' I –"

"Imbecile."

The show went on…

"My name is Unity. Me brothers an' I were born in the Horse Hospital an' I is fourteen-years-old. All me life been lived in darkness, hidden away in a cellar, quiet as a mouse, nobody knew about me. I do, read, write, sing, cook, think, sink an' swim just like anybody, just like you. I has a loving family an' there ain't nothing I don't know 'bout the Big Smoke, the waterlogged lanes at high tide, the Projack Building, the ferry boats, the docks and the Seven Dials. All mine to explore by night on me pony, so nobody'd see that I is paralysed down one side, a paraplegic, one of them revolting Deviations, property of the Mantle, a disposable kid, an' a perfect little guinea pig for the lab. Hey ho, I's out of there now, far away an' free."

"Hi, thank you all for what you's done for me, the safe house who took me on an' called me Jai. An' I want to thank thems that got me out of the Big Smoke, an' them that let me find my dignity on the road. My muscles is wasting with the DMD but I is high, due the friends I has now, who sees me as I am an' makes it all worth while. That's all I has to say."

"My name is Marley, I has the Downs. My Ma tried to shop me to the Mantle, me Dad and I went on the run…

"Hi, I'm Kieran, and my sister's called Misty. Say hello Misty." "Hello." "I have Noonan syndrome. Projack would like to fiddle with the genes, invade the heart, see what happens when they's rearrange a thing or two. But I'll be back one day and when I do, I'll rearrange them an' pick their bones, you'll see…"

"My name is Dylan, I is nine and me sister Willa is eleven. Watch out, be careful, don't talk to strangers, people go missing. They do, and where do they go? Our parents were gone one day an' it were fishy. "What's happened?" we wondered, an' "Where is you?" We waited many days but they did not come back. We gone in search of them an' looked all over, it were a lonely occupation an' we was afraid an' often spooked out by footsteps. Willa didn't talk no more an' we was loused up, freezing an' hungry when the safe house took us in. I want to know where is our mum and dad, but it don't look too good…"

"I'm Felix and I am ten years old. Have you ever heard of something called Asperger's Syndrome? That's what I have. I used to be afraid of the Mantle. Not all of them, of course, because I don't know all of them, but I was afraid of Flintstones and his second-in-command, Mr. Poisonous Turkish Delight. Asperger's means, No talking in public, don't say a word Felix, keep your mouth shut, eyes right Felix, or everyone will know… Not any more, though. I can talk as much as I like round here…"

"Yes an' no, Felix. I's his sister Christiana. Any idea what it's like pretending that your lovely annoying brother don't exist at all? Anyway, who's on next?"

"Me, my turn! I'm Nimh. I never seen a bird before, I never been waist-deep in the water on a horse, I never been in a forest, an' I like it. I never even met another kid afore, 'cept me brother Hal, who's five. You can live a long, long, long time with Cystic Fib but sometimes it'll floor you to the ground. It ain't half good to know what the wind feels like or to be cold in the pouring rain. I used to live in a water tower, but now that I got out I likes it what I see. It's great, ok? An' I am seven, goodbye."

"Many of the folk who put this show together were bought into the world by a midwife, who been waterboarded for information concerning the kids you has just been listening to. And that is the truth, the whole an' nothing but the truth."

The show concluded with Gloria's growly voice leading a litany she wrote. She sang one line, Angelina sang the next, then the Priory choir come in for the third one and it were a thing to break your heart…

"Life goes on out there/ timeless the tide rises an' falls/ the daylight comes/ another day goes by/ a lonely man/ leans his frame into the slanting rain/ on the foreshore/ the single women walks their loyal protecting dogs/ at night the Smokes/ come out to churn the steady river/ them bored stray kids/ burn out the worn-out buildings/ some keeps their heads/ above the water/ an' some do keep/ their heads well down/ some is successful/ an' some is on the way/ some is found/ an' then some is not/ an' all of it/ a world away from here/ the days pass by like everlasting evenings/ my mother lies/ quite still beside me now/ her breathing rises/ an' her breathing falls/ she sleeps serene/ her life poised in the invariable dusk. Amen."

Dorcas (the Akashic Record)

For one moment, a brief moment, I seen my family like they was at the wrong end of a telescope. Then the long landscape of my life spread out for me to walk through, an' it rolled up behind me as I passed. The Grim Reaper comes for every seed that's sown but the severance of his scythe is a loving thing that releases the spirit from the Mother Ship. 'I will not go far, Tobias, and I will always watch over you, Angelina and Gloria, my daughters…' An' I departed with the sound of their sweet singing in my ears.

Dr Cole Levet

The snow was a blessing, and there was a great quietness and beauty to the soft determination of its fall. The streets became impassable for snowdrifts and as the city sank beneath a pristine quilt, New Year's Day came and went unmarked.

Life lay in winter's suspension, the sleeping earth contracted and slowed its frozen breath to rest, and I let grief have its way with my heart, for there is no denying the course it takes. Nor did I attempt to fill the absence at my side, and when in time life became more gentle, I found a way to honour the space that my friend Dorcas left behind.

Dorcas was greatly loved and the Priory Chapel filled to overflowing at her funeral, not only with us, her closest friends, or the families of those whom Dorcas had delivered safely into this world, or her colleagues from the Horse Hospital, but also Booker and the Lone Woman of Combat, the ladies of the night from Borough Market, people from the Oriental District that she liked to frequent, Jabba and her girls, Smokes and Tinkerage, Topaz and the Saracen clan. An' the broadcast had touched the hearts of many more, who came to express their solidarity and helped to bring a smile of pride an' disbelief to Tobias, Angelina, Gloria and poor old Dorcas's mother, who looked about in tearful dignity and quiet surprise.

Later, when Delilah bore Dorcas's coffin away, a great many people flocked to follow her cart in a torchlight procession that snaked all the way up the frozen river to the Chelsea Physic Garden, where we laid Dorcas to rest in a grave amongst the medicinal plants and herbs.

Grandma Tookie (the Akashic Record, the Mantle)

"This charming Day of the Dead procession," Mason growled, jerking his thumb toward the offending funeral cortège, "been provoked by that broadcast. A real act of defiance. Believe you me, if it weren't for the weather we'd have a riot on our hands. I've always been a reasonable sort of man, who exercised a suave an' subtle, softly, softly style of law and order."

"Very suave indeed, sir."

"We've been far too distracted by the Projack Project. A chink has appeared an' now we has to move fast to close it."

"How's that sir?"

"Well Turkish, it's been ever so long since we called in our debts and flexed a bit of muscle round here, eh?"

"A long time indeed guv, a long time."

"An any one who thinks we're all hat and no cattle has another think coming. We'll start at the bottom and work our way up to the top, and by the time we is done, no one will ever trifle with the Mantle again."

"The Mantle again…"

"Turkish, has you turned into a parrot?"

"No sir. I was merely wondering where the Dark Elite is when you need them."

Topaz, Chief of the Saracens

The winter wonderland experience became an absolute nightmare when it lasted for three long perishing months. 'Course there is always them types as enthusiastically embraces disasters like some gosh-almighty opportunity to be made the most of, but even Canada was showing some signs of relief when April seen the end of his ice skating/ice fishing/ice sculpting season an' the beginning of his boating activities. Any rate, all sane people were very glad for the breaking up of the river ice.

The terror temperatures were particularly hard on the Tinkerage, who been starved into eating many of their beloved dogs. An awful cruel blow for folks who was obsessed with the esoterics of dog-breeding, an' passionate gamblers who liked nothing better than to race their dogs on a slightly glorious old track, reminiscent of a rusty lopsided Christmas cake. The dogs was the one thing that perked em up, an' to have to eat them?

The Tinkerage pitch lay between the chemical waste-dumps an' deserted warehouses north of the canal. It were unbelievable volatile an' liable to moments of spontaneous combustion, which caused a lot of lethal fumes for its consumptive population. But they was not about to move on, for their hopes lay in finding the One Big One that would make them rich, perhaps a diamond, an opal or a big amount of gold. Meantime, they survived by wheeling an' dealing the fruits of their pickings from them exploding an' reeking mountains of rubbish, an' the likes of Slim Pickings in his day, an' Jean de Fer, always give 'em a fair deal for any scrap metal they bought in.

Early one morning that Mental Health Act known as Asbo an' Rickers come careening down river on a large lump of polystyrene. "Oi, ya swivel-eyed varmint," they's hollered, "gawdssakes wake up! Mantle's mashing up the Tinkerage! Come on tripe, bestir yourselves afore they's all deleted."

"Thanks for the tipoff, keep your hair on," I says.

"It's nuffink, keep your turban on," they's replied. I chucked em a rope, an' aware that these two was making history, it being the only single instant they'd ever made themselves useful, I thought to encourage it while they was in the mood. "We'll get up there. Meanwhile you two sweethearts can take me skimmer an' fetch Dr Cole. Then get them twins of Canada's to guide you on up there through the water maze."

"Skimmer?"

"Yeah, an' asap. Here's a couple of fizz balls, now scoot."

"Reet ho, big chief," said they, an' shot off towing their polystyrene behind them.

I'd like to believe that the appearance of the Saracens were so unhinging that the Mantle stowed their bludgeons an' fled in fear an' trembling between the alleyways of rubbish, but more honestly it were a tactical retreat, explained by the absence of their real fighters, the so-called Dark Elite. Which were a remarkable peculiar fortuity, on top of which there were not a single Hissy Boy. Had they been there, the Tinkerage would a been subject to a slash-an burn-fest that don't bear thinking about.

As it were, they'd had a horrible whacking but was alive. "Tar for the help," they says, stunned. "What was all that about, what's we done?"

"Nothing," I reckoned. "A bully is prone to kick a man when he's down, is all." We got the beaten comrades comfy as poss, fed up the fires for warmth an' rolled smokes for them with broken limbs, while their wizened ribby kids came crawling out from under the dust to join us. Then, with that uncommon care the extreme poor shows for another, they helped each to douse their wounds with Grave Robbers Blend, a rather-you-than-me potion they makes themselves, until the dear Doc finally come chugging out the woodwork along with a whole company of kids, his DIY juniors, who gone to work patching, bandaging and stitching left, right and centre, while he tells them all about the merits of Grave Robbers blend an' gives them a short course on bone-setting.

I were beginning to think that Asbo, Rickers an' me skimmer was on the joyride to end all joyrides, or catapulted about half way up a some tree by now, but the sound of its purr come to my blissful ears when they came ramping up the canal an' bucked to a halt.

"Oi Big Chief, meals on wheels," they grinned a tad unnervingly, an' revealed the panniers to be full of bacon, onions, sausages an' flat bread galore. "Don't ask," they says.

"Wouldn't dream of it. Good kids, nice kids." It were a boon breakfast, but not one of them oh-the-hokey-cokey, lovely early-dawn fry-up end-of-story moments, 'cause it were the start of a programme of rough raids the Mantle were going to carry out, an' the herald of some particularly mental times.

Loco Vance, Captain of the Dark Elite

One minute you is freezing to death – it's ok, it's ok, you is in it together, one big family, part of the herd – then, heavens to betsy, the next you is a bunch of raw individuals, an' there ain't no denying the human condition do take some getting used to. It were no mass wake-up call for all clonekind, but a thing that come whispering on the snow only to some. an' it did not include a single Hissy Boy, they being a result of some human error, descended from one single batch of clones that been tainted by the Taipan snakebite vaccine, which is what makes em such good trackers, an' rear afore they strike. That's why they sharpen their teeth an' is called Hissy Boys

They also needs to be warm, so they was not out in the snow to hear it.

We overwintered in the forest, acclimatising, finding our feet an' getting our heads around the whole human situation we was in, and been much assured by the idea that there were plenty of people who had not got the hang of it either, an' was definitely still on the humanity cusp. But what to do, what to do, what to do? we wondered. 'It's not just up to me anymore, but I can think of one person who might be able to sort this thing out for us, or at least be open to the idea that we was not who we used to be.'

"Captain Dan an' me," I explained to the men, "signed into the army at thirteen, an' throughout our youthiness we was deployed in seeing off the determined invasions of starving fugis, who was all hell-bent on crashing the country for its food potential. One time, about a hundred boats washed up on shore, full of Africans, an' every single one of 'em had perished on board.

"By the times we was nineteen years, we were total foolproof top-of-the-range seasoned campaigners, an' the Council and Mantle was dead keen to accept Dan's offer of putting the country's infrastructure to rights, they being jumpy paranoid about any threat to their autonomy, an' a project like that would keep Dan well-occupied an' out the way for years. What's more, he were the best man for the job. Perfect all round. So they made him Captain Dan of the Wall and they made me Captain Loco Vance of the Dark Elite, an' we gone our separate ways.

"Captain Dan were really into the infrastructure. He'd been doing my head in for years on the subject, saying that 'protecting the country from erosion an' invasion is all one and the same thing,' it weren't till I seen what he were building that I got what he were on about, an' ain't his wall a landmark thing?

Seeing it were a long-term engagement situation, he encouraged the Swags – that's soldiers, wives and girlfriends – to come along and manage the camps. Which were typical true to him, being born natural civil an' blind to the distinctions of rank-an-file, men, women, ethnics, turbans an' fez. I would suspicion that he'd been relentlessly bending their ears all the way up the coast, with his parlari of a 'civilised society, a socialised democracy, the common good, eco-ethics' an' all that jazz, so that his world army all had a handle on the nature of the future they was shaping."

We never were required to think afore, but what to do, what to do, what to do seemed to be to find the wall, an' walk along its long slow curl into infinity. A long an' necessary walking away from what we was, an' when we finally come into his camp, we laid down our arms very loose an' easy gentle, an' I said, "Respect. Captain Loco Vance of the Dark Elite, we come in peace." Which were mighty lame, but mighty sincere.

"With all due respect Captain, what does you want here?" No mistaking that Captain Dan were taken aback an' a mite sharpy narky, but I kept my dignity, an' holding his gaze man-to-man, I touched my heart an' head briefly. "Been a change of heart an' mind, and we is offering our services as a act of free will an' as free men, Captain sir."

"Has you got religion or something?" he queried.

"Good question. Not particularly," I replied.

"It's a mystery then," said Captain Dan, an' smiled. "But I do see you is all free men, Captain," an' he saluted. "I do see that an' I take my hat off to you." His face lit up. "You're welcome here, an' I'm honoured to accept your services. At ease." I took his hand and shook it as men do.

We was housed in Nissan Huts with beds, plenty of pelts and wood-burning stoves, which sure beat freezing to death out on the marshes – luxury, but the integration were not easy. Everyone were ostracising, suspicious an' hostile. 'Cept the Swags, who was of their own minds, and seemed quite a lot intrigued by the tattooing we had from head to foot.

The long wall work were over now an' the army been biding their time, reconditioning their weapons, hunting, fishing, keeping fit an' playing a lot of football, for which they was fanatics. By-an-by, we entered a Dark Elite team at the bottom of the third division. Somebody scratched that out an' wrote 'Dark Effete' instead – ha ha, what a wit, what a joke, what the hell, because in the end it were the beautiful game that broke down all the barriers between us. What's more, the Swags begun to support us, an' with their faces all painted in spiralling tattoos, they's chanted out a full-on stream of sweet an' low encouragements while unleashing their gift of obscene tongue-lashings upon our red-faced opponents. Win a few, lose a few, up the blithering league tables we gone.

The end of April seen the arrival of the chirpy Canadian Captain with a shipment of goods. Captain Canada were not one to be fazed by our presence in the camp, indeed he looked pleased about it. "Super, I's all for the ententes cordials. Respect, how do, lovely juvely to meet you," he smiled frankly, very plain an' friendly-like.

We helped to unload some octagonal piles for a bridge an' some reflective panels for an ironclad boat. "See here," he said, "Phoebe de Fer came up with this stuff. It's light an' tough as titanium an' reflects the surroundings same way as water does."

"Wow, this is a real advance. Ain't it top of the range?" an' very pleased with what he saw, Captain Dan asked, "And you're telling me some kid invented this stuff?"

"Not just any kid. In time you will be dealing with her, you savvy? She's the natural heir to the Wayland Forge." Then handing over the blueprints, Canada explained how the design got streamlined for efficiency. "That's Column de Fer's work. Knows a thing or two about design. I think he also done a number on your bridge."

"So I see. Better then my design… Fewer joins, the less riveting the better. You give them the go ahead for another three boats."

"So tell me, Loco," asked Captain Dan, "would you and the Dark Elite rather be in charge of building an architectural statement going nowhere, or refitting the Vorsprung durch technik boats?"

"Aye?"

"It's old English."

"Reet. No contest, I has an interest in building that bridge well. If I ever retires, it's gonna be here, out in the open, free as the millions of birds on the water… How old are we by now, anyway?"

"Shhh!" Dan put his arm over my shoulder to whisper, "We is forty-something, man, and that is a Top Secret piece of army intel."

The end of winter seen the departure of some three hundred mounted 'troopers', well-armed, well-capable multinational boys aged atween fourteen and twenty-one, all of them born in camp, who was to escort a number of families to the far North. They also been detailed to survey a safe passage through the Big Empty while establishing a number of posts along the way, an' they was to be guided by a brother-an-sister team called Gracie and Ryan.

"Good luck, guys. A tamer land will make all the difference," said Captain Dan when they rode way, an' then turning to me, he added, "Plus they're well out the way, should a war break out."

Tucker (the Akashic Record)

The starry script do record a faithful account of a individuals story in all its detail, yes it do, but it ain't necessarily agreeing with what a person thinks they themselves is all about. The stars themselves has different priorities, which ain't about whether you is part of the herd or a highly unique sort, or coping well with hard times, or achieving fantastic deeds or even what you does for others. It is all about timing, good timing, an' it is about staying with the natural order your life do take, doing the right thing at the right time. That is what moves the stars an' makes them shine a little brighter.

Grandma Tookie and I been so very engrossed in the lives of others, we hadn't noticed the big cloud of red paper lanterns that were heading our way until they drifted through the starry writing and came to settle all about us, totally obscuring our view of life on earth. "Well whatever next?" said Grandma Tookie, and for the first time in a very long time she cracked a smile, an' the pair of us begun to laugh.

Franny

The death of your own child ain't a thing to get over; an' though it will take you to hell an' back, strip you down to bare bones an' raw nerves, you is left with your love, that survives as a forever bond across the void. The death of Tucker were not a thing to come to terms with, it were a thing to live with.

We waited for those riding north towards us, an' amongst them were at least three ownsome youngsters, living with the loss of their parents an' braving their way up through the harsh terrain in search of a way to carry on, an' a simple thing called home. We waited an' watched while spring unfolded an' we waited through the lengthening summer evenings, an' it were almost high summer before our patience was rewarded. When the company did come riding in, there was such a spirit about them, a new wind trailed at their backs. For rather than being a place at the end of the land to hide in, we was a place to come to, a place on a map.

I ran out to greet Ryan, who had a down-to-earth girl called Abby with a baby on her hip at his side, an' Gracie, who were in the company of a young trooper. An' poor Jules were so overcome by their return that he sat down on a stone, rolled himself a smoke an' sobbed, "It's a proper glass-half-full day."

"Is you Jules?" said a young lady, slipping off her pony. "I'd hate to see what a glass-half-empty day looks like to you. How do, I's Marley," she beamed.

"Oh," said Jules. "Roll-up?"

"Thanks, I smokes like a chimney," she replied, an' sat down next to him.

"Well how do one an' all, I can't believe you're here." Joe came forward to welcome them, "We've been looking forward to this moment, hoping, really hoping you would all get here soon. Now which one of yous is Nimh, who likes to feel the wind on his face?"

"Me," said a small pigeon-chested boy from his perch on top a big soldier's horse.

"We heard you on the radio. World-famous the lot of you, by now. Now see those houses up there? Jules, Smokey, Gabriel and I has been busy putting something together for yous. They ain't entirely finished, they ain't got no windows yet, but they has a roof…"

Sixteen young troopers had escorted the families on the last leg of the journey. Eight of them returned to help establish a safe route south, while the other eight decided to remain, an' surely somewhere amongst them were a mate for Ruby.

They settled in by degrees, skilled people of good will with everything to offer a grassroots community: Tom a dad with some boat-building experience to add to Gabriel's, Jamie a foodie an' a dab hand at salting an' smoking and making paté, a couple of young lads to join Smokey's fishing fleet an' Lara's willing hands to help Jesse with gardening. Marie and Fionn were both teachers who joined forces with Sandy and Corbin at the schoolhouse, new patients for old Dr Levet to care for an' plenty of builders for Joe to boss about. Plus I don't believe anyone had ever had a proper hair cut until the arrival of Romola, and due to Otto's social nature our inward community begun to look out.

Otto were Marley's dad but Jai, Willa an' Dylan had gravitated under his wide wing and it were easy to see why, for he were older, easygoing, enthusiastic an' confident. First he got the whole school involved with a glass-making project, and with the help of some books on Roman history, they discovered the right proportions of sand, limestone and soda, which they stuck in the furnace to heat till it melted. Then they poured it out evenly onto a flat stone slab to cool, which Otto cut down into 'windows,' that never was completely clear or without some air bubbles or the circular pouring ripples, subtly tinted with greens or blue which made them different and something beautiful to look through.

Joe and his apprentices fitted them into the four new houses and the little croft that Otto shared with Marley an' his charges, an' then the whole operation went local.

Lewis an' Ruby been quick to see the potential in glass-making an' gone to Otto for help in designing a sleek new range of bottles for Smokey Old Peat. "Don't flood the market. Keeping it rare will make it highly desirable," Otto advised, an' showing them how to pack their bottles into cases cushioned with popping corn, they sent their first official export down the army line to a certain Brother Thomas, who been a good friend to Ryan, Gracie an' Tucker when they was on their way down.

Well blow me but a couple of months on, a Herring Bus come into our little harbour with Brother Thomas himself on board, a mighty man with a mighty voice who shouted "VISITORS," an' disembarked with some of the brethren an' six fine Ayrshire cows for us. Their comings-an-goings been a regular fixture from then on.

Otto and Marley learned spinning an' weaving techniques from the elderly crofters, Marley learned to weave traditional heathery tweeds and Otto learned to weave art, which were the beginning of a cultural exchange between us and some Nippon weavers he knew down south. And they in turn been in touch with China Town.

We kept our exports small. Smoked Mackerel paté, smoked salmon or trout, glass bricks, woven tweeds and honey all left like missives between the isolated monasteries of old, but it were all communication an' the way to go.

Phoebe de Fer

I believe that the beautiful funeral we gave Dorcas been one poke in the eye too many for Mason Flint. He may also have had a feeling hazing up from his subconscious that the fat years was under threat an' the lean years was a-coming in, so didn't he bring the Mantle down on the people heavy as a steam hammer, hitting on the homeless, kicking down doors an' hauling sleeping 'offenders' from their beds. Terrible things went on outta sight, around the corner, up in godforsaken buildings or in basements just beneath our feet, an' in a constant round of stop-an-search routines, all up an' down your body them meaty mobster hands would creep. An' I minded it, I minded it a lot.

Hard to tell if the heavens were reflecting the Earth or if the Earth were reflecting the heavens, but it were hard going on the ground an' hard going beneath a sky that glowered down with weighty clouds, all charged with a thunder that never did roll.

The shadow they laid down on us were intimating but we learned to walk through it, quiet, almost fearless, an' gone on with our lives almost normal, and somehow or other the city miraculously exhaled into summer, a transformation, about as astonishing as a desert in full bloom.

Angelina

Maintaining the life quotidian were a tall order when conditions was so edgy, but for my family it been a way of keeping it together while moving on, an' moments of levity were to be had, small things like the occasional escapes of the City Farm pigs, who was devious an' plotted an' schemed meticulously afore effecting the collective getaway. Clearly they'd had it with the heat, for on our way to the Wayland Forge we seen the whole herd standing belly deep in the river, oinking triumphantly to one another, socialising an' chilling out.

I'd been looking forward to returning to farrier work an' knocking out a few bits of bling in the creative company of my soul mates, but the sight of all them pigs enjoying themselves gave me the idea to make some fairy-lights for Delilah's cart.

Electrics were not a number one thing on my to-do list an' the learning curve were perpendicular, an angst-riddled struggle, what with spinning a magnet and rearranging the north and south poles of electrical charges that's required to make a dynamo, but after one hundred years of self-imposed exile in a dark corner of the forge I come forth victorious. "Thank you, thank you, thank you," I whispered on my way out the ring on a stretcher.

Milo was kind enough to cast me a bottle-shaped cylinder to house my dynamo, an' when we fitted them on the cart, the bipolar donkey took to the wavering fairy nightlights. She would, she enjoyed the attention they generated, an' with her ears turned forward she stepped a little lighter beneath the enormity of it all.

I was tempted to leave on a high an' bow graciously out of the whole farrier scene, but the lights became a must-have thing an' when the orders began to roll in, Jean de Fer were so happy he'd helped me achieve something – you know, what with our mum dying an' all – he promoted me out of intermediate apprenticeship and my advanced apprenticeship had begun… Great.

Harley and Tyler

The heat were on and the pressure were high, an' for Ma, who were full of her own fire, it were a lethal combination. For she been of the migraine disposition, an' with her head stuck inside a bucket of ice, she moaned mournfully through the fine steam rising from her head, "I shall be fine with the dogs for company. Bye bye boys, don't let me get in the way of your education."

"The dogs is absolutely super," said Papa, "an I's here two just in case they has any difficulties opening the pain-blasters or making more ice. So long, guys." He raised his eyes to the heavens an' waved us away from the open door.

The Venus Man Trap were the place to be, for not only were it a time-out place-away-from-it-all to see our friends, but Liberty had cocooned herself inside in order to concentrate on refining her produce. Her aim were to subdue the fragrances to a mere whiff of the sea, or a suggestion of lemon balm an' a hint of the wild bog rose, but so far the giant leap forward for womankind were a marvel of alcoholic vapours and giddy staggering about beneath a powerful sweet haze, which in a moment of ill-timing reached its all-time chaotic zenith the very same day that Turkish swooped to make his inspections.

Turkish moved like chess piece when he were on duty – two steps forward, one to the side – an' on this occasion, it were the long diagonal Bishop-to-Queen that brought him gliding to the porch. He were very officious about opening the door, an' triggering the little bell which rung violently, he gave a slight jump of alarm. Then, one step at a time, he advanced, a pawn in a homburg, a pair of very dark shades an' a massive plaster across the bridge of his nose. "Good heavens, Sergeant Turkish. What a delight," Liberty beamed at him, weaving slightly an' probably deliberately leaving out his 'detective' prefix. "What on Earth has happened to that poor nose of yours? A little Arnica for the swelling?"

"I don't think so, love. I'm here in the name of Health and Safety an' it don't look too good me, dear. Reeks of alcoholic fumes." He had a point, it did. Turkish snuffled the air as best he could beneath that big plaster and were in the process of making a very obvious note to close the place down, when ting-a-ling-a-ling, Morgan arrived, an' bestowing a brief look of extreme romantic goofiness on Liberty he says, "Alone an' unprotected, a child so fair?" Then turning his gaze on Turkish, he regarded him with steely distaste. "Hmm, I did not have you down as a vain man. A nose job, well I never." Morgan berated him loudly, "Beware of vanity, it leads to no good. Now Mr Turkish, don't you have some real criminals to catch? There's the door. And Turkish – don't come back." Turkish went crimson. Checkmate. He bowed out an' closing the door smartly behind him, he gone off to wreak havoc in the name of Health and Safety with the creative wiring system down at Jabba the Sluts.

"If you don't mind me saying so, it does rather smell like a Stop-and-Retox in here. What are you up to?" asked Morgan.

"Well," said Liberty, opening the windows, "Thank you for coming to the rescue, we are in the process of refining our range of perfumes…"

"Of course you are. A really good perfume is a minor enchantment, throws a bit of glamour into the mix, so to speak."

"That's interesting," said Liberty, "I hadn't thought of it that way." an' to my ears, there been a deal of regret when Morgan responded, "Glamour is not something you are in need of. Pregnancy suits you. Make the most of it, it is a time to treasure."

"Yes, thank you, I will." Liberty looked at him kindly. "Was it some skin cream you were after?"

"Yes, I suppose it was." an' to my eyes, Morgan wavered briefly in a moment of fragility in which he seemed old an' tired beyond his years, until he reanimated with a gentle smile an' said, "Well, I better let you get on with it then. Good luck now."

"I reckon," said Tyler watching Morgan walk slowly away beneath the trees, "I reckon the solution to making a really fine an' rare perfume is to distil it all thrice over." Liberty's whole face lit up with that suggestion. "Oh Harley," she said, embracing him, "we live to fight another day."

"Yeah, sure we does, absolutely. Onwards an' upwards, go Liberty… I's Tyler, by the way."

Ariel Levet

A seed is a fine thing in itself. It contains life and death and the absolute assurance of another whole new seed. A seed is a seed is a seed, an' while the Chelsea Physic Garden remains much the same as when it were first planted, it is ephemeral an' always moving on. Naturally, the gardeners has changed but the work has not, an' quite a lot of ours been taken up with quenching the garden's thirst.

Obviously I been one of Dad's new discoveries, for I'd been included in some midnight jaunts down the Horse Hospital, an' even while we walked about watering the plants, the focus were on teaching me everything he knew.

"Healing hands are a wonderful but unreliable gift. They will ease the pain but they cannot knit bones, nor will they move the mountains. It's a good thing to know your stuff." Dad were off. "Most of our remedies are based on a system of Like Treats Like. That's why we treat snakebite with snakebite, or use Sulphur for sore boils that erupt like tiny volcanoes on the skin, an Arsenicum Album for Uncle Jean, whose limp is due to Arsenic poisoning."

"Well Dad, there's many ways to skin a cat."

"What?"

"Just a difference in the diagnosis. In my opinion, Uncle Jean never did get over his nearly-drowning accident and therefore he has one foot stuck in the past, which makes him limp. An' what's more, he's gonna go on limping until he frees himself up from it."

"I see. Well that never would've occurred to me in a million years," Dad replied, while letting the water pour all over his foot. "A case of the psychosomatics. How would you treat him then?"

" I'd keep it spiritual, Dad. Healing hands an' talking therapy is the way to go."

"Oh yes, spiritual indeed, an' also a good piece of psychiatry. We could try it. To be honest, my remedy is not doing its job. Anything else on your mind while we're about it?"

That question was a opportunity to sow a seed, for what been uppermost on my mind was that over in the Projack Building there were a very sick kid called Hope, an' though I been sworn not to blow his cover, there could be ways around it. I were burdened with the secret of him, so I said to my Dad, carefully, "You know, the world turns round an' there is no stopping time, but I regret them As Above So Below days are over, and get burdened out with the idea that it is all up to us to effect the changes we wants to make. I feel lonely small beneath the weight of it."

"I can understand that, but if improvements are to be made, then Earth is the very best place to be to make them. What kind of changes do you want to make that burdens you so?"

"Well Dad, I like healing an' I like helping, an' I can't help thinking that if we can evacuate all them ailing kids outta the Big Smoke, an' seeing as some mysterious persons been gone and liberated all them creatures out of Projack, it ought to be perfectly possible to spring all them human lab experimentals out of Projack too. In fact, I'd say it were a duty."

"Aye?"

Asbo

The back wall of Linda Miscellaneous's apartment were end-to-end covered with a sewing picture she call a Bayou Tapestry. I been blind to art until I seen this one. It were full of rolling heads, severed limbs, rivers of spurting blood, an arrow in a eye, a hawk on a hand, all sorts of weaponry an' interesting battle details. Linda explained to me just how queenly elevated seamstresses once been, for no king went nowhere without at least a dozen of them. They couldn't draw in them days, so them sewing ladies sat on the nearest hill with a good view an, I imagines, well out of range, an' gone hell for leather at the sewing, recording whatever were going down in the battle below… According to Linda.

Mistral (the Akashic Record)

The Big Smoke is conspiracy city an' covert operations capital of the world, a haven of clandestine endeavours, a tissue of deceptions, a multi-layered web of secrets an' a conniving arachnid heaven. Boy, even the pigs is devious.

However's, pull all them threads together an' the Big Smoke tapestry is even more riveting havocy then Linda's, crowded with Mantle mobsters dishing out an unreasonable authority, pregnant perfume-makers, fairy-lit donkey carts, cage-fighting Hissy Boys, psycho kids, dancers, lurching binge babes, an' Saracens spit-polishing their Skimmers. There maybe a few boats sewn into Linda's tapestry but the river runs from top to bottom of mine, an' the Big Smoke's boats is part of its fabric. Some is old familiars an' some is a mighty surprise.

Just when we's all forgotten about them, Full Metal Racket came zooming out the pinchy atmosphere, foghorns blasting an' lights flashing (there being no such thing as Rock Stars Anonymous), an' they gone zigzagging up-river, sending a wide wash out behind them what gone clean through the Shad Thames an' slapped about halfways up their stairs. An' Abracadabra, Open Sesame, Alakazam, the Raggers stampeded outside to check it out. The wonderful powerful boat were all glittering, black as death, with a winged skeleton figure-head an' tombstone balustrades. It been decorated in absolutely gorgeous graveyard themes, such as spectres peeping out of red-lined coffins an' tasteful roses hanging out of dead eye-sockets, with plenty of blood dripping from vampire fangs an' all topped with thrilling Jolly Rogers. Which bring about a rare emotional moment for the Raggers, who wiped their eyes, streaming with tears of joy.

The Full Metal Racket crew were identifiable by their leather jeans an' skull-an-bones T-shirts, while a coven of pouting rock dames stalked about on deck. Howevers, there were others onboard, just out of sight, who did not belong in this picture, an' they was Russki mafia, who barked at each other in a uncouth Russian Mat.

The whole caboodle dropped anchor, midmorning, midstream an' midtown, an' was soon surrounded by a flotilla of junky sailing contraptions packed with euphoric Leggers an' cruising Smokes who skimmed over to see an' be seen.

Jean de Fer's electrical services was sent for, an' Canada Blanch gone to sort out a leak situation in case they sank afore the gig, which been announced for Midsummer's night, in two day's time.

That night, Rickers, who was partial to rock stars an' late night boating, were hanging out on her big lump of polystyrene in the oil slicky waters by the Full Metal Racket outfit, when she were almost shipwrecked by Mason Flint, Turkish an' Nicky, who come nosing along in a Port Authority tug and slips into the shadows beside her. Well, hush, hush, they skulked there in silence while the Russkis, shhh, very carefully lowers a cargo down to Nicky who been respectful of the contents an' cautious about stabilizing it. The whole process took no more than five minutes afore they split, along with the Russkis, an' heads upriver for the Projack Pier.

Meantime, Rickers had grabbed a hold of the anchor chain an' were bobbing about on her polystyrene when her patience were rewarded with the sight of Necrophilia, the leader of the band, who gave the departing tug a big V, saying, "Good riddance Vladivostok! I is so relieved to get that horrible stuff off me boat. Honestly, the things one has to do to get a gig in the Big Smoke these days, 's unbelievable."

"Tell you what, though," responded the pyrotechnic with relish, "we does have a gig, man, an' it's going to be a lot more fissile then the stuff we just off-loaded."

I is drawn to Nicky in the same way as some people is drawn to hurling themselves off great heights, an' the intel that me erstwhile father, who do nothing but leave a trail of death in his wake, is in possession of fissile materials, do bring about a big black hole right of centre in the tapestry.

The metal populace come trickling in from the sticks – countrified Wiccans, extra-terrestrial types, Goths from the twilight, happy ravers an' heavy-duty drifters – who all passes by Borough Market to score their preferred substances an' then moves on to claim a pitch along the Embankment or scramble up the vines into the vacant buildings, to settle in by prime-view empty windows an' hang a cauldron over a fire to brew a meal of frogs an' toads, I bets.

A half hour before blast-off the amp stacks was floated out, an' so no one should miss out, they were anchored facing north, south, east, west, and come humming into life with a low-level feedback that got everyone scrambling for their perches, including the Hissy Boys, who was the security. Oh my days…

All ready to make another bootleg, Harley, Tyler, Phoebe Ariel and Column moored their leaky old Lighter off Gabriels Wharf. Solo, who had a thing for Necrophilia's voice, were settled up on the roof of the Winged Messenger Service. Angelina, Gloria and Eden were in Milo's new penthouse suite over the stables, but not for long… An' reassuring the technicians with a hasty "Trust me guys, two fizz-balls at a time, every half-hour, powerful as lightning. Now give me a sec to get away. Good luck, lads!" Jean de Fer leapt into his Lighter an' hit the gas.

Reema, Liberty, Mara and Linda sat in the Chelsea Physic Garden, earplugs at the ready, Smokey old Peat to hand, an' Cole tied his long hair into a ponytail, donned his leather jacket an' headed out with Tobias an' Canada "to mingle for a while," which they did not…

There were no sun, there were no moon, nor was there a single star, only the slow dimming of Midsummer's night into the sultry darkness. "Good Evening the Big Smoke! Fasten the seatbelts an' strap yourselves in, for we aims to break all sound barriers. Are you ready to rumble? On my count now – five, four, three, two, one… We have lift off!" A wide ring of fire ignited around the boats an' a single beam of blue lightning shot skywards, powerful enough to blind the angels. The crowd lifted their heads and roared their appreciation as the spectre-like hologram of Necrophilia climbed hand-over-hand down the light, eerily singing in his high weird girl voice what make him so famous. "Half a league, half a league, half a league onwards," he quavered, "All in the valley of death rode the six hundred…" Now the backing girls picked up the tune. "Into the valley of death rode the six hundred…" The bass-players galloped out a sound of hoof-beats. "Not tho' the soldier knew/ someone had blundered…" The drummers rattle a military tattoo, an' when the work of the pyrotechnic began lacing its way about the boat in gunfire, flashes an' a deal of dry ice… Hey, the darkest show on earth had begun.

The event triggered a quantity of alternative activity. Topaz and the Saracens raided Borough Market, an' hard-driving the addicts in panic attacks through the seething crowds, they deposited them, willy-nilly, into the care of the Black Friars for a regime of hard work and three gourmet meals a day, all punctuated by bells which called them to regular feverish prayers – "Please God get me out of heres" – until they resigned themselves to the devotional detox.

"Bless you Brothers, can't hang about." Topaz grasped the hands of Dominic and Sebastian, then the Saracens returned to Borough Market an' persuaded the fuming outraged Balkan dealers, oriental opium barons and independent operators into the good night with an ugly punch-up, and then politely an' extraordinary embarrassed, they hustled out the local girls.

The Saracens been very thorough about torching the place, sending a potent pall of dope smoke over the ecstatic fans, who believed it were all part of the entertainment. But it were not, it were a good deed an' a smoke-screen which had the Hissy Boy security rocketing away to deal with the fire, an' while Full Metal Racket gave the Big Smoke a night to remember, Dr Cole, Eden, Tobias, Gloria, Angelina, Jean de Fer, Milo, Canada an' Booker did most coolly snatch as many of the living dead as could be saved from Projack's labs, refilling some of them empty high-security beds with the Russki guards, who been karated into unconsciousness, professionally chloroformed an' strait-jacketed by the sweet hand of the Lone Women of Combat an' her beautiful friends, the Buddha's Fist an' Total Zero Tolerance.

Towards dawn the concert wiped itself out and to the east, which is on the right-hand side of my tapestry, Booker, Tobias and his daughters was rippling along the endless tracks through the romantic Essex murk, toward St John the Baptist's Orthodox Monastery. An' though I searched them ramshackle carriages for the kid called Hope, he were not among the sorry load.

Ariel Levet

One by one, Column's puppets did make their dazzling appearances, each one breathing its very own particular life an' character into our show. My brother Eden learned all the lines and became a very engaging narrator, telling the story in his fine clear voice, an' Milo, who has a cool head on his shoulders, became the reassuring stage-manager we required, while the rest of us become the invisible puppet-masters, passing the puppets between us so they's could move seamlessly. The twins been practising some special effects, hopefully of the gentle breeze variety rather then tornados, an' our Ma, who had tornado tendencies herself when a dress rehearsal were looming, relaxed, for the story of Faust been gathering a magic all of its own an' were becoming a piece of work which were, quite frankly an' confidently, unlikely to have hit the stage before.

Reema Levet (Director)

The scene is set: an anticipatory scene of familiar friendliness. Everyone had a drink, which was good, as they were going to need it. The assembled parents and friends began to amble through the garden to find their seats, while Solo slipped quietly into the shade, for he too had come to see our show. The audience settled down an' focussed themselves on the event that lay ahead. Even the trees seemed to bend a little closer to pay attention, while the patient puppets waited, poised an' ready in the wings.

"Good afternoon. It is a great pleasure to welcome you to see our work-in-progress." Eden strolled out and bowed deeply. "Ladies and Gentlemen, we present to you…"

The History of the Damnable Life and Deserved Death of
Dr John Faust (Part 4)

The Dark Angel drew the remnants of the night into the shadow of his wings and opening his wings, the Angel of Light released the dawn to the skies.

"Look at Faust now." The Dark Angel folded his wings about him. "Look at him, with bloodied sword in hand and Gretchen's brother lying dead beneath his feet. His soul is mine to have and hold until eternity. Have I not won the wager fair and square?"

"Nay, not so hasty, my friend. Twenty-four years is your Mephisto bound to serve Faust still."

Sheathing his sword, Faust stood amongst the summer

flowers, while the gentle wind eddied in the wheat and small birds sang in the early light. "Do not weep when you awake," he said, looking to Gretchen's window in sharp anguish. "I love you, sweet child and though I flee in hast, I love you still and will not forget."

Mephisto cringed in horror: "Love! Don't talk of love." His face smeared into a cunning maliciousness. 'Now will I spirit Faust away to the witches' mountain, where he will drown his love in lust and forget fair Gretchen ever walked upon this earth.'

Faust and Mephisto linked arms and ran full-tilt until the ground sped away beneath their feet, and hurling through the skies, flew until at last they slithered to the ground in the mountains. High over the bareback mountain, the witches rode their crooked broomsticks, wild glittering black stars of the night, shrilling with inhuman voices, for it was Midsummer night on the Bare Mountain, the Witches' Sabbath – a night of wild celebrations for the Devil's own.

A blind man played his fiddle on the crossroads, crows on his shoulders and slit-eyed cats mewling at his feet, while beak-to-beak, claw-in-claw, locking horns and tails entwined, the revellers waltzed around a vast and spitting fire. The ground exhaled in sulphurous effervescence, hobgoblins crept beneath the smoky shadows, tiny sprites lay dazed inside the mushrooms they'd been nibbling and all around, a undertone of half-grasped mutterings filled the night.

Faust: "Mephisto was royally received into a crowd of cloven-hoofed consorts, and a young witch of haunting beauty drew me into her untamed arms, but even as we whispered and embraced, the pale translucence of her face turned into that of a forsaken child who reached for me in anguish. 'Where are you, where are you and where are you now, my Faust?'

A distant bell rang in the dawn and we found ourselves alone in the great silence of the mountain. 'Fly man, fly

Mephisto, we must make haste, for Gretchen needs us now!'

But for one night's dark passion on the Bare Mountain, one whole year goes by on Earth, and when we came nigh her, Gretchen was in jail, condemned to death, for she had drowned our little child in the cold cold waters of the brook. And I pitied her, I pitied her so, and my heart spilled over with remorse…"

Milo de Fer (Stage Manager)

It were all going swimmingly, you could have heard a pin drop. Reema was wiping the tears from her eyes while the rest of the audience was perched on the edge of their seats, stunned at what all they'd seen. They was waiting, suspended in a state of silence, for the grand finale, when with a strangled "Ouch", my Ma gone into labour. In wide-eyed disbelief – "Oh my giddy aunt, can't be, can it?" – she stood up. "I'm so sorry. The show is transporting, brilliant. Honestly, it's just like being there, but I'll have to see the end another day." Ma smiled dazzlingly an' apologetically, then clapping enthusiastically, she sailed towards the house with Reema, Mara, Linda and Uncle Cole, who were applauding thoughtfully, in tow.

It took a moment to disengage from the show but we was not marooned for long, for Canada, Tobias and Dad (who were wired) came backstage to pay their compliments. "Say, could you just tell me how do it all end?"

"Nice try Canada, you'll just have to wait an' see."

"Sure, no problem. How about you explain the special effects instead, then? I has all night, I ain't going nowhere until this babe arrives."

"I don't reckon anybody is," said Tobias.

"Chin chin," added Ariel, draining the dregs of a glass of wine. "Let's clear up, get some food together an' sit it out."

I guess it were uppermost on everybody's mind that the baby were a very early bird, an' there were no Dorcas to smooth its way into the world.

Hope

Where they all went I don't know but the 'patients' was vanished, and I became a invisible man inside the Projack machine. Perhaps Nicky thought I'd gone with the disappeared, but with the arrival of his long-awaited uranium rods, the whole episode of me registered no more than a blip in a land far, far away.

Nicky's attention were with the nuclear genie he had in his lamp, an' dressed in his best dark suit of velvet, his mane of hair well-tamed over the ears, he paced around his lab, loose, elegant an' powerfully efficient as a black panther moving in on its prey. In his hands he toyed with a glass vial containing a neutron, and at his feet the Thames water flowed through the pipe that cooled his small pressure vessel. Nicky paused, poised, for a moment's juggling with his neutron, before the point of no return, when he released it and set the fissile process in motion.

The uranium rods were fully inserted into the pressure vessel to keep them cool and the rate of nuclear reaction down, while Nicky loped here an' there checking valves, reading gauges, adjusting levers and tweaking the taps, until he were satisfied that all was working smoothly. Then raising the uranium rods a little, Nicky watched with the kind of detached curiosity that made him so lethal while the water temperature began to rise, and the steam built up enough pressure to travel down the steam line. "Aren't I clever, aren't I clever?" He spoke so sinister, I seen he were mad beyond repair. The turbine heaved into action and the generator begun to spin. "Let there be light… Let there be light… Let there be light. Five, four, three, two, one – Good Evening, the Big Smoke!" He spread his arms and bowed.

The Projack Building lit up like a lurid Christmas tree, with a glacial light that radiated through the windows and transformed the glass-domed atrium into a cold bluish moon, an' I crouched behind my grill, shielding my eyes for fear of becoming one blind mouse. "Oops," Nicky chuckled unsettlingly, an' powering the place down to a more normal glow, the wraithlike shadows he been casting dimmed into a blur. He drew his hands into a tight fist, then flicking his fingers open, he pronounced, "And God saw that the light was good."

"You batty batty cake, you's lost it." I seen enough an' retreated back to my bubble and bed. It never once occurred to me that I were gonna survive, for I been winding slowly down in sickness, but I were determined not to die until I found a way to take the whole place with me. And that were not a vengeful thing, nor were it an altruistic thing. It were a matter of being a ten-year-old boy, worth more then a pair of seeded ears.

Jean de Fer

Our baby were too small and frail to come into the world unaided, an' the whole point of childbirth is to have a fine an' healthy child, so a caesarean section were the way for her to go. "It's alright Cole, I'm all for it." Liberty flashed a brave smile, and offering up a trusting arm for the morphine, her senses began to dull as her bloodstream carried it away. The atmosphere was one of peace and the room full of friendly lamplight, and while Cole focussed his attention on preparing Liberty, there happened one single blinding flash of lightning, the like of which I've never known. One, two, three, four, I were counting for the thunder clap, when the lonely little wail of my new-born babe came to fill an eerie void.

She were a creature of soft burnish, a delicate thing on a wing an' a prayer, refined as newly-annealed copper, a tiny fish struggling in the high seas. I held her against my heart awhile before swaddling her up tight an' laying her into Liberty's arms.

When Milo, Column and Phoebe came in to see her, "Look at that," Phoebe said in wonder. "She's got lovely turquoise eyes, like Mum."

"You mean," said Column, "lovely turquoise eyes, like Column."

"All babies has blue eyes when they're born. The more fetching dark ones, like mine an' Phoebe's, don't come along till later," said Milo, and masking his angst at the size of her, he asked "What did you make of that weird lightning, then?"

"I don't know if it was lightning. Lightning is so lively, an' there was something chilling about that flash," answered Cole.

"On the other hand," said Canada, poking his head around the door, "the weather's been awful sticky an' we is due for a storm."

"Well," said Tobias, coming in too, "how do, little one? Ain't you a brave little bird, an' how is your lovely mother?"

It is a great thing to be born with so many friends to greet you, pass you around an' let you know that this is where you do belong. There been drinks all round an' a cup of chai for Liberty, who were still woozy with the morphine, an' sometime in the wee hours our daughter got nicknamed Bird, which were the name that stuck with her for the rest of her life.

Grandma Tookie (the Akashic Record)

The death of a star comes in brightness and with flair, because a supernova will take one last dazzling waltz through the heavens before it's extinguished and moves on into the Cosmic Midnight, a place beyond our reach. New stars appeared in great variety: binary stars for my grandsons Harley and Tyler, while Serco Tagging has an energetic pulsar all of his own, Loco Vance a quasar in the elliptical galaxy the Dark Elite had formed, and Big George, Grandma Amber's dear old boyfriend, seems to have acquired an ambling wandering star. But mostly stars are born as nebula, and on the decline they had dwindled down to a mere six or seven hundred clusters...which coincided with the Big Smoke's falling birth-rate.

Bird was the last child to be born for five long years, for she was the last one of an era, and while Jean de Fer, a man of iron and a fixed star, focused all of his will-power on reeling his tiny daughter in off the high seas, the rumours flowed freely up an' down the river – Liberty's baby's terrible sick... A caesarean... A little girl... She won't survive... Came during that strange flash of lightning... They say she's blind... and gathered pace until word trickled down to Nicky's ears that Jean and Liberty's child was a Deviant.

Hope, who was a thing of thistledown, hurried through the Projack Building as fast as his feet would carry him, and arriving at Morgan's door out of breath, he began to pound on it, "Wake up, Morgan Grey! Wake up, wake up, you godforsaken pineapple."

"Homunculus?" Morgan opened the door. "Are you still here?"

"Please hurry, Nicky has gone to claim what he thinks is his own."

"Slow down. What are you talking about, homunculus?"

"It's me, HOPE. Liberty's baby, Nicky's gone to snatch Liberty's baby. He's crazy, an' he means to drown her like a kitten."

"What Liberty, her baby?" Morgan fled down the stairs two at a time. "Fly man, fly like the wind!" Hope watched him go. "An earn yourself the heart of gold you always longed for."

Liberty de Fer

The day came when Bird was quite robust enough to take home, and so as to avoid any hassles from the Mantle, Jean an' I decided the river would be the safest way to go. Plus it were a pea-souper, which been to our advantage, an' settling into the Lighter, we took off down the gentle river.

What happened next came in a series of images, grainy as old snapshots an' sounds all muffled by the fog. A boat came out of nowhere an' bore down on us. "What the heck is you playing at," shouted Jean.

"Playing? This is no game, I have come for the child," came the voice of Nicky Nigredo, who circled his boat around us.

"Over my dead body, you madman," I blazed up fiercely, and shielded my sleeping babe from him.

"The child is a Deviation and belongs to me," Nicky replied, and tightened his circle.

"No she isn't, an' even if she were those days are over," said Jean, and grabbing an oar he lunged at Nicky, catching him full across the head.

"Over? I've only just begun," hissed Nicky from the bottom of his boat, but as he got up reeling, a figure launched itself from the ironwork of Chelsea Bridge an' fell upon him like a bird of prey. I believe it were Serco Tagging. The thick fog rolled over them, when the disembodied voice of Morgan Grey called out, "Get them out of here Jean, you are in terrible danger," followed by an awful crunching wham as he rammed his launch full-tilt into Nicky's. Seconds later, I saw Serco Tagging struggling to push Nicky's head under the water as they were swept away in the current, then Morgan clutching his heart in pain before he sank beneath the water, an' the fog closed over him.

342

Hope

"Right, " I thought, "let's blow this pop-stand," an' circling all down and down the long iron walkways, I arrived before the gates of Hell, in Basement Two. Walking into the cold blue light of Nicky's lab, I raised the control rods high as I could an' locked them up irreversibly, an' then did triumphantly an' irrevocably swallow the key.

I crawled behind an extractor fan, where I's waited as the temperature rose until it became hot enough to trigger the Projack fire alarm, very hopefully emptying the place of all those busy-bee lab technicians. The wiring began to short an' fires broke out when Nicky came squelching in, all drenched, bootless and baby-less. Narrowing his eyes at the situation, he muttered, "You save your baby and I'll save mine," and opening wide the sluice-gates, the waters flooded in to cool the boiling tanks. "The slave shall be the master and the master shall be the slave," hummed Nicky, but it were too late, the whole place was shuddering apart with the accelerating speed of the turbine, and I crept out. Nicky leapt to lower the control rods to cool in the water, but they were locked tight and could not be forced down, and while he looked about, wildly searching for whoever it were had betrayed him, I closed the doors behind me, turned the key, an' slipped the bolts home to make sure the gates of Hell remained tight shut forever.

I been at the end of my capabilities then an' slumped down on the floor, but I thought it weren't nothing to be the one who blew the place for good, an' resigned myself to Kingdom Come when a reassuringly calm stranger appeared through all the rattling, falling masonry. The smoke were in my eyes an' the visibility were poor, but he wore a clean white suit an' I thought it were probably God. Then I realised he must have come down from the labs. "Come on my boy, you're not dead yet," he said, an' linking arms we ran like the wind along the corridor, upstairs, upstairs, through the atrium with all the shattering glass raining down upon us and out the main entrance. "Keep running! Good lad, now jump," he called, an' as the ground speed away beneath our feet, I saw all the other lab technicians high-tailing it along the towpath, as the big chimneys of Projack collapsed in on themselves with the imploding of the whole building.

The flying man spread out a pair of huge white wings and carried me high above the blast that mushroomed silently beneath us. "What the heck, I's stone dead, innit?"

"No, no," he said reassuringly. "Not at all, you feel heavy enough to me."

"Oh, but did I get him, did I get him, did I?"

"For the time being. The likes of him come and go."

"D'you mean a nine-lives thing, like a cat?"

"Yes, that's very apt," he replied.

"What's happened to Morgan?"

"Ah no, I'm afraid his heart gave out."

"But I sent him to his death," I howled, an' my tears began to flow.

"No, you did not," came the reply. "Morgan's final days were blessed with love, and it was love that set him free." I grappled with that for a while, an' when I thought I understood, I asked, "Well whatever happened to that angel they's trapped on the earth so long ago. Is he free to go now too?"

We moved on up through the cool wet clouds and broke out into the clear glow of the setting sun. "I've never seen anything like that before," I said, hoping, beyond hope that I really was alive and not the victim of an as-above-so-below, subjective/objective, dead-or-alive what's the difference kind-a-thing. "It's so beautiful here…"

"Oh I know," said the flying man. "Makes you want to stay forever."

Linda Miscellaneous

The occasional collapsing of buildings is one of them things one takes in one's stride. It ain't anything to write home about, an' generally I looks out the window, waits for the dust to settle an' watches to see which space has opened up in the skyline. I don't suppose for one moment anyone were prepared for the fall of Projack, though, which fell with the raw energy of a force of nature, an' the weight of its falling exploded into a powerful dust-storm that thrashed through town like a dying behemoth, eliminating all the light, such as it were, an' bringing an end to my sewing day.

The conditions was still of Armageddonish proportions when I awoke in the morning an' found the frailest of little people asleep beside me. 'Man, who's this, and what's it doing in my bed?' I wondered. Perhaps he were from the boat people, for he were dressed in a loose Nippon-weave shirt of linen and fisherman's trousers of white. It been quite clear that he were in a dreadful state. His head were shaven and there been a translucency about him that accentuated the many puncture-marks from needles that made him look more pin-cushion than boy. Obviously he'd been fed intravenously, and he also seemed to be leaking blood from wounds on his back. Then it occurred to me that he'd been blown right out of Projack an' straight into here.

I sent a bird for Dr Cole to come asap, and then I makes myself a strong black coffee and a mug of cocoa for the boy and settling down on the bed, I kept watch over him. Despite the extensive abuse, he were no victim. He looked victorious, even princely, and though his sleeping eyes lay in dark blue hollows, when he opened them, my lawd, they was of a cinnamon that took my breath away. "Hope?" I whispered, and he smiled back, graceful as a sunrise. "You is even more lovely than I remember you."

"You too," I said. "You too."

Tobias

A little bit of nuclear power do go a long way. Our city been so peeled back by the sandblasting it appeared contoured an' moulded from rock. The buildings was soft-edged and sculptural like shells, what windows remained was opaque and frosted from the peppering, the undulating river were littered with round-backed shipwrecks, an' only one or two leaves been left on the trees, but the facelift were a mighty improvement of gentle curvatures an' feminine lines of strata. It could be that all the debris been deposited far out at sea, or perhaps just spiralled off into the outskirts of the atmosphere, but I don't mind an' it don't matter much, for the Big Smoke were a clean slate, an' I is quite certain that with the bare-bone vision of the place come the inspiration that we'd been gifted something well-worth fighting for.

In all fairness, rehab is not a option when the road to absolute power gets blown up an' all of your hopes and dreams lie buried beneath a pile of toxic rubble. Understandably, Mason Flint were not feeling our vision. Indeed, without Projack breathing down his neck, he sensed his hour were come, and he were not inclined to relinquish the throne nor hand over the keys without a fight, so he musters every Mantle Man an' Hissy Boy to him, to counteract the fierce resistance he were experiencing on the streets.

Captain Dan

Slim Pickings came riding in off the Fens with the kid called Mistral, a wordy creature who were already in full flow. "Jeez, I'm gonna need hip replacements, this is the worst nag I's ever had the misfortune to ride, man is 1 inch-to-inch saddle-sore or what?

"Howevers, afore I croaks, I has one or two final words to impart, namely that only yesterday, Projack gone an' blown itself sky high, along with the Father of the Year, caboom, good riddance. So the intelligence do indicate that now would be a perfect moment to head for them city lights in any invisible boats of war that maybe's floating about in the vicinity, get Loco off the meccano bridge he's playing at, and make one or two encouraging noises in the direction of the rest of this veteran outfit. Limber up Captain, it's a long ride south innit sir? Yessir it is." There was both mystification an' elements of cheek to Mistral's parlari, but I got the gist of it, an' looking to Slim for a reality check, he validated her story with a wry smile an' said, "You're on."

Our new destroyers were pocket-sized twenty-man rigs, and they was marvellous manoeuvrable. The fizz-ball technology allowed us to move swift as the wind and imperceptible as a phantom in a snowstorm, as we slipped along the eastern sea-reach and dodged into the Thames.

Even at the best of times Tilbury Docks had always been a disintegrating heap of forlornity, but now it seemed to have accumulated an enormous quantity of junk and debris as well, which afforded us a deal of camouflage and made a perfect place to hide.

While we awaited the arrival of the combat troops, my wheelhouse became a war office, where I spent long hours with Jean de Fer, Topaz, Canada Blanch, Booker and Kim, pouring over the

348

extraordinary meticulous mappings of the railroad systems that Tobias had made, an' piecing together the information that they had gathered. I also warned them in no uncertain terms to get their children out.

The Mantle begun to scuttle through the city an' take up positions, dig in, clamber into empty spaces an' ram machine guns home on tripods. Their snipers slithered onto the rooftops and with a great deal of furtivity, they rolled the big guns out an' trained them on the river, because them E.S.P. Hissy Boys was sensing our presence even though they wasn't seeing us.

It do take a serious state-of-being to bring about an intelligent set of strategies, for success lies in the geometry an' the perfect timing an' synchronicity of your men, and as my troops rode south to join me, I let each one march through my mind's eye, to do them the justice of a well-conceived plan that would save lives an' rout the Mantle out.

Column de Fer

All secret ambitions we mays have been harbouring about recording the war was scuppered when Ariel, Harley, Tyler, Phoebe an' me learned, with some relief an' a deal of intrigue, that we was to be evacuated into Eden's world. Which was big of him.

Instead of blindfolding us, Eden chose to leave in the middle of the night, and after saying our earnest goodbyes we went with him into the Western Wilderness. We walked until the birds called in the daylight with a variety of song that was unfamiliar to my ears, an' when the morning light revealed we was well into the boonies, our spirits rose with the curious magic of the place. We came by a settlement of intriguing low-profile types, who greeted Eden with jagged toothed grins an' offered us a breakfast of doorstep bacon sandwiches. "Where exactly is we going?" I asked, as the long morning drew on.

"We ain't so far away now. She's an artist. Got a great roof garden, you'll love it, you'll absolutely love it there," Eden assured us, and it weren't too long afore we came upon an overgrown high-rise an' stepped through the thick curtain of vines that hid the entrance.

Opening the door on Grandma Amber and Big George were a wondrous discovery, like opening the door on a whole new universe, and being in their company was at least as extraordinary riveting as any war. And in the morning we found Hope had come to join us.

Brother Sebastian and Brother Dominic

There are twelve degrees of silence, and the absence of all those silences is the silence before war. And that silence, the thirteenth, is the one that accompanies you beneath the pall of smoke, bringing the wounded victims to the Priory. It is the silence that remains with Dr Cole an' all of his team at the Horse Hospital, who stitch torn flesh and prize the bullets from their oozing holes. It is the silence of the field medics who run between the lines staunching blood and closing the eyes of those who've died, and when all of the rattle and hum is over, forgotten and gone, it is, after all, the great silence that stays with you forever.

Grandma Tookie (the Akashic Record)

The language of war is recorded by the stars in anapaestic tetrameters, a four-footed beast that calls to the birds of prey in the sky and summons the wild dogs to slouch beneath its rigid wings, but through its horns some blinding leaps of faith are taken, and behind its stickled back come unexpected boldness and acts of great imagination.

The first evacuations coincided with the first casualty of war, the Stop an' Re-Tox, which from this perspective looks to have been blown up in an independent initiative of sneaky Brother Dominic's. But it was followed by a steady volunteering from the wasted teenage-girl department, who detoxed an' sobered up enough to grasp there were some benefits to war. By day, they took to working in the Priory kitchens, plucking chickens, skinning rabbits, peeling potatoes, dishing up bunny burgers or the vegetarian option. By night they scrubbed up and like the twelve dancing princesses, they crossed over the river to dance the night away.

Jabba the Sluts, stayed open, but the girls there changed their tune and marched around in fishnet stockings, feathered helmets, shiny-buttoned military jackets and not much else, singing, "Oh soldier, soldier, won't you marry me…?"

The Raggers, that distant constellation of cold dark stars, remained neutral but defended "The Independent State of Shad Thames," with a vicious array of crossbows and catapults from which they launched ball-bearings, rock salt, nails, steel bolts, fireworks, serrated knives and anything else that came to hand at all incoming traffic, to great effect.

One Thursday morning (a women only day), while Mason Flint and Turkish had their backs turned, Reema, Mara, Linda Miscellaneous and Liberty, with Bird strapped firmly to her, successfully took the Public Baths. The Swags were quick to join them, and it became a haven where a soldier could step out of the fray for a hunk of bread, a bowl of broth and a stiff mug of chai, and take a luxury bath.

Captain Dan's plans did not include entrenching himself in prolonged guerilla warfare, and he maintained his assault with the relentless determination of a runner who wills the finishing line towards him. And that amount of energy attracted the awesome power of the Fates and Lady Luck, who graced the scene with her attention too.

With Projack gone, each passing day saw the peeling away of layers of fug and the slow but sure clearing of the skies until, on the 29th of September, which is a Quarter Day, the sun set in a blaze of reds and oranges that flooded down the Thames and illuminated Loco Vance, who appeared as a flame while leaping valiantly across the decks of the reflective fleet, rallying his men, calling out the orders and was, without a doubt, captain of the ship that shimmered and shone quite incredibly beneath his feet.

It was a revelation for the Hissy Boys, who saw the Captain of the Dark Elite entrusted by the army as an equal, and "To hell with the Mantle," said they.

Asbo

There been no shiftiness, slithering nor side-winding to the Hissy Boy exit. No siree, they managed to appear like they knowed what they was about, an' achieved the crossover with some dignity, gathering under Loco's banner looking mighty pleased with themselves, while everybody else been left standing in a long moment of eerie silence, gawping gobsmacked, like some extraterrestrials arrived an' they's all wonderings what to do about it.

The Armistice happened as the leisurely Sun gone down over World's End an' one or two stars come out to shine. Then some of the Mantle appeared an' laid down their weapons, while others backed out of their positions very gingerly, very cautiously, very realising they all been skull-duggered, and scarpered off in the rising Moon. No one even bothered to pursue them. The war were, so over, and by morning they was gone, their illustrious leaders was gone and the Port Authority tug was also gone.

"Good riddance Vladivostok," Rickers jeered out the window an' waved the big V, when the Lone Women of Combat come swinging though the window, no sweat, saying, "Vladivostok! I don't think so. Word is that one Serco Tagging is escorting them out to sea… Maybe he'll drop 'em off on Anthrax Island, where they belong. Who knows?"

"Ha, what?" Her arrival been an outrageous breach of the securities which however I overlooks, for as females go she been okay, an' smiling kinda officious an' formal, she dusted herself off an' announced, "Hi smart brat pack. Respect from the Oriental Quarter, who say, 'It furthers a man to cross the great water/ The inferior man hides in a rice sack/ The superior man leads his people to new beginnings.'"

"What the heck is you on about?" asked Rickers.

"It's Dao wisdom," she explained. "Meaning, you has the keys to the Oriental Quarter in exchange for running the coyotes and hyenas out of town. And guess what?" She paused brightly. "I can get you on the guest list at the Bath House."

"I see. Well, respect… The keys is a honour an' all that" – I folded my hands and nodded my head, like they does – "but do the superior man get anything to eat an' anything superior to wear for his people?"

"The bargain is, food of course, but new threads after the bathing party."

"Okee dokee, go an' catch your own hyenas then."

"Oh all right, no bath needed then. New threads an' food, take it or leave it, my last an' final offer."

"We has a deal," I replied, and spits on my hand to seal it with a high five. Bam! Was she strong, my hand been stinging for weeks after.

Dr Cole Levet

My perception of peace came in qualia, its signs plain to see. There was a clarity of sound and the air smelled fresh. Peace tasted great, it came with freedom of movement and restored the crooked balance. Peace reached in and touched my heart, it filled my words with cheer and I warmed, I warmed greatly, as my senses renewed their eager interaction with the world.

Eden took Jean and Reema to fetch the youngsters home again, and in so doing they achieved a long overdue truce with their mother. And Grandma Amber had her influence on our children. Artists can always be depended upon to see things in a different light, at an inconvenient angle, and to lead the eye toward a overlooked perspective. Grandma Amber had spent quality time affirming the uniqueness of our young folk and encouraging them to remain true to themselves no matter what. The only one who did not come home feeling okay with who and what they were was Hope.

A little investigation showed that Hope's wounds bore no signs of healing. Indeed, they seemed to be eating away what little life-forces that remained to him and so I gently informed Hope and his apprehensive mother that we needed to operate in order to put things right.

I thought it was curious at the time, but just before Hope succumbed to anaesthetic he said, "Sometimes we are asked to be too brave". And while Solo accompanied Linda back and forth and around the garden, Milo and I worked on Hope's skinny back.

Beneath the ears that had been seeded on Hope's back, a further amputation had taken place, of such brutality as to leave behind two raw and festering splintered stumps which had to be removed, and it was with tears streaming from my eyes that I carefully cleaned the hollows spaces that were left behind. "Was it wings he had?" Milo's eyes opened wide with the question. "Could he have been a flying boy?"

I nodded and wiped my tears away to concentrate on reconnecting the muscle tissue across his shoulders blades. "Perhaps his father was an angel," I mused out loud.

"Hmm, this ain't Faust, you know. I is guessing that his father is Solo," Milo said, glancing through the window. "Check it out, him and Linda. Definitely more than an item, they has chemistry."

"Well yes, I see that. I hope these wounds can heal up properly now."

"I'll sew him up so well no one will ever suspect what he has lost…" But Hope would mourn his loss forever. Sometimes we is asked to be too brave.

Column de Fer

The Big Smoke eased into the variable autumn an' the army rode off beneath the big wet rain clouds, in search of their cadets who was busy somewhere up country. Loco Vance, the Dark Elite and most of the Hissy Boys sailed away in the pouring rain to live the dream, and once they all settled themselves into the swamps an' long grasses of the Wash, they dedicated their lives to bridge-building. Later when I became Loco's architect an' engineer-in-chief, I been mercilessly ear bent on on the subject of his whole lyrical philosophy of bridges. "Man, you'd be wrong if you thought a bridge is just about getting from A to B. It's a thing in itself. Seen properly, they is mind-bending, a way between horizons, an elevation of your consciousness, a portal to another world…"

I don't know whose been the brains behind it, but someone kitted the Raggers out with flame-throwers, army boots, leather combats an' fab, fab, fab 'I Love Peeking Ducky' hoodies, all of which been a lot for the hyenas to the handle, who fled whimpering back to the sticks where they belonged. The gales been extreme in their roaring but it gave you a feeling of being alive, and life went on. The hammers rang out in our Forge while Dad, Tobias and Phoebe worked hard on reconditioning the blades of some old flying-machine they'd unearthed.

Mara's barges gone to-and-fro with random stocks for trading, and the big boats come in laden with bright-red iron ore, for it were boom time, an' a great deal of mending and rebuilding been happening all over.

There been no attempt to establish any rules or regulations. The

Big Smoke was suspicious and fed up to the back teeth with them. We's cobbled together a Town Council by asking the guilds to vote for someone to represent them, then the boat-builders, the lamp-lighters, the entertainers, the loggers, trappers, Smokes, Leggers, China Town, the medics, the Raggers an' every other tiny minority, you name it, had a place on our council, which come together on an ad hoc basis. Otherwise, we was just got on with it.

Milo de Fer

There is some things that waits for no man. One, just let me tell you, is the cheese soufflé, and then there's Death, of course. Another, heaven help us, is the Society of Medical Practitioners, who is old-school an' borderline OCD on matters of punctuality. So I, a champion sleeper, been very careful to rouse myself extra early in order to walk the four or five miles an' arrive in good time to take my exams.

The gruelling goes on for three days an' nights, so as to make sure you cuts the mustard in them full on A-&-E circumstances. I been practically hallucinating by the time I emerged, but I had gained my tall black hat an' three gold feathers, which symbolised that I were the fully-fledged medicine man. The triumph were a bitter-sweet thing though, for a period of self-reliance is also required, an' I been charged with the task of travelling the land, gathering information on regional ailments and local cures.

The last thing I wanted to do were to leave my friends, my family an' my designer pad to go wandering off on me tod, just to satisfy some mystical medicinal initiation ceremony requiring time alone in the hinterlands. "Man oh man, ain't this the pits," I mumbled an' grumbled all the way home.

I been a man asleep on my feet when I stepped into the Forge, where everyone from my constellation had been waiting and began applauding, but I proceeded round the table to shake each one by the hand as been my duty. I also seized the opportunity to embrace Angelina an' kiss her right on the mouth. "Eh eh, steady on lad, that's me daughter," said Tobias.

" Phew, well done Milo," she said, and glaring furiously at Tobias, pulled me up close in a defiant hug. Yes!

" Hello Hope. Ain't you looking fine and well now?" I stuck my hat over the crop of golden curls he'd grown. "Thank you all for coming today, but you see, not only is this the day that I became a medicine man but," and I fiddled with my three gold feathers to steady my emotions, "they has ordered me out into the sticks to research the local remedies, so…"

"Take it easy, it's all reet. You is my brother an' I loves you." Column came to stand beside me. "We'll all come. Let's go visit our grandfather Lear in Greene King Keep. I bets they is ram-jam full of local remedies up there."

"And then maybes," my cousin Ariel piped up, "We heads up north to visit our grandma, Dr Clara Levet. Man, she's bound to have lots of local remedies an' all."

"You know what?" said Eden. "It could be a very long time since a show been done in them out-of-the-way places. Why not take the show on the road at the same time?"

"Well in that case, we's gonna need Harley and Tyler. Could you spare them for a while?" said Phoebe, and fixed her most charming melting gaze on Canada, knowing that he had a soft spot for her and were unlikely to refuse.

"I need a drink afore I can say a definite maybe," he replied. "We is definitely in line for a long holiday," Angelina and Gloria announced.

"'Course you is. Singing's right up there at the top of the exhausting job list." Tobias were not convinced.

"You'll need me along to take notes Milo," Hope put in. "I is Latin savvy, I has a genuine interest in plants an' local remedies, an' I has karmic connections with Greene King Keep."

"You does?" said Linda, perplexed. "Too bad, forget it. I only just found you again." But then, perhaps recalling his childhood been plum stolen away, she said, "I need a chance to think it over."

"Fine." I been very happy then to raise my glass and say, "You is all the best friends I could ever wish for. Eat, drink and be merry."

"Hear hear! an' praise the lawd an' halleluiah, a shot of alternative medicine at last," said Canada and raised his glass. I been so overcome with the examinations, exhaustions an' elations that without no further ado nor nothing, my legs fell away from underneath me an' I passed out stone-cold on the floor.

Grandma Tookie (the Akashic Record, the Far North)

T he last of the geese flew along the estuary, and the cold damp bands of mist settled across the field. The schoolhouse was full to overflowing and its doors wide open to the dusk. Joe, who was on the short side, sat up front with Franny…

The History of the Damnable Life and Deserved Death of Dr John Faust (Part 5)

Faust paced up and down his alchemists lab, followed by a large cat who mimicked his every move. Faust paused and mumbled in despair, "Long have I contemplated the laws of the natural world for the secrets of eternal youth and sought in the substance of ancient tomes the key to making gold, and all to no avail. But I will turn to the dark arts and conjure up the knowledge I so desire, may the Devil help me." And with a bang and a puff of smoke, the cat transformed into Mephisto…

Causing Joe to jump and Marley to grab Jules's hand, every time Mephisto made his dark and princely appearance. "No, no don't do it, fly man fly!" Ruby and Lewis yelled out when Mephistopheles tempted Faust to sell his soul. Old Dr Levet listened to the sound of her grandson Eden's voice bringing the tale to life. Gracie, Ryan and Abby sat absorbed in the unfolding story, while Brother Thomas stood at the back of the schoolhouse with the local populace, who muttered darkly and clenched their fists in anger when Faust seduced little Gretchen.

"Oh how extraordinary, they are inviting in the weather," Otto realised with a sense of wonder, when an uncanny wind whipped through the schoolhouse and spirited Mephisto and Faust away. The children watched enthralled as witches looped the loop, and shrank from their inhuman voices. A collective gasp went up when the puppet of blind Death stood at the crossroads, with Angelina's hands protruding from his sleeves, playing the Devil's jig on the violin, and they laughed when Hope came on dressed as a puppet sprite, and lurched about offering red and white mushrooms. "Tripsy whimsies, one-a-penny, two-a-penny. Tripsy whimsies anyone?" And the house shed silent tears when Gretchen sang to her baby and laid her in the waters deep. Then the scene was blanketed in a fog that opened to reveal the prison cell where Gretchen, mad Gretchen, lay forsaken on a pile of straw. "Where are you now, where are you now and where are you, my Faust?" she called into the cold and damp…

Gretchen: "I think I hear the hangman's footsteps descending down the stony stairs and oh how my heart quickens with relief, so do I long for death's release." But it was Mephisto and Faust, who sprang the bolts from her door.

Faust, pitiful of her madness and sorrowful for her plight: "Come away, come away with me. Poor child! Quickly now, for we must go before the jailor wakens from his sleep." But Gretchen looked at him in great alarm, for one year on the glamour had gone and she knew him not. "'Tis I, Faust," he said to her, but she just stared at him a long and hollow time.

Gretchen: "When something in his eyes perhaps still shone of Faust, and something in his voice persuaded me that it was indeed he: 'But I cannot go with you, who have no love within your heart and only come in remorse and out of pity.'"

Then Mephisto fumed and flamed in anger, revealing who he

really was, and Gretchen turned to him and said, "Get thee gone! My soul is not for sale, it is for God to weigh."

"And you are cursed and mad and damned forever," Mephisto said, and recoiling in dread, he hastened from the cell with Faust.

Then the Angel of Light walked with Gretchen to the gallows, took her hand as she walked up the steps, and folded his wings around her as she fell from the hangman's noose.

The schoolhouse was silent. Nobody moved. They waited, wrapped in thought, as the long evening settled into night.

The moon also rose over the ocean, silvering the waters and stippling the forest. It bathed the high plains blue and rippled uninterrupted over desert, rock and rift, until climbing above the mountains, it found Mephistopheles and Faust – no, wait, to where the moonlight fell on Morgan Grey and Nicky Nigredo, who stood at the edge of an abyss that plummeted beneath their feet into the endless dark. It was the loneliest place in the world.

"Nicky, I am in fear and trembling. Why have you bought me here?" asked Morgan.

"One thousand years of eternal youth. Have I not served you well? Now your time is up and you must serve me. I am the servant of darkness, and the flames of hell await you," said Nicky, and folding his arms around Morgan, he made ready to leap, when the Dark Angel rose in fury from the abyss. "Get thee on thy four paws, cat, before your lord and master. Your hubris has lost us the wager fair-and-square, and your foul meddling has wreaked havoc… A child was drowned." Nicky's olive eyes opened wide, and screaming in pain, he returned to the form of a cat.

"It is over, it is all done. Be with me now," the Angel of Light said to Morgan. "Through your love a child was saved, and thus your soul is mine. "

Then Solo alighted on the mountain-side, and bowing before the Angel of Light, he said, "Master."

"Ah gentle Solo, too long have you been trapped upon the Earth. What is your will, my friend?"

"The children, my lord, both the cat's child and my child, they have no guardian."

"I see. And poor Linda has no secret lover." The angel smiled. "Love truly has no circumference. Go, you are now free to do as you wish."

Solo

One night on the Bare Mountain is equal to a year on Earth, and I found my charges bickering with Riley in the Library at Greene King Keep.

"The End," said Mistral emphatically, and heaving a great sigh, she asked, "Has you got it all down at last, Riley?"

"He has it all down, but it ain't the end," said Hope.

"It ain't?" Riley put his pen down patiently.

"Nope. We ain't quite done yet, is we Mistral?"

"We is. If the people wants to go the extra miles they can find it in the starry writing."

"Except, Mistral," Hope was at pains to explain, "most people don't even know the Akashic Record exists. So we is making an Earthly recording, an' Riley is getting it all down here properly."

"But the people is the all-walking, talking, living record here on Earth. An' believe you me, they is writing it all up properly in the stars."

"That's very perfectly true for you an' me an' one or two others, but it's also perfectly true we all love to sit in the Library and read all about everything from beginning to the end."

"Oh man, you is putting our whole extraordinary beautiful relationship at risk... The End!"

"I think what Hope means," said Riley, "is that the end is yet to come."

The Akashic Record – FAMILY TREES

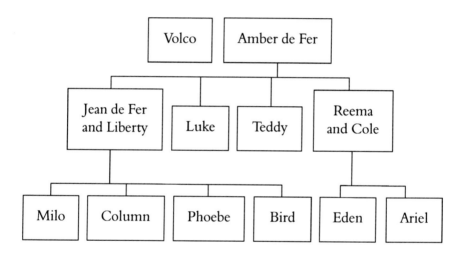

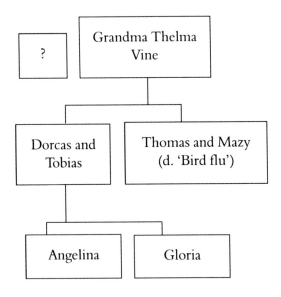

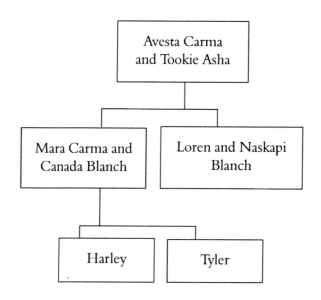

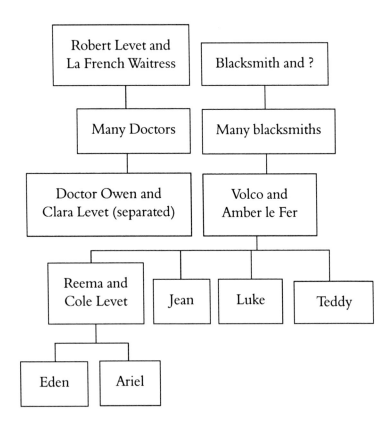

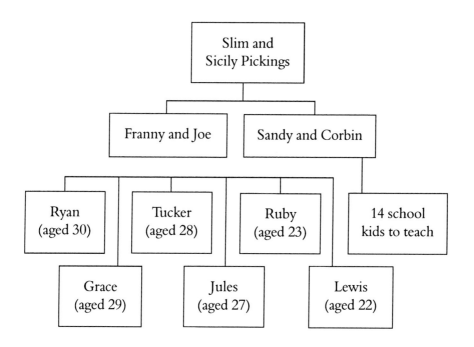

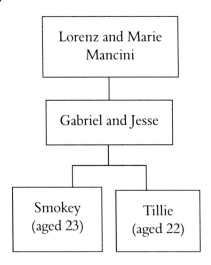